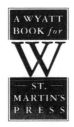

A WYATT
BOOK *for*

W

— ST. —
MARTIN'S
PRESS

Saturday, November 9, 1907

...tter Annabelle is evidently

...that we shall all remember

...to the end of our lives. Her

...has been simply dreadful!

...part of the difficulty is

...and her father want the

...be held either at the Tuileries

...Vendôme Empire Room. I

...to explain to them that this

...insuitable — that her debut

...at home, as mine was,

...was, though Hortense's

...party was a rather limited

...because Hortense herself

...have je ne sais quoi that

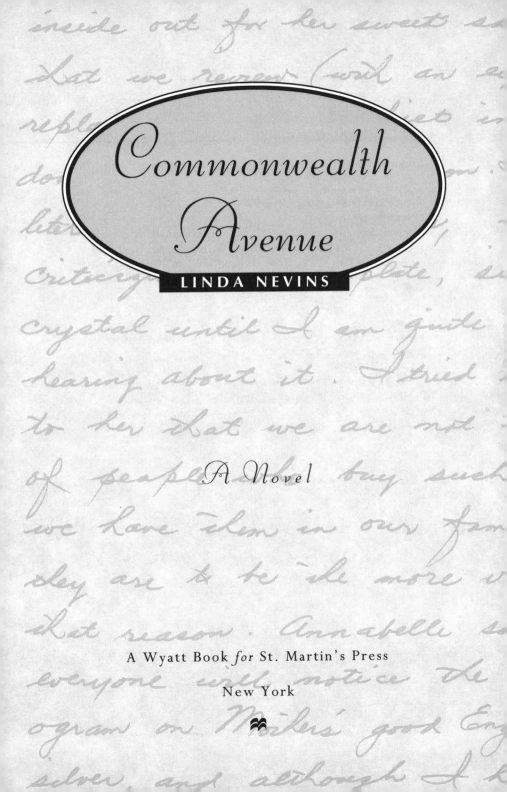

Commonwealth Avenue

LINDA NEVINS

A Novel

A Wyatt Book *for* St. Martin's Press

New York

COMMONWEALTH AVENUE. Copyright © 1996 by Linda M. Nevins. All rights reserved. Printed in the United States of America. No part of this book may be used or repro- duced in any manner whatsoever without written permission except in the case of brief quotations embodied in critical articles or reviews. For information, address A Wyatt Book for St. Martin's Press, 175 Fifth Avenue, New York, N.Y. 10010.

Library of Congress Cataloging-in-Publication Data

Nevins, Linda M.
    Commonwealth Avenue / by Linda M. Nevins.—1st ed.
        p.   c.m.
    ISBN 0-312-13949-7
    1. Family—Massachusetts—Boston—Fiction.   2. Women—
Massachusetts—Boston—Fiction.   I. Title.
PS3564.E8544C66   1996
813'.54—dc20   95-25686
                                                                                    CIP

First Edition: April 1996

10   9   8   7   6   5   4   3   2   1

This book is dedicated to the
memory of my grandmothers

Martha Virginia Whiteside Nevins
1870-1929

Bessie Nadel Socolow
1876-1968

Acknowledgments

I am immensely grateful to the many people—some friends, some strangers—who contributed, often in the most ineffable of ways, to *Commonwealth Avenue*.

Diana Barnes; Rose Ellen Branson; Alec Cheloff; Andrea Coates; James Downey; Barbara Ives; Fred Meyer; Maria Arpante Meyer; Roberta Oppenheim; Robert Oppenheim; Jane Otte; Arnold Relman; Joseph H. Rhodes, III; Bonnie Socolow; and Robert Vose, III.

A number of these generous people have suffered under my repeated expressions of thanks, but others of them, I suspect, may be surprised to learn that I consider myself in their debt.

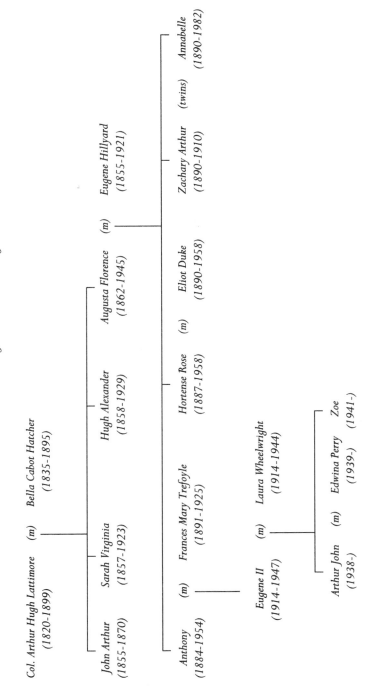

The Hillyard Family

Col. Arthur Hugh Lattimore (1820-1899) (m) Bella Cabot Hatcher (1835-1895)

John Arthur (1855-1870)

Sarah Virginia (1857-1923)

Hugh Alexander (1858-1929) (m) Augusta Florence (1862-1945)

Eugene Hillyard (1855-1921)

Anthony (1884-1954) (m) Frances Mary Trefoyle (1891-1925)

Hortense Rose (1887-1958) (m) Eliot Duke (1890-1958)

Zachary Arthur (1890-1910) (twins) Annabelle (1890-1982)

Eugene II (1914-1947) (m) Laura Wheelwright (1914-1944)

Arthur John (1938-) (m) Edwina Perry (1939-)

Zoe (1941-)

The Wheelwright Family

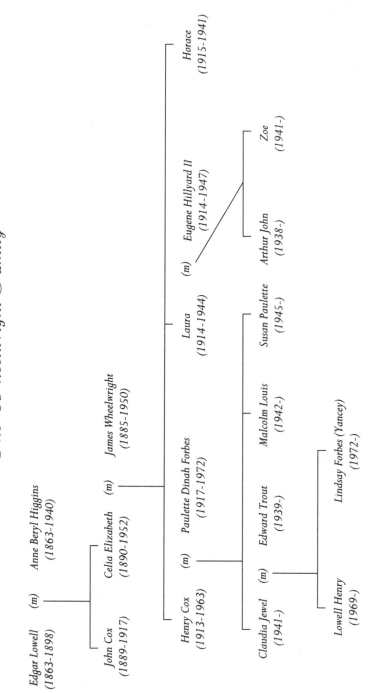

Edgar Lowell
(1863-1898)

(m)

Anne Beryl Higgins
(1863-1940)

John Cox
(1889-1917)

Celia Elizabeth
(1890-1952)

(m)

James Wheelwright
(1885-1950)

Henry Cox
(1913-1963)

(m)

Paulette Dinah Forbes
(1917-1972)

Laura
(1914-1944)

(m)

Eugene Hillyard II
(1914-1947)

Horace
(1915-1941)

Claudia Jewel
(1941-)

(m)

Edward Trout
(1939-)

Malcolm Louis
(1942-)

Susan Paulette
(1945-)

Arthur John
(1938-)

Zoe
(1941-)

Lowell Henry
(1969-)

Lindsay Forbes (Yancey)
(1972-)

The Trefoyle Family

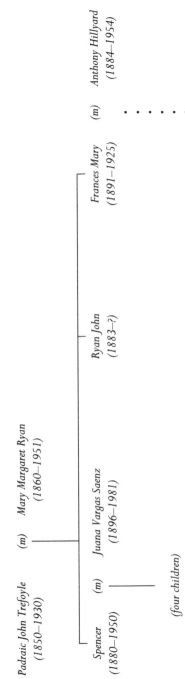

Padraic John Trefoyle
(1850–1930)

(m)

Mary Margaret Ryan
(1860–1951)

Spencer
(1880–1950)

(m)

Juana Vargas Saenz
(1896–1981)

(four children)

Ryan John
(1883–?)

Frances Mary
(1891–1925)

(m)

Anthony Hillyard
(1884–1954)

Part One

THE GILDED AFFAIR

Old families last not three oaks.

—SIR THOMAS BROWNE, *Urn Burial*

Prologue

(FROM THE DIARIES OF AUGUSTA HILLYARD)

Friday, May 30, 1902

It is quite scandalous how late I have lain abed this morning. Eugene was up and about his business at his usual early hour, but I was not equal to anything more than lying here in a beam of warm sunshine, snug under the coverlet, and indulging my remembrance of the events of last evening. A woman wonders whether she wishes the milestones of her life to be so publicly celebrated, although everyone did say that I looked quite beautiful (for forty!). But it is intriguing to me that we all engaged ourselves in such strenuous gaiety to celebrate Augusta Hillyard's entrance into middle age—if mere entrance it is. I sometimes feel that I am no stranger to the country of lost youth . . . and yet my mirror tells me otherwise.

The celebration was larger and more extravagant than the preparations had led me to expect. Although the party itself was not a surprise and all the family were eager to toast my special day, I was not aware until the last moment that Eugene had invited so many of our friends, and the house was quite choked with champagne, flowers, and a great number of self-styled Boston aristocrats.

We have been receiving calls and felicitations since Monday afternoon. Anne, of course, has come with her darling little Celia nearly every day to help with the "preparations," though my Veronica is at her wit's end with all these invasions of her kitchen. After nearly four years without Edgar, arriving at an entertainment as "the Widow Lowell" is still difficult for Anne. (Naturally, no one so much as breathes it, but their thoughts are deafening.) Thus she retreats to the warm comfort of Veronica's kitchen, chatting on and on in her sweet, timid way, but making such a tumble of Veronica's arrangements!

My dear brother Alex came to a small family supper Wednesday evening and brought with him Mother's pearls, left in trust for Alex's wife (should he ever throw caution to the winds and actually choose one!). Yet our Alex has attained the age of forty-four without a wife and so felt that it would be very much in the spirit of the occasion to bring the necklace here for me. These dear little beads were given to Mother by Papa as a betrothal gift almost fifty years ago, and therefore the sentimental value is greater than any other, but they are, all the same, pearls of great price.

Just before the guests began to arrive, I made a furtive trip downstairs in my dressing gown, only to be shooed from my own pantry by Winifred and Veronica. Potter—who always says that one should not have champagne unless there is snow outside in which to chill it—was carrying in huge cases of the best, and I'm afraid I was quite in the way! The tradesmen had been running in and out all day with flowers and ices, and (although I know I was not supposed to see, and fortunately no one knows I did) I caught a glimpse of a beautiful white cake, festooned with real roses and some of our lovely clematis from Nahant. Oh! the excitement in the air!

I quickly ran upstairs to finish my toilette, and my girls fussed over me unceasingly as I dressed. I planned to wear my new blue silk, but Annabelle, who at eleven is already developing a very piquante sense of fashion, thought I should not wear it because after all it was not as "fancy" as the pink, or even the black velvet. Of course, I pointed out to her that May is far too late for velvet and so was able to inject a note of motherly instruction into the gay and frivolous proceedings. My Hortense, however—already a young lady, though unfortunately a rather plain one at fifteen, a time when a bubble of coquetry should be just about to burst—chose to observe at a distance, though I saw her clasping her hands in delight at the party ahead. Even at this tender age, Hortense is a confirmed wallflower (one fears by choice), but a sweet one all the same.

Then, just as the girls had fastened the last ribbon (having dismissed Winifred from her usual duties for the occasion), and had leapt into the air with joy and anticipation for what seemed the hundredth time, who should arrive but my darling Zachary—much out of breath, not entirely clean, and at new heights of untidiness—eager to catch me, before I descended to my guests, to give me the most charming gift, which I shall cherish forever: it is a shell from our seashore at Nahant which I know he prizes and which has been in his treasure box since he was a tiny boy. He told me, very sweetly, with his little face buried in my stomach (his twin sister is *so* much taller than he, and Annabelle is really remarkably cruel to him on this point), that he knew this was a very special day and he wanted to give me something very "meaningful" and after devoting considerable thought to the problem, he realized that this wonderful pink shell would be the perfect choice. He knew he was late (and dirty and not yet dressed!), but he told me it had been so encrusted with barnacles and who knows what detritus, as he said, "of the briny deep, Mama," that he'd been down cellar with Potter all this week, polishing it up. This morning it glows, nearly humming with the roar of the tides, on my bedside table. I fancy I can hear the ocean at a distance. I think I love that boy more than my own life, but however wicked it is to be so blessed with four strong children and to love the last the most . . . Ah! that I should dote so on this boy invites God's punishment. . . .

But then, hearing laughter and the hum of happy voices swirling up the stairs to my door, I looked out the window amazed to see the number of carriages falling into line up and down Commonwealth Avenue. From my vantage point, I could see nearly down to the corner as the Pickmans, the Snells, the Binneys came along the sunlit walk, all bearing gaily wrapped packages. I had no idea that Eugene, whose affection for me is so well controlled and so ambiguously expressed, had gone to such lengths to create this great fête in my honor. (That Eugene may also achieve social, political, and financial advantage thereby is not important this morning. I will not be suspicious and small-minded at such a festive time.)

I shooed the children from the room, fluffed the curls over my ears one last time, pinched my cheeks, straightened the pearls, and, feeling at last prepared to go downstairs (to "make my entrance"!), I turned to see my husband in the doorway, smiling in a way one seldom sees. Eugene took me in his arms and kissed my neck and gently pulled my pearl

5

drops from my ears with his teeth. As I stood speechless and smiling, he handed me a small blue velvet box, which I recognized at once as from Tiffany's in New York, where Eugene had gone last month, as he said, "on business."

Well! The earrings within were sparkling with a life of their own: diamond earbobs set in platinum. The stones are the size of almonds, fastened with clasps of smaller pavé diamonds encasing a black pearl. I held them in my hands, feeling the weight of them, and stared wordless and open-mouthed at Eugene, who looked down at me with his wry sardonic smile as he fastened them to my ears. He kissed me on the cheek and took my arm to escort me to my party. Not one word passed between us.

As I lie in bed this morning, writing these words, I have (with a great frivolity none would believe of me) fastened on my diamond earrings once again, and they send the sun's fire to the farthest corners of the room. . . .

I observed to myself last night that we are so rarely all together, and indeed, in some ways, we were not together even then. I had a moment of solitude moments before Eugene came in, just to hold my shell and clasp my pearls, and realize that this fine party is the more notable for those who are not here to share it with us. My dear parents were not there, Papa but three years in his grave (whom I miss most of all!), and sweet John Arthur, my "big brother" . . . I was a child when he died and I can still taste the salt in my mother's tears as I tried (most ineffectually, as I remember) to comfort her. When John Arthur died, she sat holding Sarah, rocking her for hours, though Sarah was by then a hefty girl and far too big to rock. . . . Yes, and what of Sarah, who did not send a letter as I thought she might? Is our estrangement yet so fresh for her that she forgets me on this shining day? But I cannot think about that now! I must stop this! . . . It was a day for counting blessings and letting losses take the hindmost. I have more blessings than there are pearls in my mother's necklace.

Yet if there is a flaw in this immoderate joy, if there is one thing which perhaps saves me from excesses of complacency, it is that Anthony (who did not put in his appearance until very late last night—toward midnight!), showing even now clear signs of the cruel and handsome man he will become, performs his role as eldest child and heir with a sourness that is very hard to trace in any branches of our family. My faerie child? My changeling? Is it from the Hillyards that Anthony derives this streak that borders on the vicious? (I cannot believe that it is his Lattimore blood that puts that conniving glint in his black eyes.)

This is in many ways a failure that mitigates all my joys. The lack I feel of a deep love for this child tarnishes my devotion to the others. Seventeen years ago when Anthony was born and I was a young and hopeful wife, smiling with joy as he gurgled at my breast, could I have foreseen that he would develop a voluptuary's glower while still a boy? That there would be a depth in him that I, his mother, could not plumb? His devotion to his father, which borders on worship, forces me to throw my trust to Eugene, which, diamond earrings notwithstanding, I am loath to do.

And yet, on this glorious spring day, sun and diamonds competing, as it were, for the greater glory, it seems impossible to acknowledge sadness, pain, or doubt, or to weep for my lost sister Sarah, far away in Europe, angry and alone. And how could I, on such a day, bear to look into Anthony's black eyes, knowing I will not find the kindness and the love a mother seeks in her firstborn's face? I can perhaps, however, hope that these stains on the escutcheon of my happiness today will keep me honest.

ONE

*L*ate on a warm, quiet afternoon, eighty years later, almost to the day, Augusta Hillyard's great-grand-daughter sat cross-legged on her bedroom floor. She had been there for almost an hour, her lap filled with dozens of deep pink roses and tulips that spilled from a long, white florist's box. Scattered over the flowers were the individual sheets of the ten-page contract she'd gotten just that afternoon. She had come home, all excited, from the lawyer's office in Beverly Hills to find the box leaning against the front door. She went directly to the bedroom to put the big manila envelope safely away in the bottom drawer of her bureau, but she'd taken the contract out to read one more time, and there she was, still sitting motionless on the floor, miles away.

She took a deep breath and cleared her throat and looked down at the small white card she'd been holding all that time.

Roger had tried to make it look like a full-frame movie credit done in fancy Victorian script:

Zoe A. Hillyard: Production Designer

On the other side he'd written, "Dinner reservation is for seven. Don't miss the sunset! Love, R."

Zoe got to her feet, knee cartilage creaking from the hour on the floor. She took the flowers to the kitchen and ran warm water in a tall cut-crystal vase and plopped in an aspirin.

Roger had given her the vase back in early December as a special gift to celebrate both their first Christmas together and Zoe's milestone fortieth birthday. When she first opened the package and gasped and held the vase up to the light, Roger had simply smiled and kissed her and promised to keep it filled with flowers.

Holding the vase with both hands, she carried it into the living room. She set it carefully on the long worktable and moved slowly through the room, picking up a book here, a length of dark red silk moiré or a sheaf of crumpled sketches there, and then stopped and just stood still, her hands on her hips, smiling at the chaos.

There had been a time when everything in the room had been ordered and perfect. The room had begun, ten years ago, as a pale green sanctuary, the few pieces of furniture impeccably in line, each ornament selected and placed with the eye of an artist and the care of someone who believed that at last she had a home. But now it was a mess, and had been for almost four months, inundated so extravagantly with Victorian clutter that you had to pick up your feet to walk across it.

Three enormous bulletin boards hung on the once-bare walls, bristling with a forest of pins that held brocade swatches, lengths of lace, notes, drawings, photographs. The coffee table was invisible under piles of art books and auction catalogues, half a dozen pasteboard-bound scripts, bundles of fashion plates from the 1890s, and at least a dozen library books, many of them overdue, including Edith Wharton's masterpiece *The Decoration of Houses,* and a 1902 first edition of *Eminent Actors in Their Homes,* filled with ancient daguerreotypes of the studies and parlors of old, patrician theater people, all of them dead for decades.

More books were stacked on the fruitwood secretary, and cuttings of watered silk were draped over the back of the sofa and the arms of every chair. Meticulously constructed scale models of interior sets, complete down to tiny pieces of furniture and microscopic bibelots, were set on every flat surface. Over the worktable, on the wall between the windows, hung a framed pencil sketch of a woman wearing an old-fashioned artist's smock and holding a palette. She stared intently at her easel, the end of her brush in her mouth. And at the bottom, written in nineteenth-century copperplate script: *The Artist in Contemplation.* Roger had given it to her about a month before, though he laughed and

9

refused to answer when Zoe demanded to know where he had found such a treasure.

Zoe brought the flowers back to the bedroom and then knelt down to pull open the heavy bottom drawer of the dresser. All of her "location clothes" were there, the silk underwear and heavy sweaters from L. L. Bean she took into the mountains and deserts, a down-filled vest, warm socks. An insurance policy was in a folder with the pink slip for her car. But under these, buried so deep as if begging to be forgotten, or perhaps so deliberately hidden as to be never out of mind, was more.

She took out a large fabric-covered box filled with her cousin Claudia's many notes and cards, a collection years in the making. She opened the little clasp on the box and picked up Claudia's last Christmas card, gently rubbing her fingers over the fake snow that glittered on the cheerful winter scene and rattled in the envelope. She pulled the drawer open wider still and felt along the bottom for the flat handkerchief box she knew was there.

Inside, among a few old letters and a postcard of a tall ship sailing into Boston Harbor, was a yellowed snapshot of Zoe and her brother Arthur as children, grimy and sticky at the end of a fine summer day. She wasn't quite sure what year the picture had been taken. 1946? Perhaps in 1947, after everyone but Annabelle was dead and little Zoe and Arthur were left alone with her? She'd had the picture for so many years she could not remember when she didn't. The children were standing soberly at the top of the wide stone steps of Grandmère's beautiful house on Commonwealth Avenue, Boston's most famous boulevard, bordered with trees and flowers and privilege, one splendid Victorian mansion after another. Zoe had not seen the house, or her brother, for ten years, and she stared intently at the photograph, suddenly feeling almost short of breath.

For years Zoe had alternated between long periods of not thinking about her brother at all and almost unbearable fits of missing him intensely. A reminder might come at any time—an expression on a stranger's face, a bit of Chopin or Scarlatti on the radio—and the memory of Arthur Hillyard would froth up and overtake her. Such moments left her stunned, physically breathless, as if she had suddenly been pulled from swirling water.

But as years passed, the estrangement from Arthur acquired an inertia of its own; the longer she resisted any impulse to contact him, the easier that resistance was. Yet the more she delayed, the less possible it seemed to stop the spiral of missing him and doing nothing about it.

She knowingly used their cousin Claudia as a surrogate, sending her cards for all occasions, sometimes even when the only occasion was that she'd had a flush of missing Arthur but no nerve to crack that spiral. She made sure Claudia always knew how to reach her, without ever inviting her to do it. She sent breezy notes whenever she had a new phone number, or started a new movie, or read an interesting book—knowing Claudia would tell Arthur, would never so much as consider keeping it a secret.

But there were moments, too, when Zoe's resistance to Arthur paled before the lack of him. Once she wrote him a long impassioned letter, something between raging and begging, and tore it up. She'd even called him on the telephone the night one of her pictures opened, the one about the Aztecs, knowing he would get a kick out of seeing it, would appreciate the kitsch and the silly savages. But she hung up on the third ring, pretending to herself he wasn't home. Then, five months ago, when she read the story of *The Gilded Affair* for the first time, she took the old photograph from the handkerchief box, pulled the phone into her lap, and sat like that for almost an hour before she knew she couldn't do it.

But night before last, after the second meeting with the lawyer, when she began to believe there would really be a contract, she called him again. The phone number in Boston hadn't changed in over fifty years; Zoe dialed it from memory and stood with her eyes wide open listening to the ringing far away. She imagined Arthur running down the stairs from his room to the phone in the kitchen, or leaping up from his favorite spot on the back stairs where he liked to sit on a warm fine evening, smoking cigarettes.

When Arthur answered the phone, Zoe squeezed her eyes shut, almost afraid to inhale, knowing he would recognize her breathing.

"Hello? Hel-lo-oh? Anybody there?" Then he obviously turned his face away to speak to someone in the room—Annabelle, of course. "It's no one, 'Belle . . . must be a wrong number." And then his voice again, warm, friendly, close to the receiver: "Hello? No? Okay, bye." Did he think it might be she—did he say her name when he hung up, whispering so Annabelle wouldn't hear? "Zoe? Was it you?" Did he say that? Did he guess? Hope?

Twenty years before, exhilarated by the prospect, Zoe Hillyard had gone off to Italy convinced that she had the talent to make a career in film design. Her great-aunt Annabelle, not caring what Zoe did, glad to have her gone, had nevertheless blustered and fumed about the senselessness of throwing your life away for "art."

"Mother was always running off to art shows, galleries, looking at pictures," Annabelle sneered the night before Zoe left, sipping a dry sherry, her silver eyes sparkling with malice and memory. "She could never get enough of that art nonsense, and you're just like her."

"Grandmère would be happy for me," Zoe said, her back to the carved fireplace in Augusta Hillyard's once-grand drawing room.

"Then, go, for heaven's sake," Annabelle said, barely glancing at Zoe as she shouldered her aside and swept up to her room, leaving the empty glass on the table in the marble foyer for someone else to find and put away. "Do exactly as you wish."

As the old woman passed by she paused and leaned close to Zoe's face, speaking in that whispering hiss she seemed to save for their rare conversations. "You're *just* like her."

"I hope so," Zoe answered with a small, defiant smile. "I certainly do hope so."

The very next day, Arthur took Zoe to the airport and kissed her cheeks with a brave smile, gripping her shoulders with a cheerfulness, a *brio* she knew he didn't feel. He handed over her huge portfolio stuffed full of sketches and dreams and fantasies.

"You really going, Zo?" he said, tears springing up in his blue eyes.

"Arthur, we talked about this," Zoe said, kissing his chapped cheek, tasting salt. "It's not forever, kiddo."

"But movies—Zoe, you don't even—"

"I can do it . . . I'm going to do it, Arthur. I am."

"You've got no money, Zo, and I've got none to send you, almost none, hardly any at all."

"I've got a little, enough to get me settled. Arthur, look, it's the rest of what was supposed to be for college. Annabelle was happy as a fat old clam to give it to me."

"Zoe! Jeez . . ."

"Arthur, it's all right. This *is* my education. And you can come visit just like we planned. We'll eat spaghetti with authentic sauce and stroll down the Via Veneto!"

Arthur, unable to contain himself, threw his arms around her and nearly wept into her hair. "You're chasing rainbows, Zo, rainbows I don't think anybody else can see. . . ."

Zoe pulled back and looked up into his wet blue eyes.

"Not even you?"

"Well, except for me," Arthur answered, sniffing hard.

"I'll meet you backstage at Carnegie Hall, right after your concert, Arthur, how 'bout that, and—"

"My *maiden* concert—"

"Right, and after that we'll have supper and go to the movies to see—"

"The picture you got your first Academy Award for! Sets and costumes . . . fabulous and unspeakable . . ."

Zoe burst out laughing at that and pulled his soft bulk back into her arms. "You going to be all right without me?" she whispered into his neck.

"Zoeeeeee. Shoot, you know I can . . ."

She dug her fingers into the sleeves of his jacket. "*Are* you? Alone with her?"

"Aw, Zo, c'mon . . . she's not so bad. She needs me, we'll be fine. I'll be fine. Maybe I'll chase a few rainbows of my own. I decided, Zo, I'm really going to practice, every day."

"Oh, Arthur, I miss you already." Zoe clasped him to her, all her strength rushing into her arms to embrace this precious dreamer brother of hers.

"The Hillyard kids, ladies and gents," Arthur said in his favorite fake announcer voice. "Together again for the first time!"

And that was twenty years ago, not yesterday, or last week. Twenty years. Impossible.

Zoe closed her eyes for a second and then bent down to gather up the scattered pages of the contract, tapping them straight, trying to believe that after twenty years of traveling to this moment she might, at long last, have arrived.

In the earliest years only dreams and Yankee stubbornness had kept her going. She never paced herself, never stinted, never turned down any opportunity at all, however slim it seemed. She spent long nights on movie sets in Italy, England, Morocco, even in Turkey and Sardinia. Sometimes she was there only as fourth assistant to the set designer, or lackey to the art director, living for weeks on end in a tent or a trailer, staying up all night. Often the paycheck was either a joke or a figment of the producer's imagination, or even a promise starkly broken; sometimes she worked on spec—unpaid—no promises at all. But she always took every chance that came her way, and some that barely did, and thought herself lucky to have even that.

She soon spoke Italian well enough to get brief illegal day jobs, just enough to live and have some money for materials so she could work on her own sketches for the interiors of palaces and hovels, bordellos, souks, seraglios, and bunkhouses, for vaulted chapels, formal gardens, porticoes, baldachins, gazebos, yurts, and castles. She took orders from stoned cameramen and overweight producers and production designers who had less talent but (so many, many) more connections than she had. The exhilaration of the work, the new worlds she helped create, were—at least for a while—payment enough.

Five years after kissing Arthur goodbye in Boston, Zoe sold her few possessions for a plane ticket and went to London to study period design and the history of furniture, gardens, costume, and architecture. As she had as a lonely child in Boston, she went to two and three movies a day, but now analyzed everything from the style of the saddle blankets to the lighting of the heroine's pearl choker, sitting alone in the dark theaters for hours, making notes by the glow from the screen.

A few years later, back in Italy, she managed to worm her way into the crew of *Death in Venice,* hoping Luchino Visconti might glance just once in her direction, though he failed to. But she knew quite a few people now and the opportunities seemed slightly better. When things were going well, Zoe treated herself to daydreams of producers drinking crème de cacao by aquamarine swimming pools, mentioning her name with awe: "Call Zoe Hillyard for the nineteenth century, Sam—she really knows what she's doing. A costume picture? Historical sets? Believe me, Lou"—or Federico, or François, or Ingmar—"no one is better. No one." And she did get work, though sometimes only for a few days, for Fellini, Antonioni, others, painting sets for them around the clock. But they never spoke her name.

And then, somehow, soon after that, her psychic energy ran out, though Zoe admitted only to exhaustion, knowing that giving up was out of the question. She thought everything would be all right if she could just look into Arthur's sky-blue eyes again, be called by one of the funny old nicknames he loved to make up for her—could put his welcome-home bouquet of swaying river grasses in a mason jar on an antique bureau and sleep in her childhood bed. That she really didn't mind that Annabelle would be snoring under a ruffled coverlet one floor above she took for an indication of how badly she wanted to go home.

A month before her thirtieth birthday, she finished a shoot in Rome as fifth-ranking set dresser on a De Sica picture and fled home to Boston, fully expecting that Arthur would listen to her plans with joy, with celebration: Arthur-and-Zoe, folks, the Hillyard kids, together again for the first time! But in what seemed no time at all, an hour, maybe two, it was clear that the reunion Zoe longed for had turned into a standoff.

She went upstairs and pressed her forehead against the wood of Augusta Hillyard's bedroom door, the one Annabelle had locked the day she died, to which she kept the only key. Weeping silently, Zoe wondered if Grandmère had known it might someday come to this: she and Arthur screaming at each other with genuine anger, down the length of the vast, high-ceilinged drawing room.

On that icy November night ten years ago, Zoe walked back down the wide stone steps onto the wet pavement of Commonwealth Avenue, leaving Arthur speechless with misery on the back stoop, and Annabelle sniggering into her pink gin upstairs in her bedroom. Zoe got on the first flight to Los Angeles without her brother and had not seen him since.

Four years after she got to L.A., Zoe got work on a shoot in Baja, hired on this time as first assistant to the production designer. Though she'd found work off and on, paid more dues, this was her first decent picture after the return from Italy, the bolting from Boston. The movie featured renegade Aztecs, outcasts turned cannibal, and it was Zoe's idea to have them wear human body parts on thongs around their necks.

"That's a great touch, babe," the director said, squinting into the hot Mexican sun. Zoe leaned against the side of the camera van and watched him rub zinc oxide onto his nose; she thought things might just be looking up.

And although the Aztec picture turned out to be nonsensical at best—a foolish script, impenetrable fake theology, sodden actors—the saving grace was that the designer let Zoe do exactly as she pleased. He was an old man who despised the desert; he stayed in his air-conditioned trailer drinking quart bottles of the local tequila and reading Spillane, while Zoe, inspired by all the unexpected freedom, hung shriveled human hands around the neck of the "chieftain," and what was really a miserable movie turned into a cult film a year later and got picketed by the Catholic Church. For that the producer thanked God every day of his life until he died a few years later in his house in Cap Ferrat, a rich man.

Not quite a year after that, on her next picture, Zoe actually had a mini-trailer to herself, high in the Sierras, on a movie shot through snow and Vaseline. It was, the critics raved, nearly an art film; there were the usual whores and speculators, English-speaking Indians and gamblers with dueling scars, but everyone said the production values were first-class. Zoe (staying up all night with history books and old stills from a thousand forgotten "adult" westerns spread out all over the cot in the trailer) found a way to isolate a weathered look of cold venality that actually got the production designer nominated for an Oscar. A number of people promised not to forget that it was mostly Zoe Hillyard who made it happen, and Zoe herself thought she might be learning how to play the game at last.

But within months after the arty western wrapped, things seemed to settle down too fast; the production designer, well aware of his debt to Zoe Hillyard, turned his back on her and took his well-connected friends away. The few projects that came along after that—a detective farce, a teenage monster thing, one romantic comedy—were done with half her mind and just one hand. Disheartened, Zoe could not believe she had worked twenty years for trash like this. It was, for the first time, a trial to make the effort. For the first time, ever, she began to wonder if she should consider giving up.

When she was invited to a big party in Laurel Canyon, given to celebrate the end of a friend's picture, Zoe almost didn't go. But she knew it was a truism in Hollywood that anyone might be a contact, a connection—you can never tell who people used to be or who they might become. And it was there that she met Sidney Hooke.

Resplendent in dove gray and black foulard, Sidney had arranged his tidy person in a carved Mexican chair, next to which Zoe was sitting with a burrito that dripped guacamole onto the fistful of paper napkins in her lap.

"Fascinating group, isn't it?" Sidney said in a bored tone, looking critically at Zoe's dress. She looked back, taking a tiny bite of her burrito, smiling with amusement at his peeved and narrow face. Compact and tanned, elegant in a superbly epicene fashion, Sidney sipped at a Campari, hastily poured for him into a glass that Zoe could see was much too full. He was bending over his drink in a prim, fastidious way, holding a small hand over his ascot. Zoe chuckled and offered him some napkins.

Sidney was basking temporarily in the heat of being the "in" decorator to the Hollywood elite. But in spite of the glitzy life, it killed Sidney to know that he was little more to them than hired help. He loathed being introduced as somebody's *decorator;* he was sick of being on the fringes of the glamour. Sidney wanted in.

That he thought Zoe might be some sort of entrée to Hollywood's inner circle amused her, but she was wise enough, and worried enough, to allow him to encourage their new friendship. As time went by it became clear that he knew very little about period style, about furniture, about anything. But he did have beautiful taste, and knew a remarkable number of people in the business. Zoe soon realized that if she helped him out, Sidney might find a way to pick her brain to *her* advantage.

"Come, Zoe darling," Sidney might say, speaking of some producer's wife in Bel Air. "She wants her new music room to look 'Victorian'— whatever the Christ that means to her. Come, my angel, come look at her repulsive mantelpiece, her sickening window treatment. Come see what we can do with it. The bitch is loaded and her husband just made an absolutely fabulous deal with Paramount."

And Zoe went and quietly gave advice, not protesting when Sidney split the fees unfairly, not even when he blandly took all the credit for himself. For who could tell when a debt might be considered to have taken shape? But after a few months of this, Zoe felt more suspended than ever, waiting for a chance she could no longer even fantasize about. Though no explicit harm was done, the time was lost, and her dreams seemed more remote than ever.

And then, early last fall, on a smogless, windy Sunday afternoon, Zoe strolled along the Santa Monica palisades with an old pal she'd worked with on the Aztec picture, years before. She sipped a paper cup of coffee while Jerry rambled on and on, furiously licking an ice cream cone that melted as he talked. Zoe barely listened as he launched into a gossipy story about a new project, rumored to be almost off the ground and ready to cast.

"It's like the perfect high-concept, big-budget costume picture," Jerry said in his eager way, "about high-class Victorian thieves. 'Sposed to be a sexy scandal kind of thing."

Zoe sat down on one of the benches in the shade. "Thieves of what?"

"Art. Paintings, sculpture . . . y'know . . . things."

"Oh, you mean *The Gilded Affair?*" she asked.

"How d'you know?"

"It's been kicking around town for years. I thought it was dead in the water, but Victorians . . . wow." Zoe's eyes narrowed a little with an interest she chose not to show, not then.

"Crazy, huh?" Jerry sucked on the bottom inch of his ice cream cone and looked out over the sea. "I think I'm going to finally get an assistant director gig out of this," he said, "if I can just get in to see him."

"Him who?"

"Julian Frye."

"Oh, no chance. What've you been smoking?"

"I'm tellin' ya," said Jerry, giggling. "I thought it was kind of weird that he was doing it, but you know me, I'm open-minded." Jerry swallowed the last morsel and wiped his fingers on his jeans.

"Julian Frye. My God," Zoe said. "He's supposed to be completely impossible to work with, Jer. Everybody says he's a maniac, a son of a bitch."

"Who cares?" Jerry said calmly, digging in his pocket for a match. "He's also a fuckin' genius. I got a friend of mine at Fox says he's doin' the script himself. He's probably ripping off the three-four writers he already canned, but what else is new? More power to him."

"But nobody out here cares about Victorians," Zoe said. "The nineteenth century, literary scripts, for God's sake."

"Well," Jerry said, dragging on his cigarette, "I know Victorian's a hard sell, and it don't come cheap either, but I guess one of the writers he fired looked at doing it modern and it didn't work. So he's back to late Victorian. I hear he's even got serious financing. English actors. All that shit. He and the D.C. are getting the crew together."

"Does he have a designer?"

"I dunno."

"Can you find out?"

Jerry shrugged. "No problem."

And Zoe lay awake all that night, her precious old copy of *Masters of Victorian Design* on the pillow beside her. In the morning she called Sidney Hooke and invited him to lunch.

"Oh, lovely Julian," Sidney said, so casually, a week later. "He must be back from Singapore."

Zoe, well used to this posturing, smiled indulgently. "You've known him for years, haven't you?" Zoe said, reaching for the wine bottle. "Please have another glass of wine, Sidney."

"Oh, heavens, yes, for years, darling," said Sidney, wiping his small mouth on the linen napkin, sipping his chardonnay.

"I'd love for you to introduce me to him, Sidney. You know, an introduction's really all I need."

"He's very busy, my angel, so busy. . . ." Sidney wiggled his fingers at a friend across the room, biding his time. "He's working on the script day and night, you know."

Zoe had nagged Jerry unmercifully until he brought her a copy of the treatment. He couldn't get the script—still under wraps—but copies of the treatment, which gave an overview of the plot and principal scenes, were being leaked, he said, all over town.

"Sidney, this picture is perfect for me, and Frye doesn't have a designer yet."

"Oh? I thought he surely did." Sidney smiled and looked straight back at her.

"Well, I happen to know he doesn't." Jerry had already investigated; he'd sworn to Zoe it was true. She was a little irritated with Sidney's phony games. What was he holding out for?

But Sidney was thinking about it. He gazed at the decorated ceiling and sipped his thirty-dollar wine and thought it all the way through. He had supported Julian Frye's last picture, which had ultimately grossed (as Roger later said) a bazillion dollars, but Sidney had little to show for it other than his house in Malibu, the closet full of Armani, and the Swiss accounts. He'd deserved an associate producer credit the last time and hadn't gotten it because Frye was such a bastard. But Zoe Hillyard and her talent (which Sidney had come to feel was partly *his*, after all) were quite another matter. He knew the odds were slim to none of Frye locating a Zoe Hillyard–caliber designer on his own. Not at this late stage. Sidney realized it would only take a sentence or two to let Julian Frye understand that associate producer credits were acceptable as currency at times like this.

He looked carefully at her across the table. "Julian's films make pretty good money, but so far he has no Oscars, you know."

"Fine," said Zoe. "He has to get one sometime. Why not now?"

Sidney was unaware that from the minute Jerry dropped off the thirty-page treatment, Zoe had spent nearly every waking hour soaking up the characters, the settings, thinking about the use of color and light in the tall Victorian rooms. The story was full of marvelous possibilities. They would need glittering ballrooms and dark conservatories, intimate parlors and chateau-like country places—all forming a luscious backdrop for the dire events of the plot. Zoe got out all her books on fabric design, wall coverings, period furniture, and architecture and went to the library to get more. She even had daydreams about the heroine, Beatrice Holland, imagining the two of them in vivid conversation.

She looked over at Sidney and pushed his dessert two inches closer so he wouldn't have to move a muscle to eat it. She kept looking in his eyes until he tasted it, lowering his eyelids in delight.

"Yesss . . ." Sidney said softly; he licked a morsel of whipped cream off his thumb and smiled into his wine. "He just might be able to use you. I'll tell him what good friends we are."

Late that night, Zoe stood in her bathrobe by her open kitchen door. "Oh, please," she whispered into the foggy night. "Oh, please, this could be it."

Zoe was introduced to Julian Frye at an extravagant party at Sidney's beach house. Chromium track lighting cast leaping shadows as Sidney moved enthusiastically from group to group, twirling the women to show off their dresses, praising the men for their footage and their deals. Zoe sat alone in a bamboo chair on the lanai and watched the winter sun sink into the sea.

When Frye finally arrived, hours late but for once without an entourage, Sidney pulled them both aside and sent them walking down the beach, rubbing his hands as he watched them moving along the sand far below the lanai railing. He was delighted: they *both* owed him now. And the irony was that Zoe believed it was all up to her, this task of snaring Frye, not knowing that having seen the small folder of pre-liminary sketches she had let Sidney borrow, Frye needed nearly no snaring at all. But Julian Frye's own life was a scenario more thickly plotted than his films.

He enjoyed his reputation as a flamboyant, dominating risk-taker, and he paid several people handsomely to keep such images alive. The *auteur* of his generation, Frye did it all—script, production, direction. He supervised every detail of every picture, from the musical score to the narcotics preferences of the actors. But he was still, no longer on the sunny side of fifty, looking for the big one.

Julian Frye was a man with six cars, four homes, eight Oscar nom-inations, and three ex-wives (each from a different continent); he car-ried several pints of his own blood with him when he traveled. He also had ten million bucks in the below-the-line art budget for *The Gilded Affair* which he was willing to exchange for Oscar-winning production values. For an Academy Award was the one thing he did *not* have—and meant to get. This time nominations alone were unacceptable.

Frye relished the notion that only he, spiritual heir to De Mille and Lean, would dare to do a film like *The Gilded Affair*. He was well aware that pictures about Victorians (who were not also cowboys) had a small (indeed, invisible) constituency in Hollywood. But he knew also that the vicious game that swirled around Laurence Thane and Beatrice Holland, the naive lovers whose romance anchored the story line, would surprise everyone. The script had it all: power and duplicity, sex and violence, stolen art treasures and rich people in love. All he needed was the look.

Frye arrived at Sidney's beach house on that balmy November night actually eager to meet this woman who Sidney had promised him would be just perfect. Not that he trusted the old queen, of course.

"She's wonderful!" Sidney had chortled, rubbing his hands. "An artist, you can take my word for it, Julian! Brilliant!"

But Frye was determined to see it for himself. He hadn't gotten where he was by taking someone else's word for anything. He made it his business to get prints of all the pictures Zoe Hillyard had ever worked on and sat alone in the screening room of his huge leased stu-dio on Melrose Avenue fast-forwarding to sets and costumes, scrutinizing every frame for authenticity, for detail, for taste. And dammit, that sneaky little Sidney had been right: she had a perfect sense of time, a feeling for period and mood that all the others lacked. She seemed to have grown up in that gilded world herself.

Still, never mentioning what he had already seen, Frye told Zoe he was doubtful.

"Of course," he said, watching his panatela burn out in the damp sand, "there's dozens of designers out there, but I want a new eye. I'm sick of these bastards who've done a few *Gunsmoke* episodes and right away they think they know Victorian. But listen, if you want to rough something out, give it a shot; I don't mind taking a look."

And when her first drawings came, Frye was not a bit surprised to see that Zoe's eye was perfect; her evocation of the atmosphere, her clear sense of the physical weight that must surround the unhappy lovers—the clothing, the furniture, even the architecture drenched in opulent Victorian restraint—was everything he'd hoped.

At a meeting in his leather-lined office at the studio he turned to her, almost overwhelmed with greedy admiration, although he thought he hid that well.

"I won't kid you, Zoe," he said. "Your stuff is pretty good. I like it. I need more, though," he said, shrugging apologetically as if some higher power were calling the shots. "I need to see more."

"Not without a contract," Zoe said, steeling herself for disaster. "Not on spec." For just a split second she actually lost her train of thought wondering where she got the nerve to talk to him like that.

"I'll be happy to pay you something for the sketches," Frye said, looking at her over a large drawing of Laurence Thane's library.

Zoe reached over and took the sketch out of his hands. "I'm sorry, Julian, that's not really what I had in mind. I'm very glad you like my work, I really am. But I want you to hire me. I want a contract and I want a full-frame credit as production designer."

Frye was astonished, but he didn't say no. He was enjoying his game too much to have it end. However, a week later when he invited her to lunch, ostensibly to discuss her "contract" over lobster crèpes, they had a disagreement about practical sets. It was Zoe who brought the subject up, pointing out that Frye had to film the picture in an authentic Victorian house, that studio sets would not convey the sense of enclosure the story line demanded, the tight, suffocating density of space. Frye disagreed and seemed genuinely angry this time; Zoe was on director's turf with both feet. But even though she feared she was being too difficult and perverse, Zoe stuck to her guns, knowing she was right. Frye was furious and let her know it.

Two days after that, Sidney, theatrically massaging his chest, showed up at Zoe's apartment to "encourage" her to listen to what he called "reason."

"He's the *director*," Sidney wheedled, as if that were really just another word for God. "Maybe it would be smart to work on a few exteriors," he begged with the tone of one who thinks he knows what he's talking about. "Work on the country houses, the winter scenes, horse-drawn carriages in the snow . . . whatever!"

And though Sidney called daily to nag some more, and Frye waited the whole thing out, Zoe paced the Santa Monica shoreline in a January drizzle, immune to all entreaty.

Even Roger, whose judgment she trusted completely, had a hard time persuading her to let Frye be the boss.

"Why is he doing this to me?" Zoe cried, curled into the corner of her sofa. "He knows he's wrong. He's just playing with me! He can't expect to film this picture in a studio. Dammit!" She was exhausted, nearly in tears. "I just want to *do* it—make it happen. I've given him wonderful, wonderful stuff, I know it in my bones, Rog, I feel as if I've been there. Why doesn't he . . ."

"Oh, Zoe, honey, for God's sake, don't let the practical set thing be a deal-breaker. Don't sabotage yourself."

"You think I'm doing that?" she said, looking furious and horrified at once.

Roger sighed. "I think you're close."

"Yeah, maybe so." Zoe sighed and clicked her back teeth, looking into the middle distance. "I guess I know that."

"After all," Roger said, "do you want to do horror movies, biker pictures—Christ! television!—all your life? Don't let this get away from you, Zo. Use your head."

Then, in February, no contracts yet in hand, Frye announced (telling Zoe that it was temporarily a secret) that he planned to bring the passionate attraction of Laurence and Beatrice to its logical conclusion. Never mind that graphic sex might cause a problem with the ratings board. They could be made to see things his way; the box-office receipts would bear him out.

Zoe, seeing her chance to mend some fences, responded with a portfolio of drawings and collages of Thane and Holland alone. Their scenes à deux were planned in new colors, new dimensions, in different light from dinner parties, balls, and evenings at the opera. They were to be separate, isolated, and intimate—immune from the events that swirled around them.

When he saw Zoe's drawings, Frye, completely out of resistance, marveled again that this woman had so well envisioned the elegant nineteenth-century universe he expected her to re-create. It was as if she had time-traveled and was only reporting what she'd seen. But that very afternoon, when he shook her hand to seal the agreement and kissed her on both cheeks, she looked up at him with an expression of such self-containment that for just a moment Frye had a small, unnerving second thought. He knew that eventually he was definitely going to have some sort of trouble with her, but he went for the clause about a full-frame credit almost without blinking, though the lawyer spluttered when Frye instructed him to write it in.

ZOE A. HILLYARD: PRODUCTION DESIGNER

It was fine with him.

Zoe uncoiled her cramped legs and looked up at the clock on the dresser, surprised to see that another half hour had slipped by in dreamy rumination. She had promised to be at the restaurant by sundown.

In the bathroom, she pressed a warm cloth against her cheeks, put on fresh moisturizer and mascara, and suddenly paused, staring deep into her own eyes. Zoe knew how she looked, that she was handsome rather than pretty. She had an angular, pale face, with perfect, poreless Yankee skin; her tall, slender build would be called "willowy" in a novel or a press release. But her eyes—those wide black Hillyard eyes—she had seen only in her own mirror and in dim photos of her long-dead paternal grandfather, the mysterious and terrifying Anthony Hillyard.

The resemblance had always been remarked upon by anyone aware of the connection. Over the years, Zoe had wondered about him from time to time, but her memories were few, those of a child, many no doubt the memories of other people. But she had heard enough, from Annabelle and others, to understand that despite the power and glamour of which so many stood in awe, those who had loved Anthony Hillyard were few indeed. Zoe had no way of knowing that she and Anthony had one more thing in common—only Augusta Hillyard herself, the legendary Grandmère of whom Zoe recollected only scented warmth, had ever loved them both.

Zoe put the mascara down and went back to the bedroom to get dressed. She put the contract into the bottom bureau drawer along with the box of Claudia's notes, but even though she tucked the handkerchief box in underneath, she kept out the photograph of herself and Arthur and propped it against the clock, staring at it as she zipped her skirt, slid her bracelets on.

"Dammit, Arthur," Zoe whispered to the boy in the picture. "This is no good—this is awful. You should know what happened to me today."

She blew her nose and spritzed her neck with Roger's favorite cologne, grabbed her jacket, and headed for the door. When she got to the front hall she turned suddenly, her car keys jingling in her hand, and went back to the bedroom. She stood in the doorway and watched while the last little ray of sunlight washed across the faces of the children in the photograph.

TWO

*R*oger Horvath rested his elbows on the terrace railing and looked out over the sea. In his eagerness, he'd arrived at Sal's new Villa Marie a little bit too early, and for half an hour there had been nothing to do but admire the view as the sun slowly sank away, en route to cast its light on Asia.

He wished Zoe were with him right that minute; she loved to see the evening colors change, the magenta horizon blurring into the green-white sparkle of the sea. She wasn't late yet, but if she didn't hurry up, she'd miss the final glorious moment when the sun disappeared into the ocean.

When Sal came over to say hello, Roger gave him two bottles of Veuve Clicquot to put in the automatic chiller.

"Zoe'll be here before sunset, or so she said," Roger told him.

Sal squinted at the cerise sky over the ocean. "Then she better get a move on," he said, and disappeared with the champagne.

Roger leaned again on the railing, hoping as he had all day that nothing had gone awry and that after enduring months of Frye's manipulations, Zoe would arrive to meet him with good news. She had been driving into Beverly Hills to the lawyer's office every day this week, and every night Roger had listened to her reports on the negotiations. Frye's reputation as a son of a bitch, Roger thought to himself, was well earned. Sidney Hooke had confided to Roger that Zoe was a shoo-in for the production designer job, but that Frye was making her work for it, right up to the last minute.

Roger had known Sidney as his consultant and reluctant confidant for years, and had disliked and mistrusted him almost as long. But as Roger's small art gallery became more and more successful, and his reputation for taste and honesty grew, Sidney ran to him more and more often for advice about the paintings he convinced his rich clients they could not live without. That it had been through Sidney that he and Zoe met tormented Roger in a way he knew to be both needless and neurotic. But he couldn't bear it that he might be beholden to the likes of Sidney Hooke for anything. It had become clear that Sidney also expected Zoe to be grateful to him for introducing her to Julian Frye, and Roger knew that Sidney Hooke didn't do things for free—ever. He was the sort of person who remembered what he was owed and tended, moreover, to wonder what people had done for him *lately*. In fact, Sidney had called tonight, just as Roger was getting out of the shower, to see if the "deal was done," as he put it. It was not insignificant, Roger thought, that Sidney did not get his news from Frye.

Sal came over to pull Roger away from the railing and led him to a table on which he had placed a perfect antipasto, concocted of Roger's favorites. "Eat the prosciutto," Sal advised. "I know Zoe don't like it; I fixed it so it won't mess up the design if you eat that first." He put a pretty little glass of sherry down next to the antipasto. "On the house. Drink up—it'll line your stomach."

Roger sat and picked with a cocktail fork at the slices of prosciutto and cheese, wafer-thin avocado and tomato, and chewed slowly on the tiny bones of the one traditional anchovy that Zoe also wouldn't miss. Calmly eager, he sat waiting for her, sipping the sherry, feeling a little chilly, feeling good.

As soon as it seemed adequately clear that Frye would stop playing games and give Zoe her contract, Roger had racked his brain for something with which to make a perfect celebration. He had his heart set on something Victorian like Parma violets, but when he tried to buy them, eight different florists looked at him as if he were crazy. He gave up and settled instead on the unusual dark pink roses he saw in a shop in Bel Air; the florist had only nine to sell him, so Roger supplemented his bouquet with all the pink tulips in the shop. He had one more pink rose with him, which he laid at her place beside the silverware, smiling at it while he picked at the antipasto, remembering his first view of her.

He had stood, almost a year ago, on a glorious May afternoon, unnoticed in the doorway of Sidney's beach house. Zoe, her shoulders slightly turned away, was stretched out on her stomach on Sidney's antique rug, shiny dark hair hooked behind her ears, reading *ARTnews*. She had looked up suddenly and noticed Roger in the doorway. The light was behind her, dazzling almost-summer light, and for a minute all he could see was the shine of her hair, until he came closer, and then he saw her lovely crescent smile.

The very next day he took her to dinner at Sal's old pizza place on Venice Beach, and sat like an enchanted boy, watching while Zoe sipped at Sal's house wine, a really nasty resinous Chianti she said smelled just like Italy.

"Have you been there?" she asked, smiling at him over the glass. "To Italy?"

"Well, a few times . . . to the museums. About five years ago, I spent six months in Florence."

"Firenze," Zoe said softly, gazing just to his left, to a view of Florence only she could see. "A wonderful place," she said. "What were you doing there?"

She listened in perfect concentration while he told her about his gallery and the years of trial and error and training that had led him to it.

"You know, at first," Roger said, "I thought I just wanted to paint, to be an artist myself. I didn't know there was anything else. I started by trying to copy masterpieces, and I put all my allowance, my paper-route money, every nickel I could get my hands on, into art books. Lord, I even tried painting by candlelight," he said, "the way Goya did."

"Uh-huh . . ." Zoe said, nodding and grinning at him.

"Well, that was okay until the night two candles fell off my cowboy hat onto the bedspread, and believe me my dad put a stop to *that* nonsense in a hurry."

"I can imagine," Zoe said, laughing with a delight that made Roger feel he was back in his old bedroom trying to copy *The Naked Maja,* standing there in his sneakers at two in the morning with blackout candles anchored to his hat.

But when it became clear that he didn't have it, certainly not enough of it, Roger absorbed the disappointment as best he could and soon learned that he could make a career from the love of art alone. There followed years of study, internships, six months at the Uffizi, two years at Christie's in London, and then, soon enough, a small but solid niche in Los Angeles as an appraiser and dealer in fine art.

"So now I have my little gallery," Roger said, almost blushing at her expression, "and it's growing. It'll grow more. I handle mostly eighteenth-century stuff, early nineteenth, rococo . . . neoclassic."

"Your period," Zoe said, her eyes narrowed with interest. "A beautiful time. But I can't imagine having the courage to give up a dream like that," she said, her fingers grazing his arm.

For some reason, Roger was a little bit embarrassed when she said that. "I have other dreams now," he had answered, shrugging slightly. "How could I not? And I love it; I really do."

That first night they talked until Sal threw them out at one o'clock. They sat at the table, hunched toward each other, gabbing away about art, movies, friends new and old (Sidney Hooke among them), the stories just tumbling out. But Zoe didn't talk about herself that night— certainly not in the way that Roger did—and not for many nights thereafter.

But even though they soon found themselves constantly together, the days now seeming incomplete without a phone call, a cup of coffee, a flower left on Zoe's doorstep, it troubled and confused Roger that Zoe had so slim a need to talk about herself. She spoke readily, vivaciously, about art, movies, politics, history, anywhere her thoughts, or his, might take them. She could be a voluble and witty gossip, trenchant in her observations of the crazy movie people she had known over the years. She was capable of hours of attention to Roger's own ramblings, her attention never wandering as he told her all about his work, the foibles and self-indulgences of his clients, his hopes, his plans, the living of his life. But except for anything to do with movies, Zoe almost never spoke about herself.

Sometimes thinking about her late at night in the privacy of the small back room of his gallery, Roger wondered if this remote, lovely Zoe Hillyard might be the Great Love he'd waited for, the object of passion that his nature so deeply needed; but he also wondered what it might say of him that he'd become so quickly enraptured by a woman whom he barely knew. Almost every time the conversation turned to Boston, where Roger had spent quite a bit of time himself, doing a fellowship at the Gardner Museum in his early days, Zoe would find a way to change the subject.

Yet something made Roger feel content to wait. For he was a patient man who, at forty-four, had tolerated a good deal already and did not particularly think of this as endurance because by then, two months into that swaying, inexplicit mating dance, Zoe's integration into his life seemed complete. He told himself that Zoe was *there,* no matter what had yet to happen, whatever anguish or joy might lie ahead.

By the time full summer came, when roses and jacaranda choked the parks and gardens and even the median strips on the freeways blazed with color, Roger admitted to himself that he was completely in love with Zoe Hillyard—besotted, bewitched, voiceless with passion. But it still worried him that he so loved someone about whom, by his lights, he knew so little. Oh, he knew her skin, the shape of her mouth and the feeling of her teeth on his and the precise strength of her hands and what she would cry out at—what she could not resist from him—where and what and how hard or how gently or how long.

They would spend hours at a time in Zoe's cool dim bedroom on her fresh sheets, Roger startled every time by her capacity for such stunning intimacy, her ability to be both voracious and exquisitely tender with him, touching his body sometimes so gently that he was brought from the senselessness of passion to the threshold of thought by his very wondering if and where she'd touched him.

When she was with him she was inventive, strong, unshockable, welcoming him with long, soft shrieks of delight, her black eyes wide open, glowing into his. But when each encounter ended, Zoe—unlike other women he had known, all cuddlers, all sleek purring cats—would only kiss the palm of his hand, or run her artist's fingers along the smooth angle of his beard, and go away, leaving him emptied of himself and full of her, flat on his back in bed. She always eventually came back, sometimes after just a few minutes, sitting on the edge of the bed, touching him in the last place she had before. And each time she did that it seemed to Roger that her leaving was a dream and only her return was real.

It seemed as if she couldn't get enough of him and his long strong bones and his large, gentle hands, and his heart would *leap* at that as if such things were knowledge enough. And although he was wise enough to understand that intimacy is not knowledge, he believed that resisting the temptation to press her to some sort of declaration was simple wisdom: he dreaded losing her. It seemed a direct act of self-preservation to wait.

And then, for some reason, late in the summer, Zoe had begun to talk about her family. The transition was so imperceptible, so subtle, that Roger could not mark the moment. At first only small anecdotes slipped out as if she hardly meant to tell them, just fragmented stories of her childhood years in Boston, held together only by Roger's intense desire to make sense of it.

Most often she spoke of Arthur, her older brother, and of Claudia, her first cousin and childhood playmate. Occasionally she mentioned their great-aunt Annabelle, who raised her and Arthur after both their parents died. And then there was Grandmère.

"Grandmère?" Roger said one afternoon, propping himself up on one elbow to look down at her and listen.

Zoe had smiled and hummed deep in her throat. "Umm, yes. That's what everybody always called her. My great-grandmother, Augusta Florence Lattimore Hillyard . . . oh God!" Zoe had laughed a little then, suddenly closing her eyes.

"I can remember," she said after a minute, "well, I pretend I remember, she always wore a perfume called *Nuit de Noël,* Christmas Night. Oh! I can't imagine why I said that. I was so little when she died, how could I . . . Annabelle must have said something once and it just stuck way back in my . . . I can't bring back any memories of her, no matter how hard I try. Grandmère's room was always locked when we were growing up. Beats me why, but Annabelle closed it up when Grandmère died and hid the key, I guess, and Arthur and I were forbidden to go near it."

Zoe laughed a little and sat up cross-legged in the middle of the bed. "Of course, we did anyway; we'd sneak up to listen at the door, late at night when Annabelle was asleep, to check if we could hear Grandmère breathing."

"Locked it up? Untouched?" Roger was amazed. "Like Queen Victoria and Albert?"

"Exactly like that. Big mystery. Anyway, Arthur and I grew up in her house, you see, on Comm Ave. Grandmère's beautiful house. Must be a hundred years old by now. No one ever lived there but Hillyards."

She'd gotten out of bed then, reaching down to smooth his forehead with the back of her hand before she gathered her robe around her and went quickly out of the room.

Roger lay there with his hand covering the place on his forehead where she'd touched him, realizing he must have walked by the house a hundred times, not knowing. He might have passed a closing gate, or seen Arthur Hillyard in his old tweed jacket on the steps, buttoning it up against the sudden damp, or squinting into a hot white New England summer sky, humming a tune. Had he seen Annabelle, perhaps, proceeding like a full-rigged battleship (as Zoe said dryly) down the great avenue, the peasants scattering as she sailed by . . . and never known?

One bright November afternoon, shortly before she met Julian Frye, Zoe told Roger that it was ten years that day since she had seen her brother and that they hadn't so much as spoken since. Astonished, Roger pressed her, but though she quickly retreated, Roger knew it was important, a loss compounded by a keen, still-fresh regret. He was not so convinced that she had truly left the hundred-year-old house on Commonwealth Avenue and all its generations buried under the cobblestones of Boston. And though it was quite a while before she offered any details, Roger found the strength to hope that Zoe might have begun to love him back. He chose to take her stories of Boston and Arthur and Grandmère as a sign—even though she never spoke the words.

It was almost completely dark, and Sal came over quietly and lit the small flame-shaped lamp on the table; the pale blue pleated shade glowed in the dusk. Roger held the rim of the empty sherry glass against his mouth, realizing he'd been taken completely out of himself by his thoughts. He turned from the darkened ocean and looked across to the front door. Several laughing couples came in together, blocking the entrance, and then he saw Zoe kissing Sal, moving through the crowded tables with long, eager strides, her arms outstretched to him.

"Oh, Roger!" she cried, still yards away. "Oh, my dear, thank you for the flowers!"

"They came!"

"They did—they're beautiful, *beautiful!* I put them in the vase. And what a *wonderful* color—you must have looked all over town for them!"

He laughed and put his arms around her. The breeze from the ocean blew her hair into his face—it felt cold and silky to him.

"And the card was, uh, accurate? 'Zoe A. Hillyard: Production Designer' is carved in stone?"

Zoe stood back from him with her hands still holding his sleeves, grinning. "In granite. And a full-frame credit!"

Roger laughed again and brushed a strand of hair away from her eyes. "That's wonderful, wonderful. I knew it. Didn't I tell you I knew that?"

Zoe drank her first glass of the champagne without stopping, and Roger, chuckling, filled it up again. She took a sip and then saw the rose beside her plate. She picked it up, putting her hand over her mouth for a second, and then looked with a broad smile into Roger's eyes. She twirled the stem in her fingers and brought the blossom to her nose.

"Okay, tell me," Roger said. "Everything."

And Zoe, pushing the menu aside, told him all about the final details of the contract, Frye's last-ditch attempt at game-playing.

"I was so freaked when I left the office I didn't even pay the parking lot attendant," she said, laughing at herself. "I just peeled out. I guess I'd better go back tomorrow . . . or mail it. Eight bucks."

"Speaking of which, how's the money?" Roger asked, crossing his long legs. They had talked about this at length, Roger quoting industry catechism to her on salary track records.

"The money's pretty good—could be better I guess, but that's okay. And a quarter of a point, which I didn't actually expect, so . . . but it's good—it's fine. I'm not in this for the money, after all." Zoe laughed suddenly at the obvious truth of that.

"Well, what's that 'nonperformance'?" Roger said, frowning, knowing Zoe did not focus on such detail, did not always adequately protect herself, or when she did, did so excessively—too little or too much.

"The language is standard, Rog, no big deal." But then she giggled again. "How can I possibly 'nonperform,' for heaven's sake, when I do this shit fifteen, twenty hours a day?"

She put the rose down and reached for her champagne glass, taking just a sip. "It's more than I even hoped for, Rog. It's fine. The credit is what matters most. The credit is the best part . . . aside from the actual work, of course. If he's screwing me a little on the money, I don't really care." Roger sucked in his breath and said nothing, reluctant to lecture her tonight.

When their food came they ate in silence for a little while, smiling at each other, catching each other's glances, Zoe turning away every few minutes to stare at the glimmers of random light on the water.

"So who's playing 'the heroine'?" asked Roger, his mouth full of *pollo valdostana*.

"Beatrice Holland? Nobody knows. Frye's still keeping it a big secret. That son of a gun is having the time of his life with it. He's got eight, maybe nine agents he's playing around with—price is no object, by the way—for Miz Holland. The man absolutely does not grasp the concept of saving money."

"Good news for the production designer," Roger said, sipping his ice water.

"You bet it is," said Zoe, laughing, raising her glass.

"Anything new with that practical set business?" Roger asked, still chewing on his chicken.

"No. He's sandbagging me, but I don't think there's too much I can do about it," she said, wrinkling her nose, putting her fork down. "It's not in my contract, of course—I mean, it's not appropriate for that— but I can tell you, Rog, I'm not ready to give in. I know I'm right. After all, he can't do a picture like this in a studio . . . he can't. Look, he's not stupid, he'll come around, he'll figure it out, eventually." She winked at Roger and picked up the rose again, waving it by its stem like a magic wand.

"You're amazing," Roger said. "Stubborn, stubborn, stubborn. Well, I guess it's really a question of finding the perfect location, right?"

Zoe nodded vigorously and took a sip of her wine. "That's right. I'd be crazy to rant and rave about practical sets if there isn't a good one out there that I can suggest to him."

"You mean shove down his throat."

Zoe laughed. "Well, of course, yes. That's what I mean."

It had become full dark on the ocean's face, a sliver of moon casting quivering shadows. Zoe raised her glass to admire the champagne bubbles in the change of light and looked over at Roger, who was meticulously cutting his chicken into tiny pieces, his auburn beard crisp and shiny in the light from the lamp on the table. As he glanced up at her, she had a flash of him as Laurence Thane, the disconcerted, unfulfilled lover of *The Gilded Affair*.

But it was just a zip of an image—and not accurate at that. For Roger had a tolerance for risk that Laurence did not have; Roger did not confine himself to contemplation, did not lack, Zoe was sure, the passion to let nature take its course.

Roger realized she was staring at him and smiled. "What?" he said, pursing his lips.

"Nothing. Nothing. . . ."

"Zoe . . . what, honey?" Roger wiped his mouth with the corner of his napkin and pushed his plate back.

"Oh . . . well, when I got home this afternoon . . ."

"Tell me, Zo."

"I found an old picture of Arthur and me when we were kids, standing in front of Grandmère's house, oh, I don't know when, maybe thirty years ago, more. . . ."

She broke off and filled his glass with the last of the Veuve Clicquot, taking a deep breath before she spoke again.

"He'd be so tickled if he knew about this," she whispered, looking back toward the ocean. "Well, maybe he would. Who knows?"

"He would, Zo. Maybe you should . . . ?"

"You know, when we were kids," Zoe said in a choked voice, putting down the champagne glass and reaching into her purse for a Kleenex, "we used to spend hours together, up in Arthur's room, trying to imagine how it would be when we 'grew up,' all our wild wishes coming true."

"Well," Roger said. "Why don't you tell him?"

But Zoe just shrugged and turned away to stare at the ocean again. She stood up and leaned her elbows on the railing as he had done before, watching the whitecaps of the receding tide.

"You could call him, Zo," Roger said again, softly.

Zoe didn't answer him. She only stood there with the slow wind ruffling her hair, and even when he came up behind her and kissed her neck, she didn't say a word.

Later, after Roger paid the check and they said goodnight to Sal, they walked down the winding steps beside the restaurant, side by side on the narrow wooden path. The night was clear and silent, the soft sounds of the tide brightening the quiet. Roger put his arm around Zoe's shoulder and pulled her off the path onto the sand. They walked down to the damp, packed shoreline, where foam crinkled and fled out to sea again, back and forth. The sound of the occasional traffic on Pacific Coast Highway swished dimly behind them. The ocean slurped at the shore in little curls of water they could barely see in the dim moonlight. Roger turned and put his other arm around Zoe and felt her relax against him.

"I'm so happy for you, sweetheart," he whispered.

Zoe felt the roughness of his warm jacket against her cheek and slid her arms around his waist.

"Did I thank you for the flowers . . . and the one beside my plate?" she said, waving the rose behind his back.

"Yes," he said into her hair. "Yes, you did."

"Thank you . . . again." Zoe's mouth was open against his coat. She heard the slipping of the waves, the slight crunch of the sand, as Roger shifted his weight to hold her closer.

He kissed her slowly and carefully, almost as if he wanted to feel each millimeter's sliding of her mouth, each fraction of degree of warmth from her breath. "Zoe, darling Zoe," he said, so softly he could not really hear the words, only feel the vibration in his own throat as he said them to her. Zoe kissed the side of his mouth and turned herself in his arms until her back was to him and they were both facing the ocean, looking at the narrow streak of the moon's light on the lapping crests of water.

Roger pressed her gently against him, his eyes closed in her silky hair, one hand flat under her breasts, the other on her throat, his long fingers stroking her jaw, over and over, caressing her lower lip while he rubbed his face in her hair, breathing in a strange, melded scent of roses, shampoo, olive oil, and champagne. Zoe took his gliding finger between her teeth and held it there for a moment. All at once she turned back to him, her arms encircling his waist again, her mouth half open.

Roger took her hand and led her a few yards over the sand to the shelter of the pilings under Sal's terrace. He wrapped his arms around her and kissed her with perhaps a bit more roughness than he meant to, but even as she kissed him back, she pulled slightly away and looked up at him, reaching for his face with both hands.

"Come make love with me," she said. "Come home with me."

pointed out (in what I thought was an unnecessarily ironic manner) that he could not afford Italian palaces such as Mrs. Gardner is building for herself out on the Fenway. I replied, all sweet reason, that I did not expect an "Italian palace" but that I did expect to be able to invite my friends and *his* associates into our home without fear of shabby fringe trailing on a dusty Turkey carpet. Eugene replied that I could get rid of the damned carpet for all of him, and cut the fringe off with a pair of scissors. Suffice it to say, the conversation degenerated rather badly after that.

I know perfectly well that this is not an Italian palace, nor is it one of those confections down in Newport that the authors probably had in mind. But there are a few cues that one can certainly take, not only from the book, but from the homes of some of our friends as well. I do not want my children growing up with tattered wallpaper and chipped parquet, and I warrant Eugene doesn't either. All the same, he would probably insist that this is "not money well spent"—a phrase of which I am quite weary, thank you very much! Money that will help assure the social position and the domestic comfort of his family *is* money well spent, for heaven's sake!

Monday, December 22, 1902

Eugene has gone to the vault (I think somewhat prematurely) to take out my Birthday Earrings (as they shall no doubt be known within our family circle forever) for Mrs. Gardner's party. Mathilde writes that she and Freddy will be coming up from New York in a private car, and I have invited them to stop here with us beforehand for a light meal, since Belle Gardner is not known for the provisioning of her table. She has asked us all to arrive at nine o'clock punctually, so there should be plenty of time. If Eugene is unwilling to redecorate, even for this special evening, at least the Lattimore Coalport will be out and washed and sparkling on the table in the dining room—correction: the dingy dining room. I cannot help but recall that when the Gaylords were here two years ago, Mathilde was far too ladylike to comment on the appearance of my parlor. I daren't say anything now or Eugene will accuse me of trying to impress Mathilde Gaylord and I will have lost ground in my strategy. I shall be adroit. But oh! I am furious with that man!

THREE

(FROM THE DIARIES OF AUGUSTA HILLYARD: 1902 TO 1905)

Sunday, November 30, 1902

I am very sorry to be obliged to say (even in these secret pages) that I am extremely vexed with my husband. We have had a significant disagreement on the subject of refurbishing our home. It was a gift of my papa's generosity (as Eugene very well knows), and while we all love it a great deal, there is no question that some modest redecoration has become essential. It is too florid, too robust! It is quite out of fashion! When we had words about this last evening I reminded Eugene that he enjoys cutting a rather pretty figure at his club and wants me to look my best at all times. Why, I asked him, with somewhat more heat than I'd intended, does he not wish his home to look its best as well? And yet Eugene, he of the well-trimmed mustache and the English tailoring, does not quite seem to grasp the comparison. He accused me of loving appearances, of snobbery. I accused him of vanity and hypocrisy, and the resulting dialogue was quite disgraceful.

Last spring, when a new edition of that lovely book on the decoration of houses came out, I knew the time had come to consider renovations. After all, it has been nearly six years since we replaced the parlor drapes! Sad to say, however, my husband does not share my views. When I approached him with my idea of redoing the downstairs rooms according to some of the suggestions in the book, he laughed at me and

Well, we seem to have survived Belle Gardner's New Year's Eve gala at Fenway Court. The woman runs her entertainments as some people ran their governments in the fourteenth century. We did hear some very lovely music—there was Schubert (my perennial favorite), Bach, and even Mozart—and people seemed to enjoy the performances very much. I thought I saw my husband squirming ever so slightly during the Bach, but I must say (not without chagrin) that all in all he was obviously thrilled to be there.

I was going to wear my rust silk again (it's nearly new, having come from Mlle. Roulleau just two months ago), but Eugene frowned on that, and it was he who finally decided on the black chiffon with the jet bugle beads at the neck, which I thought a bit outré for a woman of my age, although everyone seemed to think that I looked very nice indeed. And, of course, "The Earrings."

Freddy Gaylord was in his element, very happily closeted with his old cronies. (Whom I've no doubt he misses, holed up in New York. Hail-fellow-well-met is our Freddy!) I can't imagine what Jack Gardner would have to say about all this folderol were he alive to witness it. All of them were drinking like fools, although the champagne was somewhat second-class. (It was plentiful, however, unlike the food.)

The Gaylords did come to us earlier, as planned, and we had a very nice scallop soufflé, one of Veronica's triumphs, and a raspberry torte. I didn't want to load them down with the party still to be endured and, after consultation with Veronica, decided to leave the canvasbacks in the snow. We will save them for Sunday.

Many of our somewhat older acquaintances (mossy of back and long of tooth) were there, which I think pleased Eugene, making him feel rather nicely included. The fact that his background is so different from mine has been, off and on over the years, a somewhat sticky issue, but now he seems to have charmed his way into *le cercle* on his own, and I cannot begrudge him that satisfaction. His new friend Willie Bigelow was in attendance; Eugene was pleased as could be. I rather fancy, too, that Eugene admires Freddy Gaylord; it's beyond me how anyone could (I doubt Mathilde does), yet who am I to judge, Freddy having cut such a swath in his time! However, I personally fail to see his attraction. There is something in Eugene, however, that vibrates off Freddy's chord.

Unfortunately, there was a very tense moment at the end when

Mathilde and Belle appear to have had some words *(en français),* and I am mortified to say that my own French is not good enough to have picked it up. I don't imagine, however, that we will be seeing Mrs. Gaylord and Mrs. Gardner in the same establishment again for quite some time to come. When I asked about it later, Mathilde was unwilling to enlighten me, pursing her mouth in that way she has. Oh! I do wish I had more French!

Monday, March 2, 1903

For some reason, Belle Gardner has taken me up. Though Eugene professes to "hate" art, he will not allow me to refuse her invitations (an interesting point, I'd say). Nonetheless, thanks to my association with the vibrant Mrs. Jack, I shall have an opportunity to meet the great Mr. John Sargent. He is in town to do some commissions, as well as the new library murals. I understand from Belle that he is staying in Marlborough Street with the Crowninshield Endicotts and is going to do Minnie Endicott's portrait. I am invited to take tea with them on Thursday and "observe." I can hardly imagine what this might be like, but Belle says Mr. Sargent does not mind having an audience while he paints. I am quite dazzled at the prospect, having admired so many of his pictures.

Thursday, March 5, 1903

Well! William Crowninshield Endicott met me at the door himself! (Eugene will simply perish when I tell him.) Dear Minnie was all set up in the drawing room wearing a lovely gown. Mr. Sargent did not actually touch brush to canvas while I was there, but it was clear that he had made a beginning. Belle herself came to check up on the proceedings with some other friends, making quite an entrance, I must say. Mr. Sargent is a tall but somewhat portly figure, slightly older than I (though not more than five or six years, I shouldn't think), and rather fetching, with a full black beard and a twinkling eye. I confess that in spite of myself I found him extremely attractive, as I understand legions of women have done before me. (I hesitate to approach Belle Gardner on this point however, my desire for gossip quite well intimidated by the fact that she is known to be member of the legion.)

Mathilde and Belle appear to have had some words *(en français),* and I am mortified to say that my own French is not good enough to have picked it up. I don't imagine, however, that we will be seeing Mrs. Gaylord and Mrs. Gardner in the same establishment again for quite some time to come. When I asked about it later, Mathilde was unwilling to enlighten me, pursing her mouth in that way she has. Oh! I do wish I had more French!

Monday, March 2, 1903

For some reason, Belle Gardner has taken me up. Though Eugene professes to "hate" art, he will not allow me to refuse her invitations (an interesting point, I'd say). Nonetheless, thanks to my association with the vibrant Mrs. Jack, I shall have an opportunity to meet the great Mr. John Sargent. He is in town to do some commissions, as well as the new library murals. I understand from Belle that he is staying in Marlborough Street with the Crowninshield Endicotts and is going to do Minnie Endicott's portrait. I am invited to take tea with them on Thursday and "observe." I can hardly imagine what this might be like, but Belle says Mr. Sargent does not mind having an audience while he paints. I am quite dazzled at the prospect, having admired so many of his pictures.

Thursday, March 5, 1903

Well! William Crowninshield Endicott met me at the door himself! (Eugene will simply perish when I tell him.) Dear Minnie was all set up in the drawing room wearing a lovely gown. Mr. Sargent did not actually touch brush to canvas while I was there, but it was clear that he had made a beginning. Belle herself came to check up on the proceedings with some other friends, making quite an entrance, I must say. Mr. Sargent is a tall but somewhat portly figure, slightly older than I (though not more than five or six years, I shouldn't think), and rather fetching, with a full black beard and a twinkling eye. I confess that in spite of myself I found him extremely attractive, as I understand legions of women have done before me. (I hesitate to approach Belle Gardner on this point however, my desire for gossip quite well intimidated by the fact that she is known to be member of the legion.)

Friday, January 2, 1903

Well, we seem to have survived Belle Gardner's New Year's Eve gala at Fenway Court. The woman runs her entertainments as some people ran their governments in the fourteenth century. We did hear some very lovely music—there was Schubert (my perennial favorite), Bach, and even Mozart—and people seemed to enjoy the performances very much. I thought I saw my husband squirming ever so slightly during the Bach, but I must say (not without chagrin) that all in all he was obviously thrilled to be there.

I was going to wear my rust silk again (it's nearly new, having come from Mlle. Roulleau just two months ago), but Eugene frowned on that, and it was he who finally decided on the black chiffon with the jet bugle beads at the neck, which I thought a bit outré for a woman of my age, although everyone seemed to think that I looked very nice indeed. And, of course, "The Earrings."

Freddy Gaylord was in his element, very happily closeted with his old cronies. (Whom I've no doubt he misses, holed up in New York. Hail-fellow-well-met is our Freddy!) I can't imagine what Jack Gardner would have to say about all this folderol were he alive to witness it. All of them were drinking like fools, although the champagne was somewhat second-class. (It was plentiful, however, unlike the food.)

The Gaylords did come to us earlier, as planned, and we had a very nice scallop soufflé, one of Veronica's triumphs, and a raspberry torte. I didn't want to load them down with the party still to be endured and, after consultation with Veronica, decided to leave the canvasbacks in the snow. We will save them for Sunday.

Many of our somewhat older acquaintances (mossy of back and long of tooth) were there, which I think pleased Eugene, making him feel rather nicely included. The fact that his background is so different from mine has been, off and on over the years, a somewhat sticky issue, but now he seems to have charmed his way into le cercle on his own, and I cannot begrudge him that satisfaction. His new friend Willie Bigelow was in attendance; Eugene was pleased as could be. I rather fancy, too, that Eugene admires Freddy Gaylord; it's beyond me how anyone could (I doubt Mathilde does), yet who am I to judge, Freddy having cut such a swath in his time! However, I personally fail to see his attraction. There is something in Eugene, however, that vibrates off Freddy's chord.

Unfortunately, there was a very tense moment at the end when

At one point when Belle and Minnie and the other ladies had gone for a moment into the conservatory to admire the progress of Mr. Endicott's famous anthuriums, and our host had excused himself to his library, Mr. Sargent quite amazingly approached and asked me if I might not be amenable to having my own portrait done. I know that it costs quite a bit of money to do this, and I can't really imagine that Eugene would agree (however much he may be pleased at my "friendship" with Belle), particularly if he were to meet the engaging Mr. Sargent face to face. There is a magnetism about him that even a married woman of my experience finds difficult to elude. I, sad to tell, was somewhat coquettish in my response, and blush to say that some dormant drop of debutantism in me came bubbling to life in his presence. He placed his hand on my shoulder (a liberty Eugene Hillyard would *not* admire), and turned my face to the window to catch the north light. Oh, I blush anew as I write these words!

I hardly think that John Sargent needs to advertise his services as a portraitist, for I am told he is quite well-to-do. And yet he did express an interest. I will mention it to Eugene, though I shall most carefully choose my time.

Friday, April 24, 1903

Many of Eugene's friends from the Good Government Association were at the Tremont last night, and yet a number of the tickets had been bought up by some other people who, I frankly felt, were not really our sort. I recognized Mr. John Fitzgerald making his way through the throng in his usual gregarious fashion. I do hope that the young woman with him was his daughter; one certainly expects that a man with Mr. Fitzgerald's aspirations and pretensions does not attend the theater with a lady not his wife!

The play was bearable. *Mrs. Deering's Divorce* is a foolish trifle, but Mrs. Langtry, of course, was exquisite as always. Everyone says that she is a lady no better than she should be, but that's certainly her business. One hears this kind of thing about other actresses, but Mrs. Langtry is widely rumored to be the *amoureuse* of King Edward; a rumor so flavorful cannot be ignored.

We did have a jolly time of it later, however. Eugene was host (he

insisted!), and we went to supper at the Parker House with the Endicotts and the Pickmans and dear brother Alex as well, escorting a Mrs.
Kinsett, who is, according to Anne, possibly divorced, although Alex
introduced her as a widow. Mrs. Kinsett was very gracious, indeed quite
congenial. Her costume was distinguished by seed pearls, which I don't
personally care for, but I thought they looked well on her. She wore
one of those "toques" now coming into fashion, odd and somewhat
avant-garde, but not unbecoming. She is a woman of possibly under
thirty years . . . a trifle young for Alex? But, God bless him, the poor
lamb is probably lonely. He has chosen not to marry, despite opportunities aplenty, and may have lived to regret it just a bit.

A new associate of Eugene's was at the theater, and later at the
Parker House as well, and I do not care for him one bit. I tried to speak
with Eugene about this in the carriage home, but he refused to discuss
it with me. Evidently the man's name is Trefoyle. I cannot fathom Eugene's interest in him. Eugene makes such an effort to ingratiate himself with our better element in Boston that I was quite astonished last
night to see that he was cordial in public to this rather vulgar man.

Friday, August 28, 1903, Nahant

Mr. Hillyard and I have quarreled regarding his invitation to the Trefoyles to join us here in Nahant for what is traditionally the last
weekend of the season. I do think I've the right to expect that when
we retreat up here each summer I shall be left to the essential task of
pulling myself together without having to play the gracious hostess to
brigands and riffraff. I expressed myself very clearly to Eugene, though
he seemed quite unmoved when I said I would not have the Trefoyles
in my *house*. (Of course, there is nothing I can do to keep them out of
Nahant, but they will not be guests in my home!) Eugene finally understood that I was absolutely not to be persuaded, but he got that black,
silent look I hate, where his eyes change color and the muscles contract
in his jaw.

The man Trefoyle is of course impossible. And having met his wife,
I can warrant that I would not enjoy sitting on this or any other veranda
with her. I know I am wicked, inflexible, and a damned snob, but I can't
help it and I don't care. Eugene is, as my boys would say, "tight as a

42

tick" with this Trefoyle, and I must devote myself this autumn to trying to loose my husband from that grasp.

Wednesday, October 28, 1903

Although I was feeling rather weary this morning after the exertion of being charming to everyone at the Binneys' reception last night, as Eugene was dressing to go into town, I took the opportunity to speak to him again about Mr. Trefoyle. I am not happy to say that Eugene was entirely too brusque with me on the subject and told me that as long as I had diamonds and blue silk to wear to my ("my"!) friends' entertainments, I should hardly be commenting on his associations. He was simply infuriating. As if he could possibly deny that Trefoyle is a scalawag of the worst possible sort.

I've decided that although I am perhaps a goose to pursue it, I will not retreat from the question of Padraic Trefoyle however unpleasant Eugene may decide to be. When Eugene introduced me to him at the theater last spring, I looked straight into his tiny bright blue eyes and saw clearly the stone wall behind their sparkle. Depend upon it—one develops a relation with such a man at one's peril. His powerful attraction for Eugene is impossible to understand.

Sunday, February 7, 1904

Trefoyle-Hillyard & Sons is the name of their new company. My efforts over the last many months have fallen on deaf and greedy ears, and in spite of my endless protestations Eugene has been persuaded to formalize the relationship. (Or perhaps he needed no persuading at all.) Eugene's own business, I suspect, is swallowed up in this new entity. I have read of "illegal trusts." I confess I'm not at all sure what that phrase might mean, but I find it coming into my mind more and more these days.

Thursday, March 10, 1904

Eugene has been buoyant for days. Perhaps he aspires to outwit Mr. Roosevelt and has perchance devised a way to do so . . . he and the re-

43

doubtable Trefoyle. The plot is thickening, and in my darker and more sober moments I know myself to be too sanguine and too frivolous. Trefoyle is the serpent in what I fancied was my garden, and my husband is, as Anthony would say, "in bed with him"—a phrase not nearly vulgar enough for the circumstances.

Tuesday, December 20, 1904

Having spent nearly the entire afternoon with darling Zachary collecting pine boughs for the holidays, I am here at last with my feet up on the chaise, savoring my well-earned exhaustion! With our stalwart Potter at the reins, we bundled into Eugene's new victoria (possibly not the best choice of vehicle for a rural expedition) and traveled out into the country. Oh, we must have been nearly to Lexington before we were satisfied with the greens we saw. Zachary has been assiduous all evening, arranging the fragrant pines on all the mantelpieces and wrapping them around the banister. This rather put me back in mind of the renovations I would like to do, but Eugene is steadfast (ordinarily a virtue in a husband) and will not hear of it. This penurious fit is quite out of character for him and has become a fairly sore point between us. Perhaps in the new year I can convince him to widen the bottom four or five steps as so many people are doing now. There is plenty of room in the hall to "fan them out," and it would be very handsome. After all, I can't think what sense it is to make one's money in construction and not to take so much as a passing interest in one's own home! If all else fails, perhaps I can use my Lattimore money to do it.

Friday, December 23, 1904

Zachary and Veronica made a foray down cellar today to fetch the ornaments from storage and were quite thrilled to find some of Mother's old Christmas decorations in a forgotten corner—tiny glass balls and lovely silver garlands. Zachary spent most of the morning patiently winding them through the pine boughs on the banister, and the effect is very bright and festive, just perfect for our family celebration. They also discovered Mother's bisque angel, which I had not laid eyes on for nearly twenty years; I assumed it lost. I remember her saying that it was a souvenir of her wedding trip to Italy—and precious. I washed the angel with my own hands, not trusting even dear Veronica with this piece of what I think of as "history visible." The angel is too fragile for the tree, so I have set her on the rosewood commode in my bedroom. I may leave her there quite past the holidays.

My tolerance of Belle Gardner is bearing some sort of fruit. I feel somewhat hypocritical encouraging our friendship for "gain," but of course she does surround herself with quite fascinating folk. I have met some interesting artists and writers and the like who add a dimension to my life which it would not otherwise have. Many of them are really rather strange, and in some cases quite unbecoming, but I would hardly know how to sally forth into their society to meet them on my own were it not for Belle and her indefatigable pursuit of the "bohemians."

At any rate, the exhibition this afternoon at the Copley Society was quite delightful. I had the reluctant but radiant Annabelle in tow, looking a bit more sophisticated than her mother would have preferred, but of course Belle Gardner simply adored her. Belle was there with some friends from abroad and treated me very cordially indeed (one can never be sure if our Belle will be cordial or otherwise on any given afternoon), but I dislike it in myself that I *was* pleased and have seen fit to record my satisfaction in these pages. She enjoys referring to me as "our elegant Augusta" and seems to do this with a droll, perhaps disparaging tone in her voice. Belle is a homely little wren, but there is no denying that she is a remarkable woman in many ways. She is energetic and stylish all at once, and of course—as the ever quotable Anthony would say—stinking rich.

But the Monets were lovely—all swarms and washes of color. Our neighbor, Fannie Mason, a great chum of Belle's, had me in for coffee very informally the other week and showed me *her* new Monet, which she has seen fit to hang in the music room, of all places. Fannie does try so hard. Yet it seems to me that becoming a "patroness" of the arts would be a very wise and most enjoyable thing to do. Eugene is just now behaving as if he may be in funds, and I suggested that we consider a small collection as so many of our friends have done. I quote his rejoinder here: "I am not a goddamned Medici and I will not throw good money away on the doodlings of a bunch of sissies."

He exaggerates. One need not be a Medici or a Borgia pope to have a few nice pictures about the parlor. This has all the earmarks of becoming a bone of contention between us. At this rate we shall have enough for a whole chicken.

Monday, June 5, 1905

We have had colossal rain for nearly a week. It seems that everything is limp and damp and malodorous and spirits hereabouts as soggy as the grass on the Mall. I had some time alone today, what with the children off at school and Eugene away with Anthony. The two of them are in Hartford on an errand about which I am to know nothing except the fact of their departure. My speculations on my husband's business have come to nothing and I am trying to teach myself to forswear speculation altogether. Nonetheless, he has been gone for two days already and is not expected back within the fortnight. Feeling quite as damp as everyone else, my hair trailing tendrils down my neck, I spent a good part of the day at the desk in the library, going over household accounts and trying to rectify with Potter and Veronica some of our expenditures from May, which appear entirely too baronial for these straitened times.

As I sat there, biting in concentration on the end of my pencil, Potter entered with the post and, following the distracted motion of my hand, left it on the corner of the desk, where it remained, ignored, till nearly dinnertime, when I was astonished to find a letter, postmarked Buffalo, from Mr. John Sargent, whom I have not seen nor heard of for more than two years. He writes that he has thought of me often and was hoping I had reconsidered my refusal ("though a laughing, 'pink' refusal it was") to sit for him. It seems he will be in Boston later on this week and begs leave to call on me on Saturday.

I hardly know how to describe my reaction, even in these pages, but it was the heart of a schoolgirl beating in a woman's breast. I found the thoughts flying through my mind; calculations came to me all at once. Thoughts of deception, not to put too fine a point on it, are strangers in the dismal landscape of my brain; I am untutored in deceit through grievous lack of opportunity.

I mean to do it. The question is when, and how, and where? And where will the fee come from? I'm sure John does not expect to paint me gratis, but I know only that I intend to do this. I have seen his portraits so often in the homes of our friends; his picture of Belle (which so thoroughly scandalized poor old Jack that she did not dare to hang it till he died) is exquisite, the subject notwithstanding, and I find a covetousness blossoming in me like some dark flower. I am resolved to ask Alex for a portion of my share of Papa's estate that I may buy this portrait for myself. And Eugene Hillyard and his raving disapproval (for there is no doubt of it) may take the hindmost!

We have chosen my pink beaded gown. The choice came about through a most shocking disregard for propriety: John Sargent has become the only man above the age of seventeen to come into my bedroom, with the exception of my husband. There we went through my wardrobe, ultimately choosing the shell-pink silk with the beaded shoulders, nearly without hesitation. This confection, though not brand-new, is certainly well-fashioned and becomes me. The décolletage, I must say, seems somewhat extreme even for a formal portrait, but John took the gown and gently held it up to me and exclaimed at "the perfection of it, dearest Augusta, the perfection!" Moments later, when I showed him my "Birthday Earrings" (feeling somewhat foolish lest he think me too vain or proud of them), he seized one in each hand, and holding them up to my ears insisted that I wear them for the portrait. I am unhappy at the thought of carrying them back and forth to the studio each day in my reticule, but carry them I shall. It is so fortuitous that they should have been out of the vault for the Pickmans' dinner party three weeks ago and Eugene too preoccupied to put them back before he dashed off to parts unknown. Indeed, we have heard this morning that he is to be delayed at least another week. Ah, how the gods conspire!

John wishes to paint me full-length. We spoke at first about a seated portrait, such as some that I have seen and admired of ladies posed on elegant damask bergères or on gilt divans. But he feels that my figure, as he said, "demands the scope of height"! As a consequence, the finished portrait will be more than six feet high. John says he fancies for me a somewhat Roman backdrop, filled with flowers and a ruined column, which he will then blend into the shadows, or perhaps a Chinese screen or sideboard to provide a contrast to the dress. The setting is to be a surprise for me when we begin. Tomorrow!

Thursday, June 22, 1905

The portrait is exquisite . . . absolutely exquisite. John has also devised a frame which will give the perfect finish to the colors in the picture— the deep, muted greens and golds in the background and the pink glitter of the gown—all set off by the diamond earrings. Oh! I count the hours till my painting dries and can be framed and hung. We do have the perfect wall down in the drawing room on which Eugene has insisted on displaying that wretched *nature morte* his mother loved. I whoop for joy that it will soon be gone! He may keep it in his precious library.

Although in my heart I know this to be the ultimate extravagance of my life (in every way), perhaps never to be repeated (in *any* way), I feel that from the moment I had his letter, there were never any choices. I cannot understand it yet, but I know that there are a great many ramifications here which I have yet to absorb; my life to date does not prepare me for these thoughts and feelings. I know that there is more to this than simply a painting of a woman somewhat past her prime, yet when I looked into the portrait's eyes, I saw the self I was and may yet be—a "self" I do not want to lose.

Tuesday, June 27, 1905

Eugene, quite predictably, went right through the roof (as brother Alex would say) when he returned to find my portrait hanging in the drawing room. The scene that ensued was notable for the breadth of vocabulary on his part and the depth of silence on mine. I know that the smile (of self-satisfaction? Ah, but who cares?) never left my lips, and after Eugene had vented all his wrath and outrage (at my prodigality, I suppose), I calmly reminded him that I am neither pauper nor chattel and that indeed he may consider this my father's posthumous gift to me as I had used Lattimore money to pay for it. Eugene had the gall to ask me how much Lattimore money we were talking about, but I told him plainly that I did not consider it his business. I refused to tell him and shall again—for he will ask again.

His fulminations having now subsided (as it is passing midnight), he sleeps the sleep of the righteous and I have just returned from a visit to the drawing room to look at my portrait again.

Shall it become an "heirloom"? Who can say? I had no thought of that when I agreed to sit, and yet the hours in the studio (too brief by far, though John said something about his speed at his canvas echoing his rapport with his subject) will remain dear to me forever. Mad though the notion would appear to others, I feel deeply that this is a portrait of a woman to whom exquisite love was made. Oh! Disgraceful, Augusta! . . . Ah, but I do not want to lose the expression in the eyes that outshines the diamond earrings. Tonight, in the dim light from the street lamps, my painting seemed to glow in its place against the patterned wall. I almost could not bear to leave it.

$\mathcal{H}$atless in the fine, late snow, Arthur Hillyard stood on the sidewalk in front of his great-grandmother's house looking straight up into the swirling sky as the crisp, sleety flakes fell onto his face. He shifted his bulky parcels and held out his hand to watch the snow melt on his warm palm. The fuzzy green beginnings of leaves he had seen in the early afternoon were now sugared over, the trees along Commonwealth Avenue transformed into shimmering white silhouettes all down the Mall. Arthur opened his mouth to catch a few flakes on his tongue before he took out his key and shoved into the house.

The foyer was dim and silent but for the distant hum of a TV game show. He set the groceries on the marble floor and wiggled out of his raincoat, looking quickly through the small pile of mail someone had left on the hall radiator, seeing at once the thin white envelope with one of Conrad's many addresses stamped crookedly in the corner. He held it for a moment, stiffly in the tips of his fingers, and tossed it back on the radiator as if it were nothing.

In the kitchen, Arthur turned on the overhead fluorescent ring and put his parcels on the drainboard. He rubbed at his head with a tea towel until his thinning, silvery hair fizzed back up to its customary halo above his face, then poured a splash of scotch, stashed in a cupboard only he could reach, into a Porky Pig glass and leaned back against the sink, sipping slowly.

Edwina woke up, scrambled out of her basket, and came waddling over to him. He buried his toes in the folds of skin on her tummy, cooing at her under his breath. When the whisky was gone, Arthur licked the last drop from the inside rim of the glass, polished his spectacles on a paper towel, and, Edwina at his heels, went to look for Annabelle.

She was dozing in a shabby velvet chair in what once had been the formal parlor of the house. They'd moved her downstairs about five years ago when it became too difficult for her to get around, and now the transformation of Augusta Hillyard's tall Edwardian drawing room to boudoir was complete. Arthur turned off the color TV and snapped on one of the frosted glass lamps beside the unmade bed. He stood looking around at the clutter, the soiled quilts and ruffled sheets, the huge down comforter that trailed onto the dusty Persian carpet.

He leaned over to kiss Annabelle's forehead, smiling at the blue eye shadow and circles of pink rouge on her cheeks. Her mauve satin wrapper was pulled tightly around her girth, held in place with a rhinestone button the size of a walnut. She smelled of Elizabeth Arden and Doritos. Arthur called her name in a soft stage whisper: "Annabelle?"

Annabelle shifted her weight and made soft, wet noises; Arthur put his hand on her shoulder and leaned over her again. " 'Belle!"—more sharply now. " 'Belle, where's Mona? The place is a mess. Where is she?"

Annabelle snorted and looked up at him, blinking slowly. Her pale gray irises were rimmed with a colorless iridescence, dull and vague. He thought how benign she always looked when she was sleeping.

"Who?"

"Mona."

Annabelle refocused her eyes, wiping the inner corners with an old tissue.

Arthur spoke more softly now that she was awake. "She's supposed to stay with you until seven o'clock. She didn't make the bed or do the dishes, or anything."

"Well, she quit." Annabelle hoisted her large body into a more upright position in the chair and reached for the TV remote. "Snippy about it, too. I certainly hope you brought my soap."

Arthur sank down onto the edge of the tumbled bed. He ran his fingers through his hair. "What do you mean . . . 'quit'?"

"Something about money. Tacky is what *I* say, and good riddance. Where's my soap?"

"I've got it," he said, standing up, still holding on to his hair. "I got you two cakes."

"I was almost out of it, you know. Should have had new at least two days ago."

Arthur straightened his knees and padded back to the kitchen, Edwina, annoyed but dutiful, following. He retrieved the Chanel soap from one of the shopping bags and brought it back to the parlor. At eight bucks a bar, he knew he could ill afford to keep this up.

He put the small Saks Fifth Avenue bag on the table next to her chair and leaned over, his hands on his knees. He tried again.

" 'Belle, what happened to Mona?"

"Happened? Nothing happened to her whatsoever. She's fine. Fine and dandy." Annabelle pressed the buttons on the remote control.

"Is she coming back tomorrow?"

"Of course not. What a silly question, Arthur. I discharged her, as she deserved. We had words."

Words . . . words. Annabelle's euphemism for the shrieks and recriminations that had driven away three housekeepers just since Christmas.

Swearing under his breath, Arthur went back to the kitchen and began to unpack the groceries, twisting the thermostat on the oven to "Potpies." He had made a little chart for Annabelle to use during the interludes between housekeepers, and the oven dial was marked for "Fish Sticks," "Pizza," "Potpies"—all the junk she insisted would best sustain her fleshy, aggressive frailty. From time to time Arthur took her out to dinner, but his credit had become as frail as Annabelle herself and she turned up her aquiline nose at anything but the Copley Plaza or the upstairs dining room at the Ritz.

He sipped at another scotch while he waited for the oven to heat and started in on the lunch dishes, still in the sink, scummy with macaroni and cheese. As soon as the pies were in the oven, Arthur looked in on Annabelle one last time, satisfying himself that she had dropped off again. He left a plastic bowl of Fritos on the table next to the Chanel soap and went back into the foyer.

Edwina was already there, whimpering with annoyance, and he slipped the leash over her neck. As she yanked him toward the door, he glanced toward the thin white envelope on the radiator and then, with a deep breath, stepped out into the icy darkness.

The snow, no longer falling, had left the slightest glaze on the great trees that lined the avenue. Arthur pulled Edwina across the empty street and into the Mall, where he left her on her own to nose about in the crackling grass, trailing her sequined leash behind her. He lit a cigarette and paced up and down the path, shivering just a bit inside his raincoat, whistling a Chopin scherzo through his teeth.

The Mall cleaves the broad boulevard of Commonwealth Avenue from Kenmore Square to the Public Garden, the great Victorian tidal wave of the avenue cresting into mansions on each side. The elegant houses, fronted with brownstone, stucco, marble, and brick—almost hidden in summer by the hundreds of century-old trees—were clearly seen tonight in the cold air, their strong lines framed by the barren branches.

On a January night in 1912, a bolt of snow-lightning had similarly cleft, but could not topple, a fine old elm on the Mall, directly across from the Hillyard house on the south side of the avenue. It still stood, riven, the south-facing branches bare but reaching, as if immortalized by the energy that flashed in from the winter sky all those years ago. From childhood, Arthur had stared at the tree from his room on the top floor of the house, half believing he could reach out from his window and touch the topmost branches, the bare and the leaved. And on this early spring night, the air smelling of frost, nearly all were bare, woody and dry, though the few odd leaves left over from autumn were still clinging tenaciously to the highest boughs.

Arthur rubbed out the cigarette and glanced at his watch, mindful of the pies in the oven. He picked up Edwina's wet leash, and they turned into the corner of Dartmouth Street and then walked back westward through the early-evening bustle of Newbury Street, the glow of restaurant doorways illuminating the sidewalks.

Edwina pulled Arthur along the walk, strutting her stuff, lapping up the stares and exclamations she always drew from strangers. Spoiled little Edwina was a two-thousand-dollar shar-pei bitch that Annabelle had insisted she had to have and that she now ignored. But Arthur had become fond of the prissy little dog, and he dutifully fed and walked her, finding a bit of wry amusement in remembering that she was, after all, the namesake of another expensive female, his ex- and unbeloved wife.

In the years when he still believed life gave him choices, he had come to his short-lived marriage confident he could create a household with those two so fiercely selfish women—his great-aunt Annabelle, whom he would not desert, and the intoxicating Edwina, whom he believed he could not live without. But it never registered with him that his gentle nature would be no match for the bitter disaffinity between them. Desperate to please his new bride, and deaf to Annabelle's screeches of protest, Arthur spent a great deal of money remodeling the second floor, even raiding the closed-up rooms of Grandmère's enormous house for the best of the oriental carpets and Victorian knickknacks with which to decorate the "bridal suite." But how could he have imagined that he could satisfy Edwina with the vigilant Annabelle, still spry in those days, ever at their heels, invading in all ways and at all hours?

Yet he supposed it was hardly polite, even at this long angle of retrospect, to blame The Fair Edwina, she who had put up with Annabelle's depredations for nearly two years before telling Arthur (her valises already in the taxi) that she could not bear it another second and would not be back. He swallowed the loss of Edwina with what was actually relief, the disappointment briefer than he could, at first, admit. Yet now, nearly eight years having passed, Edwina had somehow transmogrified from wife to imaginary playmate—his sexual fantasies now focused only on her—a form of fidelity in which he took a strange, belated pride.

Annabelle was sleeping again when they returned. There was a tiny piece of Frito on her chin, and Arthur, shaking his head, lips pursed, brushed it away with a fresh tissue. He let her sleep and went off to the kitchen, pleased to find the potpies nearly ready and not burned at all. He turned them onto faded Limoges plates and neatly folded two paper napkins, which he anchored to the vinyl tablecloth in the dining room with his great-grandmother's sterling forks.

"Dinner is served, madame," Arthur announced from the parlor doorway, and hurried back to the dining room to light the fire he had had the foresight to lay that morning. He touched a match to the dry logs, and the fire blazed up, crackling and warm, just as Annabelle, gripping her aluminum walker, tottered through the dining-room archway and toward her chair.

"Claudia called," she said in a voice that was crisp with disapproval.

"Oh? While I was out with Edwina?" Or last week, or this morning, or two years ago? "Sit down, dear," he said, guiding her pink bulk to the head of the table, moving the basket of Wonder bread closer to her plate.

As he settled her in, Annabelle looked at him with the angry, uncertain look which Arthur had (almost) learned not to notice. Back in the kitchen, he filled a tumbler with ice and poured in the exotic Swedish mineral water which Annabelle required and which he could . . . not afford. He'd tried to fake her out once with some cheaper carbonated stuff from Maine, but she'd caught him at it, bitterly insisting that she knew the difference, knew he was trying to deny her what she needed and deserved. Or, had she found the empty bottle and seen an opportunity to badger him? It made no difference. He could afford none of it.

"She's having a birthday party for that Yancey of hers," Annabelle said, attacking the top of her pie with a fork, salting vigorously what she had not yet tasted. "Next week."

Arthur felt a small rush of pleasure. He smiled broadly at her and spread his napkin on his lap. "Claudia is? A party? Great! I'll call her later . . . that's great." He buttered a piece of Wonder bread and folded it in quarters.

"Uh, anybody else call, 'Belle?" he said as cheerfully as he could, even though he knew it would not be in character for Conrad to call on the same day that a threatening letter was delivered—that was not his style. The agony must be prolonged. Conrad would never deny himself the pleasure of dragging it out: the letter today (lying even now on the hall radiator where Arthur had left it, not fifty feet from where he sat poking at his food), then a phone call tomorrow. And soon a mutilated animal on the front steps? Oh, God . . .

Conrad, once friend and savior, the light at the end of a long tunnel of debt and error, had turned into a roaring freight train coming toward him. It had begun with a casual conversation in a bar in Cambridge where Arthur had gone to lubricate his worries over money, taxes, bills, over Annabelle and the style of living he could not deny her, over his

fleeing choices—those now invisible and those still in the process of disappearing. It had been a conversation into which he slid as if greased,
all traction gone.

"Sure, Artie," Conrad had said. "Happy to help out! It's *such* a lovely
old house. How much you think you need? Eighty? Hundred grand?
Happy to cosign for you. Happy to. Listen, read this over, Art, and sign
it. And have another drink."

Remembering, Arthur abruptly put his fork down and went out into
the hall. He took Conrad's envelope all the way up to his room and held
it against the lightbulb in the dresser lamp, imagining he could read the
words inside through the skin of the envelope: "Pay or Die"? Or, possibly, just one word: "FOUR"? Or one short, pithy sentence: *"THE
HOUSE IS MINE!"*

Opening it, holding it in his hand unprotected by the envelope, was
more of an occasion than Arthur could rise to. And why do it? He was
filled with the prescience of the truly guilty, the deeply defaulted. He
knew damn well he was four payments behind. He dropped the unopened envelope on the bureau and went back to the dining room.

When his after-dinner chores were done—Annabelle snuggled into
fresh sheets with the TV remote beside her, clean dishes neatly stacked
beside the sink—Arthur dragged himself up to his room as the cramp-
ing swimmer seeks the shore. His efforts at cheerful dinnertime conversation were obliterated; the three flights of stairs put the finishing
touch to his exhaustion.

He lay fully dressed on his narrow bed, smoking a cigarette, listening to a cassette of Dinu Lipatti playing the Chopin *ballades*. His eyes
traveled over his collection of sheet music and scores, piled up to the
dark wainscoting in one corner, and the poster of Vladimir Horowitz
in a baseball cap . . . all the dusty mementos of years that had blurred
and slunk away from him.

He tried to lose himself in the beauty of the music, but suddenly a
familiar tightness spread through his chest and he swung his legs over
the edge of the bed and hunched over, his hands flat against his pounding heart. Would he feel like this, he wondered, if Mona came back, if
he ate more protein . . . if the house were safe?

Arthur had been raised with the clear understanding that Grandmère's house was a sacred object, fortress and shrine together. Although

it was still tall and handsome, the strong elegance was crumbling, nearly stone by stone, as if in rhythm to Arthur's loosening grasp of what was left of the Hillyard fortunes. That his nearly complete squandering of the precious Hillyard Family Trust had all been for Annabelle made not one bit of difference.

He lay back and lit another cigarette, trying to calm himself with a brief but deeply carnal fantasy about Edwina, whose hot skin he only vaguely recalled. His nearly eight years of celibacy had been punctuated by a number of adulterous sessions with women about whom he knew nothing except that they were strangers. There had been a time when Arthur Hillyard, both amazed and inspired by his success with women, had reveled briefly in a view of himself as the Don Giovanni of Commonwealth Avenue; but for quite some time now, he had retreated into his grotesque fidelity to Edwina, though only for lack of initiative. His once exuberant sexual energy was gone, rechanneled into the greater effort of endurance.

In all the years that he and Annabelle had been alone together—in the twenty years since Zoe left to go to Italy, the ten since he'd last seen her—Arthur had tried, with all the whimsy that sustained him, to keep his devotion to Annabelle as honest and powerful as it once had been.

Arthur was certain that the central event of Annabelle's life had been her long and passionate affair with Spencer Trefoyle, the mysterious lover whom Annabelle, even now, always referred to as her "beau," her "gentleman friend." Arthur knew little about the history of that forbidden liaison except that after their parents died and he and Zoe were left alone with Annabelle, Spencer was suddenly always there. Even in late middle age, Spencer was a crackling, powerful figure. Arthur and Zoe spied from the shadows, confused but riveted, as the drama between Annabelle and Spencer played itself out. Dark, silent, sinister, Spencer Trefoyle came and went as he pleased, often disappearing for months on end only to return to a pathetically grateful and adoring Annabelle.

But when Spencer died, some light went out in her. At the time, Arthur was just twelve years old, pubescent and confused; Annabelle had no one else to cling to, and Spencer's death made little Arthur heir to the role of loving her. There was simply no one else. Zoe, who backed away from Annabelle's very presence, was ignored (as Annabelle ignored all females), and Arthur became son, escort, straight man—

and now caretaker. Annabelle's passion for Spencer Trefoyle was more than her one vulnerability, one saving grace: it was the hook on which Arthur had long ago hung his own affection and his willingness to be everything she had. But Annabelle herself was almost outliving his endurance.

It distressed Arthur that what had begun with devotion, with such love for her, had twisted itself into this trap of guilt and forbearance. He had been too slow on the uptake—had missed every clue, had let years of once complete solicitude slide into mere willingness, thence to an edgy compliance, and finally into this terrible exhaustion. But it didn't matter how he felt. His options were all gone, because Annabelle—ninety, sick, and nasty—really did need him now.

With a groan and a guilty quickening in his heart, he leapt up from the bed, ran down the three flights of mahogany stairs in his stocking feet, bumping his toe on the turning of the ornate newel post, and skidded to a stop outside the doors of the drawing room, where he paused, listening for breath.

Annabelle was slumped against her many pillows, her mouth slightly open, one of her old silver picture frames facedown on her stomach. Arthur squatted by the bed and looked at her wrinkled eyelids, pinched elegant nose, and frizzy hair. About once a month he took her to the beauty salon at the Ritz Carlton Hotel to have her hair washed and curled. From time to time they put in a lavender rinse while Annabelle waved her plump hands about and regaled the hairdresser with stories of her conquests and social triumphs as if she were the belle of a ball still going on.

Arthur understood that the passage of the last fifty years was not real to Annabelle. Though the hairdressers and housekeepers, the various tradesmen and doctors who tramped through the marble magnificence of the old Hillyard foyer thought she was a selfish, strident old bag, Arthur knew that to herself she was still the sparkling queen of Boston society, her girlish beauty untouched by the many decades that had passed. If there were some inner core of awareness in her, if she ever looked into the fancy mirror in her bathroom and saw the fat old woman she had become, she did not let on. Arthur was sure that in her own mind Annabelle Hillyard was still the beautiful woman who had once dazzled men from Washington to Bar Harbor.

Arthur gently pried the silver frame out of Annabelle's limp fingers and turned it over. He pressed his thumbs against the glass that covered Spencer Trefoyle's malign and almost handsome face, knowing that if he wished to he could push right through, cracking both the glass and the photograph behind it. But that wouldn't make a whit of difference to anything.

He breathed on the glass and shined off his fingerprints on his trouser leg so Annabelle would not know he had touched the picture. He set it back among the others on the cluttered table by her chair, all of them crusty with tarnish, placed randomly among the Dorito crumbs and pieces of Oreos, old *TV Guides* and wadded-up pink tissues. He pulled the ruffled hem of the comforter up to her chin, kissed her forehead, turned off all the first-floor lights, and took himself upstairs to the music room.

Arthur stood in the doorway and stared at the old Chickering concert grand, the ivory keys gleaming dully in the light from the landing. He always kept it polished, sneaking in from time to time with his bottle of lemon oil and a special cloth. He walked across the vast parqueted floor, his footsteps silent on the Kerman rug, and placed one hand on the side of the piano. He drew himself up, tall and straight, his froth of silvery hair gleaming in the spotlight. Holding his other hand against the white waistcoat of his splendid formal suit, he bowed graciously to his audience, then flung out his arm in modest acceptance of the applause that thundered from all the balconies. Roses fell at his feet, and the audience went wild.

Arthur closed the door to the music room and went across to the library to look for another cigarette. In recent months he had gotten used to lying on old Eugene's cracked leather chaise, smoking, the ashtray on his stomach, and speculating about getting out from under Conrad's thumb. He would stare up at the embossed ceiling panels and plot far into the night about how he would get the money for the mortgage, how he would save Grandmère's house by means fair or foul, if not from the record-breaking ticket sales on his concerts, then by some stroke of unnamable fortune. Scheming about how to get the money to silence Conrad occupied many of Arthur's hours, but for now he saw no way but to continue to endure, to plod as bravely as possible through the thicket he had made of everything. All the same, he felt sure that the letter today (unread but well imagined) was the beginning of what might be the end.

He stood just inside the double doors of the library and gazed around at the velvet draperies, the carved ceiling cornices, trying to remember where he had hidden the cigarettes. He was sure he had left a few Winstons on the top shelf of the Chippendale breakfront. He turned the little key and found them almost at once, just behind the old bisque Christmas angel which for many years had stood guard from the doily on top of Zoe's dresser, protecting all her treasures: her ninety-six-color pastel set, the X-Acto knife with which she had once carved her initials in the dining-room table, and the jar where she kept her ill-gotten movie money, dimes and quarters she won playing double canasta with Claudia and their school friends.

Arthur carefully took the angel down and brushed some dust from its faded tulle wings with one finger, realizing he was having another of those strange, surprisingly powerful moments of remembering his sister. Though they had not been together for such a long time, during the last six months or more he'd found himself suddenly engulfed by vivid, unsought memories. Out of nowhere would come aching speculation on how and where she was . . . what was happening to her.

Last Christmas, Claudia had told him she'd gotten a wonderful letter from Zoe, cheerful and filled with news. Arthur had listened to that with half an ear, reluctant to ask the details, though he knew Claudia would happily answer. What did he fear to learn? Perhaps that Zoe's life was glorious without him?

Arthur had never told Claudia that in the last ten years he'd seen nearly every movie Zoe ever worked on, standing for hours at the big newsstand in Harvard Square, religiously reading the Hollywood trade papers to learn the complete cast and crew of every film about to be released. Just last fall he'd traipsed up to Medford to see a repeat of something he'd missed the first time around. In his mind's eye, Arthur could still see the lonely metallic sky, the palette of silver-white snow and ice-blue shadows against the darkness of the timberline, and, oh, yes, there was a woman, a dance-hall queen, something like that, standing in the snow with the long gold fringes of her embroidered shawl glittering in an ocher dawn. And he *knew* that Zoe had created that— mined those eerie colors out of her own mind, her own memory.

Arthur lit one of the dried-out cigarettes and sat down on the leather chaise, holding the angel on his knees. It was only about ten inches high, its little porcelain face wise and inquisitive, a sphinx with tulle wings. As he lay back on the chaise, still holding the angel, Edwina came waddling in, grumpy with sleep, missing him. She climbed up and tucked herself between his knees while he smoked the cigarette and stroked the angel's brittle wings, thinking of Zoe. Her pale face seemed to hover in the air before him, wreathed in smoke from his cigarette.

"I'm trying, Zo, I am really trying . . . but I think I just might be losing it this time."

oe pressed her front door shut
with her foot and fastened the chain lock. She dropped her bag on the
floor and leaned back against the wall with her arms out to Roger. He
walked into them and leaned against her, holding her head in both
hands, licking her mouth, her eyebrows, not really kissing, humming
a tango under his breath.

"Roger . . ." Zoe whispered.

"Want to have a little drink?"

"You actually think I need a drink?" Zoe said, chuckling, reaching up
to touch his mouth with one finger, running it along the edge of his bottom teeth. "After all that first-class champagne I drank?"

"Well, no, you certainly had plenty, but I think I'll just . . . what do
you have? Oh, any of my Kahlúa left?"

"Oh, yuk. Kahlúa?"

"Mmmm. Where is it?" he said softly, gently biting her breast through
the silk of her blouse.

"Well, you certainly turned out to be a tease, didn't you? I'm rather
horrified to—"

"So where is it? In the kitchen?"

"Oh . . . mmm, ouch! . . . Yes, in the kitchen."

Roger kissed her cheek and ambled off down the hall; Zoe heard
small clinking noises from the kitchen. Feeling oddly remote and calm,

she walked slowly to the bedroom, where she lay the limp pink rose on the table and undressed, putting her shoes neatly, heel to heel, beside the chair, methodically hanging up her clothes. She felt very tired, with a strange, sexy weariness. She smiled to herself, thinking that the nearly full bottle of Veuve Clicquot she'd drunk probably had a lot to do with that.

She put on a robe and stood barefoot in front of the bureau, taking off the few pieces of jewelry she wore—a watch, long gold hoop earrings, two bangle bracelets. She put them, with the same calm lethargy, into the little tray where they belonged.

The old photograph was leaning against the clock where she'd left it. She picked it up and with narrowed eyes gazed into Arthur's childhood face, running one finger down his plaid shirtfront to his scuffed oxford shoes. She tried hard to remember that summer afternoon, the reason for the Band-Aid on her own knee, the color of the droopy ribbons on her pigtails. Still holding the picture, she went over to open the windows a crack and looked out into the alley. The swishing of poinsettia bushes against the building echoed the sound of the ocean's movement against the strip of shore behind Sal's restaurant.

A moment later Roger came in with a tall glass of water in one hand and a bowl of plump green grapes in the other.

"I decided I don't need any stimulation," he said, kissing the back of her neck and stooping to rest his chin on her shoulder. When he saw the picture she was holding, he put the grapes and water on the bedside table and came back, encircling her from behind, one hand inside her robe rubbing the top of her breast with the tips of his long fingers.

"Oh, that's the picture. Look at you. How pretty . . . how sweet."

"Yes," she said, leaning back against him. "And Arthur."

"When was this taken, do you know?"

Zoe shook her head and said nothing, blowing out her breath in a long, soft exhalation.

"Is that your Grandmère's house?" he said, taking the photo out of her hand.

"Um-hmm." Zoe turned around inside Roger's arm, her forehead tight against his chest. She reached inside the waist of his trousers and pulled his shirt up until her fingers touched his skin. When he leaned down to kiss her, his mouth was sweet and cold from the water. Zoe moved her hands up to his face and ran her fingers through his beard and around his neck, leaning back to look at him, smiling so faintly he could not be sure.

Over her shoulder he saw the picture of the children on the dresser where he'd dropped it, the little girl squinting so hopefully, earnestly, into the sun, her black eyes intent and eager. Then he looked down at Zoe, at the faint shadows the last thirty or more years had dusted under those same black eyes. He felt her cool, strong hands move on the back of his neck, smoothing his skin.

"I love it when you're like this," he said, "sort of dreamy and tired. What else are you, hmm? What else? Come tell me . . . come tell me, darling."

He walked them backward the few steps to the end of the bed and sat down, gently pulling Zoe's hips between his legs, his face nestled against her stomach. Zoe put her hands in his hair, holding his head tight against her. They stayed like that for a long time, each lost in private thought.

Zoe pulled slightly away and knelt in front of him. When he reached for her she shook her head and wordlessly, slowly, unbuttoned his shirt and took off his shoes and socks and undid his belt and his trousers and when she had undressed him completely pulled back the covers for him, guiding him silently to the exact center of the bed, where he lay smiling gently up at her with a combination of such adoration and willingness she almost couldn't take her eyes away. She took the dark pink rose from the table and sat next to him, moving it across his shoulders and chest so delicately he had to close his eyes to feel it. She reached over to dunk the head of the rose in the glass of water and stroked his arms and flanks with the wet flower, leaving minute droplets all along the tracks of sensation the rose left on his skin.

Roger opened his eyes and looked up at her with an expression, Zoe thought, almost of apprehension, and then she realized it was only love.

"Zoe . . ."

"Shhh . . ." She drew the rose between his legs and up over his thighs and his belly, following the path of the wet rose with her own fingers. Roger closed his eyes again and imagined they were in some cavernous wet place underneath a waterfall; soon he heard the spilling of water over the cataract, saw through his closed eyelids the soaked thick petals of the gold and purple flowers that bloomed from every crevice in the cliffside; the broad leaves of the flowers were glossy with rain, drenched in the endlessly falling water, battered but still glistening.

It was almost midnight when Roger got up to close the window against the growing chill. He brought the bowl of grapes back to the bed and lay with his head on Zoe's stomach, the grapes balanced on his chest. Zoe was almost asleep, but she felt the bed creak under his weight and opened her eyes, smiling when he reached backward with one big grape held in the tips of his fingers.

"Want something else?" she asked.

Roger laughed a little. "Why in the world would I? Here, have another one."

"Oh," Zoe said, biting down on the tart fruit, "I almost forgot. His nibs is having a party this weekend, to celebrate the start of the picture. He says he might announce his choice for Beatrice Holland. Would you want to come with me?"

"I'd love to, hon, but I can't. Got to go to Palm Springs."

"Oh, Rog, that's great. You're going to see that Delacroix?"

"Just found out today for sure . . . if it even is a Delacroix. Those people are making me crazy, Zo. They're such idiots they actually put some money down on it."

"You mean they paid for it? Without your advice?"

"Well, they took an option from that old woman in New York— from her lawyer. I'm not sure that's even legal, but it doesn't much matter at this point. I'm driving down tomorrow. I'll be back Sunday noon, I guess, something like that."

"That's amazing," Zoe said, taking another grape from his fingers. "Is there an undiscovered anything—anywhere? I thought all the great ones were catalogued on computers, whatever."

"I know it, but you'd be surprised. More masterpieces rot in attics than anybody thinks."

Zoe laughed. "Holy cow, I wish I had an attic. My goodness. But do you think it might be real? Is it even likely?"

"Sure. Time will tell, but it's possible—Delacroix was incredibly prolific. If it is real, though, I was thinking I might do a show around it. There's a Fragonard in a private collection in Santa Barbara I think I could borrow. We'll see. So, will you go over to Frye's alone?"

Zoe slid down until she was inside his arm. "I don't know. Maybe.

I have so much work to do, and most of tomorrow's going to be taken up by that monster production meeting . . . no pun intended. So, I don't know. I might."

"What about Sidney?"

"Oooh, what a lovely thought. Maybe Sidney would like to be my date. He can eat chili and rumaki," she said in a perfect imitation of Sidney's affected vowels.

Roger laughed. "Well, he'd rather die than miss that party. He'll go with you or without you. Chili or no chili."

Zoe flopped onto her stomach and looked down at him with a doubtful grimace. "You know, Rog, I'm not too pleased with Sidney's role in all this. It's really been bothering me. He seems to think I owe it all to him, but I don't think so, and I can't . . ."

"Sweetheart, please stop worrying about Sidney."

"Yes, but I—"

"Zoe."

"You don't think?"

"No. Look, he's not a problem if only because he's so damned selfish. That's why you *can* trust him. He has only one motive, and he would never, ever do anybody a favor that was not primarily a favor to himself."

Zoe slid gracefully out of bed and took an old kimono Roger hadn't seen before from a hook behind the door. She sat on the edge of the bed, hunched over, and snapped another grape off the stalk. "Well," she said, "Sidney did help me, after all, introduced me to Frye in the first place. Maybe I should do something nice for him."

"Zoe, please. You cannot possibly compete with all the nice things Sidney does for himself. Just be careful. He does believe you owe him something now, and whether you and I think so or not makes no difference."

"You think he and I are even . . . don't you?"

"Darling, of course I do, but when did Sidney ever think he was even with anybody? I'm not saying you should worry about it particularly, just be aware—"

"Actually, he called me up last night to 'remind' me, he said, about 'his' associate producer credit, trying to put me in the middle. He wanted me to bring it up at my own contract meeting, can you believe it? I don't know what to think, Rog, how to react to all this."

Roger frowned at that. "Zoe, sweetheart, Sidney's credit is not your lookout. You're an artist and he's a would-be hanger-on, for Christ's sake. This credit thing is between him and Frye now. There's no need for you to get involved at all."

"I guess you're right." Zoe got up again and stood by the window, her forehead pressed against the glass. She could barely see the poinsettias in the darkness. "I don't want him giving me a hard time, though," she said. "I have to concentrate on the picture, Rog. I can't be looking over my shoulder all the time, wondering if Sidney . . . oh, dammit anyway." She turned and looked at Roger, just catching the grape he threw to her. "I know how selfish and squirrelly he can be," she said, "and I swear to God if he tries to screw this up for me, I'll . . ."

"Zoe . . . Zo, come over here, listen to me just this once. It's early days yet, don't forget."

"I know, but . . ." She came back to bed and sat cross-legged beside him.

"Just pace yourself, honey. You've worked on dozens of pictures; you know how it is, how it goes." Roger broke off with a sudden peal of laughter and sat up, swinging his long legs off the bed.

"Christ, if I were you, my friend, I'd be worrying about what to wear to the Academy Awards next year. Forget Sidney."

Zoe started to laugh, too, and he bent down to kiss the top of her head. He went out of the room to take a quick shower, but paused in the corner of the hall and listened as back in the bedroom Zoe laughed a little more and blew her nose, and all he could think of was how blank and solemn his life would be without her.

Before Roger left he came up behind her where she stood by the worktable in the living room and turned her to face him, smoothing her hair with both large hands, over and over, then blowing every fine, loose strand away from her forehead, her temples, brushing her hairline with minute, adoring kisses.

"I love you, Zoe."

Slowly, she wrapped her arms around his neck and clasped him to her so he couldn't see her face.

"I know," she whispered. "I know you do."

Roger sighed and pulled away. "Listen, I'll try to call you from Palm Springs," he said, moving toward the front door.

"You want to stop by Sunday when you get back?"

Roger paused when she said that, but he didn't turn around. "I could."

Zoe slipped her arm around his waist. "Will it be around lunchtime?" she said softly.

"It could be."

"Well, I have to work like a fiend all weekend, and most of tomorrow is that principals' meeting, but I'll deserve a break by Sunday."

She felt Roger stiffen, hesitate. Then: "You think you'll deserve it by two o'clock?"

"Absolutely. No doubt about it."

He nodded, slipped away from her arm, and opened the door; he leaned down to give her one brief, brushing kiss, and was gone.

After she locked the door behind him, Zoe went back to the bed and lay perfectly still in the center where the sheets were still curved to Roger's shape, his weight, still smelling faintly of roses and cold water. She stayed there quietly until she thought she'd stopped crying and sat up, flicking the last tears away from where they had run into her hair.

She took the bowl of grapes into the living room and lowered herself against the crushed cushions of the sofa, pushing the piles of architecture books and fabric samples on the coffee table aside with her feet. She ate the grapes slowly, individually, making three or four bites of each, consciously squashing the pieces in her teeth, trying to come to grips with how she felt.

In the years before she met Roger Horvath (the scenario of that moment on Sidney's lanai itself a kind of omen: the bright setting sun leaving Zoe in shadow, Roger in its glare), Zoe's experience with love affairs had taught her that they were an end in themselves and led to nothing. She thought of them as finite, and though she knew it was irrational, she had begun to worry that with escalation of their relationship she might lose Roger, too. She could not bear the thought that he might recede to being less to her than he'd become, but although she knew he had come to love her with a fidelity that seemed to demand the same in equal measure, all she could do was cling to him at arm's length, engaging him in every kind of loving but the declaration of it.

For months, Zoe had tried to tell herself that she wanted from Roger only what she decreed he should give her—that the pace, the rhythm, could be hers. But Roger wanted more; he wanted what any person so in love would want, and he had patiently, constantly reached toward her, almost with her own sketched gesture of Laurence to Beatrice. And whenever Zoe retreated from that powerful fidelity, Roger only smiled, held out an open hand, advanced, and drew her back.

This was the polonaise they'd danced nearly from the day they met, but lately Zoe had begun to fear he'd had enough. There had been something in his voice tonight, something felt in the slight alteration of the tension of his muscles as he moved away from her and left her standing in the hall, that hint (which she'd been waiting for with a trepidation that bordered on precognition) that maybe he was not content to dance until he dropped.

Sometimes, as now, alone and honest from exhaustion, Zoe knew that all her endless agonizing over the development of her affair with Roger was more about fear of risk than about love. But had she not taken bold (some would say insane) risks all her life? Hadn't she run off to Italy, to Boston, to L.A.? Hadn't she defied the likes of Julian Frye? In the process, of course, she had lost her family, her brother, her past, and perhaps even some essential part of her own self. Those numberless losses she had borne, and (almost) learned to live with; but she doubted she could tolerate the loss of more, the loss of what she was now at even greater risk to lose . . . and where would she ever—with her history—find the courage to risk it all again?

Oh, God, she whispered, a grape held in her teeth, oh my God, what if he gets fed up with me? What if I lose him? What if he doesn't understand about the movie . . . or, what if he *does,* and still won't wait?

Zoe put the bowl of grapes on the coffee table and leaned forward over her bent knees, staring ahead as if the answer to these questions were hanging somewhere in the air of the room. What if I have to choose? she thought suddenly. Or what if the time comes when there are no choices, only necessity, and no risk left except the risk of having nothing?

Of course, if she chose what Roger so clearly offered, she would no longer be officially alone, no longer free (though free for what she frankly wasn't sure). She had not always been alone; had been at one time half of Zoeandarthur, half of "the Hillyard kids." But that was over now, and for years being alone was the only certainty she'd had. But then Roger came, and now *The Gilded Affair,* beside which all risk paled.

Zoe had come to realize through the winter, through the months of that vicious footsie game with Julian Frye, that, stripped to its essentials, her contract was not with him. She saw it as a compact with herself, with her twenty years of working for it. It seemed insane to Zoe that a woman merely forty years of age could reach a watershed, a showdown. But there was definitely a kind of crisis here, and all that risk and . . . last chances. No need to sugarcoat it (as Roger might say)— *last chances.*

She ate the last grape and rummaged around in the mess on the coffee table for her tattered copy of the current version of the script of *The Gilded Affair*. In the bedroom she smoothed out the sheets, opened the window again, and, barely glancing at it, took the photograph of herself and Arthur and put it back in the old handkerchief box in the very bottom of the bureau drawer.

She got into bed with the book and a handful of dried-out cookies she found in the kitchen cupboard. She pulled the blanket up and tucked it around her hips and read through to the end of the opening scene— a Christmas reception at the Fifth Avenue home of Beatrice Holland's wealthy parents. It was almost midnight when, truly exhausted, she fell asleep at last, wondering how most cinematically to render the two lovers, poised under the blazing chandeliers of the great ballroom: Beatrice's dark green velvet gown against the banked white flowers . . . her fan of eagle feathers, and the band of diamonds in her hair.

SIX

(FROM THE DIARIES OF AUGUSTA HILLYARD: 1905 TO 1907)

Saturday, July 15, 1905, Nahant

Tomorrow is Mr. Anthony Hillyard's twenty-first birthday, and tonight at the Club (one of those interminable Dutch-treat suppers, followed by everlasting croquet), Eugene plans to toast him with the champagne he has been saving for this purpose since President McKinley was voted into office. Anthony has developed into a rather wild and difficult boy, encouraged in his behavior by his father's insistence that he is a boy no longer; the fact that he gave Anthony a fine razor set three years ago purports to be some arcane proof of this transition—a *rite de passage* which mere women cannot hope to understand.

Anthony has been spending his summer in town with his father, considering himself far too grown-up to join women and children except at the weekend. He is finished with Boston University (and they with him)—to what end I can hardly imagine, although unless I miss my guess the faculty of that institution are gratified to have him gone. Even this doubtful mother's eye cannot help but see him as a dazzlingly handsome young man—he looks very much like his father and reminds me that I was fairly well dazzled myself all those years ago . . . oh, dear, *such* a long time. At any rate, this poppycock is to occur tonight under the pretense of simplicity and good-fellowship and I shall do my best to endure it.

I'm sorry to say I've given up *The Golden Bowl*. I was *so* proud of myself for daring to take up Mr. James's latest challenge, but though I plowed through with determination for a week or more, I find I simply can't go on. Of course, I'm ashamed of myself for having backed down, but *McClure's* and the *Ladies' Home Journal,* with the odd peek at the *Atlantic Monthly,* are doing me quite well. I find myself somewhat short of mental fiber this summer, but fortunately I've got some embroidery to do for the chair covers in the dining room (part of my unceasing campaign on behalf of my house from which project I shall *not* be turning tail!). Embroidery and ladies' periodicals are the level to which my tiny little mind has sunk. Zachary is reading Count Tolstoi; *Anna Karenina,* I think he said. Intellectually, that may have to do for both of us.

Anne and the Lowell offspring were here today with darling Celia quite holding her own among the other young people—all chums of Annabelle's, who came for the afternoon. Celia is *such* a lovely girl. I wish she and Annabelle could find a common ground, as they are contemporaries and classmates, but they are so different. I'm afraid that dear Celia is lovely in a way that my own Annabelle, for all of her great zest and beauty, is not (and may never be?). I have half imagined that Celia and Anthony might someday form a "suitable" if not predestined pair, but I frankly can't imagine subjecting such a gentle creature to the Visigoth that my Anthony has become. (I see I have written "*my* Anthony" . . . he is not mine at all.)

Leaving the youngsters to their own robust devices, Anne and I spent the entire afternoon, with Potter's assistance, adding some wisteria to my pergola trellis. Anne brought her Rhinelander along to help, and I think Potter was fairly peeved at the presence of an unwelcome colleague, priding himself as he does on his green thumb. The deeper purple of the wisteria will be splendid with the pink and lavender of the clematis. Great trailings of wild morning glories and honeysuckle have arrived unbidden, but they are so very fresh and charming I have decided they must stay. I believe a metaphor lurks here, but am too busy with my other duties to pursue it.

The Trefoyles have again leased a cottage here for the month. I daresay evil old Padraic is not particularly enchanted to be hobnobbing with the Yankees (I do think he would far rather fleece them than drink with them), but his social-climbing wife rather fancies herself and has come up here with her only daughter on what may be a "mother's errand," though a premature one. Their Frances is actually a sweet child, appropriately silent, though she looks sickly to me. They paid a call last Thursday afternoon, and I was not in a position to refuse, as Eugene was here. Anne also dropped by with her cousin Amy ("the poetess"), and Minnie Endicott, so we made quite a party. Frances was very sweet to me, confiding her feelings about some young swain or other, and in an attempt to pass the time and circumvent her mother's society, I took her for a brief walk down to the pergola and we examined the new wisteria and my wonderful clematis. Her reactions were very endearing; there is a finer flavor to her perhaps than to her parents.

Sunday, August 27, 1905

Well, I've just returned, all aflutter, from a week with Mathilde at Chatham Cove. It was simply splendid—I don't know when I've enjoyed myself so much. As always, Mathilde's hospitality was Lucullan in its generosity, her beautiful house brimming with guests. The event of the week was the annual flower show in Harwich Port, and dear Mathilde's roses were a rousing success—quite extraordinary this year—tea roses as well as large, fat red blooms on the longest stems I've ever seen, which easily took first prize. I traveled home yesterday with an armful of her peach-colored jacqueminot roses (Mathilde knows I love them best); I will never know how Potter managed to get us back before they died, but here they are—and wonderful!—in Mother's good Minton vase next to the bisque angel on my writing table.

When I am with Mathilde I feel as if I've risen to another plane. She always seems, alone with me, to "let down her hair" a bit; the reserve, the cold "bossiness" (of which some complain) flees and all the warmth and buoyancy come out. Somehow, Mathilde by her very example encourages me to be more than I am, although I sometimes wonder if I should not indeed be deriving this inspiration from within my own family circle. Yet, it makes me wonder, too, if I must forgo any "soaring of spirit" (as my dear friend says) unless I can learn to be all things to myself despite my family. Inspiration and Serenity must be found within, I think.

Yesterday morning, just before Potter arrived to drive me home, Mathilde and I were strolling in the garden and I told her all about my wonderful portrait, which she is looking forward to seeing the next time she comes to us in Boston. She seemed so readily to understand the little I managed to say about J.S., touching but lightly (and with a far too girlish reluctance) on the strange fantasies with which I have become given to beguiling an odd hour. I confessed to her (for confession it was) that so often, just as I am about to fall asleep, I find images of his face flashing across my vision . . . memories of his warm hand on my shoulder. I was less than articulate on this point, but Mathilde put her own hand to my cheek and by way of answer smiled warmly into my eyes and plucked a young rosebud from a nearby bush and tucked it in my fingers.

Wednesday, October 24, 1906

What a splendid trip we've had! Four glorious days in New York to celebrate our special twenty-fifth wedding anniversary! Wonder of wonders, Eugene insisted we must go and outdid himself in generosity and flair. We stayed not at the Belmont (Bostonians are so provincial in thinking there is no other hotel in all of New York!), but at the Waldorf, where we were treated quite like visiting royalty in a suite filled with fresh flowers and awash in champagne. One imagines that such excesses are not to be found, certainly not with regularity, in Boston! I'm sure it would all take a more profound "getting used to" than I am likely to have the opportunity to master.

My husband was ardent in his attentions to me; the nights were quite as splendid as the days. Lying sated in the dark in my husband's arms (still so strong and hard) has become more rare with the passing years and so our second "wedding trip" was the more memorable. I think Eugene has on occasion found it exciting, though perhaps unbecoming, in me that I enjoy those times so much. I was (it hardly needs to be said) reared to believe that a lady does not enjoy her conjugal duties, much less initiate the occasion of their performance, and yet, certainly in our early years together, it was not a "duty" for me. Early on, however, I realized it was a mistake to initiate these amorous encounters with Eugene, because it did not elicit the response desired: Eugene is happiest as hunter and conqueror, and I learned rather swiftly (and regretfully!) to let him play that role. Yet, if other women feign pleasure (as Anne has confided to me she was wont to do with Edgar), I feign a reluctance I would so willingly trade for assault—and thus must enjoy my passion on my own.

My own delight in these activities is undiminished with time; indeed, I own (in these pages!) a resurgence of interest here in the middle years of my life. I am only sorry that moments of complete fulfillment are so few and far between. (Good heavens, but I am expert at euphemism this morning!) Eugene and I no longer feel, perhaps, the enchanting mystery of that night twenty-five years ago. Now I know Eugene all too well and have experienced too many swings of the pendulum of passion (oh! now *there's* an ill, vile pun, which I, with my slight literary pretension, have the pride to regret having written). And yet I understand, from some of my more candid friends, that gentlemen of Eugene's age require motivations for consummation of the marital function (blessed euphemism) that younger men do not. It is impossible for me to tell if Eugene is in any way feeling the affliction of his age in this regard—but he did *not* in New York! Two nights ago, as I lay in his arms, his mouth upon my breast, it seemed as if I had known him forever, and yet he is so different in his incarnation as "lover" from the other self I see in Boston that I sometimes wonder if I know this man at all.

Saturday, December 29, 1906

Alex and Eugene . . . Eugene and Alex . . . I have been musing all the week on that pair, locked together in the library, often for hours at a time. They are thick as thieves (an infelicitous comparison?), and becoming in a sense two sides of a single coin. They have been friends, of course, for years—they knew each other as young men: a formidable tie. It is not to be forgotten, after all, that it was Alex who brought Eugene Hillyard to our house on Chestnut Street when I was a girl, and it should not surprise me now that they are cheek by jowl at all times. Yet it is difficult to know who is the leader and who the led in this relationship. Is there a great trust and friendship between them, something true, or are they perhaps at some sort of "Mexican standoff," as Anthony would say, competitive and watchful?

Monday, February 18, 1907

The events of the last fortnight have been most unsettling. I fear that Alex has involved himself in Eugene's association with the man Trefoyle and that Lattimore money may now be finding its way, by some circuitous route, to pockets in South Boston. Papa's decision to name Alex as trustee was perhaps an obvious one all those years ago when I was a busy young matron with a large household and small children. But I despise (even as I nurture) my suspicions that Alex has become a principal in Trefoyle-Hillyard. He and Eugene are daily down to the Irish section, plotting and scheming, day and night. Now that the redoubtable John Francis Fitzgerald has been in office one full year, enjoying his role as "Mr. Mayor" with what I must say is the most unbecoming glee, it seems that Eugene is involving himself even more deeply with the upstart Irish Democrats, even as he panders to the established Republican interests in the Back Bay.

I almost feel sorry for Eugene; he sometimes has a tightness around his mouth that is very hard to interpret, particularly because he has never been the sort to confide his feelings and I am forever obliged to wait and watch and rely on hindsight! I am forever catching up! Alex is the more likely to say what he thinks, but possibly he would not choose to say it to me, and I daren't suppose that his reluctance is to be equated with guilt over a misuse of Papa's money. I think what I really mean, as I ramble on and on, is that I don't trust either one of them. I seem powerless to influence the affairs of my family as I have every right to do. And I despise that—I *loathe* it.

Saturday, November 9, 1907

My daughter Annabelle is evidently determined that we shall all remember her debut to the end of our lives. Her behavior has been simply dreadful! A good part of the difficulty is that she and her father want the party to be held either at the Tuileries or at the Vendôme Empire

76

Room. I have tried to explain to them that this is most unsuitable—that her debut should be at home, as mine was, as Hortense's was, though Hortense's coming-out party was a rather limited occasion, because Hortense herself does not have that *je ne sais quoi* that one normally associates with debutantes.

Annabelle, however, who has this in abundance and knows it, is demanding that we turn our lives inside out for her sweet sake and that we review (with an eye toward replacement) every *objet* in our home, down to the last teaspoon. She quite literally means the teaspoons, having criticized Mother's plate, silver, and crystal until I am quite weary of hearing about it. I tried to explain to her that we are not the sort of people who *buy* such things—we have them in our family and they are to be the more valued for that reason. Annabelle says that everyone will notice the "L" monogram on Mother's good English silver, and although I have labored to make her understand that makes it all the more precious, Annabelle will have none of it—neither my explanations nor my silver.

But her frightful behavior is unsubdued by my protestations. Yesterday morning she was far too crisp to Potter and Veronica, but they at least have enough experience of Annabelle to allow the invective to roll off their backs. Unfortunately, however, Winnie's young sister, Flora, is nearly in tears from all of this. She is newly arrived, and very sweet and biddable, but quite unused to someone of Annabelle's particular *façon*.

Worst of all, Annabelle has also become fond of comparing herself with poor little Celia Lowell, who does not have innate advantages of person. I rather fancy the Lowells have more money than we do (common of me to say so, but it's true), but I don't think that's quite the point. Celia Lowell is a plain little bird, but will be coming out herself, right after Annabelle—all part of the insane round of parties for which we brace ourselves even now—and Annabelle is being quite mean-spirited in suggesting that because of her own physical attractiveness she deserves something different from, additional to, or better than dear Celia.

Monday, November 18, 1907

As of this morning the issue of a location for Annabelle's *gala* is still unresolved, and time is growing very short to make the necessary reser-

77

vations. I may be quite mistaken, but it did occur to me that Eugene is insisting on holding the party at a hotel rather than at home because on the whole it would cost less. He knows that properly refurbishing the house would take a great deal of money and would also give me what I have so long campaigned for—a victory he will not concede to me? Eugene also says (this is a remarkable man, indeed!) that we have no ballroom as our friends have. Another ploy that he's using to try to get around the redecorating fuss is the fact that we are not on the "sunny side" of Commonwealth Avenue. Of course, it is commonly said that "the place to be" is the water side of Beacon or the sunny side of Commonwealth, but *this* is the house my father gave us and it is our *home!* It is certainly not an Irish hovel, though Eugene seems determined to do his best to turn it into one. It's all quite outrageously pretentious, and I am sorry to be obliged to record such tripe in these pages.

Friday, November 29, 1907

. . . and so preparations continue apace for Miss Annabelle Hillyard to be unleashed upon society. Her brother teases her unmercifully; even though he's staying in Cambridge, he comes home every weekend, which gives him a perfect opportunity to prey upon her in this manner. I try to maintain a matriarchal distance from these squabbles, but I find myself turning my face away more and more to hide my smile. Zachary accuses her of being vain, shallow, and frivolous, and his vocabulary is broadened by his efforts to annoy her. Annabelle, for her part, screeches at him that he doesn't understand anything at all of "life," and that he is a pig, a worm, and a little boy. He then reminds her that she is eight minutes older than he and therefore "ancient" and they are off and running for another round. Zachary is being perhaps a mite too clever with all this, and yet his point about the essential foolishness of a debut does not distress me, because on the whole I suppose I agree with him. I was presented to society myself, as was my sister Sarah and of course dear Hortense—as were all our friends and as little Celia Lowell will be ere long—but Annabelle is indeed a "belle" this season and her brother is determined to amuse himself (and his mother) at her expense.

SEVEN

*F*riday-evening rush hour found Arthur on the subway platform at Harvard Square jammed into a crowd of almost a hundred people. The moment the train screeched into the station, they all surged onto the cars at once, and Arthur, carried along in the crush, was shoved bodily into a seat. As the train lurched out of the station, he sank back, his head against the dirty window, and closed his eyes, allowing the rumble of the train to lull him into a comfortable blankness. He felt warm and a bit sticky; his hips and shoulders hurt in the dull, nonspecific way that forgotten muscles do after weeks or months of disuse followed by the burst of activity he'd put them through that morning.

Bright and early, teeth clamped on a cigarette, he'd called Mona's agency, chuckling at the receptionist in what he imagined to be an urbane manner, identifying himself as "Mr. Hillyard from Commonwealth Avenue." But after a deferential murmur and a few moments of dead air, she came back on the line to tell him that Mona was unavailable and that the agency would be unable to supply another housekeeper. And by the way, at his earliest convenience, the agency would appreciate a check from Mr. Hillyard in the amount of $865. Thank you very much.

So Arthur sighed, went out on the alley steps to smoke another cigarette, and then rolled up the sleeves of his old Celtics sweatshirt and got to work on the kitchen, Annabelle's bathroom, and the back parlor, pausing only to gather all the laundry and get it ready to be dragged over to the public laundromat on Newbury Street. Then he vacuumed the carpet runners on the stairs and along the first-floor hallway and fixed Annabelle's lunch and started in on the debris that had collected outside the back door, throwing it all in the trash bin in the alley. But his hips and shoulders hadn't really started to ache until now.

Arthur felt himself drifting just a bit, his aching gluteal muscles massaged by the rhythm of the clattering train. Still, in spite of his exertions with the laundry, and the bad news about Mona, and having but skimmed the surface of the dusty, messy house, it hadn't been all that bad a day. He fixed Annabelle a nice egg salad plate for her lunch and sat with her, sipping an Alka-Seltzer, while she ate. And then afterward, she seemed so chipper and good-humored that he thought it might be a perfect time to go over to Cambridge for the afternoon. Once Annabelle was settled into her chair with a box of Oreos and the new *TV Guide,* he dashed for the door, calling, "See you for dinner, 'Belle!" over his shoulder.

And here he was on his way home to her in the lavender dusk of an early-spring evening, the Red Line train careening through Kendall Square and out onto the bridge. He missed at least half the sunset because of the large teenager who blocked his view, but he flexed his tired calves and thought what a good day it had been after all.

Arthur was a part-time teacher in an "alternative" junior high school, tucked away in an old pre-Revolution house behind the Radcliffe Yard. He went there as often as he could, which had been less and less in recent months, to teach music appreciation to the rich adolescents whose desperate parents may or may not have known that the unaccredited and underfunded "school" was just an expensive baby-sitting service. When he got there early in the afternoon, the one practice room in the cellar had been vacant, and he ducked inside, elated, hanging his old tweed jacket on a hook behind the door. The instrument was a peeling Baldwin upright with yellow keys and "Fuck You Show Pan" carved into the keyboard lid. It was badly out of tune, but Arthur, oblivious, sat down and for forty-five minutes lost himself in the *sarabande* from Bach's Third Partita and the little bit of the *Appassionata* he could remember, drifting, quite impromptu, into a little burst of boogie-woogie that made him laugh.

Annabelle wouldn't let him play the piano at home anymore. Years before (had it been *years?*) he had practiced regularly and got quite a few gigs with amateur classical groups in Cambridge and Boston, or accompanying singers, enjoying the fake show-biz atmosphere, even in the sleazy clubs he sometimes played in. A few months ago, around Thanksgiving time it must have been, Arthur got the bright idea that a Christmas party would be nice. Just a small one, he thought, Claudia and her family, a few old friends perhaps, to repay their many kindnesses, to share some festivity. They could even have a "musicale"— drink eggnog around the piano, toast the season. But he was just about to send out invitations when Annabelle raised the roof, screaming about the noise and all those trashy people and missing her *Bob Hope Christmas Special* and many other things, and in the ensuing crisis, Arthur, hoping to avoid further hysterics, decided he'd better not play at all anymore, except at school.

At Park Street almost everyone flooded off the cars and up the steps to make connections on the Green Line. Arthur wandered back and forth, stretching his hips and smiling benevolently at the music of a group of youngsters who had set up their instruments near the snack stand. They had a wild and cheerful look, enjoying their playing, nodding vigorously to each other with great mutual admiration. Arthur dropped two singles into their open guitar case just before the opportunity came to shove his way into the rear door of an overflowing car. He gazed out the window at the musicians as the train roared back into the tunnel, knowing that he had probably never been remotely like them—fresh-faced, eager, his ponytail swinging in his own breeze. It seemed all he could remember of his early years was the long winter afternoons he and Zoe spent up in his room at the top of the house, spinning dreams together about how they would have lives filled with adventure, risk, and star-filled skies. But the details were a blur to him. Mostly Arthur just knew that he and Zoe held on to each other while adult life boiled on four floors below.

Disturbed at these reminiscences he had not wished for, Arthur found himself, swept along by the suppertime crowds, up on the street in Copley Square. Nearly home, nearly back to Annabelle again. And it was just the two of them now. No Mona . . . and no Zoe. When he thought that—a radar blip in his mind's eye of smooth dark hair, a curved, affectionate smile, intense black eyes dancing with schemes and expectation—the fantasy in old Eugene's library last night came back to him and he had to lean against the side of the kiosk for a moment. Vividly, he remembered the sense he'd had of Zoe in the room with him as he held her angel in his hands.

He decided that he would actually *ask* Claudia the next time they talked, speak Zoe's name out loud. He'd called Claudia back just after lunch, before he left for Cambridge, to double-check the date and time of Yancey's party, and they chatted for a while, Claudia's high-pitched musical voice bubbling through the wire.

"And Uncle Jim's coming! Oh, Arthur, I'm *so* pleased, we haven't seen him in months—you remember he missed Christmas. Well, he's been down in Clearwater all winter and I spoke to him Tuesday and he's coming for sure and it'll be wonderful, Yancey is *so* excited!"

It was just like Claudia to talk without breathing; being with her often wore Arthur out, but it also renewed him somehow, encouraged him in his unending effort to find the strength (as it seemed to him these days) to live through his life. Whenever he was with Claudia he came away warmed, inflated with the heat and light she generated. He had not asked about Zoe today on the phone, though he wanted to—could not, for some reason, find the words—but he definitely intended to, next time.

Arthur understood that it was significant to Claudia that their parents had been brother and sister. When Laura Wheelwright married the second (and much diminished) Eugene Hillyard in 1936, her brother Henry, Claudia's father, gave her away. After Eugene's and Laura's early deaths, the kindhearted Henry Wheelwrights unfailingly included Arthur and Zoe in their family circle. Arthur still cherished vague memories of rainy childhood days spent playing Go Fish and Old Maid with Zoe and their Wheelwright cousins, or dashing boldly—all of them holding hands and screaming with delight—into summer surf.

The Wheelwright largesse had continued, unabated, into the next generation. Claudia had Arthur and Annabelle out to her rambly house in Newton for Christmases, Thanksgivings, and all birthdays. She made it a habit to "drop in" unannounced at Commonwealth Avenue, but never empty-handed, always bringing flowers or cologne for Annabelle, or still-warm loaves of her nut bread and cranberry muffins for Arthur.

She would perch on a dining-room chair in the messy drawing room near Annabelle's bed and cheerfully rattle on about her patient, adoring husband, Eddie Trout (whom Annabelle dismissed as a commoner), and her boys—Lowie, the solemn, bookish twelve-year-old, and Yancey, the demon in the Red Sox T-shirt, soon to be ten—and Arthur would listen to her, chuckling and nodding, imagining he had a family himself.

It was interesting to him that his cousin's gifts and invitations and surprise visits persisted in the face of Annabelle's rude disregard for "those snooty Wheelwrights." But Annabelle's disgraceful manners never bothered Claudia at all. If she perceived or was at all intimidated by the old woman's resentment of the years of help and support she'd gotten from Henry and Paulette Wheelwright, she never let on; Claudia had never been one to keep score. In her view, family was indivisible, and to be endlessly cherished and forgiven. In the ten years that Zoe had been gone, Claudia had become Arthur's *de facto* sister—their cousinship blurred for him into something greater. With a full and honest heart, Arthur acknowledged what had become an ongoing, ever-growing debt to Claudia. He frankly did not know where he would be without her.

Feeling sort of giddy as he enumerated these familial blessings to himself, Arthur plunked down three bucks for a bunch of flowers at the open stand on the corner of Dartmouth Street. The miniature carnations were somewhat the worse for wear after a long day in the sun, but a lovely pale pink that he thought Annabelle would like. Feeling that some sort of celebration was called for (after all, he had had *such* a good day!), he took himself along Boylston past the Old South Church to the Chinese restaurant opposite the library.

Arthur was thankful, though with a rueful sort of self-awareness that vaguely irritated him, that at least he still had his old ability to seize his pleasures, however rare they had become, in whatever guise they might appear. A few minutes at the piano, half a sunset, carnations, and Chinese food might be an anemic substitute for the epicurean life he had once imagined for himself, plotting with Zoe so many years ago, but they were pleasures all the same.

He passed the time waiting for his takeout order by drinking an icy Kirin beer at the small bar and watching the bustle of activity in the lobby. When the food came, Arthur rummaged in his various pockets for some money, but soon realized that he'd spent the last of it on the flowers and the beer. Smiling broadly at the bored Chinese girl behind the cash register, he nonetheless produced his MasterCard with a flourish. He knew it was worthless, having gotten a rather threatening notice just the week before, but as he signed the chit he kept his smile plastered on his lips and whistled some themes from *Carmen* under his breath.

Clutching the warm paper bag, Arthur gained the sidewalk and turned briskly into Exeter Street, heading for home, not entirely sure if the prize was worthy of the deception. It was all of a piece with the "misunderstandings" over the color TV, the cassette player, the microwave oven (which he ultimately had to take back to the store), and so many other things, all votive offerings to Annabelle and her utter lack of awareness of their situation.

Arthur had resolved some years before, back when he first began to realize he might have to mortgage Grandmère's house, that Annabelle was not to know how bad things were. He had successfully hidden all his financial woes from her for five years now, but the string was playing out faster and faster and the resources with which to slow its uncoiling growing weaker and less real. Even as he hightailed it down toward Commonwealth Avenue, still humming "The Toreador Song," Arthur knew that the situation was becoming less stable by the day. That very afternoon, he'd gotten paid by the school for the efforts of the last two weeks; the check for almost three hundred dollars after taxes was even now safely in the pocket of his corduroy pants. But what was three hundred dollars against the pile of bills (all unpaid and many of them unopened) sitting in a plastic dishpan in his room? Against the letter from Conrad, still tightly sealed, in plain sight on his dresser top?

Arthur somehow could not bring his tired and unwilling mind to embrace it all. After all, it had been a good, *good* day; many nice things had happened. Annabelle was in a jolly, even kittenish mood; he'd played the piano, uninterrupted, for almost one whole hour; he was looking forward to some shrimp and lobster sauce for his dinner, for God's sake! How could Conrad and a mortgage on a one-hundred-year-old house exist in the same world with *that?*

Thus musing, Arthur soon found himself on the sidewalk in front of the house, looking up at the dim fanlight, seeing even in that dusky light the chipping of the wooden pilasters on either side of the wide front door. Feeling the heat of the food against his chest, he felt he could steal a few more minutes of solitude and went across to the Mall to sit for a while on the fancy stone bench that his great-grandfather, old Eugene Hillyard, had donated to the city so many years ago. Sturdy and solid, the bench had endured the decades; though its carved curlicues evoked gentler times before wars, pandemics, and acid rain, it was now pitted in its concrete footings, festooned with dry elm and maple leaves. The discreet brass plate was still riveted to the back:

TO THE CITY OF BOSTON * THE HILLYARD FAMILY * JULY 4, 1908

As he sat down, Arthur tried to reinflate the small bubble of contentment he'd nurtured all the way home, but with the tiny glimmer of clarity that never left him, no matter how stubbornly he mocked himself, however fanciful he might become (his pianist's mind open at all times to distraction), he knew that he could no longer push away the question of money. He had been facing the world—palms out, pushing hard—for a long time now, but the world was pushing back and its force was growing.

Just that morning, while his load of towels and underwear sloshed in the laundromat, he'd gone to a pay phone and called Conrad, finally reaching him in his Cadillac. For at least four months, since the last time he'd actually come up with a mortgage payment, Arthur had been watching his supply of excuses splinter and blow away. He no longer had the chips with which to pretend to bargain—and he knew it. This morning's concession on Conrad's part, hissed over the bleeping connection to the car phone, was only another form of creative sadism. Conrad had, finally, backed off a little, but only for his own amusement; he lacked imagination for anything but his enjoyment of Arthur's frantic gratitude.

But he had also been quite clear about his timetables and the kind of retribution Arthur might expect in the event of additional default. Until today it had not been absolutely clear to Arthur (oh, yes, it had! it *had*!) that he could really lose Grandmère's house, yet the ferocity with which Conrad's powerful palms pushed back at him was not to be mistaken.

"I've had enough of your crap," he shouted at Arthur through the car phone. "You'll be out in the fuckin' street, Artie, got it? The street!"

And Arthur's difficulties with the people at MasterCard, the heating-oil guy (now in an end-of-season tizzy about his money), Annabelle's various former doctors, not to mention the mighty New England Telephone Company, paled beside Conrad and his death grip on the Hillyard mortgage.

Pulling himself from the muck of his reverie, Arthur became aware that the food still held against his chest had cooled. Time to go in. He stood, stretching his stiff haunches, and went across the dry grass and the empty street and up the rotted stone steps (how could Conrad even want them?), digging in his pocket for the key. The foyer seemed darker to him somehow, more silent than usual, though he heard the buzz of the television from the parlor.

" 'Belle? Annabelle?"

He heard Edwina's squeaky whimper before her wrinkled little body rounded the corner from the back hall. She sidled up to him, growling, and then backed off a few inches.

"Annabelle?" he called out, running down to the wide doors of the drawing room. "Edwina, where . . . ?"

He found her at the bottom of the back stairs, wedged between the door to the butler's pantry and the newel post. One leg was twisted beneath her body and her arms were stuck above her head, caught in the turning of the posts. Her eyes were closed, the lids blue and still.

Annabelle had soiled herself as she lay (for how long?), and there was a large dark stain over her robe and gown. Though she had only a few raw pink scrapes on the skin of her wrist and elbow, there was a gash on her forehead that had bled into her hair, her eyes; the collar of her robe was covered with still-damp but crusting blood. Hardly realizing that he'd moved, Arthur squeezed beside her, getting his right arm under her neck and raising her into a sitting position. She stirred and coughed (not dead, not dead!), her tongue flicking in and out of her mouth.

Holding his breath with the effort, Arthur carefully laid her as flat as he could on the carpet at the bottom of the stairs. He ran through the butler's pantry to the kitchen, splashed some cold water in a glass, and hurried back. As he bent over her, his breath ruffled the wisps of hair around her face. She opened her eyes just a fraction, the pinpoint pupils glittering at him from under pale, twitching lids.

"Annabelle, does anything hurt you? You fell down, dear." Arthur brought the glass to her lips, but with a strength that astonished him, she pushed it away, and rivulets of water trickled down her face. He tried to dry her cheeks with his sleeve, but Annabelle's whole body stiffened with a rigid spasm and just as suddenly went slack. Her eyes rolled up in her head and all her great weight fell against him.

"Oh, God!" Arthur screamed. "Annabelle! Annabelle! My *God!*"

oe's bedroom was the only part of her apartment not yet invaded by *The Gilded Affair*. She had furnished it with several years' patient gleaning of flea markets and yard sales, spending hours stripping, painting, and shellacking the chests and small tables and one pretty Sheraton chair no one else seemed to want. There were no antiques, and nothing new, just junk made into treasure by skill and polyurethane enamel—and the need to do it.

The warm peach and tangerine tones in the room were accented by a terra-cotta pot of paper-white narcissus, purchased just last week, already blooming, and several small mementos of her years in Italy—glass figurines from Venice and a few shells from Mediterranean beaches—which were placed adroitly around the room. Over the white iron bed hung a shadowy watercolor of the Palazzo Vecchio in Florence.

The early April air was cool, and Zoe lay barely wakeful under her comforter, waiting with dreamy patience for full consciousness to come. That it was Saturday morning, a time once reserved for little errands and the pleasure of small chores, no longer mattered; after yesterday, it was quite clear that weekends were now irrelevant and would be for at least a year. She pulled the comforter closer under her chin and gazed across the room to the stripes of light coming through the miniblinds, thinking vaguely of her conversation last night with Julian Frye.

Being in cahoots with a force of nature like Julian was in many ways the greatest risk of all. But Zoe had begun to understand that however it went against her grain, the conflict between them was to be relished, remotivated if it faltered, though a need for that seemed unlikely; Frye thrived on conflict, savored it, exuberant at knowing that he reversed the ions in the air of every room he entered. Zoe, seeing the morbid humor in this, could only hope that the tension between them would make the movie better by overturning every rock, exposing every possibility.

After a while she got out of bed and padded to the kitchen to make coffee. While it brewed she changed the water in the crystal vase and carefully placed Roger's flowers out of direct sunlight on a low table by the door to the living room. The roses were holding up awfully well, she thought; so far only two had died.

She drank her first cup of coffee while she wandered through the apartment with a watering can, humming to her plants. Then she put on her jeans and a new T-shirt she'd gotten from the gaffer at the studio yesterday. All the guys on his electrical crew were wearing them— white shirts with *GILDED* on the front in gold paint. She refilled her mug and settled herself at the large worktable in the living room.

Zoe had prepared a thick, oversized notebook large enough to contain a special loose-leaf copy of the shooting script. The broad margins of each page were filled with notes, drawings, paint chips, bits of fabric, all heavily annotated and analyzed. Sipping at her coffee, she went to work on ideas for the scene in the music room at the Fifth Avenue home of Beatrice Holland's eccentric grandmother, Lavinia Van Riis-Griffith, where Laurence Thane and Beatrice, in the midst of a crucial rendezvous, are interrupted by DuBose Mortlake, the arrogant "villain" of the piece, who lusts after Beatrice and craves her for his own.

Yesterday, out in the studio parking lot, Jerry (who had gotten the assistant director job after all) told her he'd heard a rumor that Frye was thinking of taking Hitchcock's old trick to its limit and actually casting himself as DuBose Mortlake. Jerry had pulled her aside before they went in to the meeting, looking furtively over his shoulder as he talked.

"Get this," he whispered into her ear, a joint hanging from his lip. "They're saying he wants to play that Mortlake part, the art thief, the rich con artist. Can you believe it? Maybe he identifies with it, huh?"

Jerry laughed in the odd infectious yelping way he had, and Zoe laughed with him. The heavy sensuality of the character evidently appealed to Frye in ways that Zoe really did not want to think about.

"Could be," she answered, shaking her head. "Could be. He probably wouldn't be half bad at it, either."

"Want a hit?" Jerry said, leaning against Zoe's shoulder, showing her the hand-rolled reefer in his palm.

"I do *not,* and you'd better put that away, bean-brain, or he'll fire your ass," Zoe said, laughing and slapping Jerry's arm.

"He won't," Jerry hissed back. "He needs me."

"Dear heart, he doesn't need anybody," Zoe said, yanking the joint out of Jerry's mouth and pushing him ahead of her into the building. "At least not anybody in particular. Behave yourself," she whispered, taking Jerry's sharp little nose in her fingers and giving it a twist. "I mean it."

The studio was crowded. Zoe saw many people she had worked with in the past and exchanged air kisses and greetings all the way down the narrow hallway to Frye's office. She stopped for a moment to chat with the wrangler, a seedy old rodeo cowboy who was in charge of the many horses and carriages needed for a historical film. He kissed her cheek, told her a tasteless joke about Victorians, and, cackling, loped off in a cloud of bourbon fumes.

Zoe was well aware that Julian Frye had spent the best part of the last three months making damn sure that everybody in the business realized that *The Gilded Affair* was not going to be mere grist for the mall movie mills. He had confided to the woman from the *Hollywood Reporter* that he expected at least ten Oscar nominations and seven or eight actual awards, Best Picture, of course, among them. That this interview had appeared on the front page surprised nearly no one. Hype and glitz were air and water to Julian Frye, and everyone in town knew it. Many had begged to work on *The Gilded Affair* because of it.

When Zoe arrived in Frye's office, the other principals were already there, except for the costume designer, an ageless Sicilian named Marco Pelitti. Marco, nasty and revered, was an old hero of Zoe's from her days in Rome. It was a coup for Frye to have ensnared a man like Marco, who had worked with them all—De Sica, Visconti, Buñuel, Bergman—even Frye's idol, Fellini himself. But Frye regarded Marco with a deep personal dislike and had just about decided not to use him when Zoe talked him into it, some weeks before. She pointed out that although Marco was known to be a shrill martinet in his quest for authenticity (even his inner seams, some said, were faithful to the period), it was necessary to tolerate his personality if the perfection the man could deliver was to be achieved.

Zoe had played to Frye's elitist ego, reminding him with an ironic smile that no gunslingers, no San Francisco hustlers from the gold rush days, were mentioned in the script. Marco's experience with period costume went far beyond endless segments of *Have Gun Will Travel* and *Bonanza,* she said, obliquely threatening, knowing that Frye abhorred television and feared it as a last-ditch destiny should *The Gilded Affair* implode.

At last he was persuaded, and he had grudgingly signed Marco for what Jerry told her was an astronomical fee, "even for a hotshot." It seemed that Frye was taking no chances, however loudly he might bluster. This picture, Zoe thought as she settled herself on the leather sofa next to the sullen, famous Norwegian who was doing the cinematography, might in many ways be Frye's own "last chance." But if he was angry that Marco wasn't there, he had too much pride to let it show.

For almost three hours, Frye held forth on his ideas about structure and movement, the overall design and concept of the film. At lunchtime they took a break for deli sandwiches and coffee, but after just twenty minutes, Frye snapped his fingers and everyone turned toward him with absolute attention as he began to talk about the major scenes—the Christmas ball where Thane and Beatrice meet for the first time; the encounter in the snowy park where Mortlake kills the forger with a knife; and the lovers' secret meetings at the Metropolitan Museum of Art and the small inn outside Boston. Everyone took notes, barely looking up from pads and sketchbooks as Frye talked on and on.

He then dimmed the lights and showed footage, virtually still wet from the lab, of the exterior locations that had been identified so far. As she watched, Zoe began to realize that all the strained camaraderie, the phony group discussion, the pretense of direction-by-committee had been a setup: Frye's intention to dominate the shoot was all that mattered. It was clear that he would be the ultimate and only authority on the set, and Alan, the poor, unsuspecting location manager, was now revealed as the sacrificial lamb, dragged here to the slaughter so Frye could make his point.

The film rolled for several minutes, the utter silence broken only by a faint grinding sound from the projector. Zoe could see at once that the locations were terrible—all wrong in every way. The skies, the swing of the landscape, failed completely to create the look Frye said he wanted. When the torment was finally over, Frye let the 16mm film flap through the projector for several minutes before he reached over and turned it off.

Nearly gagging on his paper cup of Pepsi, Alan nervously defended his choices, not even waiting for Frye to make the first comment, apologizing for his failure to find more snow, though he'd been on the road for weeks and this was only the second day of April. Although the winter scenes would not be filmed for months, they were symbolic and important. It was essential to define them, to test light and lenses, to get the process started. Alan knew that, but he had failed most miserably to get it right.

Zoe could sense Frye thinking how to play this, trying to decide whether it would be more effective, more cruel (more fun?), to cut poor Alan's footage to ribbons bit by bit or to bring the hatchet out at once. Frye seemed to choose the former; he was subtle, careful, deadly—and worst of all, Zoe thought, completely right. He started the film again only to stop it every two seconds to point out the shortcomings of the angles, the color, the light, the very earth itself, multiplying his criticism frame by frame. Alan put down his soda and shrank deeper into his chair, feeling Frye's hot sneering eyes upon him.

By late afternoon even Frye seemed exhausted by the tension in the room. He digressed into some old anecdotes of filming in snow, telling lurid tales of a shoot a few years ago in Wyoming (one of his Oscar nominations), glancing occasionally at Alan, who realized he was only temporarily off the hook. Though he obviously planned to fire Alan soon, no doubt in full view of a much larger audience, Frye had clearly decided to punish the poor guy even further by letting him twist in the wind for another day or two.

Abruptly snapping on the room lights, Frye said he'd had enough. He motioned Zoe out into the hall, leaving the others alone to contemplate their lesson. After a brief, muttered conversation, Zoe followed Frye out to the parking lot, and they drove in separate cars to a little bistro not too far away on La Cienega.

At the restaurant, Frye settled back with a Kir, still fuming over Alan. Zoe asked the waiter for a ginger ale and then listened with distaste while Frye castigated both Alan and his footage, making no distinction between them, growling that Alan was a tasteless disobedient loser, raving on and on until, somewhat suddenly, he seemed to have emptied himself of his anger and frustration. He yelled across the room to the waiter for another Kir and a cappuccino and started in on a few more old war stories of what some people in the industry had begun to speak of as his "glory days." Zoe recognized most of it as an adulterated version of his press kit, which she, of course, had read five months ago. But tonight she viewed it all much differently, confronted as she was with the thick-shouldered reality of the man himself and the still-vivid memory of all the months of anguished uncertainty she had endured, which she now realized were probably far from over.

There were those, Zoe knew, who considered Julian Frye somewhat past his prime. He obviously knew it, too, making a rather obvious effort to impress Zoe with a lecture about the tribal culture of the late nineteenth century, the cruel hypocrisy of those old social customs, the zesty Victorian snobbery. He spoke at length about the irony of the title, about a "gilded time," as he called it, thick with deceit and self-delusion.

As the darkness deepened outside the lace-curtained windows of the restaurant, they started in on the topic that now emerged as Frye's hidden agenda for the evening. So subtly that Zoe could not restrain her admiration for the polished dishonesty of his style, he turned the conversation to a discussion of the color schemes for the scenes between Thane and Holland.

That these were to be isolated from the design and concept of the rest of the picture was a point long since conceded. Zoe had already spent several sleepless weeks working out a Dantean setting for the lovers—a dark bower saturated with deep wines, maroons, and russets. She wanted fashionable New York in the 1890s to look like hell: plush, opulent, elegant, but hell all the same. She had drawn Laurence and Beatrice nearly writhing in red rooms, embracing under red sunsets; even the romantic garden labyrinth scene, though set in winter, was to be sanguineous with hot summer light.

At the time, Frye had almost salivated over her ideas, but it now appeared he'd changed his mind. He said he'd been thinking about it and decided he wanted those scenes to be dark and gloomy, black and white perhaps, lit with mere points of light—the shine of a diamond or a pearl choker, one small gleam of bared teeth. He wanted to shoot these scenes from Titan cranes.

"Too much distance," Zoe said at once, shaking her head, knowing she was on director's turf again. "Too removed. You want to shoot it tight, Julian, at ground level—all of it up close."

When she said that, Frye looked up quickly and saw again the self-contained expression he had noticed in the lawyer's office just two days before. He saw it and was both invigorated and displeased. He enjoyed the one-sided game he played with Zoe Hillyard too much to have it stop, but all the same he felt a surge of anger, which he bit back quickly, knowing she was the one principal he would really hate to lose. He could do without the Norwegian, who was such a downer, and that fag bastard Pelitti; he could live without the gaffer or that pothead kid he'd hired as AD. But not without Zoe Hillyard. He felt a shiver of apprehension—something more—but hated that so much he forced it down and felt it slide away.

Frye had spent more time planning this movie than any other he had ever made. Every camera angle, every optical, every pull of focus, every close-up of Beatrice's tear-filled eyes was vivid in his mind, and he expected Zoe to bring it all to life. But he quite forgot, it seemed, that it was she who had planted many of these seeds herself. Zoe stared into the bubbles of her ginger ale and heard him speak of scenes fully formed in *his* imagination, and recognized her own early drawings. He spoke of the colors, the lighting, the very blocking of the scenes between the lovers, and she saw her own model of the back parlor at the Griffith mansion, Laurence's reaching hands.

"Snow is cold," Frye said, referring to the pivotal erotic scene in the garden of the deserted country house.

"But passion is hot," Zoe responded, not without humor, a small smile widening her mouth. "They absolutely can't keep their hands off each other, Julian."

Frye looked at her with hooded eyes; he'd been up since four that morning and knew he was more tired than Zoe and thus possibly compromised.

"Maybe both?" he said, hoping she would see conciliation in his artless smile. He had never been sure about how far he could push her. Zoe Hillyard's gentle integrity annoyed him; it drove all her energy into the work itself with nothing left for games. Of course Frye knew blood red was better than ice white. He knew it perfectly well.

"Before and after the scene in the labyrinth, when they first do it?" he said, not quite willing to give up. "How about black and white before and dark red after?"

"Like *The Wizard of Oz?*" Zoe said, and winked, reaching under the table for her bag.

In spite of himself, Frye laughed, a booming sound that startled the dozing waiter and brought him running with the check.

"Actually, we could try it," Zoe said. "Do you think so? Maybe we could go up to Big Bear next week; there should be some snow even this late in the season. We could shoot some color up there—pretend it's the labyrinth scene, see how it plays."

"Good," Frye said, pushing his chair back, still annoyed but smiling, biding his time. "That's good, we'll do it."

When they got to the parking lot, Zoe said good night and bent down to unlock the car, but Frye grasped her arm for a moment, holding her back.

"I want you to understand, Zoe," he said, "that I want that Oscar and *I will have it.* I have no intention of fucking this up, not me and not anybody else working on the picture. Nobody . . . not for any reason." As he spoke, his irises caught the reflection of the sodium lights from the street lamps; his small eyes glittered as he talked.

Zoe bit her lip, her face hidden for the moment that she turned to put her key into the lock, then she took a deep silent breath and looked up at him again, her mind filling with an apprehension she could not push away.

"I can't imagine why you think you need to say that to me, Julian," she said slowly. "Is that a threat?"

"I can't afford it, Zoe. I have a lot at stake here." He leaned toward her, his weight balanced by his hand holding the car door shut. "So do you." He looked at her intently for a moment and then squinted up at the sky, as if deciding whether or not to tell her something else.

"Look, I don't want to be too premature here, but I thought I'd let you know—and you can keep this to yourself—that I'm thinking of doing something with late-fifteenth-century Italy . . . possibly the

Medicis, Leonardo da Vinci, all that stuff, but very intimate. I know I'll be able to put the financing together based on the early footage from *Gilded,* so . . ." He let the end of the sentence slide away unspoken, knowing Zoe would not miss the implications.

Zoe looked up at him and said nothing, still snagged on the spike of trepidation that had not even had a chance to become blunt from his comment a moment before. But at the same time it angered her to see that he had not, after all those months of manipulation, understood that she did not respond to threats. Why did he believe he had to coerce her best effort? Why would he dangle such solid-gold carrots—the Medici! Ducal palaces! Savonarola and da Vinci!—with *The Gilded Affair* barely two days off the ground and the ink still wet on her contract?

All at once she realized that however capable he found her, however much he praised her work for its authenticity and style, her position on the picture, contract or no contract, would in some sense never be secure at all. He could blow her away with the same deliberate malice with which she knew he was going to get rid of the location manager. He just wanted to be sure she knew it.

But then, for the first time, it occurred to Zoe that for all his posturing, his self-aggrandizing fakery, Frye had actually given careful thought to what she wanted out of this—though of course he'd twisted it to his own advantage. He knew that if *The Gilded Affair* established Zoe as the premiere production designer for historical films, if some fine day schmoozing producers did in fact say "Try to get Zoe Hillyard," the world would know she owed it all to Julian Frye.

Standing there with her shoulder still turned slightly away from him, Zoe suddenly realized that in some serpentine corner of his brain, Frye did understand her enough to see that she wanted the chance to prove herself so thoroughly that coercion would become impossible. But then, if all went well, gratitude would take its place.

"I think you're right, Julian," she said then, as smoothly as she could, "not to want to get ahead of yourself. We have a lot of work to do. One step at a time," she said, smiling up at him.

Frye took his hand off the car door and looked into her eyes with that odd mixture of challenge and respect she knew she had to grow accustomed to. But Zoe's defenses, like old seashells, had had too many years to grow, there were too many layers there; seamless, powerful, they held him off. If he thought she would fall to her knees on La

Cienega Boulevard at eleven o'clock at night begging for a chance to redesign the Renaissance, he was mistaken.

Just then Frye smiled and offered the tiniest ironic bow, holding the door for her with exaggerated courtesy. She smiled and got in, and then closed the door with a solid thwacking sound and drove away.

Still deep in thought, Zoe got up to get herself another splash of coffee and went back to the worktable, hunched over her notebook, rereading the scene in the music room. She took out her first sketches and noted the black-and-white marble inlaid floor, the gray silk jacquard upholstery on the formal chairs, the enormous ebony piano. The weight of time, of wealth, of artifice enclosed the lovers in the stark but heavily furnished room. Turning back to the worktable, Zoe quickly sketched Beatrice Holland seated at the piano in a red satin evening gown and wondered if Frye's idea might work at that—black-and-white color schemes before the first time they made love, and dark, ensanguinated red thereafter.

She sat back with her pencil in her teeth, thinking that it was interesting that the question of practical sets had not come up last night. "He's probably saving it for later," Zoe muttered to herself, stretching her legs under the table. She put the pencil down and leaned back in her chair, looking up at the framed drawing of the artist with the palette who gazed with such perfect concentration at her work.

"How'm I doing, kiddo?" she whispered, and winked at the young woman in the picture. "How do you like it so far?"

NINE

(FROM THE DIARIES OF AUGUSTA HILLYARD: 1909)

Sunday, September 12, 1909

There is little doubt that Eugene's somber mood (by which we have all been oppressed for several weeks) is due to the recent inauguration of Mr. George Hibbard as the mayor of Boston. Mr. Fitzgerald lost out because of what the *Transcript* called "improper municipal contracts." And now that a Republican, and a Yankee at that, is in the mayor's chair, my dear Eugene, I rather fancy, does not know which side of the fence to jump to. Yet it seems clear that Eugene mourns Fitzgerald's defeat because of Trefoyle's own strong connection to him. The word "patronage" comes to mind, and yet I dare not believe it.

Tuesday, September 21, 1909

I am torn between wanting to know and not wanting to know—between feeling that it is my right to be informed of my brother's doings (however irregular) and rejoicing that I am to be spared information which would cause me, I suspect, no end of distress. I rail against my helplessness and yet retreat into it, but there is no denying that in the last year or more I have begun to see an expression in my brother's eyes that I do not remember in him as a child, as a young man. I wish that Papa had made *me* his trustee. I yearn to have something to say about my own prospects beyond the housewifely chores with which I try to content myself. And yet I must believe that the Lattimore Trust is safe. It *must* be . . . Alex would never do that to us.

I may be imagining this, but I have the impression that Eugene may have become odd man out at Trefoyle-Hillyard. There are unsavory and possibly illegal relationships here. And yet when I complain of his silence, when I demand (however cautiously) to *know*, I am patted and chucked under the chin and told that I look lovely today. But he cannot silence my thoughts.

I feel that Trefoyle and Hillyard look to Lattimore for social advantage, for introductions to fresh investors. Poor Alex belonged to a rather déclassé club at Harvard and so was fairly near the bottom of the social barrel. I can't think that there is much advantage there, and yet we know how significant those "old school ties" become in a society where a gentleman's circle, for all of his life, consists of the boys he scrapped with in the schoolyard. I should think dear Alex hasn't nearly enough of that to offer, and, God knows, Eugene has even less. But I know that something is afoot and I will not rest until I know what it is. Just last night, preparing to retire, I passed the door of Eugene's library; wishing to bid him a good night, I put my hand on the door and then thought better of it when I heard angry voices raised within. My brother Alex's was among them.

Sunday, November 7, 1909

A terrible thing has happened, and even though I know I am but in the first flush of feeling, I have taken a step from which there will be no turning back: I have demanded that my husband leave my bed. He will be staying henceforth in his precious library, and there he may remain, as far as I'm concerned, until the end of both our lives. Eugene Hillyard is out of my bedroom, and—except for the lingering legalities—out of my life.

Last evening we went to Symphony with the Pickmans for a special concert. We heard some wonderful Mendelssohn and Satie and the soloist treated us to a lovely trio of Chopin scherzos. We had fine seats in the orchestra and plans for supper afterward at the Somerset Club. (Eugene, of course, is not a member—I'm sure they would not so much as consider it—but Bob Pickman has been a member for many years and we were to have been his guests.)

Well, and who should come upon us at the interval but Mr. Padraic Trefoyle, with his usual *entourage,* including Mrs. T. and several of his henchmen and their wives, and Eugene's behavior was absolutely mortifying. He greeted Trefoyle as effusively as if he were his long-lost brother—as if he hadn't been with him all that afternoon. And when he introduced Bob Pickman (who visibly cringed), Trefoyle pounded poor Bob on the shoulder and he and Eugene virtually dragged him away from Louisa and me and into the outer lobby. Bob looked actually frightened at this robust assault. I went after them and tried as smoothly as I could to insert myself into their conversation, hoping to draw Eugene away. But then he shouted at me, told me to wait for him at our seats, and actually shoved me in that direction: *this* in full view of the thirty or forty people standing in the lobby.

I remember how furiously the thoughts raced through my mind as I tried to decide how to respond: Shall I take Louisa and sail as regally as possible back to our seats? Shall I smile sweetly and chat with *Madame* Trefoyle (God save me)? Or shall I—as indeed I chose at last—run for hearth and home? Gathering my skirts, with my husband bellowing behind me, I ran out of Symphony Hall onto the sidewalk. Fortunately, I spied Potter in the line of carriages waiting at the curb, jumped without assistance into the back of the victoria, and screamed at him to take me home.

I think at that moment what distressed me most was the fact that I had raised my voice to Potter. But it hardly mattered: we had revealed ourselves more than enough. When we arrived at the house, I ran upstairs and locked the bedroom door behind me, nearly collapsing to the floor, wanting only to scream and shriek, but fortunately I had enough presence of mind to be afraid to wake the girls.

Evidently Potter went directly back to Symphony Hall, just in time to catch Eugene, who was poised to hail a cab even as Potter drove up. At any rate, they came back here. Eugene raced up the stairs, bursting in with boot and shoulder, to find me at my dressing table, taking down my hair.

The dispute that ensued was unlike anything in my experience: he called me names that I will not repeat even in these pages. I screamed back at him like a fishwife and would again. . . . That is not what I regret. I can hardly decide the order of preference in which I regret things this morning. Can I go back nearly twenty-eight years to regret marrying Eugene Hillyard?

My *God!* I am entitled to trust my husband not to disgrace me, am I not? Am I not entitled to look forward to an evening of Mendelssohn and Chopin without fearing that I will be humiliated in front of my friends? What else do I have but my tiny little place in this tiny little social world? I have only my small life here, and Eugene is taking it from me (or making it unbearable, which comes to the same). But what a blinding irony to face in this cold Sabbath morning light: everyone thinks of me as "Oh, such a charming woman!" "Our elegant Augusta!" "Our vivacious Augusta!" Vivacious indeed, screeching like a fishwife.

My loathing of Trefoyle is not mere snobbery; it is not the social connection. Not alone. If Eugene wishes to involve himself with the Trefoyles of this world, that must be his affair and his alone: each of us is free to go to hell in the handcart of our choosing. But he should never— *never*—entice sweet decent people like the Pickmans (and all the others) into the lair of a creature like Trefoyle. I am guessing, but I have come to believe that those "investments" (wheedled out of our friends on social occasions where I simpered as the hostess!) are false and doomed to failure—destined for Trefoyle's own pocket.

It occurs to me that I might share the fault here; my anger at the Trefoyle connection has gotten completely out of my control. Of course I have begged Eugene to break it off—perhaps too vehemently. But it is clear that I have overestimated my wifely influence; it seems Eugene no longer has enough regard for me to be susceptible to my wishes, otherwise I might have prevailed upon him to stay away from Trefoyle and his cronies. But could I not have been adroit and indirect, wise and clever? Could I not have done *something?*

I would have risen above all this, I think, all these thoughts that clattered through my mind as he approached the dressing table where I stood to face him, my ivory hairbrush (like a weapon?) in my hand. But then he struck me for the first time in all our years together. My husband struck me with the back of his hand, and I fell awkwardly against the bed, my leg twisted beneath me—it still aches a bit this morning. He seized the front of my dressing gown and ripped it from me, kissing me violently. Holding my head in both his hands, he kissed me again and again, and though I struggled to free myself, he held me fast and forced himself upon me.

I think he'd had a glass or two, but Eugene is not a drinker and I have seen him manage quite a bit—that wasn't it. There was a fury in his eyes—they flashed, they darkened. I was terrified and exhilarated all at once. It all took barely minutes, and then I somehow gathered myself and, dragging the coverlet to my chin, I roared at him to get out of my house.

Monday, November 8, 1909

All of Eugene's clothing has been removed to a wardrobe in the library. His toiletries are gone from the bath, and his trinkets from the chiffonnier. Neither Annabelle nor Hortense has commented on what they may have heard or guessed—Hortense from timidity and Annabelle from an inability to take an interest in affairs that are not her own (never a blessing until now). And for a reason which I can't quite put my finger on, I have had Potter remove my portrait from the drawing room. It is hanging beside the fireplace, directly across from where I lie even now, a pale and much diminished woman.

Sunday, November 21, 1909

Eugene and I have not, it hardly needs to be said, spoken since the unspeakable events of a fortnight ago. But some repairs must soon be made to the ruin that has been created of our marriage. Some patching of the facade is needed now, if only for the sake of the rest of our family.

He came to me today. I happened to be in the back parlor doing some handwork, and he knocked, although the door was open, and I looked at him—I think calmly, but without encouragement—and he came in and paced for a while. He looked at me, he looked away, he leaned on the mantel. He pulled back the fire screen and poked at a log and cleared his throat . . . and I said nothing. Then he came over and stood straight before me and simply said that he was "sorry." He had the sense not to say that it will never happen again because we both know that nothing will ever happen again. Whatever remorse has bubbled to Eugene's resplendent surface will be his to bear alone. Eugene Hillyard has forfeited his claim on me as partner and as helpmeet.

I think this short encounter was notable for what was unspoken, although Eugene, feeling perhaps that some embellishment was called for, closed and locked the parlor door, and then repeated his apology. I murmured platitudes in answer. I know Eugene remembers (as do I!) that we have known passion and joy together in the past; from that have come our children, our home, and our life here. As none of this can be abandoned, there is now nowhere for us to go but onward. We held each other's eyes for a moment, as in a poem of Donne's, and then he went away and I picked up my sewing.

Thanksgiving Night, 1909

We had a fine and bounteous dinner this afternoon, proof that life goes on. All of us gathered together to thank God for our blessings. I suspect that no one is as taken with recent events as I, and that is indeed a blessing.

Zachary sat on my right at dinner, where he held forth very amusingly on his adventures across the river. He is making nice friends at Harvard, chief among them dear Anne's son, John Cox Lowell, who has been so kind to Zach—very like the older brother he has not really had. This is another blessing.

Annabelle, a vision in moss-green velvet, my citrines sparkling at her throat, was enthroned on her father's right. This is a tradition that goes back many years to when the twins were tiny tots and begged one Thanksgiving to be allowed to share the ends of the table. Annabelle was charming and witty and not out of temper in any way at all—another blessing.

And, wonder of wonders, Hortense was accompanied by what I must suppose to be a "suitor"! She asked me very shyly (and quite prettily, really) just last week if she might be permitted to have Mr. Eliot Duke as a guest at our Thanksgiving celebration. He is away from home on the holiday; his family are Southern people and he has been for some months in Boston on family business. He and Hortense were introduced, as a matter of fact, at Anne Lowell's. I said he would certainly be welcome to take dinner with us, and we all found him most congenial.

Anthony was alone and unpartnered, looking fit and handsome, but rather Mephistophelian. He has decided to grow a mustache, which gives him a sardonic look that I'm sure all the young ladies find quite irresistible. Our Anthony is, as Lord Byron once wrote of himself, "mad, bad, and dangerous to know." Ah, but poor Anthony (not unlike Byron) is a bit of a fool for all that, and fancies himself far beyond reason.

Alex was there with Mrs. Kinsett, she of the seed pearls and the toque. I suppose it is proof of my expanding sensibilities and up-to-date approach to things that I made her welcome at my table. I don't know why I take even facetious pride in this; I am in no position to criticize the behavior of others. There is, after all, no evidence that Della Kinsett is not a lady. Buried under all this folderol, no doubt, is my growing lack of trust in my dear brother.

As is also our tradition, the servants joined us for a toast. We had some very nice champagne, and Potter, Veronica, Winifred, and Flora shared a glass in the dining room. They are all, indeed, part of our family.

After dinner we had our usual puzzles and parlor games and a small musicale as in past years. Hortense enjoys demonstrating her modest skill at the piano. She has always performed her lessons faithfully, and in the past we have had a bit of Schumann perhaps, or more rarely Chopin, with Zachary accompanying his sister on his harmonica. I saw a smile on Mr. Duke's red lips as Hortense assayed a mazurka . . . unkind of me to be so surprised at the satisfaction in his glance.

I sit now in my favorite chair, sipping a last brandy, wrapped in a warm robe, watching the street sparkle with new snow. I have a small lagoon of time here in which to reflect, and indeed a strong need for reflection has crept upon me on this fine, cold Thanksgiving night. There is much to be grateful for, but I seem unable to take comfort and joy in the great good fortune that I have: family, friends, children, good health, and our beautiful, warm home. Oh! what else could I possibly want?

Truly, I am not discontent, but I am wary. I feel as if there is something missing, and yet we have so much. I am disturbed by the most remarkable feeling of dread that something awful soon will happen, but I have no faith, and even less courage, with which to give it shape.

$\mathcal{S}$aturday morning, the rising dawn barely brightening the eastern sky, Claudia Trout sat in her spotless kitchen, sipping at a cup of cold black coffee. She'd slept so poorly that she'd given up about five o'clock and come down to putter in the kitchen. But for over an hour now she'd been staring out the window at the budding purple leaves of the Japanese maple in the yard, unable to think of anything but the horrific events of the night before and of her cousin Arthur, lying in sodden sleep upstairs.

She got up and leaned against the chilly glass of the window, watching the light curl slowly around the neighbor's garage, reaching for the big lilac bushes in the far corner of the Trouts' backyard. Her eyes moved from the dry shrubs to the bare brown tulip patch, and then up into the April sky.

The backyard was to be the scene of her son Yancey's tenth birthday party one week hence. That it might rain, or snow, had not occurred to Claudia when she planned the party. She had lived in New England all of her life without giving a moment's consideration to the kaleidoscopic weather that was the source of so much Yankee humor. In Claudia's imagination even the white lilacs would pop out for Yancey and grass would sprout magically under the lawn chairs as the family ate potato salad in their shirtsleeves. And most wonderful of all, Uncle Jim Forbes would be there with them, back from another season as the most eligible (and probably the friskiest) of the elderly bachelors who cruised the winter boulevards of Florida.

When Claudia's mother, Paulette Wheelwright, died ten years before, Jim had come east to his younger sister's funeral—and never left. He had spent a lifetime in the Midwest, moving out to Kansas City to practice law right after the war, his visits through the years infrequent, his absence, all those decades, unexplained. Jim was an old man now, older than his own father had lived to be, and childless—nearly "the last of the line," as he liked to say (though the exaggeration was typical)—but overjoyed at his new status as the patriarch.

Jim's favorite twilight occupation, second only to a well-chilled vodka stinger, was endless reminiscence, which repeated itself with ever more embellishment, and perhaps invention. He'd sit and sip and talk for hours about the Forbeses, the Wheelwrights, the Hillyards, the revered Lowells—all the great, flowering Victorian families of whom so few remained. And now, of course, Claudia thought, with Annabelle gone (as the young doctor at the hospital last night had nearly promised she soon would be), there would be fewer still.

When Arthur called right after eight o'clock, his voice thick with a hysteria only barely controlled, Claudia knew at once that there was no question of leaving him to handle things alone. The most she could gather on the phone was that Annabelle had fallen, was perhaps dead, and the ambulance was on its way. Claudia jumped into her silver Toyota, leaving her husband, Eddie, standing speechless in the driveway, and zoomed up Route 9 from Newton, arriving at Commonwealth Avenue just in time to bundle her shaken cousin into the car and follow the ambulance to the emergency room. By the time they had filled out all the papers and a comatose Annabelle had been wheeled away, it was nearly midnight, and almost one before they got back to Newton.

Arthur had insisted on going back to the house to get Edwina. He absolutely wouldn't hear of leaving her, and so Claudia had prowled the downstairs room alone, waiting for Arthur to gather his things, horrified at the mess. She hadn't been there for several weeks, but even though Arthur told her he'd done some cleaning himself the day before (their housekeeper having left for reasons he refused to specify), it was just awful. Mail and soiled bedclothes were strewn all over, and Chinese food cartons dripped lobster sauce down the sides of the old-fashioned radiator in the vaulted foyer.

Remembering, Claudia pulled another Kleenex out of her pocket and stared out at the Japanese maple. "My God," she whispered to herself, "Grandmère would just turn over in her grave if she could see what's happened to her house."

For all the years of their marriage, Claudia had regularly told Eddie long, rambling stories about the glory days of the Hillyards of Commonwealth Avenue. It was all so vivid to her that Claudia sometimes felt as if she herself had eavesdropped from some dark Edwardian corner of the enormous drawing room while they all passed before her: Augusta, the mythic "Grandmère," and her powerful husband, Eugene; Aunt Laura Wheelwright Hillyard (believed by Uncle Jim to have been a genuine sinner); nasty old Annabelle (tales of whose youthful beauty absolutely defied belief), and her infamous lover, Spencer Trefoyle . . . all of them, marching by.

Claudia considered her self-imposed stewardship of what remained of "the Families" to be a sacred trust, and though Eddie entreated her constantly to mind her own business, Claudia insisted that it all *was* her business. Deserting what remained of the Hillyards was unthinkable to her, and her devotion to Arthur was a mixture of pity and esteem that Claudia herself didn't entirely understand. But she felt honor-bound to keep it up, and did so with a cheerful heart, though last night's drama had been the greatest test so far of that devotion.

She knew it wasn't truly up to her to supervise Arthur's grief and isolation, but it was unimaginable that anyone could think him capable of living through all this unaided . . . although, come to think of it . . . it wasn't as if Arthur had no one else at all.

Suddenly, Claudia's tired blue eyes lit up with inspiration.

She went to rinse out her cup and stood paralyzed at the sink with the water still running, staring out the window at the Japanese maple.

"Maybe it's time," Claudia whispered again. "Maybe I ought to call Zoe. . . ."

Uncertain, she wandered back to the window and leaned against the glass, thinking hard, wondering if she could—or should—resist the impulse sweeping over her.

Of course, it was true that Zoe had been away for years . . . many years. But so what? Wasn't she entitled to know what was happening to the family . . . to the house? Oh, how Zoe loved her Grandmère's house! When they were all kids, she used to spend hours sketching the ornate, curving staircase, and the strong lines of the incredible marble fireplace in the dining room. "Perspective, Claud," she'd say. "I've got to get the perspective right." And she'd take out her big pink eraser and rub away at it . . . and do it again, and again until she was satisfied.

Claudia's eyes filled up at the memory. She bobbed her head up and down, massaging the idea. "Yes," she said, louder this time, "I think I'd definitely better let Zoe know what's going on. She'll hate me some-day if I don't. And she'll come, I just know she will, when I tell her . . ."

But wait, wait. Be careful.

Claudia knew she had automatically embraced Arthur's problem as her own, forgetting that however much he and Zoe had loved each other when they were children, however close they'd been, that argument ten years ago had virtually destroyed the powerful bond between them. Claudia didn't know the details, and (though Eddie refused to believe it) she'd never actually asked Arthur to tell her. She'd just be guessing. But had the time perhaps come to interfere? Did she dare do it? Did she dare *not?*

Claudia went upstairs, walked silently in her slippers to the far end of the sunny upstairs hall, and stood with her ear to the paneled door of the spare bedroom. She slowly turned the knob and leaned just a few inches inside. Arthur lay fast asleep, his fine hair deep into the big pil-low, a wedding-ring quilt that had been pieced and sewn by their shared grandmother, Celia Wheelwright, smooth under his chin. He looked as if he hadn't moved a muscle since she'd tucked him in—in exactly that position—almost six hours before.

Closing the door noiselessly, Claudia went down the hall to her lit-tle sewing room and stared at the phone beside the rocking chair, bit-ing her lips in concentration. After a couple of minutes, she squatted down beside an old-fashioned commode that she kept in a corner of the room, a beautiful little piece with a marquetry top and scrollwork on the door; it had belonged to her mother. Inside was an old Crane's sta-tionery box where she kept every card and note Zoe had ever sent her. She sat on the edge of the chair and slid the box onto her lap.

From Florence to London to Rome and now Los Angeles, Claudia's cheerful, frosted Christmas cards and flower-bordered letters had fol-lowed Zoe Hillyard through twenty years of her life. And Zoe never failed to respond; oh, her cards and notes were usually brief, often hurried, but there was never a possibility that Claudia (and by extension, Arthur?) would not be able to find Zoe if she had to. Zoe herself had made sure of that.

Just three months ago, at Christmastime, Zoe had sent a real letter, warm and newsy. Though there were no messages for Arthur, there was one rather cryptic final sentence: "I hope everyone in the family is well and happy."

Claudia told Arthur all about the letter, as she always had, scanning his face for evidence of delight, or pain, or anything at all. But his reaction was right in character. As usual, he listened with absolute attention, clenched his teeth inside his cheeks, put his hand on hers for just a moment, and got up and left the room.

Claudia had always been sure that, had she been there to intervene, she could have prevented whatever terrible thing had happened during Zoe's visit to Commonwealth Avenue ten years ago. And with the ample tools of hindsight—a silent Arthur, a preening Annabelle, a longer interval than ever between notes from Zoe—Claudia had deduced that it had been horrible indeed. But though she knew no facts at all, Claudia had faith that loose ends remained. She believed in the river rather than the pool of life, in continuum rather than containment. Hers was not a cinematic, not a literary mind: she could not visualize conclusion.

Claudia was well aware that Eddie disapproved of her self-appointed role as go-between, and in a tiny corner of her mind she suspected he just might be right. And she'd really tried—had been as circumspect as her nature permitted—but it was no use. For she knew in her heart that she had not been put on this earth to mind her own business.

She lay back in the rocking chair, staring at the ceiling, and suddenly remembered a snowy Saturday morning, oh, it must be more than thirty years ago now. She had been sent from Grandma Celia's house on Bay State Road to spend the day with Zoe and Arthur. When she got to the house the front door was unlocked; the downstairs hall was dim and silent, and neither Annabelle nor the housekeeper was anywhere in sight. Claudia crept down the long hallway to the back parlor and peeked around the doorframe.

There they were, Zoe and Arthur, listening to *Let's Pretend* on the big wooden cathedral radio. They sat shoulder to shoulder, hip to hip, on the floor, their backs pressed against the rim of the loveseat, hold-ing hands, transfixed by the storyteller's voice. Zoe's black eyes were glowing with concentration in her little face, a small crescent smile of wonder curving her mouth.

And remembering that, Claudia, whose impulses were all to feeling rather than reflection, who swallowed whole what other, more analytic souls might chew to ribbons, knew that Zoe could not bear to be for-gotten. And that someday Arthur would thank her for what she was about to do.

ELEVEN

(FROM THE DIARIES OF AUGUSTA HILLYARD: 1910 TO 1912)

Friday, June 17, 1910

This afternoon Zachary and I spent an hour in the Public Garden, where we strolled amid the flowers in bright sunshine. My dear boy is now just halfway through his time at Harvard and has begun to think seriously about his future. He tells me that he has decided to take up the study of American history. He has done quite a lot of reading on his own, chiefly at the Athenaeum, where they have (with a note from one of his professors) permitted him to look at some original manuscripts of Jefferson and de Tocqueville, and it has all seized his interest and his ambition. (Eugene will fairly froth at the mouth when he hears this, but too bad.) I think perhaps it inspires Zachary to know that his grandpapa Lattimore was a colonel in the Union forces, an adjutant on General Grant's staff, who distinguished himself at Chancellorsville and in the Wilderness Campaign. That small *soupçon* of family history somehow rings in Zachary's ears; his sisters are not nearly so taken with their antecedents. At any rate, dear Zach is quite enthralled with his plans and—a trifle?—with himself, but his enthusiasm is so healthy and infectious.

I do confess, however, that I'm a bit surprised at his decision, as I once thought he might rather attach himself to more artistic pursuits. But this is probably more suitable, and I happily look forward to my role as the professor's mum! Yet I pray he does not lose his interest in the arts—he has the eyes and ears of a connoisseur and has always found such great enjoyment in music and painting. I have explained to him that art can be a great solace when one has little else.

Thursday, August 11, 1910, Nahant

I took an unusually long walk this afternoon by myself, hoping to escape the heat, and found Zachary on the lawn behind the clubhouse with sweet John Cox Lowell and some other friends, acquitting himself rather handsomely with his croquet mallet. I was surprised to see them there, as they have acquired a boat in some creative fashion not involving money and have been rowing about all summer long like a band of Phoenicians, quite uninterested, or so I thought, in other sporting activities. But he readily left off his companions to walk back to the cottage with me. As we made our way through the public meadow, steamy with black-eyed Susans and honeysuckle, Queen Anne's lace and tall, swaying wild hollyhocks and goldenrod, their scent indolent and warm, I chided him (gently, of course, but with a mother's prerogative) about his expenditure of time on croquet mere weeks before his return to college.

But it is very hard to tease Zachary successfully; his wit generally gets the best of attempts to do so and the joke is invariably turned around. With a twinkle in his blue eyes, he pulled from his pocket a book of Monsieur Zola's (*en français,* I hasten to add, not without some pride) and dryly explained to me that as Lafayette had helped so much in our defeat of the British, he thought it only fair that his studies of American history include some French! We had a nice chuckle over this, and, linking arms, chatted of Lafayette and the late roses (turning rather brown and dusty in all this heat), and croquet and Harvard, and many other matters, until we reached our own veranda.

Dear Veronica brought out a pitcher of her superb lemonade, and as we rocked and sipped we speculated on her news of a possible storm coming up the coast. With a gay laugh, Zachary observed that he hopes that the thunder and lightning (which even now I see, blue and flashing in the sky over the mainland to the west) is not a false alarm and that the deluge may come and wash away the torpor of the summer air.

Zachary is dead

Rising from a bed that held no sleep to a dawn that holds no light, I wrote those three words. I have now stared at them for an hour. The emptiness in me is so complete that I wonder that I have even these three words to write.

John Cox Lowell and another boy brought this news, these words, to us yesterday afternoon. The three of them had taken their little boat out onto the Charles in the fresh, nearly autumn air. The boys, pale and sobbing, were unable to explain how Zachary could have tipped the small craft over. They reconstructed only later that the oar had hit his head and he lost acuity, for just a moment, but long enough to go down. John Cox said that as they stood watching from the bank they had shouted and laughed at him when he fell into the water, knowing what a strong swimmer he was, never thinking harm would come, never realizing when he went under that he was indeed unconscious and would not come up again. Of course, at last they dove in to try to reach him, swimming as quickly as they could to the spot where he went down. They found him nearly at the bottom, dragged him as best they could to shore, trying desperately to press water out of his lungs, breathing into his mouth, but it was futile.

I am to spend the rest of my life without my boy. That's all I know. My delight, my comfort, my companion, my dear friend, my child— all gone. . . . I wanted so much for him! Yes, he had walks with his mother through wild flowers . . . yes, he had the joy of books and music, of spring sunshine and vivid conversation . . . and yes, the joy of knowing he was loved . . .

BUT IT'S NOT ENOUGH!

I speak to no one, though all the family gather at my door. I have no thoughts, no feelings, no words but three. I don't know why my heart is beating. Zachary Arthur Hillyard is gone and I will never be happy again.

*   *   *

Saturday, September 2, 1911, Nahant

Hortense and Annabelle and Potter and Veronica, all quite sedate and somber, came to me yesterday to suggest that we make a garden here for Zachary. Hortense had with her the pretty little book of the "Language of Flowers" that Zachary gave her as a birthday gift some years ago and we looked through to plan his—I can write this word, I think—Memorial.

We have chosen a spot behind the cottage, sloping toward the sea, protected from the winds by some lovely aromatic evergreen myrtle he loved, their blue-black berries just coming out. Hortense, her nose in her little book, announced that myrtle signifies love. And Annabelle, seeming to remember her Shakespeare, wanted to plant rosemary and five cypress trees to signify our mourning. Potter, standing tall and silent behind Veronica, smiled and nodded to her when I asked them to choose what they would like to plant. "Lily of the valley, Mum," says Veronica, with a glance at Potter. "For return of happiness."

And I chose only, as I lay wide awake last night with my volume of Shelley, to reflect that my boy is "made one with nature" now.

Thursday, January 4, 1912

Tonight after dinner (Hortense, Annabelle, and their mother dining *à trois* on a nice trout), I took my girls with me into the back parlor for coffee to see if I could elicit the ghost of a "life plan" from either one of them. (My daughters are definitely not of a feather: I am no student of ornithology, but as far as I know, peacocks and sparrows do not flock together. How in the world Eugene and I produced such a very motley crew I will never know.)

On the subject of Hortense, I am, I suppose, resigned. I don't think it would be fair to say that I have "given up" on Hortense, but certainly I'm not setting quite as much store in her as I am in Annabelle. Hortense seems entirely content to sit with her handwork, her sole proficiency, and wait for the post and a letter from her Mr. Duke, who has been back in Savannah these many months. In the two years that Eliot and Hortense have been keeping company, I have grown quite fond of him, and I pray that the dear boy has the romantic fortitude to pursue a woman who does not have the sense to run from him! She placidly sits and receives what she is given. And yet I do not think it is indifference; I think, rather, it is a complete absence of a normal coquetry in her nature.

This is, of course, more than compensated for by the machinations of her sister, who can hardly keep the young men straight and who, indeed, as I understand from Veronica, had one going out the back door while another was coming in the front! (This happened just last Wednesday afternoon, but I have elected to hold my tongue . . . possibly not a wise choice.) I asked Annabelle tonight if she wouldn't care to visit our new Simmons College over on the Fenway. Of course, it is very new, open less than a decade, I believe, but it is considered quite respectable for young ladies, and the fact that it is exclusively female is, to my mind, not a drawback, although it was all the reason Annabelle needed to turn her nose up at my suggestion. It disturbs me that she has no interest whatever in education or good books, nor in music and the arts. I have extended myself to invite her to some of the nice gallery shows here in town, but she will have none of it. Indeed, she is barely civil in her refusal.

And yet, of the young men who daily darken our doorway, wearing the very pattern off the carpet in the entrance hall, no one seems to be emerging as "front runner." I sense that Annabelle is holding out for a perfection that I would be happy to tell her does not exist. When Annabelle and Hortense are my age, the world will be a very different place, and I am concerned that they will be unprepared. I am haunted by an image of my daughters, sitting on the top floor of this house forty years hence, clutching embroidery hoops, with nothing to show for their years on this planet but unused tablecloths and quilts. It may be too late for me, but it surely is not too late for them unless they wish to have it so.

Saturday, January 20, 1912

As has become my habit, I lay awake last night, propped up in bed, reading. I have a new volume of Mr. Dreiser's that Sue Snell recommended to me. He is fast becoming one of my favorites, although one is reluctant to admit as much in polite society! Many people have found this latest effort rather shocking, but I find an invigoration in these melodramatic pages. But as I read on, absorbed in poor Jennie Gerhardt and her miseries, my small bedside clock was just coming up on three-fifteen when the room was illuminated with a blinding blue-and-white light. Tossing aside my book, I ran to the window. Just at that moment, another bolt of lightning lit up the entire sky in the direction of the river and, gathering its power, split the huge elm directly across from our house with a deafening sound!

This fine specimen was a mere twig when we returned from our wedding trip to France and in thirty years has grown into a great prince of a tree. Zachary used to love to scamper up its boughs while Potter, beneath him on the grass, would plead with him to come down. And for just a moment—the most fanciful of moments—I imagined that it was not only lightning splitting our great tree. As I watched, fascinated, tiny sparks and minuscule small fires ignited in an instant, only to be put out at once by the fierce, wet snow.

This morning everyone went out to look. People came trudging through the deep drifts from as far away as Berkeley Street, the word having traveled nearly as fast as the lightning itself that we had a "natural catastrophe" virtually at our front door. Eugene spoke on the telephone with his tree surgeon, imagining (as only Eugene would) that he somehow had not only responsibility but prerogative as well. (Of course, he doesn't—the tree belongs to the city!) But Eugene's possessiveness extends beyond his own doors, indeed, as one might say, to all that he surveys. Perhaps he believes he owns the very lightning!

Nevertheless, I do hope that the trimming will be minimal and in the interests of pedestrian safety only. I rather like the idea of the dead bough growing, sustained, from the living tree. We shall hear more anon from the tree surgeon, but I favor letting nature take its ever fiercer course.

Saturday, August 18, 1912

Our dear little Celia Lowell has married Mr. James Wheelwright at Trinity Church, and we have all been treated to what I must say is quite the loveliest wedding I have been to in some time—and, so fortunately, on a summer day both bright and *cool!* Anne, oblivious to these blessings, was wringing her hands, hardly knowing whether to be the more distraught over the possibility of oppressive weather or some foolish misunderstanding with the florist. Bless her, poor Anne has never learned to sit back and enjoy herself—she is such a nervous Nellie.

Potter drove me to Beacon Street last week to share in the prenuptial preparations. One of Celia's bridesmaids had a nosebleed from the excitement and had to be sent home in a hired carriage. Anne, in a frightful dither, was patting the poor girl's cheeks when I arrived—everything quite at sixes and sevens. Anne's dreadful cousin Amy, "the Poetess," was there, brooking no nonsense from anyone and with all sorts of brisk advice for the bride (though one assumes Celia has the sense to consider the source in entertaining those admonitions). Mlle. Roulleau was on her knees, fitting and tucking and pulling and rearranging the gown, which was just lovely. I remember it dimly from Anne's wedding to Edgar; she has kept it well wrapped all these years in white silk and the discolorations on the ivory satin hardly show at all. Old Mrs. Higgins got it from Worth, so of course the quality withstands the test of time. But our Celia is much smaller than her dear mother, so Mademoiselle had her work cut out for her (an unworthy pun, indeed, Augusta!).

At one point, as Mademoiselle went off to fetch more pins and the bride and I were alone for a moment, little Celia, moist of eye and trembly of lip, looked up at me and said: "Oh, Aunt Augusta, do you think he really loves me?"

Indeed, I am in no position to judge such a thing! Naturally, I have met Mr. Wheelwright on several family occasions, and a pleasant fellow he is—or seems to be. There is some talk (people can be *so* small and disgusting!) that Celia Lowell is marrying beneath herself. They forget, no doubt, that Edgar's people were only *cousins* of the Lowells, though I suppose the sainted name does mean something special hereabouts. It's true, of course, that we don't know the Wheelwrights, since they are from New London, and in trade, as I understand it, but all the same, James has shown himself to be a model gentleman whenever we have been in his company, and even Eugene (that worthy!), who is as chary with his compliments as the gods have been with cool summer weather, paid him the ultimate accolade: "Good man!" says Mr. Hillyard, as if his role as social arbiter may assure poor James his place in Boston society!

In the event, the wedding went off very smoothly. The mother of the bride stopped twitching long enough to reach into her reticule for a hankie, and the reception later at Beacon Street was perfectly managed, even though Cousin Amy insisted on smoking on the back steps with the servants.

Tonight I find a rueful, though not a sad, smile on my own lips. I have known Celia Lowell since before she was born. I remember when

Anne was anticipating her birth—just before the twins were born, and we were both "great with child"—that Celia barely moved in her mother's womb. She barely moved for Mlle. Roulleau. One wonders if Mr. Wheelwright will inspire her. And yet there is a heartfelt gentleness, a kindness, about Celia that shows more strength than all the flutterings and twirlings of my own extravagant Annabelle. Naturally, the fact that they are contemporaries makes me reflect on Annabelle's chances of unearthing a "Mr. Wheelwright" of her own. In fact, as we drove home from the reception in the warm twilight, Annabelle (who is becoming more mean-spirited by the day) did make a very unsuitable remark to me about the fashion of Celia's gown. At least she had the horse sense to tell it to me in private; but she added that she definitely does not want to wear my wedding dress when she marries. I refrained from comment and took not a little pride in the fact that I was able to hold my tongue in spite of the exquisite temptation offered.

TWELVE

*Z*oe worked on the scene in the music room for an hour or so, and then drove to the open-air flower market a few blocks away to buy an armful of the deep red anemones and tulips she'd seen the day before. Her eye was caught by some remarkably expensive fuchsia peonies, and after the slightest hesitation, she bought half a dozen of those, too. Though they were not indicated in the script, Zoe thought she would try the flowers on the ebony piano, using them as a centerpiece around which Laurence and Beatrice could move; the scene could be blocked around the hot, red mass of blooms that symbolized their passion for each other.

Back home, she got a plain ceramic pitcher from the kitchen and sat on the floor by the coffee table with the flowers spread out all around her, a book on Edwardian flower arrangements open in her lap. She worked with complete concentration, losing herself in the abstraction of color and form.

The light changed subtly, continuously, as the sun inched past the windows, and Zoe stood back from time to time, looking with satisfaction at her arrangement. It was so quiet in the room she could hear the stems sliding against each other as she positioned a few of the gorgeous hothouse peonies, one by one.

Thus absorbed, Zoe actually jerked and a flower dropped from her hand when the phone rang just before ten o'clock. She tolerated three or four rings and then ran back to the kitchen to answer, assuming it was Frye, or possibly Sidney, or even Roger, calling from Palm Springs.

She listened for a split second to a long-distance hum of dense white roaring on the line and then said, "Hello? . . . Yes, hello?"

It must be Roger, she thought, out in the desert.

"Hi, Zoe? Zoe, it's Claudia. How are you?"

They talked for over half an hour, and when Zoe hung up she stayed where she was on the kitchen floor, slowly becoming aware that the peony still dangled from her hand. After a while, knees creaking, she got to her feet and went back to the living room. Only three anemones were left, and Zoe slid one of them behind the curved stem of a peony bud, just starting to unfold itself in the water. The anemone was red and open, its black center crisp, the pistils and stamens perfect—hardly real, she thought, like a drawing, almost like wax, or like the famous glass flowers in the museum where she and Arthur had gone as children, marveling that anyone could blow a flower out of glass—and then the anemone blurred and swam before her eyes.

Claudia, characteristically, had not minced words. She quickly, factually, told a silent, disbelieving Zoe too much about it—the screeching ride to the emergency room, the tubes, the respirator, the shaking of heads, and Arthur's sobbing, gulping inability to absorb what had so suddenly happened.

"I know things were never good between you and Annabelle," Claudia said, "so that's not exactly why I'm calling. . . . I mean, of course it's a shame, even as old as she is and all, you know, but . . ."

Zoe had heard little of all that but Arthur's name. "But . . . what? What is it? Is she going to die?"

"I think they're pretty sure, Zoe. They didn't say anything about when, of course, but the stroke is evidently pretty serious, so . . . probably not too long. A few days, maybe a couple of weeks, tops."

Zoe had always been irrationally reluctant to face the obvious fact that when Annabelle at last was gone, she and Arthur would be the only Hillyards left on earth. All the weight of whatever that might mean, the finality of the responsibility to bear the name and the history, would then be theirs alone. She'd never been sure why that notion called up such dread, such awe and sorrow in her, but it did.

But Claudia hadn't given her a chance to contemplate such mysteries. "Arthur's not doing too well with this, Zoe," she went on. "He . . . God, there's no other way to say it, he's falling apart, and all this only happened just last night."

Zoe had just a flash of Arthur's fizz of hair, his soft, absentminded smile . . . Arthur bringing her little weed bouquets and the bigger "half" of his Hershey bar . . . Arthur sharing his skate key, painted bright red with Annabelle's nail polish so he wouldn't lose it . . .

"Anyway," Claudia was saying, "he's with her right now. He slept here last night, but I took him back to Comm Ave this morning to get some things, and then dropped him at the hospital. He's going to be staying with us for a while. But I just felt I should call you. I thought you would . . . want to know. And of course there're going to be so many things to take care of. The estate's going to have to be settled . . . Grandmère's house . . . all her things."

Claudia paused for a moment, and Zoe heard her blow her nose, obviously trying to hide it.

"You wouldn't know him anymore, Zoe. He's gotten very closed off the last few years. I think she wore him out—I think that's what it is. He keeps to himself, doesn't say what he's feeling like he used to, but even if he doesn't express it—well, some of it's bound to come out, isn't it, in other ways? This morning when I looked in on him he was sleeping like I'll bet you he hasn't slept in probably years. He's just exhausted."

Zoe said nothing to that, and Claudia paused again, snagged on the silence. "I'll tell you something, Zo, I'm not going to miss the old bitch and that's the truth, but she *is* dying, and Arthur is going to pieces over it and . . . gee whiz, Zoe, this is not right. It's not right—it's been too long. Ten years, my goodness. I think you should come back here."

It had been then that Zoe pulled the phone off the counter and sat on the floor with her forehead on her bent knees. When Claudia said nothing more, Zoe took a deep breath and picked her head up.

"Claudia, I'm sorry to say it this way, but . . . I don't see how I can. I'm starting this new picture, and I, well, very frankly, it's the biggest opportunity I've ever had, and if I leave . . ."

"Yes, well, there's a hell of an opportunity here, too."

Zoe, momentarily ashamed, said nothing, and Claudia, seeming to sense that, went on quickly.

"Look, Zo, I don't know what happened with you and Arthur, but I do know that whatever it was, this is a chance for you guys to put it right—or try to."

"You don't really know . . ."

"No. I don't. Believe it or not, I actually don't. In fact, Eddie asked me this morning if I knew what the problem was between you two, but I never asked, Zo, that's the truth, and . . ."

In spite of herself, of everything, Zoe thought with a smile that that had to be some kind of first, because Claudia never had been one to mind her own business.

"And Arthur never told *you*," she said, "all this time?"

"No." Claudia let that sink in.

A kind of fidelity? Zoe wondered. *Faith* in something?

"There aren't too many options, Zoe. Annabelle's almost certainly going to die very soon, and there's a terrific amount of stuff to deal with and Arthur absolutely cannot handle it alone. I'm sure I don't have to tell you that Eddie and I would do anything in the world for him, but . . . it's not the same. I wouldn't be calling you if I thought there were choices, Zo. Arthur really needs help. But I think he needs it from you."

"Did he say so? Does he even know you're calling me?"

Would he even want me? Zoe thought the words so vividly that for a moment she feared she'd spoken them aloud.

Claudia paused before she answered, considering. "Well, actually, no. You see, I didn't want to hurt him unnecessarily . . . in case you, uh, decided not to come."

When Claudia said that, Zoe began to realize that at some point in the conversation her heart had stopped pounding. The years of unacknowledged anxiety were, ironically, over, because the phone call she'd waited a decade for had come.

"Listen, can I call you back, Claudia? I'd have to . . . I'll have to call you later."

"When, Zo?"

"I'll call you. I promise."

"When?"

"Soon."

Zoe spent the next several hours flat on her back on the sofa with the old photograph of herself and Arthur propped against the fabric-covered box that rested on her stomach. She read every single one of

Claudia's notes and cards in order, lingering over those sent right after she arrived in California. From time to time she took a sip from the water glass full of Chianti that stood on the table beside her, but she ate nothing, drank no coffee. She just lay there, alone with her verbatim memory of everything Claudia had said.

When she finally got up, stiff and hungry, she stuffed everything back into the box and swung her feet slowly to the floor. She saw something that had fallen under the coffee table and got on her hands and knees to fish it out. It was a St. Patrick's Day card, from eight years ago, with a cartoon leprechaun racing down a wide-angle photograph of Commonwealth Avenue on a motor scooter. "Couldn't resist!" Claudia had scrawled across the back.

And then, from nowhere, came a zip of memory: two little girls with crisp matching ribbons in their hair literally dancing hand in hand down the middle of Commonwealth Avenue in eyelet pinafores, laughing, someone calling to them to "act like ladies!"

Zoe put her face in her hands and leaned against the sofa, breathing through her mouth. Minutes later, thoroughly disgusted with herself, she put the box back into the bottom bureau drawer. She tilted the photo of herself and Arthur against the clock where it had been before and stood with her hands in her pockets, looking at it with calm critical eyes. "Hang in there, brother," she whispered and went to take a shower.

Just before four o'clock Saturday afternoon, Roger's overheated car shuddered to a stop in a parking space around the corner from Zoe's apartment.

He climbed out and leaned against the dusty fender. It was gray and cool in Santa Monica, and a freshness in the sea breeze began to dry the sweat that pasted his shirt to his back; he peered into the moist silver sky, hoping for rain. There had been none since nearly Christmas, and it was past time for a cold, drenching downpour, the kind he remembered so fondly from the old days in New York.

Roger suspected, and had for quite some time now, that he really belonged in the East . . . in a *city*. He had been here in this sprawling place for almost fifteen years, and had never quite stopped wondering if he "belonged." He was pretty sure he was losing his sense of humor over those damn self-absorbed movie people, the pretentious phonies like Sidney Hooke, and the overprivileged maniacs who forced him to spend endless, intolerable days at their desert estates, looking at fake junk. He'd been a fool to traipse all the way out here for nothing.

Annoyed with himself, and doubly angry that he was, Roger kicked the left front tire as a token of his feelings and took off down the sidewalk.

Zoe, hovering by the bedroom window in her old kimono, saw Roger get out of the car and ran to the front door, happy he was there at last. When he'd called from Palm Springs to say he was coming back early, she was overjoyed and told him so.

"I have something to discuss with you," she said in a low voice filled with much more melodrama than she had intended.

"Discuss?" Roger said. "That serious, huh?"

"I mean . . . when do you think you'll be here?"

"About three-thirty. That okay?"

"Sure, yes."

"Maybe we can go to Frye's party after all," Roger offered, remembering, but Zoe just laughed at that, a thin sound void of amusement.

"I don't think so, but I'm glad you're coming early, Rog."

"Zo . . . ?"

"We'll talk when you get here."

Before he reached the stoop she flung open the door and stood holding out her arms to him, and he took her hands and kissed them, pulling them up and around his neck, burying his face in her shoulder.

"I missed you," he said.

Zoe could feel his weight sagging against her a little, heard the rare, dispirited tone in his voice, and slid her arms from around his neck. She kissed his face above the line of his beard and linked her arm through his, pulling him into the living room.

"So was it a Delacroix?" Zoe asked, clearing off the easy chair for him, throwing the swatch books and lengths of red fabric onto the floor. "Are you now filthy rich from your commission?"

"Oh, Christ, not a chance." Roger took off his deck shoes and tossed them backward toward the hallway.

"You didn't say anything on the phone," Zoe said.

"Oh, I'll get my usual consulting fee, of course, but the painting is garbage. They should leave the sucker out in the desert for a year or so and see if the weather improves it. And the weather was brutal. Ninety at least."

Zoe was straightening out the mess on the coffee table. She stacked up an armload of architecture books and set them on the floor under the windows. She turned to Roger for just a second as she carefully rolled up a sheaf of sketches of the Holland family parlor and slid it with great care into a cardboard tube.

"Umm. Too bad. I'm sorry, dear. I know how much you hate the desert, too."

"Yeah, well, I wasn't counting on it. Actually I wanted to come back yesterday, and I would have, but the Shulmans, weird as they are, are a good connection, so I didn't think it would be too smooth to run out on their little dinner party last night."

"Maybe you can still do a show around that Fragonard you mentioned," said Zoe.

Roger took off his tennis socks, wiggled his toes, and put the socks back on. "Yeah. Maybe. I'll see."

Zoe took the embroidered pillows from the corners of the sofa, banged them against each other, and replaced them. She punched each one into shape and set them carefully, just so, against the arms.

"Zo, what is it? I haven't seen that couch bare since before Christmas."

"I'm sick of this mess," Zoe said, her back to him. "Want a beer?" Without waiting for an answer she went down the hall to the kitchen.

Roger, alert to everything, waited only a second and followed her, leaving his shoes in the hall, flapping his damp shirt as he went. "What's up, Zo?"

She still had her back to him. "I'm just tired, that's all." She handed him a Coors and stepped out onto the tiny back stoop, a square of bruised cement where she kept her brooms, a watering can, some old clay flowerpots. She leaned against the doorjamb, inhaling the fresh wet air, and Roger waited, poised on his intuition that whatever was on her mind, it was *not* the movie.

That she would have blurted out, black eyes flashing. Her anxieties about the movie and Julian Frye were very Zoe-esque, but valid. Yet, Roger was sure that this was not about that bastard Julian Frye. He wanted to ask her what she wanted to "discuss" with him, but knew better than to do it before Zoe herself decided it was time to spit it out. This was intimacy verging on knowledge, after all, and with that thought he felt a strange, skewed comfort.

He leaned toward her and kissed the top of her right cheekbone, brushing her hair aside with his nose. He felt her small, reflexive smile, kissed her neck, and took himself and his beer back to the kitchen table.

A moment later, Zoe sat down in the other chair and leaned slightly toward him, looking with absolute attention into his eyes.

"My cousin Claudia called me this morning."

"Oh? From Boston?"

"We haven't talked on the phone for . . . years."

"And? Everything okay in Boston?"

Zoe wiped one hand slowly over her face but she didn't turn away. "Well, not really. It seems Annabelle—my great-aunt?—seems she's in the hospital. She's had a bad stroke, and they don't expect her to last too long. Claudia said there's some difficulty about her estate, and Arthur is quite upset about it all, and Claudia thinks I should . . ." The rest of the sentence slithered away. Zoe swallowed and cleared her throat. Roger set the Coors bottle on the table and took her left hand in both of his.

"And?"

"And what?" Zoe met Roger's eyes with an odd pleading expression and then gently drew her hand away.

"Claudia wants you to come to Boston?" Roger said, rising slowly, moving around the table toward her. He got down on one knee beside her chair. Zoe nodded, not looking at him.

"What did you tell her?" he asked, touching the line of her jaw with the backs of his fingers.

"I said I'd call her back, but of course I don't see . . . I mean, how can I possibly go? I have meetings all next week with Marco, plus we're probably going up to Big Bear with Niels so he can film some fabrics against snow—he has a new lens he maybe wants to use in the picture, and Frye's all excited, insists we *all* go, so . . ."

Zoe placed her hand on Roger's shoulder for a second, sighed deeply, and leaned against the back of her chair.

"Some timing, huh? Jesus, if Claudia had to pick *one* day, one day in the last twenty . . ."

Roger stood up behind her and put his hands on her shoulders. "So when will you call her, Zoe?"

"Roger, please don't nag me," Zoe said in a soft, tense voice. "I'll call her when I'm ready."

He allowed the ends of his fingers to curl down around her shoulders, feeling the delicate line of her collarbone, the softness of the ancient kimono, but after a moment he flattened his hands again and backed away from her.

"I don't think this has to be a problem, darling," he said. "If you have to go to Boston for a couple of days, go. We can call Frye right now; it'll be okay. Just . . ."

She turned to face him, her eyes bright and narrow, but then she just got to her feet and slowly shook her head.

"No. I've been waiting twenty years for this picture, for this chance. It's the best one I've ever, ever had, and now . . ."

"But Zoe, a weekend, three days . . ."

"Oh, Roger, for God's sake, I can't screw it up with Julian Frye. You know what he's like. He has no reason to put up with any shit whatsoever from me. No matter how I dress it up with stuff about my family."

Zoe ran her hands through her hair and looked up at the ceiling light. "He can get someone else in a minute. A minute! He's obsessed, Roger. You should have seen him yesterday. He has absolutely nothing else on his mind. He's so focused, it's almost frightening. I can't leave it. I can't."

"But, Zoe . . ."

Zoe shook her head again, quickly, abruptly, but then she smiled a little and touched Roger's face with the tips of her fingers.

"I'm sorry," she said. "I guess I really don't know whether to laugh or cry over this. Listen, come in here a minute."

She took his elbows in her hands and gently pushed him ahead of her into the living room and over to the worktable.

"For weeks now," she said, "I've been searching for a picture I could use to crystallize something for myself, and I finally found it the other day. Look here."

Squarely in the middle of the table was a thick leather-bound book, held open with large clips to an architectural rendering of a brownstone mansion—Roger guessed from the 1870s or '80s—Italianate roof, crenellated balcony around the third story, Doric pilasters guarding the door, reaching to the leaded fanlight.

"This is going to be Mrs. Griffith's house," she said.

"In your imagination . . ."

"That's right. I could have made it up, but I wanted to find a picture of a house that really, truly exists. I wanted it to be completely authentic. And there it is. I think I'm going to set the final dinner-party scene in that house." Zoe pointed to the fanlight and rubbed the tip of her finger back and forth across it, as if to polish the very paper of the page.

"The big dinner before the cops catch up with the thieves?"

"Yes."

Roger turned and put his arm around her, drawing her against his side, thinking furiously about everything he'd ever read about the mysterious wellsprings of inspiration, the labyrinths of the creative process.

"It looks a lot like the houses on Comm Ave in Boston, doesn't it?" he said, pulling Zoe ever so slightly closer.

"Oh, Roger," Zoe cried out suddenly, "this is almost exactly like my Grandmère's house. I didn't particularly think of that when I found the book last week, but after Claudia called this morning I went and got the book out and looked and . . . I don't think I can do it. I don't think I can go back there."

"Zo . . ."

"I can't."

Zoe turned away and went back to the kitchen, leaving Roger with one hand still on the book and the other hanging at his side. He took a deep breath and followed her, pausing when he saw her standing in the doorway again, the damp breeze barely ruffling her hair.

"After all," Zoe said, "I've been away from all of them for ten years. More, really, and I don't see how I can . . ."

She stopped, midsentence, and turned to face him. "Besides," she said, "I totally do not care if Annabelle dies. That old bitch is not my problem. Roger, that woman never showed me the slightest bit of consideration. She had no use for me at all, paid no attention to anything I did—good or bad. If I did something wrong, naughty, she ignored it, just as she ignored my good marks in school, my drawings. But she grasped Arthur to her like . . . like a lover. It was almost sick, almost scary. I was so young I didn't know what to make of it, so I coped by backing away, by leaving, you know, in my mind . . ."

Zoe coughed a little, a dry sound, and blew her nose on the Kleenex she took from her pocket.

"And then, of course, I physically left the first minute I could, left for real, first chance."

"And went to Italy," Roger said.

Zoe nodded, sniffing, brushing the Kleenex back and forth against her nose. She went to the back doorway again and leaned out toward the yard, where a fine, slick rain had started.

"It was as if Arthur were some sort of trophy Annabelle and I were competing for. As if . . . shit, I don't know. Maybe I didn't try hard enough . . . maybe that was it. Or maybe I tried *too* hard. Christ," she whispered, closing the door against the welling chill of the afternoon. "Awful, isn't it?"

Roger frowned and leaned back in the chair, picking up the Coors bottle.

"But this isn't really about Annabelle," he said. "Isn't that right? And it's not about Frye either."

Zoe looked at him with brimming, angry eyes. "There's nothing to go back *to*," she said softly, through her teeth. "There never was anything there for me except Arthur, and I . . ."

Roger knew he could not even begin to understand the intensity of regret and guilt that Zoe had suffered for so long. Ten years ago she had turned her back on a brother at once desperate and beloved, and was nearly ready, from guilt and fear, to turn her back on him again. An instinct in Roger brought him to his feet.

"I can't believe you would let yourself miss a chance like this," he said. "I can't."

"What's that supposed to mean?" Zoe's voice was parched and breathy.

"This is your chance to make it up with him, Zoe, to clear the air— however you want to put it. If you don't go back now you'll miss that chance . . . and you'll regret it the rest of your life."

"That's what Claudia said on the phone this morning," Zoe whispered. She looked up at him, and the glistening in her eyes spilled at last. "She used almost those exact words."

Roger's hands went instantly to her shoulders, and she gripped his wrists and cried without hiding her face while he stared intently down at her.

"Roger, I'm afraid to go," she whispered. "I'm scared, I'm really scared. Everything's gone, it's too late. I let it go too long."

He started to pull her into his arms, but she slipped away from him and went down the hall to the bathroom without saying anything more.

Roger leaned over the sink rim for a second, trying to think, fiercely wondering what he should do.

After several minutes, Zoe came back, her face damp, her hair freshly hooked behind her ears. She reached for the glass of wine he'd poured for her and folded her hands around the stem.

"I wonder if Arthur's still practicing," she said, smiling in a faint, uncertain way. "You know, every time I hear piano music I think of him. Every single time. I always thought he had actually quite a lot of talent, but I have the feeling he . . . gave it all up. I used to lie on the floor of Grandmère's music room and listen while he played Gershwin, Mac-Dowell, Chopin . . ." She grinned suddenly. "He adored Chopin. But for some reason, Annabelle didn't want him to do it, and so whenever she went out of an evening, with friends or whatever, he would sneak up there to that beautiful piano and play for hours on end. Sometimes he'd light a few candles and play like that, almost in the dark."

Roger smiled, imagining.

"Did I ever tell you Arthur came to Italy to visit me one time?"

Roger smiled and nodded, still waiting.

"Did I? Yeah, it was great. We spent a week or so just wandering around Florence, Siena, Fiesole, we had this funny old dented Fiat . . . it was wonderful . . . and then, ten years ago, when I decided to come home, back to the States, I had such marvelous fantasies about how it would be to see him again, but . . ."

Zoe took a sip of her wine and wiped her mouth with two fingers in a delicate gesture that Roger loved to watch.

"Christ, it was awful." Zoe sighed and leaned back in the chair. "I almost have to laugh now, it was so bad. Oh, Roger, I know Arthur's been locked up there with her all these years. Many's the time I've imagined what his life must have been. Claudia even said that on the phone—that he's not what he was, that he's different. But back then, ten years ago, Annabelle could have been dealt with, and I just wanted to help Arthur do that. I never meant for him to desert her, abandon her, I only wanted to help him make a life for himself! The piano, teaching, whatever he wanted to do, just to be true to *himself*—see what his life could *be*. But he wouldn't listen to me, and I wouldn't shut up. We got into this terrific fight, and a lot of really terrible things got said. Ahhh, we just lost it . . . completely. I remember feeling when I left that even though I was the one getting in the taxi to the airport, it was as if Arthur left me."

Zoe paused to get her breath and folded her hands, pressing them against her forehead.

"Look, Rog," she began, "the point of it is I'm not really a part of them anymore. I don't belong there. The connection with Arthur was so strong when we were little, when we were growing up . . . but now, I . . ."

"Zoe." Roger moved as if to touch her, but thought better of it. "Arthur is your brother."

Zoe heard his words, of course, but she couldn't take them in. Although she had been invited—*beseeched*—to come, she felt like a petitioner at the Hillyard castle gates, no longer enfranchised by her blood, her genes, to be among them. She realized she hadn't said anything for several minutes and looked up to find Roger's clear brown eyes intent upon her.

Roger's intuition told him to change the subject, just a little.

"So are they pretty well fixed, then? Arthur? Annabelle? You said Claudia talked about settling the 'estate.' Must be a bundle, huh?"

Zoe took a sip of wine and shrugged, nodding slowly. "Well, I think it used to be. I actually don't have the faintest idea if they have any money now, and naturally I didn't ask Claudia. I've always had the impression that there was once some serious money in the family, but now, who knows?"

Zoe frowned and got up, walking the length of the kitchen with slow straight paces, her hands folded across her stomach. "There's the house, of course, on Commonwealth Avenue, Grandmère's beautiful house . . . maybe there was something left, but Arthur was never very good with money, so who knows?"

Zoe stopped pacing and stood looking down at him.

"Dammit, Roger, I know Arthur Hillyard better than anyone on the face of this earth, even now, even after all this time, and this morning, when Claudia told me he wasn't 'doing well' . . . I could have told *her* that, and I haven't even talked to him in ten years." She took a deep breath and covered her mouth with both hands as tears filled up her eyes again.

Roger got up and took her hands away from her face. "You've missed him since I've known you, Zoe."

"But what if I go there and he says, 'Why are you here? Get away from me, go away!' What if he says that? After all, he's done it before, sort of."

"Then you'll just have to work with that," Roger answered in what he hoped was a matter-of-fact tone. "But he probably won't, right?"

Zoe looked at him suddenly, as if surprised.

"No. No, he probably won't."

Roger took his shot. "So you're going."

"God, I guess I am. I'll work it out with Frye tomorrow. I'll simply explain to him that I have to go to Boston, and I'll try to get the music-room drawings done, and do the Big Bear thing with Marco and Niels and get a flight probably next weekend. Maybe I could go for just the weekend. You think . . . ?"

"Just go and see, Zo—see what happens."

"I really have to, don't I?"

Roger just nodded, rubbing her back in a circular motion, pulling her into the hollow of his arm.

"I guess I knew it the minute I heard Claudia's voice on the phone . . . that I'd go, that I'd freak out like this," she said, almost laughing, "but that when all was said and done . . . oh, my God, I can't believe I'm going to sleep in Grandmère's house again."

And with her last words Roger began to see that Zoe's belief that she was truly alone had been the way she'd borne her separation from her family. For years, she'd retreated into a shell of survival of which the world saw only shining iridescence, but if the nacre of that shell were to be cracked, by Arthur Hillyard or by other forces, Zoe risked being left without illusion, without possibility of future reunion—truly alone. For the longer she denied them—not only Arthur, but all the long-dead Hillyards, that mysterious family she came from—the more that denial clutched them to her. It was the way she'd held on to them.

For months now, Roger had been waiting for Zoe to declare herself to him, to say she loved him—or to leave. He'd tortured himself with an image of a line drawn in the sand between them, careful not to cross it prematurely. But suddenly Roger knew—that minute—that until Zoe journeyed back and through another line, one drawn many, many years ago, he would have to wait his turn with her.

THIRTEEN

(FROM THE DIARIES OF AUGUSTA HILLYARD: 1913 TO 1914)

Saturday, March 22, 1913

Well! The Hillyards are now *literally* in bed with the Trefoyles. Anthony has been hauled off to the altar to become one with young Frances Mary Trefoyle. Eugene has fairly leapt for joy at this dynastic marriage (for so I am sure he imagines it), and none matched his enthusiasm as he pranced about among the Irish, expansive beyond the confines of his fine new waistcoat. I wore my brown velvet with the Malta lace again, thinking it more than suitable under the circumstances. Although Eugene was peeved and let me know it, wanting a far greater show of extravagance from me, I think I looked perfectly fine to play my role as the (reluctant? appalled?) mother of the groom. It was, after all, an afternoon wedding, performed in a small side chapel, since Anthony of course is not a Catholic and has no intention of becoming one, and required nothing more. And I did have my sable neck piece.

It was, all told, a perfectly stupefying affair. Mr. Padraic Trefoyle and his social-climbing wife spared no expense for their only daughter. The crème of Irish society frolicked in their cups beside a Mr. James Michael Curley, campaigning (as I was later told by Alex), even at these nuptials, to be our next mayor. But the occasion was not exactly fashionable, and I am just as pleased the Lowells and the Wheelwrights did not come. I know that I am a nasty old prune to make these observations, but there it is.

This marriage of Anthony's cements a relationship that I had hoped to destroy and which has itself destroyed my marriage (though admittedly with assistance from Hillyard and Wife in nearly equal shares). Affecting the course of these intertwinings is far beyond my power, but it is clear that the present matching-up, dynastic though Eugene may think it, has neither sense nor destiny to recommend it. I can't imagine that Frances, who is really a dear child . . . well, I cannot imagine that Anthony loves her, if love be in his repertoire at all. I predict they will produce an heir as expeditiously as possible and the twain not meet thereafter.

Monday, June 2, 1913

I have had a very timely and welcome birthday letter from my old friend Mathilde Gaylord, settled once and for all—and I feel contentedly—in Paris. I have not seen her since my beloved Zachary's funeral, when she so kindly came up from New York to be with me. But so insensate was I at that time with my own grief that I was unaware that poor Mathilde was suffering torments of her own. Only later did Anne Lowell tell me that Mathilde and the wretched Freddy were living apart, and now I learn that their divorce has been granted (the French look less glumly on this than we provincials do). For all my love of form, I am happy now for Mathilde's sake. She writes that toward the end he was "keeping" a woman on Sutton Place; I had heard nothing of that, but in our circle such intelligence would scarcely come to such tender ears as mine. Freddy Gaylord is simply disgusting.

Friday, June 6, 1913

I have been thinking about Mathilde's divorce . . . and more to the point, about my new suspicion, well founded I believe, that my husband has "another establishment" of his own and that his recent generosities to me may be proof of that suspicion. It seems that I may have paid for my new portieres and cornices in tarnished coin. Eugene disappears more and more in the evenings, as he did last night—I heard him coming in near dawn as I lay here reading.

Of course, Eugene remains unwelcome in my bed, and I know his need to be too powerful to resist welcome in another. Yet if he has indeed solved his problem in the fashion I suspect, it bemuses me to know that I may not do the same. The temptation that I experienced (and relished) some years ago, the memory of which gives me pleasure still, is not to be forgotten. I revel in the remembrance that I have felt that wonderful deep flutter for someone other than Eugene. And yet I wonder if I have that courage—or that passion (or that need?). Would I run off into the darkness, jeweled and scented? It is easy to be bold from lack of opportunity; I am fifty-one years old and I hardly think to engineer a secret lover at my time of life.

Tuesday, July 8, 1913

I have decided that we will not open Nahant this summer. Eugene may, if he wishes, if he feels he must "entertain" his friends, but he shall do so without servants and without hostess, and so the message to his cronies will be blunted. Veronica, Win, Flora, and even Potter will definitely be staying here with us. Hortense and Annabelle are not pleased with my decision, but I absolutely do not want to go there—and I won't.

Thursday, July 10, 1913

Eugene, who demands to have a self-indulgent summer amusement, and will not be denied, has announced that within the week he will be off to the island summer home of his chum Willie Bigelow. Julia is in Vienna with her brother's family and Willie is "on the loose" for fair. It is still difficult for me to believe that a man like Bigelow takes a man like Eugene Hillyard seriously (in the social sense, that is), but he seems to. They went hunting last winter, like rampaging barbarians of old, and if they want to sit this summer and fish and drink beer and curse Woodrow Wilson together, they can do it and be damned. Perhaps while Eugene is there, ensconced upon that private island, he can skin Bigelow and his fancy friends out of some additional money for Trefoyle. My God, but Eugene is a horse's ass.

We spent a most opulent afternoon at a reception at the Larz Andersons' in Brookline. The architect of their exquisite home is that distant but cordial relation of dear Jamie Wheelwright; as a matter of fact, the man also did Celia's house. She knew I would love to see their sumptuous surroundings, and with some urging on her part, and from Eugene as well, I agreed to go. Despite the fact that the new Wheelwright son and heir—Master Henry Cox Wheelwright—is just one month old this week, Celia and Jamie, the happy parents, were able to be at the festivities as well, leaving the baby safely home with "Gran."

The Andersons are extremely well-to-do and have been for who knows how many generations. They have traveled extensively throughout the world and have furnished their home with the spoils thereof. They have Indian and Tibetan artifacts in abundance: there is everything from carved inlaid ceilings to Dutch faïence, sandalwood chests encrusted with *blanc de chine,* a Chinese mirror painting that occupied an entire wall, cabinets filled with red lacquerware and jade carvings, rare porcelains and celadon! And the gardens! Really, it is all far beyond what one imagines for oneself.

I enjoyed it all thoroughly, but Eugene paced the perfection of their black-and-white tiled marble floor, sparks of resentment fairly sizzling from him, even as he chatted and smiled and browsed among the many guests.

When we came home, Eugene changed into his lounging jacket for a session of who knows what inner plotting in his library. Indifferent, I went about my business, doing a bit of reading and later, as Alex will be joining us for dinner, going down to confer with Veronica on the vegetables. Then, to my astonishment, Eugene came to me just now as I was dressing and said he thought we might consider some redecoration after all, something beyond the new portieres in the drawing room. I wisely held my tongue and am immoderately proud of myself on that account; I merely murmured something bland about how lovely it would be . . . and let it go at that.

Of course, there is no question of emulating (surely not of *equaling*) the Andersons, but I know Eugene was inspired this afternoon in ways mere mortal woman cannot understand. There is a need in him that goes beyond simple enjoyment of nice things. Eugene has never been content to settle for the odd bibelot—only extravagance fulfills him.

1 3 7

After lunch I took myself off for a long and solitary walk, making a detour to the Metropolitan Furniture Company to inquire about the fabric for the new parlor chairs, and then stopped into the stationer's to buy more paper for this diary. My "complete works" are developing into quite a bundle (good for feeding fires, I sometimes think), adding girth and volume daily, if not substance. . . . As I sit to write this, I cannot help but reflect that next week will be thirty-two years that I have kept this diary. It is just staggering to think of it in those terms!

I started off as a young bride: I made the first entry on my wedding night after Eugene fell asleep. I remember how hopeful I was, how joyful, and how stimulated by Eugene's raw presence. Goodness me, what a great deal of water has splashed over the dam since then! This afternoon when I was buying the paper I thought I might take some time to go back and read some of it again, but I lack the fortitude to do so.

I wonder what they all would say if they knew I do this. Isn't it odd that in thirty-two years no one in my family has ever questioned me about it? I think they genuinely don't know. To be sure, I have never told anyone, never breathed a word—for surely my privacy is, after all, as sacred as theirs? Still, would they be curious? Would they sneak up in my absence to read and find out what I feel? Would they scour these pages to know my thoughts and possibly to love me better? To despise me? To be shocked and horrified at what I think of *them?* I know there have been times over the years when I have been writing and one of the children, or Eugene, might have stopped in to have me tie a ribbon, to find a cufflink, to announce departure . . . but they never said anything at all—they never asked me what I wrote. I think my whole life must be blank to them.

And yet I have been faithful to it. I have poured out my heart in these pages. I have missed, of course, some days, sometimes a month or more—after I lost my Zachary, nearly a year went by—but this pile of paper has become my other self. I find it impossible to stop. And since I write so small a hand, it's all quite well contained here within its box. I tie the years and decades together and it all fits nicely in the rosewood commode. When I die they can burn that instead of me.

The most astonishing thing happened just minutes ago. I was in the upstairs parlor, amusing myself at the Chickering, where I enjoy occasionally to pick out the odd tune from one of my favorite Schubert songs, when Eugene presented himself and with a fascinating combination of bluster and diffidence told me that he had been passing the open door of my bedroom the other day and had been quite transfixed by my portrait, which hangs, of course, on the long wall beside the fireplace. Making no reference to the teapot tempest that ensued after I sat for John Sargent years ago (at my own expense, let us not forget!), Eugene said he found it very beautiful and asked if I would agree to hang it once again in its original spot in the downstairs drawing room. I was quite stunned, but I think I recovered myself very adroitly (I do have an intense dislike of allowing Eugene to sense my feelings), and told him I would think about it.

Why in the world would Eugene want me to move my painting to a public room? I'm not necessarily opposed to that; I just find it very strange that he should tender the suggestion. I do not doubt there is a hidden reason, some hope of gain—though my indifference extends to contemplation of his motives. I've come directly upstairs, however, to look at the portrait myself.

Certainly in the last couple of years it has become part of the wallpaper for me, but as I sit here staring at it (and writing these words with utter immodesty), I see there a loveliness that seems to have grown with the eight years now passed. Why should this be so? The brushstrokes are exactly where dear John placed them, and yet there is a look in the eyes of that once-young woman in the portrait that stirs something in me as it may have done in Eugene.

Gazing upon one's portrait is not the same as looking in a mirror. In a looking glass one can pull a silly face, pinch one's cheeks to make them pinker, one can smile, frown, show one's teeth. But the portrait is fixed and immutable. I cannot help but be reminded, as I gaze upon the "myself" that once was, of Mr. Oscar Wilde's chilling discourse on the mutability of character. And yet, upon inspection, I see no indication that the portrait has changed—nor have I remained the same. *Au contraire,* there is a freshness and an anticipation of delight in that painted face that I am at some pains to find in my looking glass. "The Dorian

Gray Effect" seems to be reversed here; life does not seem to be imitating art on this occasion.

This day is one of milestones for our family. Eugene Patrick Hillyard has been born to my son Anthony and his exhausted little wife, and I am now "Grandmère." This has always been a title of special respect in our family, and I cannot deny that I felt a most particular pleasure that my turn had come.

The child was born at home, of course. Anthony and Frances are ensconced in a very charming new dwelling on Clarendon Street near the river, with a spacious master bedroom where little Eugene first saw the light of day. When I arrived there at noon, Frances was pale but happy, her mother by her bedside. (Mary Trefoyle and I have labored for one year under the constraints of our pro forma "familial" relationship. I certainly hope that little Eugene's arrival does not mean we shall be seeing too much more of each other!)

My suspicion, looking into Frances's drooping eyes, is that she has now done her duty: she has carried and borne this child. Her intimacy with my son is a job of work I wager she did not relish, but it is over and the product of that consummation mercifully arrived.

Anthony put in an appearance rather belatedly; he arrived with little Eugene's grandfathers at dusk, and I left soon after, not wishing to be obliged to endure their heartiness. In spite of the new phase of life this represents for me as grandmother, I find that I am a bit indifferent to it all, and I'm not happy to say it. Be it lineage or the somewhat feeble appearance of the child himself, I cannot bear to share what should be a joyful occasion with those people. I decided to take myself back home alone, it being not so far. Eugene, a tot of whisky clutched in his grandfatherly hand, was, I think, unaware that I had left the house.

I came to the corner of Commonwealth Avenue and walked straight up the middle of the Mall, the brisk west wind in my face, admiring the lamplight shining on the snow, and thought that I was better off to be alone. Surrounded by the bright, swirling snow, I was neither mother, nor wife, nor Mama, nor Mrs. Hillyard, nor Aunt Augusta—nor even "Grandmère." I am only Augusta: to myself, and perhaps to God.

Part Two

AT THE HILLYARD CASTLE GATES

When I was young it used to seem to me that the group in which I grew up was like an empty vessel into which no new wine would ever again be poured. Now I see that one of its uses lay in preserving a few drops of an old vintage too rare to be savoured by a youthful palate; and I should like to atone for my unappreciativeness by trying to revive that faint fragrance.

—EDITH WHARTON, *A Backward Glance*

$\mathcal{D}$uring the tense half hour that
the big jet circled Boston Harbor, Zoe pressed her nose against the little oval window, mesmerized by the geometric runway lights below
that tilted with the banking of the plane against the curve of the Atlantic
shoreline. Clutched in her hands was the little stack of mementos she
had decided, at the last minute, to bring with her.

Just that morning, while Roger went around watering the plants and
making sure everything was safe and ready for her return, Zoe had knelt
in front of her dresser and taken out a handful of Claudia's notes and
cards and the old photograph of herself and Arthur. After only a second or two of hesitation, she snapped a rubber band around them and
tucked the bundle in the bottom of her bag. Several times during the
long flight from California, she had taken the little packet out and
looked at it all again, concentrating on the photograph, trying to tell
herself to take it as it came, to be calm and ready.

As the plane leveled off and the sheds and hangars at the end of the
runway grew larger, outlined with tiny lights, Zoe gripped her bag with
both hands and stared out the window at the swampy infields just visible in the darkness. Finally, the plane bounced onto the runway, en-
gines roaring, and minutes later Zoe came through the jetway into the
bright, noisy terminal. She looked eagerly around for Claudia's bubble
of blond hair, but was surprised, and oddly disappointed, to see Eddie,

all alone, squinting at the crowd of arriving passengers with bleak, expectant friendliness. She recognized him almost at once from the many photographs Claudia had sent through the years.

When she came up to him, he grinned suddenly, looking a bit flustered, but he instantly swung her satchel onto his shoulder and took her elbow in an old-fashioned way that made her smile. He led her through the crush to the parked station wagon, and soon they were through the Callahan Tunnel and turning onto the peeling green superstructure of Storrow Drive.

They talked very little in the car, but it was a quiet, almost comfortable conversation, Zoe making small talk about her flight, Eddie commenting from time to time about the changes wrought to Boston by time, and greed, and architecture. In answer to her careful questions, as if relieved to be talking about it, Eddie told her that Arthur had been spending all day, every day, at the hospital, hovering at Annabelle's bedside. He had refused Claudia's offer and was staying with Edwina at home, even though Claudia had promised to drive him into town every morning and back to Newton every night.

"He's probably happier in his own place, though," Eddie said in a doubtful tone.

"Oh, I'm sure he is, Eddie," Zoe offered, looking out the car window at the orchestra shell, the bare-branched trees along the Esplanade, and the lights of Cambridge across the river. "It's much closer to the hospital, after all."

"Yeah," he said, "that's what I told my wife. She takes everything on herself, though. She worries."

"I remember," Zoe said, frowning into the lights of the oncoming traffic.

When they pulled up on Commonwealth Avenue, directly in front of the house, Claudia had the heavy door wide open, the lights from the foyer glowing brightly behind her.

"What marvelous timing!" she called to them from the doorway. "We just got in from the hospital. I've got the coffee on already. Zoe!" She ran down two or three steps and threw her arms around Zoe and then pulled her through the door. Once inside, Claudia hugged her again, then stood back, still holding Zoe's wrists, looking avidly into her face.

"I'm so glad you're here, Zoe, really glad," she said in a stage whisper.

Zoe found herself able to smile and murmur something back, embarrassed at being made so welcome. She barely swallowed the lump that blossomed in her throat before she hugged Claudia back, much harder than she thought she meant to.

"Oh, you look wonderful," Claudia said, still whispering. "Wonderful!"

"So do you," Zoe said, her hands on either side of Claudia's face. "You look terrific, Claud."

"Can you believe we're *forty?*" Claudia hissed, giggling with pleasure.

Arthur was standing rather stiffly, formally, in the middle of the marble foyer. He took a step forward, reaching for Zoe's hands with both of his, and held them firmly in the space between them. Zoe tilted her face to look up at him.

He was as before, tall, maybe heavier than ten years ago, his smooth cheeks flushed pink, the halo of silvery hair, thinner than she remembered, backlit by the carriage lamps in the hall. The top button of his plaid shirt was open under the knot of his woolen tie, and his blue eyes were pouchy but focused behind his glasses.

Zoe had a momentary urge to embrace him, to gather him against her, and for just a second, she thought he might have felt the same impulse, but they only stood, immobile, under the dusty sconces, looking into each other's eyes, holding each other's hands.

"In here, everybody!" Claudia called out, and Arthur let go of Zoe's hands and followed her through the archway to the dining room, where Claudia was arranging plates of cookies and little fancy pastries, laying out cups and saucers and paper napkins at one end of the long table.

"Sit wherever you want, Zo," she said over her shoulder, briskly rummaging in the sideboard for spoons.

"Something stronger?" she asked, pouring coffee into a thin porcelain cup. "Maybe a sandwich?"

"Oh, Claudia, thanks, this is fine." Zoe smiled and stirred sugar into her coffee. "I'm really not too hungry. It's only about five in the afternoon for me, after all."

Undeterred, Claudia slid the heaped plate of pastries in front of Zoe and then poured cream from a chipped Spode pitcher into Eddie's tea. "Try one of those, Zo, they're gooseberry, just delish. We're in here, by the way," she said with an apologetic, hostessy air, "because the big parlor is, well . . ."

"It's where Annabelle slept . . . sleeps, Zoe," Arthur said. "Her bed's in there and all her things. Easier for her to get around on one floor, you know. . . ."

When he spoke, Zoe realized those were the first words he'd said; his voice sounded soft and hoarse all at once as if he hadn't spoken for hours.

"Of course. This is fine," Zoe said, glancing around at the baronial dimensions of Grandmère's dining room. The twelve-foot ceiling, the heavy dark wainscoting and ornate dadoes that fronted the fireplace, all faded away in the dimness of the low-wattage bulbs in the crusted chandelier. Zoe remembered the two large Piranesi renderings, framed by the moldings above the fireplace; she had sat at this very table, facing them, more than a quarter of a century ago and tried to copy the one on the left—a Roman ruin—with the India ink set she'd spent her whole allowance on. Even in the shadows she could see the yellowing cracks in their corners.

Zoe realized that she was sitting at the place that had once been hers, in the center of the eastward side of the table. For several minutes she had been unconsciously rubbing her fingers over a spot on the vinyl tablecloth, under which, if she was not mistaken (on a hot summer's day, a day of defiance and spite and some childish froth of anger), she had carved her initials with her X-Acto knife: Z.A.H. It was surely the very spot. Annabelle never did find out, either, never imagining there was evidence of any crime as yet unlooked for, but Arthur knew, of course, and for months afterward he called her "Zah" and then "Zaza," often even as Annabelle presided at the head of the table, and the children giggled with ecstatic guilt. As she looked across the table at Arthur, remembering that, she found his calm, sad eyes upon her, and then he looked away.

"And remember, we want to hear all about your new movie, Zo," Claudia was saying. "If it's okay to tell us, that is."

"Oh, sure. Of course," Zoe said, a little confused, wondering if Claudia wanted to hear about it right then and there.

"Maybe you can tell us Sunday," Eddie offered, smiling at Zoe as if to apologize somehow for Claudia's nosiness.

"That's right," Claudia said, reaching over to press Zoe's arm, "at the cookout. It's Yancey's birthday, Zoe, and we're having it out in the yard, if the weather holds."

"Indoors if it doesn't," Eddie chimed in, licking Oreo crumbs from the corners of his mouth. "Yancey will be *ten,* Zoe; he thinks it's a big deal."

Zoe smiled at him. "Of course it is."

"We'll be there," Arthur said. "Uh, I mean, if it's okay with you, Zoe?" he added quickly, looking at her with a worried expression. She saw at once how much he was looking forward to it.

"Oh, sure," she said. "Sounds like fun."

"Great," Arthur murmured, almost whispering to himself, but Zoe caught his eye. He smiled at her with a sudden, radiant pleasure and then glanced away as he had before.

"Oh, and Zoe," Claudia went on, " I almost forgot to tell you. Uncle Jim is going to be there, too, Sunday. He is just so *pleased!* He told me he remembers you well."

"I remember him, too, Claud. I'm sure he's just as charming as ever," Zoe said with a chuckle.

Claudia laughed. "Oh, goodness, he's a treat—he really is. And he's going to *love* hearing about your movie. He's so— Oh, for heaven's sake, just look at the time," she said, waving a dessert fork at the mantel clock. "I promised Lowie we'd be home by ten and it's way after nine."

She began clearing the cups and wadded napkins, but Arthur lurched up to stop her.

"I'll do it, Claud. Don't worry about it."

Arthur's rising somehow drew the others up. He stood with the heavy courtliness Zoe remembered in him, the unself-conscious and perfect courtesy.

Arthur and Claudia disappeared into the kitchen together, and Eddie came to Zoe and took her hand, his fingers soft and pressing. Zoe realized he couldn't think of anything to say.

"What time is Yancey's party, Eddie?" she asked, smiling at him.

"Oh, eleven. Well, that is, I thought I'd pick you guys up at about eleven, Sunday, for the picnic, if . . ."

"Eleven sounds fine. Shall we—I—bring anything?" Zoe wondered, unsure if that would be presumptuous.

"Oh, absolutely not, absolutely not," he said, as if to reassure her. "You and Arturo are our guests. We—"

"Okay," Zoe said, "if you're sure. So, we'll see you then, I guess."

"It'll be nice for the kids to meet you. You remember Lowie—Lowell—he was just a toddler when . . ."

"I do remember him, Eddie. I'm looking forward to seeing both your boys. I really am."

"Yes. Good."

Just then Zoe felt Claudia's soft round cheek against her own, and another quick one-armed hug.

"I'm so happy you're here," Claudia said into her ear. "See you Sunday!" And she hurried off down the front hall, Arthur and Eddie in her wake.

When Arthur returned to the dining room from seeing the Trouts to their car and locking the heavy door for the night, Zoe was standing by the sideboard, tracing with one finger the patterns of fish and fruit embossed in the majolica surface of a huge tureen that she vaguely remembered from years ago. When she surreptitiously lifted it, Zoe noticed that there was a perfect oval in the dust of the sideboard, and the curves and indentations of the design were crusted with old debris. It was the kind of *objet* the families in *The Gilded Affair*—the Thanes or the Hollands—would have, and keep on a sideboard just like this one.

"This is a wonderful old piece, Arthur," she said, turning to look at him. At the sound of her voice, Arthur quickly straightened his sagging shoulders.

"Zoe, there is more stuff in this house than you can possibly imagine," he said with a short laugh. "Annabelle won't let anyone touch a thing."

He gathered the remnants of their snack onto a tray and, popping the last Chips Ahoy into his mouth, carried everything to the kitchen. Zoe followed him with the coffeepot and the darkened silver spoons that Claudia had taken from the buffet.

The kitchen was dim, its farthest corners obscured as in the dining room, the walls smeared with ancient efforts to wash them down by someone either too lazy or too short to reach above the lintels. But otherwise the room was neat as a pin, the porcelain sink scrubbed to a dull shine, the yellow plastic dish rack clean and empty except for one glass and one soupspoon. The old Westinghouse refrigerator gleamed, as did the oven door and the ancient enameled metal table.

Zoe put the spoons in the sink and set the coffeepot on the counter where, she remembered, it had always been kept. Arthur didn't seem to know what to do with himself. He ran the water in the sink as if he were actually going to wash the dishes, but then he turned it off.

"Claudia's looking awfully well," Zoe said, leaning against the refrigerator.

"She said the same about you, just now out on the steps," he said, turning to look at her. "She's right, Zoe. You look . . . you look . . . very good."

"Thank you. I'm a little tired right about now, of course—but no, I'm fine, Arthur, feeling fine."

He nodded and looked at his hands, then took off his glasses and wiped them studiously on the end of his tie.

"Well," he said after a moment's consideration, "I imagine you'll want to get some rest pretty soon, but maybe you'd like a little drink first, a little brandy or something? We could go up to the library and sit a little . . . before you . . ."

He ventured a small smile, as if hoping she found him as considerate a host as he clearly wanted to be. Zoe wondered if he was remembering the last time they had a drink together, years and years ago in Italy, in a tiny outdoor bar in San Gimignano, a little medieval town near Siena where they'd gone one afternoon to look at the famous frescoes in the cathedral. She looked up into his eyes and knew that he remembered.

"I picked up a bottle of grappa the other day," he said shyly, still polishing his glasses. "We could have some of that."

"Oh, Arthur, my goodness. Sure, that sounds good," she said, smiling back, aware that she was waiting for him to say he remembered their time in Italy. But Arthur just cleared his throat and led the way upstairs.

As they approached the tall double doors of the library, Zoe could hear whimpering growls from inside, and she looked questioningly at Arthur.

"Ah, that's Edwina," he said in a low, chuckly voice. "I locked her up in here before you came. She can be . . . well, let's just say she likes to be the center of attention, so . . ."

He turned the heavy brass handle and pushed one paneled door into the room. Edwina did not come rushing out; she sat on the edge of the rug, looking up at Arthur with a baleful combination of pique and gratitude.

"Edwina, this is my sister Zoe," Arthur said with a dry formality, bending slightly from the waist.

"Hi, baby," said Zoe with a sudden broad smile. "Hi there." She turned to Arthur as she bent to pat Edwina, who sidled over to smell the back of Zoe's hand. "A shar-pei?"

"That's right—good for you. A pedigreed shar-pei—more papers, more ancestors, than all the rest of us put together."

Arthur stuck his hands in his pockets and looked with fond resignation at Edwina, who was licking Zoe's wrist.

"How long have you had her?" Zoe asked, scratching Edwina's ears.

"Oh, it's a long story," Arthur said as he pulled two cracked Oreos out of his pocket and set them on the carpet for Edwina. "I'll tell you . . . another time. Come."

Arthur saw Zoe comfortably settled into a shabby damask wing chair before he opened the latticed door of the breakfront. With some ceremony, he poured out two glasses of the grappa; though he stood with his back to her, Zoe could tell he was breaking the seal on a new bottle.

As she looked around the room, she noticed the obvious attempt to spruce it up—the vacuum-cleaner tracks in the large Hunting Tabriz rug, the pretty vase of eucalyptus leaves on the table. When Zoe bent down to pick up a dead leaf from the floor, Edwina came over and flopped down on top of her shoes, whimpering for attention, and Zoe rubbed her fingers into the thick wrinkles of her neck and over her little shoulders.

"Arthur," she said in a voice that came out more matter-of-fact than she meant it to, "tell me about Annabelle. What actually happened to her? Claudia didn't give me too many details on the phone. She fell down?"

"They think she probably had a fairly serious stroke," he said, turning to place a small glass on the table beside her. Zoe raised her glass a little, whispered, "*Salute,*" and took a sip. Arthur sank down onto the side of Eugene Hillyard's blue leather chaise, his forearms hanging between his knees, his own drink on the floor. He lit a cigarette and blew the smoke toward the ceiling.

"The doctors haven't said very much, but Claudia says they never do. Annabelle seems, well . . ." He ran his long fingers through his halo of hair and reached for his glass. "You'll see her tomorrow at the hospital. Most of the time she's pretty out of it, but then she sort of comes to."

And in a tight, hesitant voice Arthur told her a long euphemism-ridden story about the events surrounding Annabelle's stroke, ending with a reluctant admission that things might not be going all that well.

"They didn't actually *say* she was going to die, but . . ."

"Arthur, she's a very old woman," Zoe said, leaning toward him.

"Ninety-one last November."

"Yes. . . . It won't be forever, you know?"

"I do, I do," he said, nodding vigorously as if he really did. "But not soon, necessarily? Not now." Arthur looked up at her again as if for reassurance, a hopeful sparkle in his eyes seeming to deny the mortality of Annabelle's great flesh.

Zoe watched him while he unfolded himself and rose, going to the open breakfront to pour more grappa into his glass. For a moment he rested his weight on the mahogany ledge; he had the attitude of wiping tears away without actually touching his eyes with his fingers. Zoe got up to offer her own glass for a tiny refill, and on the shelf near Arthur's hand she saw the small bisque figurine of the angel with stiff tulle wings and chipped praying hands.

"Oh, for heaven's sake, Arthur!" she cried. "My goodness!"

She set her glass down and reached for the angel, gently scratching with her fingernail at the grime encrusted on the tiny features.

"She used to be in my room. Arthur, do you remember that? I had her on my dresser for years." She let him take it from her and watched with a smile while he licked his index finger to wipe at the angel's cheeks.

"You kept it next to that little tray of cologne samples you had," he said. "It's been here in the breakfront I think quite a while, but I can't remember how it got here. You used to say she would—"

"—watch over me," Zoe said, taking back the angel and setting it on the shelf, "while I was sleeping."

Arthur sipped at his fresh drink, tasting it as he had not tasted the first, gulped glass, and leaned against the breakfront.

"It's all here, Zo, all of it. Well, nearly all," he added with fastidious honesty. "Annabelle wants it to be like it was, so it is."

Zoe nodded, straightening up and moving slowly through the room. The tassels that hung from the keys stuck into the locks of the old glass-fronted bookcases shivered with dust as she touched them. The gracious proportions of the room were masked by the bulk of too much furniture, the heavy, rotting draperies, the dimness of the lamps.

"She always did, Arthur."

"Even when we moved her to the parlor," he went on, oblivious to her comment, "she insisted that she had to have all her stuff fixed just the way it was upstairs. I mean, she had us put the furniture at the same *angles* as when it was upstairs. It's been about five years now. She's got all those pictures of Spencer Trefoyle and those two little china dogs she always liked . . . all that stuff."

Zoe walked slowly across the huge carpet to the windows, gazing out into the darkness. She wandered back, looking idly at the rows and rows of books in their cases, pausing to scratch Edwina, who had snuggled up at the foot of the chaise where Arthur sat with his hands in his hair. Zoe raised her hand slightly as if to touch him, but decided not to and moved slowly back to the windows.

Arthur hardly knew what he felt, why he was rambling on so. Last Sunday night when Claudia told him Zoe was coming from California he had felt a surge of something almost like joy. But there was so much else swirled in with that sense of exuberant relief he couldn't sort it out at first. Once he'd gotten used to the idea that Zoe was definitely coming, he'd had all week to think and wonder, tormenting himself with little scenarios about how it would be—how difficult, how wonderful, how scary.

It had amazed Arthur that when Zoe was actually there in the front doorway, after ten whole years, she seemed very much the same to him, her eyes as black, her smile as charming, her strength as effortless as he remembered. Of course now, a couple of hours having passed, he could see the fine crackle that invades the glaze of any woman after enough time goes by. She had always had the sculpted, almost Mediterranean Hillyard looks he remembered in their grandfather, Anthony, and even in the few remaining photos of the first Eugene—and she still did. But the sharpness was less instantaneously perceived, blurred or replaced by something deeper, more contained.

Arthur sighed. "Zoe, look, it's all just like before."

He got up to fill his glass again, then sank into the damask wing chair.

Zoe, standing away from him by the bookcases, wondered what he meant. Just like before what? How could that be? How could anything be the same? And then she realized that Arthur hadn't meant to say that. She felt suddenly exhausted, ready for sleep. As she turned to go, scarcely knowing that she did so, she put her hand on her brother's shoulder.

Arthur led Zoe down the stairway and along the broad hall to the room that had once been hers. It was obvious that he had fixed it up for her; all the surfaces were swept and dusted, the crewel rug was at neat right angles to the floorboards. The pretty sheets on the turned-down single bed were patterned in shades of rose and a lovely green that matched the blanket, and the pleated ruffles on the edges of the pillow-cases were perfectly smooth, as if someone had taken time to pat them into place. A small glass vase of jonquils stood on the table by the bed.

"Oh, Arthur . . ." Zoe began, turning to look up at him.

He squeezed the tips of her offered fingers, quickly, awkwardly, and then sidestepped away from her and bowed himself out.

"See you in the morning, Zoe," he said with a strange little smile and closed the door behind him.

Zoe sank in her dusty clothes to the edge of the bed, too tired to un-pack, to take her shoes off, to drag herself across the hall to the bath-room. But after a few blank minutes she did, and at last got into bed, aware, from the creases, that the lovely sheets were brand-new, though Arthur, of course, had not said so. She lay back and reached to turn off the pistol-handled urn lamp that had once lit her sleepless adolescent nights. The very same, she thought with a small, choking laugh. She felt glad to be alone with the realization that the dread that had locked onto her last week seemed to be sliding away somehow, turning into relief, and yet they seemed similar to her because each feeling has the power to subsume all others.

"So far, so good," she whispered into the darkness of the room. "So far . . ."

And finally she slept, while her brother, lying limp with similar feel-ings on the old blue chaise, finally got up to pour himself another glass of grappa. He then sank into the damask chair where Zoe had sat be-fore and smoked another cigarette and stared for over an hour at her antique angel.

FIFTEEN

(FROM THE DIARIES OF AUGUSTA HILLYARD: 1914 TO 1916)

Sunday, September 13, 1914

The beautiful weather has passed us by for a time. In another month perhaps we may anticipate some autumn sunshine, but the damp late-summer smell is rising out of the earth and we have had rain for days. Annabelle is in a blue mood—a vivid contrast to the transports of social enthusiasm to which she was given all summer long. She sits in the back parlor listening endlessly to the creaking Victrola, reading foolish magazines, and all the while her sister Hortense placidly awaits the return of Mr. Duke. He is due back, again upon family business, late next month, and perhaps at that time he may indeed, as Anthony put it at dinner last Tuesday, "fish or cut bait" with Hortense.

Tuesday, October 6, 1914

Eugene left the house very early today. Although I seldom see him in the mornings, I happened to because I arose early myself and chanced to pass the downstairs hallway as he hurried out the door. We exchanged no greeting, just a look, but there is an exuberance in him that is so unbecoming. He is thicker than ever with Trefoyle—how vigorously they contemplate the opportunities the war provides! I went to the window in the drawing room and watched him gallop down the stairs, eager of eye and quick of step, and felt, for just a moment, the oddest pang of—shame. It is bitterly apparent that my husband is not interested in valor, pride, or country. The coming of war means nothing to him but the coming of profit.

Sunday, November 15, 1914

Well, well, well! Mr. Duke has "fished" at last and seems quite satisfied with his choice of my elder daughter. At our small family dinner here tonight, as Eliot made his "formal announcement" to us all, Hortense (true to form) simpered and giggled and fell silent and gazed at her plate, the walls, everywhere but in her lover's eyes. It is and shall remain a mystery to me why he has chosen her.

Eugene, relishing his new role as "father of the bride," has cheerfully demanded splendors which ultimately, I think, betray his self-interest, for which we are all vehicles. I have become convinced that his gifts to me (diamond earrings included), his purchase of a far too handsome new home for Anthony, his insistence on fountains of champagne for the wedding of a daughter of whom, as far as I can tell, he has been scarcely aware for twenty-seven years, are somehow all for him and not for us, not for the family. Of course, I protested, I think sensibly, when Eliot said they wanted to be married on Christmas Day, but there was such enthusiasm for this insane idea that my objections were quite overwhelmed! A flurry of preparations will begin tomorrow, and my sweet Hortense will be "well married" in just six short weeks.

The lovers (*really,* Augusta) came to me after dinner to say they wish to plan a wedding trip that will take them, of course not to Europe, but down to Georgia—to some primitive resort on the coast near Savannah, where they will make their *home.* The South! Oh, Hortense!

Friday, December 4, 1914

The recent round of prenuptial festivities has been simply exhausting, possibly because it hasn't been all that much fun. Tonight Fannie Mason gave a party for Hortense and her "young man" (as Fannie insists on calling him) in her famous domed music room, drowning us all in the grandeur of the arched walls and carved columns and pilasters, the *putti* with their miniature private parts all covered up—and those damned sixteenth-century chairs everyone knows (because Fannie tells them) she got during her European trip with Belle Gardner.

I found myself suffering through it, realizing after just an hour that the splendid party was not really for my Hortense at all. The attention of the guests drifted away from my child to the striped Venetian chairs, to the gossip of the day. . . . I left as soon as decent and hurried home across the Mall with a sour taste in my mouth that did not come from the smoked salmon canapés or the Piper Heidsieck, or the tiny choco-lates shaped like doves. I felt no gratitude—Fannie can well afford to do this every day if she chooses. This great fête was merely the killing of many social birds with the same chocolate stones, and my Hortense and her innocent happiness but the hook on which to hang Fannie's over-due reciprocations!

Saturday, January 9, 1915

I have been abed for one solid week, attended by Winnie and Flora in shifts, only now starting to recover just a bit from the effects of the se-vere chill I caught at Mr. James Michael Curley's swearing-in. Dutiful wife that I have somehow allowed myself to remain, I am too dutiful by far. I was most disinclined to go, and yet, weighing all the factors, I felt it would be suitable to put in an appearance at my husband's side at that dreadful circus of a ceremony at the Tremont Temple. But I did not promise to catch my death of cold in the doing.

Mr. Curley—giving the devil his due—has a great deal of style for a man of somewhat tender years; although he is not yet forty he has been able to distinguish himself as a person of astonishing rapacity. Perhaps Mr. Hillyard can learn new lessons in how to be thoroughly corrupted and a charmer all at once. Eugene clung to the side of the tub with his manicured fingernails when that fool Fitzgerald and his people were thrown out with all their bathwater, and no doubt he feels fortunate in-deed to have survived. Yet I suspect we have the ineffable Mr. Trefoyle to thank for that. Trefoyle, criticize him though I will, has shown him-self to be more agile than most in dancing his way through the political thicket which Boston has become. He has carved out a position among the Irish which is, indeed, dynastic. He "supervises" his many brothers, cousins, brothers-in-law, and other henchmen who champion Mr. Cur-ley's interests in South Boston, delivering votes, loyalty, and fear.

I can't think what role my husband plays in this, but they must believe that they cannot, just yet, do without a connection to the Yankees,
and my husband, by this alchemy, becomes a whore. (Not as ladylike a
word as one would guess of me, or even from my pen, but there it is.)
Eugene is leading what I am forced to call a "double life" and in the
process has become the most appalling stuffed shirt. His earlier excesses
were really much more interesting than this damned pomposity through
which I am now obliged to suffer.

The day after the extravaganza at the Tremont Temple, he was out
earlier than usual, marching down our front steps in his new coat and
his finest English boots, Potter at the ready in the new motorcar. I
learned later (interesting, is it not, that I should gather my intelligence
from my servants?) that they went directly to the City Hall on School
Street to pick up their "party favors."

Thursday, May 13, 1915

After a cold and rainy April, the May flowers promised in the verse have
blossomed after all, but when I looked out my bedroom window this
morning at the splendor of the bed of purple iris and the blooming clouds
of white lilac (a trifle early this year), sending their precious fragrance
into the air, I could not have anticipated the turn of events this fine spring
day would bring. I set off at three o'clock, new hat stylishly in place,
quite looking forward to Anne's usual Thursday at-home on Beacon
Street.

However, I have survived to report that Anne's at-home was not a
success today—certainly not for me.

I arrived feeling very ready for some stimulating conversation after
several damp weeks undistinguished by luncheons, recitals, or tea parties, and I expected these women, whom I have known all of my life,
to be at least a tiny bit interested in the disaster that befell that British
ship last week when over one thousand people lost their lives. But no.
The sinking of the *Lusitania* is not nearly so fascinating as little Nannie
Pickman's coming out! I must be more of a bred-in-the-bone prig than
I thought to care more about a burning death for hundreds than the pre-
sentation of one thin girl to what is left of "society."

I was possibly a bit outspoken on this point (particularly as Nannie's
mama was not there) as I tried to turn the conversation back to a

broader scope of topics, but they would not allow news of the war to take the edge off all that lovely gossip. Sue Snell (to whom I frankly would have given more credit) chided me for it, saying, "Really, Augusta, I should have thought you would take more of an interest in sweet Nan's happiness than you seem to."

When everyone left, I remained behind (taking my prerogative as "oldest friend"), listening to Anne blather on about Nannie's gown and prospects, wondering what would after all be the most convenient time for me to take *my* leave, so bored and out of sorts had I become. But I was spared the subtle efforts of concocting my departure, for Anne pulled up her chair and, leaning over in that confidential cozy way she has, informed me that she loathed herself for speaking so, but that it was of course her *duty* to let me know that there had been more and more talk among our ("our"!) friends about Eugene's "relationship" with the Irish. She simply launched into it!

I sat there in one of Anne's silly Directoire chairs, astonished beyond speech, my teacup halfway to my mouth, as she—with what I'm sure she imagined to be a very *intime* frankness—explained to me that people are "tolerating" (that was the very word she used!) Eugene's behavior out of respect for me, for the Lattimores, and for my mother's family—pronouncing in that connection the most remarkable words of all: that even though my mother and the Hatchers were only a "very distant collateral branch" of the Cabots (layers of cousinship separating Eugene and me from all that grandeur), it was partly on that account that we have been included as we have, particularly in the last couple of years. Evidently our appearance at Mr. Curley's inauguration did not go unnoticed by what Anne is pleased to call "our finer elements."

There were then some elongated moments of silence, though I realize now that it could not have been more than mere seconds. I got to my feet and looked down at Anne as she sat simpering up at me with what I'm sure she thought was sweet and proper righteousness, and told her very plainly that my husband's business was his own, that she was completely faithless and improper to mention it to me in any context and behind any guise whatever, that I was appalled at her insensitivity, poor judgment, and bad manners. That said, I stalked through the foyer and out onto the street, unimpeded either by servants or by entreaty from my former friend. Fortunately, the day being so warm, I did not have a wrap, the fetching of which would have marred the drama of my exit.

Tuesday, May 18, 1915

My contretemps with Anne has virtually not left my thoughts for days. If there are overtures to be made, however, they will not come from me. If Eugene Hillyard disgraces all of us forever, it will be without commentary from Anne Higgins Lowell—my childhood friend though she may be!

Monday, August 9, 1915, Nahant

Eugene drove up here last Tuesday, all importance, to say that we are to go back to Commonwealth Avenue at once. Although he and I had, right there on the front veranda, the most passionate words we have exchanged for quite some time, back we shall go, tomorrow morning. We've been packing all the week, although we seem to have made much out of little. There are quite a few pieces going back . . . my mother's gateleg table, I think the spindle chairs as well. I feel I'm wise to take it all. Eugene is not forthcoming with an explanation of these circumstances to which we must all submit, but I can't see why he could not have waited a few weeks until the end of the season. I don't understand his urgency (which for some reason he does not have the caution to disguise), but it does appear that we will not be coming back this way.

Tuesday Morning, August 10, 1915, Nahant

I was up and dressed before sunrise, gazing over the porch railing to the brightening sea. However sweet our cottage and the memories of all our summers here—and as beautiful as it can be on a morning such as this, cool and filled with light—the truth is that I have not enjoyed Nahant since I lost Zachary.

I went at dawn down to his garden, heavy with dew at such an hour, where I soiled my dress plucking at weeds and pruning the evergreen locust, which has burgeoned more gloriously than we expected. Poor Veronica was so assiduous about monitoring its progress, and now it seems we are deserting it. I also made one final trip across the lawn to my pergola trellis to admire the climbing clematis, which so thickly covers the lattices that the shade within proceeds to darkness even at midday. I think I love it more this way. Wild berries and seven sisters rose vine have joined the grape ivy and wisteria, and it really is quite overrun. Perhaps in later years we may make a pilgrimage to see if nature really does, as the poet tells us, reclaim its own.

Wednesday, November 3, 1915

It has become my habit to walk in the afternoons, all alone, wandering without much direction through the various districts of the city. It does seem, however, after my experience today, that I shall have to realign my compass just a bit. After a late lunch I set off for the library, and was turning up to Dartmouth Street when just there on the corner, what should I behold but a splendid little gaggle of ladies which included Anne Lowell, Louisa Pickman, and Julia Bigelow, chatting very animatedly on the sidewalk, obviously just come from or about to enter some sort of afternoon festivity at the Chilton Club. I have never been a member, although Mother was, along with old Mrs. Higgins, Anne's dear mama, and some of Mother's Cabot relations. How they looked forward to going there each Wednesday to visit with each other and revel in the trivialities they so enjoyed—"improving their minds," I think Aunt Sallie Cabot used to call it. Well, there I was in my sturdy walking shoes and somewhat less than fashionable green coat (which has seen much better days), confronted with the three of them, standing right before me.

Did I imagine it, or did they shrink together into a little pod of rectitude, and stand aside that I might go by, unimpeded and untouched? Everyone nodded to me, I heard a murmur of "Awgustaaah . . ." in Julia Bigelow's dreadful Rhode Island accent, but they barely met my eyes, although I seem to recall that I looked rather pointedly at them as they stood there, shoulder to shoulder, all of them smaller women than I, looking up at me so oddly, so much as if they wondered who or what I was.

I made my way toward Boylston Street and the library, quite alone, feeling my shoulders warming, prickling, as I put greater and greater distance between myself and them.

Once again I find myself snug under my old goose down on a night which has turned quite chilly. Despite the crisp snowflakes scurrying by the window, I am very cozy here at nearly midnight with these pages to warm and comfort me, for it is here that I increasingly find my solace and myself. In recent weeks I seem to have sunk—too frequently!— into a mordant contemplation of my solitude. I spend my days in unwelcome isolation and vent my feelings in this diary. I suffer my lack of worthy employment with facetiousness, but I cannot seem to rouse myself from this disgraceful torpor. . . . The snow has heightened in the last hour, frosting up the glass and rattling the windows in their sashes.

SIXTEEN

*O*n Saturday morning Zoe awoke to dusty sunshine. In natural light, the room seemed so much shabbier than it had the night before, the wallpaper stained, several of the porcelain knobs chipped or missing from the chest of drawers. She saw, too, that the small plush armchair was different if not new, though the primitive floral print on the long wall seemed to have come but recently from Woolworth's or Pier I, a decorative gesture, she thought, smiling, which Arthur had been unable to resist.

She sat for a minute on the side of the bed with her elbows on her knees and then went across to the window and pushed up the creaking sash to let cool air flow into the room. For just a moment, looking through the smeared glass to the great brick and brownstone houses far across the Mall, Zoe felt sucked in, vacuumed up into the atmosphere. It occurred to her that it might not have been so much relief she'd felt last night, in the moments before she fell asleep, as the great force of that atmosphere and of the illusion that no time at all had passed.

She pulled her bag into her lap and dug inside for the snapshot, examining Arthur's face in the clear light. She saw that the soft cheeks and fluffy silken hair of the little boy had blurred with time into the rounded jowls and thinning silver-blond halo of the man Arthur Hillyard had grown to be. And the candid expression in the eyes had changed as well;

the simplicity of Arthur's childhood gaze had fragmented into the worry and doubt she'd seen last night.

As she dressed, Zoe looked around at the brave, swept-out shabbiness of her old room and was reminded of something Roger had said about how Arthur had stuck it out, all those years, alone in this place, rising to it every morning of all the years she herself had been away. She had no way of knowing how it felt to him—whether he viewed this house and his life in it with pain, or if indeed he perceived it as suffering at all. She sensed that the momentary flashes she had felt last night of that smooth, uncomplicated childhood's ease between them only meant that there were other, different moments still to come.

Before she went downstairs, Zoe stopped at the door of Grandmère's room. She'd stood there last night, just for a minute, aware of keeping her distance, standing on the outer border of the Persian runner. But now, even as she heard Arthur fussing downstairs, getting ready to leave for the hospital, Zoe leaned toward the heavy door, her hair brushing the wood, and listened as she used to to the humming silence. She put her hand on the cold glass knob and turned it, fully expecting the door to be locked as always. But the door moved inward, with the sound of a vacuum gently unsealed, before sticking in its frame. Zoe pressed her shoulder ever so slightly against the panels, and the dry wood creaked and would have given had she pushed harder. She let go of the doorknob and almost leapt away, covering her open mouth with her hands.

When they arrived at the hospital, they were informed that Miss Hillyard had been moved to a private room. Arthur was instantly alarmed, fearing that this signaled a turn for the worse, but the young nurse on Annabelle's new floor assured him that it was only because the patient had had some difficulty with her former "roommate." Apparently, a rather heated exchange of insults had occurred, and the doctor felt it would be best to put her in the private wing. Looking around at the pale mauve walls, hung with soothing tapestries and paintings, Zoe found herself wondering about the cost of such sanitary splendor, but said nothing to Arthur, who, oblivious to such matters, was loping down the polished tiles after the nurse.

They found Annabelle sitting up in bed, an aide beside her with a bowl of apple sauce, spoon poised.

"That is diz-*gusting*—take it away—take it away!"

"Miz Hillyard, now . . ."

"It's dreadful and I won't eat it. Arthur!" she screamed, spying him hunched in the doorway. "Well! It took you long enough to— Get this away from me!"

Annabelle backhanded the apple sauce, the dish, and the aide, and the food flew and splattered on the pink-and-white-striped blanket. Arthur swooped to help the poor girl clean it up while Annabelle lay, beached, beneath the sheets, still bellowing at the nurses who hovered on each side of the tall bed, ready to hoist her up and wipe the sauce from her chins with damp towels.

Zoe stood silently in the doorway until at last the nurses and the apple sauce departed and the Hillyards were left alone. Arthur fussed around the bedside, plumping, straightening, offering juice, while Annabelle weakly batted his hands away as she reviled him for his neglect and indifference, launching into a recital of her complaints— the food, the nurses, the color of the walls, and the iniquities of her ex-roommate, who had pilfered her tissues and her candied fruit. Arthur slumped on a chair by the bed, waiting for her to take a breath.

The old woman then suddenly closed her eyes and lay flaccid and silent, a vein ticking in her neck. Zoe moved into the room and leaned over Arthur's shoulder to look at her great-aunt up close.

"Annabelle," Zoe said in a low voice. "Annabelle, it's Zoe. I came to see you." Annabelle's puffy face was blotchy with tiny whorls of broken purple capillaries; a bandage covered the wound on her temple.

" 'Belle, wake up," Arthur said, taking her plump hand in both of his. "Zoe's here. . . . 'Belle? . . . She came all the way from California to see you."

Annabelle opened her eyes, but the sharp malicious glint was gone and an opacity almost covered her pupils. She looked toward Arthur and gave him a grotesque approximation of her once arch, coquettish smile.

"Come tonight," she said in a bubbly whisper.

"Annabelle! Oh, 'Belle, it's Arthur!"

"Come in the back parlor door . . . no one will ever . . ." Her eyes closed again and great moist snores came from her open mouth.

After a moment, Arthur stood up and pulled Zoe from the room. Out in the hall he leaned against the mauve wall, his face tilted up to the blinding ceiling lights, while Zoe stood beside him, the sleeve of his old tweed jacket held in her fingers.

"This is what you were talking about last night, isn't it? She fades in and out . . . forgets . . ."

"It's been happening a lot this week. She thinks I'm Spencer Trefoyle, for God's sake, Zo. Begs to run away with me, to sneak off somewhere when Grandmère's out. And then, when she sort of wakes up, she's . . ."

Just then a tall, middle-aged man came striding toward them down the length of the polished hallway, hand outstretched, his white lab coat flying behind him.

"Arthur! Glad you're here, saves me a phone call. Ah! And this young lady must be your sister from California!"

"Zoe Hillyard," she said, shaking his proffered hand.

"Jack Mainwaring. I'm your aunt's doc, Miss Hillyard—Arthur must have mentioned. Let's go talk in the lounge, guys."

He swept them both along, chatting to Zoe about the unreliability of the airlines and the restaurants of Beverly Hills while Arthur allowed himself to be pulled down the corridor in that hearty half-embrace to a wide, sunny area filled with teakwood furniture. As they sat down, Arthur, clearly bested by the events of the last half hour, searched in his pockets for a wrinkled cigarette, which the doctor lit for him with his own lighter, regarding him for a moment with thoughtful eyes.

"Okay," he said, poking Arthur's knee with a blunt finger. "Straight skinny on our Miss Annabelle. Arthur, hang in there, pal, okay?"

Arthur inhaled deeply and nodded while the doctor's shrewd eyes slid to Zoe, who looked back at him with a cool, candid expression.

"Arthur, we're developing a little situation here, and I think we need to talk about it. We need to look at our options."

"What do you mean?" Even at that moment Arthur seemed to have the sense of expecting nothing to change that Zoe remembered in him. As a child he had always been so rigidly convinced that things would forever stay exactly as they were, no matter how furiously, or how often, events changed and swirled around him.

"Well, she can't stay here too much longer, you know? She's stabilized now, has been for a few days, and . . . frankly, Administration's all over me about how long she's been in *already*. Plus the fact they've figured out that she has no insurance, so—"

"What do you mean, she has no insurance?" Zoe realized she hadn't really listened when Claudia mentioned this on the phone a week ago. "What about Medicare?"

"Ah, well. Not in this case. I'm told that she's ineligible because she never worked and never paid into the Social Security System and was never married to someone who did, so . . ." Genuinely distressed, worried that he had said too much too soon, Mainwaring stopped talking for a moment and took one of Arthur's crumpled cigarettes, lit it, and inhaled with a shiver. Zoe and Arthur just looked at him.

"Look, guys, clinically speaking, I think Annabelle can hold her own for a while, but it's hard to say how long. Could be a few months, maybe just a few days. . . . Listen to me, please, Arthur. The brain damage is fairly substantial, but, you see, she could stroke out tonight, or it might level off where it is, or she could have a whole series of TIAs, and also we're watching her for kidney damage, from lying on the floor so long. . . . But anyway, right now, believe it or not, that's not the issue. Administration wants her out, and to tell you the truth, Arthur, so do I. I think we need to get her settled until . . ." He knocked the ashes off his cigarette and rearranged his behind in the fancy chair.

"Can she go home?" Zoe asked. "I mean, what exactly are you saying?"

Mainwaring inhaled hugely and stubbed out the cigarette in the overflowing pedestal ashtray. He shook his head and blew his nose on a large monogrammed handkerchief.

"Damn smokes. Can't seem to give 'em up. . . . No, she can't go home. . . . Arthur, hear me out. Now, I've got those girls down in Social Service looking for a nursing-home bed right now. They should have some leads by Monday. Look, even if you had somebody round-the-clock, Arthur, you couldn't handle her at home."

"You said she was stable!" Arthur said in a hoarse voice, leaning toward the doctor.

"Arthur, believe it or not, a nursing home is ultimately a lot cheaper than the kind of setup you'd have to have over there on Comm Ave. She needs medical equipment, constant attention . . . no, *listen* to me, Arthur. She can't go home, son, she can't."

Arthur put his face in his hands; his body was bent way down over his legs. Zoe scooted up to the edge of the seat cushion and put her arm around him. The doctor blew his nose again and patted Arthur's other shoulder.

"Try to get hold of yourself, Arthur. I don't mean all this to sound so harsh, but we have to face the facts here. I'm trying to show you the sensible, realistic thing."

"Go ahead," said Zoe, slipping her hand into the crook of Arthur's elbow.

"All right." Mainwaring began to tick off his points on his large, clean fingers.

"First of all, Annabelle can't do anything for herself anymore. I know she could before last Friday, but not anymore. Okay. Two: this place costs very big bucks, especially this pavilion, and you have no Medicare and no other insurance, correct me if I'm wrong." He paused as if he expected to be corrected, but Arthur just looked up at him and shook his head.

"All right. Three: we'll help you find a good clean nursing home, hopefully not too far out of town; I happen to know there's nothing in Boston. We've got my wife's mom in a place out in Wellesley, as a matter of fact, and—"

"And 'four'?" Zoe cut in softly, drawing an annoyed, uncomprehending look from Mainwaring, who was not used to being interrupted. "She may or may not live that long, right?"

"That's right," he said, pausing a moment to swallow this effrontery. "Arthur, most of the time she doesn't even know where she is. You've seen that for yourself. You want to keep her comfortable, and you want to keep yourself out of the poorhouse doing it. Sounds lousy, I know, but we're at the point where we have to think in those terms."

Arthur's gaze had not wavered for several minutes, but his eyes had lost their focus as if to shield his mind from what was said. Mainwaring suddenly stood up, his slacks falling in their perfect creases to his tasseled loafers. Arthur struggled to his feet.

"Look," the doctor said, "I just came from Dr. Weintraub over in Radiology. We're going to get another CAT scan this afternoon, see if anything's changed. Why don't you guys go get a bite to eat . . . talk all this over." He took Zoe's left hand in a quick squeeze, and was gone.

Arthur's knees bent as of their own accord and he sank back onto the davenport. Zoe stood over him, her hands deep in the pockets of her jacket, waiting for a response that did not come. Finally, she sat beside him and linked her arm through his.

"Let's take his advice about getting some lunch, okay?" she said softly. "My treat—anything you want in the whole cafeteria."

"I'm not hungry, Zoe."

"Mainwaring's right, you know. He is. A little abrupt, maybe, a little self-satisfied, but he's not a bad guy, I think, not unfeeling. And he's probably right."

"About what? What?" Arthur pulled his arm slightly away as he turned to face her. His blue eyes were bright and dry; a flush rose through his pale cheeks, still raw from his morning shave.

"About Annabelle . . . about keeping her comfortable." Zoe knew she had to be very careful. She drew Arthur's arm to her with a surge of affection that neither acknowledged.

"Arthur, I think you have to focus on that right now, don't you? Look, let's get something to eat, and then we can go back up to see her after her X ray, okay?" She pulled him up by their linked arms. "Come. I'm buying."

Arthur found a table at the far end of the large cafeteria on the street level while Zoe took a handful of quarters to a bank of vending machines where there was no line. She got sandwiches and chips and a couple of cans of soda and brought them back to the table. They ate slowly and in silence.

The room gradually emptied and people left the tables around them, breadcrumbs and little puddles of spilled milk shakes in their wake. When he finished his sandwich, Arthur lit up one of his bent cigarettes and offered one to Zoe.

"I gave them up. Thanks."

"Really?" Arthur looked slightly jealous, but smoked on. "You used to smoke, I remember."

Zoe nodded and sipped her warm Sprite.

"I actually didn't care too much for it," Arthur said, "until, well until, uh, just recently. Annabelle used to smoke like a chimney, for years, but she set fire to her bed a while back, so . . ." Arthur smiled as if in fond memory of a more vigorous, smoking Annabelle and leaned back in the plastic chair.

Zoe realized they had come to another of those stalled-out moments, just as they had last night in the library. The little conversational bubble burst and left a silence that neither of them seemed alert enough to fill. But this time it was Arthur who ventured into the breach, pausing only a moment before changing the subject, awkwardly asking her if she was doing all right in California.

Zoe looked up and saw that he heard the bald, conversation-making sound of it and was embarrassed that he'd said it, but she smiled and nodded.

"I am, Arthur. I'm doing fine. Frankly, it's been sort of a long haul, but—"

"But you're doing a brand-new movie. Do I have to wait until the birthday party tomorrow to hear about it?"

Zoe saw the little twinkle in his eye and remembered the conversation with Claudia and Eddie. She smiled; in spite of herself she was pleased that he asked.

"Well, it's called *The Gilded Affair*. The main plot's about an art-theft scandal in New York in the late 1890s."

"Oh, no kidding! Victorian crime! That's great!" Arthur was impressed; he sat up straighter and put out his cigarette.

"I remember you always liked to read those big, fat Victorian novels," Zoe said with a chuckle.

"Oh, I sure did. I came this close to being an English major, remember? You know, I actually reread *The Portrait of a Lady* a few years ago . . . or started to. Pretty heavy going. But gee, Zo, that sounds wonderful." Arthur had his elbows on the table, a fresh cigarette clamped in his teeth.

Zoe laughed, delighted at his enthusiasm. "Of course, there's lots of work involved—period costumes, finding the right furniture, locations . . . even the horse-drawn carriages have to be authentic. I think it's going to be a terrific picture, I really do. It took quite a long . . ."

But suddenly she could not go on. She realized she did not want to be so happy when he wasn't, did not want to imply that she had better things to do than be here with him, watching his life go to pieces. She stood up and gathered their cellophane wrappers and empty Sprite cans and put everything in the big plastic barrel by the door. When she came back she looked at her watch.

"All set? Annabelle should be back from her X ray. We can go see her for a bit and then get down to Social Service."

"We're not going to Social Service."

"Arthur . . ." Zoe looked up, frowning.

"I don't care what Mainwaring says. She's coming home; that's where she belongs. I'm going to fix her room up really special, get railings, nurses, all that stuff . . . maybe a bigger TV." Arthur's eyes darted from his cigarette smoke to the windows and back again as he babbled on and on.

Zoe plopped back into her chair. "Arthur, the doctor told us that—"

"No . . . no. I've been thinking about it ever since he brought it up. No nursing home. They can't make us."

"But what if . . . ?"

Arthur shook his head violently from side to side, his lips pressed tight together. Zoe remembered he used to do that as a boy when he had one of his little fits of stubborn self-assertion.

"No, no. We'll manage, we'll work it out, we'll do it."

"Arthur, for heaven's sake. Think a minute."

"I'm serious, Zo."

"Arthur, all *right*. We won't talk about it now."

Arthur just nodded and put his cigarette out, but Zoe saw the muscles moving in his cheeks. She waited for him to look at her, but he didn't, though he followed her, strangely docile, as they got on the elevator and went back to Annabelle.

Arthur held her limp, puffy hand for a moment and then excused himself and disappeared—whether to the men's room or to the lounge to smoke alone Zoe had no idea.

She closed the door behind him and sat quietly in the chair at the foot of the bed, staring at Annabelle's slack face, oddly skull-like in the weak illumination from the light over the bed.

Zoe had spent the years of her childhood dreading to be touched, spoken to, even looked at by Annabelle. On the plane yesterday afternoon, she had hoped that perhaps, after all these years, she might be able to step back a pace or two and see Annabelle's life for the shallow waste she knew it had been—and to dredge up some sympathy from that understanding. Now she stared at her aunt's once-beautiful face and wondered if she could.

Zoe later thought she must have dozed off, lost track of time somehow. She vaguely recalled Arthur coming into the room a few times with guilty stealth; he would hold Annabelle's hand or hover over her,

her hoarse breath ruffling his hair. Then, after just a few minutes, he would go out again—to smoke, to pace, whatever. And Zoe sat there.

The north-facing room dimmed with the falling of the early April light. Zoe went to the window and stood rubbing the muscles of her stiff back as she looked down onto the Saturday-evening traffic. A rusty glow lingered in the west over the Brookline hills. She wanted to retrieve Arthur from wherever he had hidden himself and go back to the house, have a drink, maybe go out for dinner—to be anywhere but here. She turned back to the bed and saw Annabelle looking directly at her.

"So you came to see me die, did you?"

"Annabelle . . ."

"Don't you give me any of your snippy talk. I don't need to hear it." Annabelle laughed suddenly with the cackling sound that witches make in children's stories. Zoe went back to the foot of the bed and looked at her with what she hoped was dispassion, though her head was pounding.

"Figured you'd come see if there was anything left . . . come wanting money, I suppose . . . after sneaking off the way you did." Annabelle laughed again and began to cough, her huge breasts heaving under the sheet. She tried to reach for her cup of water but couldn't. Zoe didn't move.

"Mama will be surprised to see me. . . . She died believing this was all there was, and hell enough for anybody. I never thought that poppycock about life after death made any sense either, but now I'm going I find I'm not so sure. . . ."

Annabelle coughed again, and then her eyes glazed and closed. Zoe waited, hoping Arthur would come back to the room, but after several minutes, when Zoe had ceased to expect it, Annabelle roused herself from wherever she had been, speaking in the same soft, whistly voice, her eyes still closed against whatever her mind could see.

". . . she used to come in to kiss us good night, before a party or the theater, and light from the hallway would catch in those diamond earrings Papa gave her. . . ."

Standing there, gripping the footrail of the bed, Zoe realized that she had no idea at all what Annabelle was talking about, and she felt suddenly awash in anger and regret that she knew nothing of the lives that had been lived in the house on Commonwealth Avenue in the decades that preceded her own memory of it. As the cracked, elegant old voice went on and on, Zoe was less and less able to place the names, the events, Annabelle spoke about.

"She hated Spencer . . . despised him . . . said he would never bring me anything but sorrow and anger, but I knew he loved me, yes he did . . . he did . . ."

When she stopped talking, Annabelle's eyelids fluttered but did not open; tiny metallic crescents showed beneath her white lashes. With an effort, Zoe pushed herself away from the footrail and leaned over the bed.

"Can I get you anything, Annabelle?" she whispered. "You want some water?"

". . . she died knowing I did not forgive her. And I still don't. . . . I expect to tell her that to her face pretty soon now."

Zoe swallowed her saliva and glanced over to the door, wishing Arthur would come in, wishing herself outside under the red sky.

"You're the spit and image of my brother Anthony . . . always were, but now you're older it shows more."

"Annabelle, would you . . . ?"

"Every line of his face, those eyes of his . . . but you're *like her,* did you know that? You always were . . . just like *her.* . . . I've been waiting twenty years to tell you that. That's why you and I never saw eye to eye on a blessed thing—"

Annabelle's voice broke into choking gasps. Foamy drops bubbled in the corners of her mouth. Zoe instinctively ran to her and thrust an arm under her neck behind the pillow. Using all her strength, she managed to prop her up enough to make it easier for her to breathe. She reached for the water glass and brought the end of the little bent straw to Annabelle's dry lips.

The old woman took a sip and relaxed her weight against Zoe's arm. The platinum eyes flicked open just to the rim of the pupil; her sour breath gusted into Zoe's face. The whole bed groaned with every slow, heavy breath she took.

"Annabelle, I'll get the doctor."

". . . just like her, so stubborn, so strong . . ."

"Aunt, why don't I . . ."

The eyes kindled up for a second. ". . . too bad she didn't live to see it. . . ."

SEVENTEEN

(From the Diaries of Augusta Hillyard: 1917 to 1918)

Monday, April 2, 1917

I have forced myself to watch this swift, greased slide to war, this eagerness of the old men to send the young men into battle. I *gasped* when I read in the *Transcript* today that there is virtually no opposition to the plan of sending American children to die in the forests of France. Even the self-styled isolationists and pacifists are now talking war and preparing accordingly. At this rate we shall make of our whole nation a Whited Sepulcher.

I try and fail to turn my face away from my husband's efforts to find a hook on which to hang a profit. That there is a component to war other than the chance for profit has not crossed his mind, and he is frantic with possibility. I am repelled by his behavior—his obvious *glee* at the opportunities ahead. He seems consumed with his frank anticipation that he and Trefoyle will "make a killing" on the war. I cringe at the hackneyed phrase "blood money," but what else can I call it?

But yet, to be honest, I think I am more disgusted with myself, that I could ever have been such a foolish little girl that I took this man to my heart and to my bed and never knew him. But now, of course, I know him all too well and am forced at last to see that Eugene Hillyard is the man he is and not otherwise. Have I been waiting all these years for him to turn into a saint or a poet? Hardly that, but I shall have to find a way to come to terms with the inescapable fact that not only did I choose him, years ago, I begged my father—begged!—to be allowed to marry him when Papa would have had it otherwise. And now I have lived to find myself grown weary of feeling shame on his account.

Sunday, July 22, 1917
Eugene now makes no pretense whatsoever of having any business that does not include Trefoyle and his henchmen. His own construction works have been at a standstill these many months. They are almost daily with "the mayor," and Eugene holds forth at dinner with detailed accounts of their meetings. Just tonight, Eugene regaled us with stories of the superb city contracts which Trefoyle-Hillyard have garnered through, I am sure, more exercise of poetry than truth. I am amazed, actually, that he talks about it so baldly; he never used to mention his business in the house. But they do, apparently, have contracts for paving sidewalks in Charlestown and Roxbury; they are involved in the tunnel extension to East Boston; they are widening roads and working on the subway, which is planned now for precincts far from Park Street.

As monument to these spoils, the decoration of our downstairs rooms is nearly complete: we now have a new Sarouk in the drawing room, several exquisite marquetry tables, one of which is just lovely in the small parlor, a number of lamps which Mr. Paine's nice grandnephew assured me were absolutely *comme il faut,* including a very handsome pistol-handled urn lamp that I do actually like quite a lot, and an Aaron Willard bracket clock which sits in splendor on the mantel shelf in the dining room, guarded by two venerable (and quite hideous) Staffordshire dogs over which Annabelle went into a most unnecessary transport. It's all quite ironic, of course, that I should finally be redecorating my home under circumstances which have completely destroyed my enthusiasm for the project. These fine trimmings have come at the expense of my husband's reputation; the fact that that is not his point of view does not in the least alter mine.

Monday, July 30, 1917
Evidently there is a plan to develop the old shipyards at Squantum for the war effort. I have no idea what contribution Eugene may be called

1 7 4

upon to make. Have they not already fleeced the "aristocrats" of all spare change? Is it his skill and experience at construction? I certainly find it hard to believe that my husband may have lessons in rapaciousness to teach them. Thus, it is divinely mysterious to me why Curley and Trefoyle, they who control the shipyard labor, continue to need Eugene and Alex. This mystery notwithstanding, however, the early profits seem quite healthy for mere hangers-on. They are, indeed, "sitting pretty"—Anthony's words, not mine.

Sunday, August 19, 1917

The Squantum shipyards become more and more a steel-and-brick reality each day. The contract for the sheds, offices, warehouses, storehouses, and docks went, of course (through what I am certain was the most Jesuitical of bidding procedures), to Trefoyle-Hillyard. The flurry of activity has paralyzed our household, as it takes Potter completely away from us here at home on a daily basis. Eugene is out betimes and does not return until very late, when he does come home. So often I hear him after midnight, making no effort to be quiet, and then he's out again with but a few hours' sleep. He is a vortex around which swirls a booming time.

Thursday, September 20, 1917

I overheard Eugene and Alex, thinking themselves well isolated in the library late last night, speaking rather disparagingly of Mr. Curley. (It must so *gall* Eugene to be beholden to a much younger man!) Now that the shipyard work is nearly complete, the various buildings all but painted, it interests me to hear them criticize the man who made it possible. Although Squantum is not Boston, one realizes that where Irish labor is concerned, Mr. Curley is never far away. He is undeniably trashy and common, but he is not at all stupid. Far from it. In the past two years he has created hospitals, clinics, parks—all for the safety and comfort of his vast constituency. And he has done this, moreover, with money extracted (by fair means and foul) from the old families.

Not all appreciate this joke, but I am constrained to suppress my smile. He has raised their taxes, he has badgered them into giving loans from their banks, and he has turned it all back on them. The rich old families of Boston—like it or not—have financed the well-being of the underclasses. I myself enjoy that rather hugely, but there are few in our immediate neck of the woods who share my amusement.

It appears that Eugene is no longer welcome at the Tavern Club. When he first joined, years ago, it was virtually the only one that would have him, except for the Pembroke Club, which is composed of parvenus like himself, but he seems now reduced to "guest" at every turn. He contents himself with lunching at the Algonquin with Alex or at the Somerset with Bigelow (who has not deserted him just yet). Although Eugene's mood is somewhat glum of late, he seems not quite to have made the connection between his own social isolation and the fact that people are "talking about the Hillyards" in ways I am grateful to be spared. All the same, I suppose that with Eugene one never can be sure; whatever serves for "feelings" in him is far below the surface—beyond the skills of archaeologists and wives alike to unearth.

However, he may be feeling some lack of the high times and camaraderie he has enjoyed so in the past, for he came to me this morning (not without his usual bluster) to propose a small "but excellent" dinner party with family and some "friends." I was astonished at the enthusiasm of my response, answering with an agreeableness that shocked us both. It seems the flow of social juices is not dammed up in me quite yet.

. . . of course, corralling the Anthony Hillyards for this grand dinner party will be simple. Miss Annabelle may or may not find it convenient to attend (she seems in perpetual anticipation of a "better offer"), although I think we may find some suitable young man for her, and Alex will come, of course. But that is family. Wherever shall we find "friends"? I thought to myself as I paged hopefully through my address book the other afternoon, seeking inspiration. Yet I did finally ensnare the Chauncey Phillipses and an obscure Appleton to share our meal, and it was with some rue that I saw a sparkle come to Veronica's eyes when I informed her this morning that we are to begin preparations for something rather small but very fine. I am considering a lovely *ris de veau,* or possibly that wonderful saddle of venison with fresh chestnuts (and yes, Potter confirms that there is *one* bottle of Calvados left), done as only Veronica can do it. Perhaps, however, on second thought, the venison might quite overwhelm the fragile sensibilities of poor Frances and that pasty little Iris Phillips. Yes, I think the sweetbreads with wild mushroom sauce. That should do nicely!

Saturday, October 20, 1917

Well, at least it wasn't a complete failure. The food was wonderful, of course, and the wine plentiful, but unfortunately merely decent (Eugene goes on the cheap in the most extraordinary ways). Horace Appleton became quite tipsy, which was the highlight of the evening, and took a bit of a fancy to Annabelle, who at the last moment agreed to favor us with her presence. I am embarrassed to say that she was unable to tolerate the effect of so many toasts to her charms.

The party disintegrated rather smartly after that. Alex and Eugene held forth at great rate on the war effort and the need for expert construction, and as their cheeks flushed and Chauncey giggled into his napkin, and the level of wine dropped in the decanter, I had all I could do to observe my proper duties as hostess and to remain at my post at the foot of the table listening to drivel until nearly eleven o'clock.

Eugene later chided me for what he felt was less than vivacious behavior on my part, and I responded very pertly that I hadn't known he'd cared about anything but money, money, and more money. He answered me that indeed money is all that matters and that I seemed to have had a very handsome frock upon my shoulders in which to entertain my guests!

I lack sufficient sangfroid to keep my mouth shut when he provokes me in this way and replied in turn that the respect of respectable people is all that matters and as the Hillyards seem to have lost that utterly he had better get used to the fact that all the money in the world will not buy it back. He glared in that way that no longer succeeds with me, turned on his heel, and left me standing in the hall. A faint whiff of his Havana tainted the air behind him. I came up here, my cheeks afire with more than the indifferent white Bordeaux. I pulled my diamonds from my ears and hurled them at the window. It is proof of the craftsmanship of Tiffany's that they did not come apart. Of course, the stones gouged the window rather badly, and henceforth, whenever I look out the window in the night with the lamps of the room all lit behind me, I shall see that scar across my own image in the glass.

Saturday, April 20, 1918

We have daily reports of activities at the front. The British have been forced to withdraw from Ypres to Armentieres, while the French, equally ineffective against the Germans, are at Rheims and Voyonne. I have a map, very dog-eared and limp, by my bedside table on which I have taken to following the march of the Demon through Europe. Every night I sit here with my marker in my hand, tracing the "progress" of the war. I can't understand why I do this, but I feel I must. If there were something else that I could do, something that had some sort of consequence, I would be filled with joy to do it . . . but there seems to be nothing at all.

Sunday, June 2, 1918

Tonight it was just Hillyard and Wife at dinner. Annabelle (it scarcely needs be mentioned) was not at home; she was invited to a "house party" in Manchester-by-the-Sea, where she has journeyed for the weekend and probably the best part of next week. I may be remiss in not demanding to know the exact identity, lineage, and prospects of every individual in her group, but I hope at my time of life I have learned to know futility when I see it. As my daughter's age increases by the day and her own prospects diminish, I feel that I can hardly deny her the pleasures she so theatrically insists upon.

As I sat silently at my end of the table, lost in my thoughts, dear Flora bounced in and out of the kitchen with a variety of dishes, but nothing seemed to tempt Eugene. This is surprising, as he has always relished his food, and yet he has grown somewhat less stout of late, which his height disguises frankly not a bit. Is evidence of declining fortunes to be inferred from his declining appetite? I myself have been tucking into my food more than formerly and have perhaps grown a trifle fleshy as a result, and yet I do not particularly consider *my* fortunes all that ascendant!

The mystery of Eugene deepens as our years together progress. This

1 7 8

evening, as I stared at him through the lovely peony buds and yellow roses in the center of the table, I found myself newly fascinated by the once handsome, now lined and distracted face of this stranger with whom I have spent nearly forty years. It seems impossible that he was sixty-three years of age last month. And yet I think he has aged without my realizing it! I amaze myself, for it is apparent that I still view him as he was when *both* of us were young. He no longer moves me in that way, but he still has the power to make me remember when he could.

Monday, July 1, 1918

This horrible war has touched us deeply. Eugene arrived home this afternoon to say that he has learned that dear John Cox Lowell died at Belleau Wood, near Rheims, just before our victory there—less than a week before! Of course, I have been reading in the *Times* of this great battle that lasted nearly a fortnight; the United States Marines captured Bouresche and Belleau Wood, but in the process of gaining this Pyrrhic victory, they lost more than half their men—and today I weep to learn that my friend Anne's only son was among them.

Oh! I am so sorry for her! Oh, poor, lovely boy! John Cox was but a year older than my Zachary—he was his mentor and his guide in the early years at Harvard. I remember how kind he was to Zach, how thoughtful, how amusing and generous! Zachary spoke of him so often and with that wonderful peal of laughter at John's good humor. And he is now gassed and stabbed and shot and blown apart in Belleau Wood . . . near Rheims Cathedral.

It seems grotesque to me—like the very gargoyles on the parapets—that one of the most vicious battles of this bitter war should have been fought near a great basilica made to celebrate Man's love for God. Is God "at home" in Rheims Cathedral? Was He sitting in a small parlor behind the apse, snug in His carpet slippers, reading the war news in *Figaro* with a cup of tea beside Him? Is that where He was when Zachary drowned? When the Confederates shot Papa's leg off? Was He taking His ease when sweet John Cox died at Belleau Wood with a bayonet in his stomach? It is impossible not to wonder where the Lord God keeps Himself while boys are being blown to pieces. . . .

I have decided I will go to Anne. If she rejects my offer of comfort, I shall suffer for it, but go I must. I knew John Cox Lowell all of his life.

I held him in my arms when he was still warm from Anne's womb. His mother has been the confidante of my youth and of my later years as well, and all our arguments, all our past travails, wither before this tragedy.

We have turned all of the upstairs rooms into a virtual hospital. Everyone but Potter, Eugene, and me is down with this dreadful influenza, which has hit Boston like an earthquake. I have not left the house, except to go out to the Mall for a moment's breath of air, for nine days. A good part of my time is spent quarreling with Veronica, forcing her to stay in bed and rest. The worst of it seems to be over for her; her fever has diminished, although she continues to have quite a lot of trouble with her breathing. Win and Flora, thankfully, seem also to be past the crisis, although they still suffer terrible chills and tremble and cry out in the night. They are weak as kittens.

Annabelle, whose iron constitution is somewhat the worse for wear, has nevertheless had a rather milder case, for which we are all grateful, although the experience has not improved her disposition one little bit. Yet her growing prickliness is taken by one and all to be a sign of returning health.

I have taken in Anne's girl, Maureen, lest she infect the babies. Celia and her brood have moved in with Anne, which I hardly think to be the wisest course, but Anne, bless her bones, is typically hysterical and wanted her daughter near. Since no one else in their household seems to have been affected, however, Maureen is here with us, sharing Zachary's old room with Winnie and Flora. The heat has been so oppressive (adding to our woes) that I could not allow them to remain in their stifling rooms at the top of the house. . . . Yet our household is among the more fortunate, even as we are so beset, for none of us has lost his life. Whomever shall we thank? I would as soon praise Druid gods as any other.

We have had a letter from Sarah! She writes from Paris, where she has been living since last spring. She has lost some friends, and sons of friends, in the war, but she herself is safe and well. Shortly before the

Armistice, she called on Mathilde at the rue d'Artois with a letter of introduction from brother Alex, and was very well received. They passed a pleasant afternoon speaking of family and, as Sarah writes, most lovingly of me.

I think the time has come for me to shed my old anger, my reserve, and yes, my pride. Our senseless estrangement has gone on for so many years that I literally do not remember what it was about. When Sarah went away I was too young, too foolish, too deluded by the snippets and spoonfuls that I knew of life to understand, and I have let a quarter century go by without retreat from my stupidity. Can I make this up to Sarah? She to me? I only know I would reclaim my sister as a token of those lost and therewith, I suspect, a part of myself as well.

Thursday, December 5, 1918

Eugene informs me that the individual to whom he sold the Nahant property three years ago has at last decided to move in. That this mysterious personage has chosen to do so in dead of winter has perforce spurred me into action, and I have just returned from a very arduous day trip with Potter—my first visit to the cottage in well over a year.

Zachary's garden, untended all last summer, is so terribly overgrown; as I walked among the shadows of our plantings, remembering the day we planned his garden, the dry vines and brittle cones and needles rustled in the cold December wind and snapped beneath my shoes. The rosemary and lily of the valley are, of course, fled with the season, their little beds but faintly outlined in the dry grass, but the quincunx of five cypress trees has, in just eight short years, created a green bower, dense and restful even under this morning's pewter sky. Just before we left, Potter went off to do one final chore and left me quite alone. I sat on a forgotten chair and smoked a cigarette, and thought of my sweet boy and felt him warmly present, though safe—*safe*—within his grave. I cannot help but think that he was better off to die in water in Boston than in fire in France.

Christmas Night, 1918

Tonight my joy is well-nigh perfect. Under this very roof I have my Hortense and dear Eliot. They arrived last night on the train from

Washington, where they had spent some weeks with Eliot's sister, and are at last here with us for their first visit since their wedding. They are now asleep together in the bed Hortense slept in, child and maiden, for twenty-seven years. I am both relieved and delighted to be able to say that Hortense and Eliot, on this their fourth wedding anniversary, appear to have remained quite enchanted with each other.

As I sat beaming down at everyone from the end of our laden Christmas table, all of us on to the third generation raising our glasses for the traditional toast with Potter, Veronica, Winnie, and Flora, I thought then as I think now: I will clutch this to my bosom. I will keep it as a pressed rose that I may take out from time to time to inhale the perfume of this day.

We took our coffee in the big parlor after dinner, joined by the Wheelwrights as well as Horace Appleton (who makes his foolish sheep's eyes at Annabelle every chance he gets), and my heart warmed with pleasure, even to such a horse's ass as Horace. Mr. Stuart Comfrey, Alex's chum from his club, dropped in, and Potter, adding the perfect coda to the festivities, surprised us with what I suspect is the last of Papa's Cockburn port and a very acceptable Armagnac that has survived my depredations.

And now I lie abed, my new white cashmere shawl snugly about me as I write, listening to the silences of my filled house, quietly savoring, as best I can, this sense of many things restored. However short-lived this feeling of peace and well-being may reveal itself to be, I hope I've earned the gift of cherishing my memories.

EIGHTEEN

A warm and golden sun, just past meridian, shone down on the Trouts' back lawn. The yard was rather small, Zoe thought, oddly disproportionate to the rambling old house before it, and still more brown than green, but it was cozily bordered with narrow beds of daffodils, just coming out, which also surrounded the budding purple lilacs in the far corners of the space.

Zoe sat in a yellow lawn chair sipping a mimosa while Claudia (who had forbidden her to help) ran in and out of the house carrying a variety of dishes and bowls, all covered with aluminum foil, which shone back at the sun. Claudia paused in her work only to shoo Yancey, and his picking fingers, away from the food.

When Zoe and Arthur, chauffeured by a beaming Eddie, had arrived just an hour before, Zoe had been introduced with a sweet ceremoniousness to Master Lindsay Forbes Trout—the "Birthday Person" himself, who stood up proudly, his thin little chest puffed out under a Red Sox T-shirt. Eddie had already explained to Zoe that he would answer only to "Yancey," a childhood pronunciation of his proper name. Yancey had a sly, confidential way of squinting when he talked; he caught his lower lip in his teeth as if to say he'd done something frightfully naughty, but on the strength of his remarkable cuteness all crimes were to be at once forgiven.

"And this is Lowell—Lowie," said Claudia, her arm around the shoulders of her elder son in a protective curl. Zoe smiled with a surge of instant affection that she would never have believed of herself and looked into Lowie's bright blue eyes.

"Hi, Zoe," he said shyly in a clear voice.

"Hi, Lowie," she replied, and then they laughed at precisely the same moment when they heard the sound.

Eddie had just begun fussing with another pitcher of the mimosas when Uncle Jim Forbes, dapper and tanned from his winter in Florida, made his entrance through the kitchen door.

"Ah, Zoe Hillyard, my goodness, this is indeed a pleasure, my dear. It's been many years . . . many years." He bent low over Zoe's hand, raising it to his lips with a broad courtliness.

Zoe remembered him well and said so, smiling at his obvious enjoyment of his status as paterfamilias. He was ensconced in a padded lounge chair, and Eddie, without being asked, brought him a tall vodka stinger on the rocks. Jim raised his glass to Zoe with a wide smile and swallowed half his drink.

"So," he said, turning to Arthur, his tone suddenly gentle, serious, "how's the old girl doing?"

Arthur said nothing, but he gave Jim a wan, brief smile and silently went to work on his mimosa.

"Pity about Annabelle," Jim said to no one in particular. "Shame she's coming down to the wire—person lives that long you tend to think they'll last forever. Well, no one does. She was a gorgeous woman, though—gorgeous! No doubt about it. Folks thought she was fairly hard to get along with, but I'll say this for her, Annabelle Hillyard was the single most disputatious human being I believe I ever met, and I want to tell you that's a distinction."

In spite of himself, Arthur chuckled and smiled affectionately at Jim. "You sure brought the nice Florida weather back with you, Jim," he said, not really trying to change the subject, reaching over to pat the old man on the knee.

"It would so appear," Jim said in a droll fashion, lying back in the lounger and looking at the blue sky. "Unseasonable as all get out—probably rain tomorrow—or snow." With that, he drained his glass, and Eddie came over from the grill to take it from him.

Zoe sat quietly, watching this little display with great attention, both flattered and hugely amused that Jim was so obviously showing off for her.

Oblivious to any and all undercurrents, Yancey skipped over to Zoe, plopped down on the ground in front of her, and rested his smooth little forearms on her knees. "Mom says you're in the movies, Cousin Zoe. Did I ever see you?"

"Oh, honey, I'm not an actress. I'm sort of behind the scenes—I help get everything ready so the actors can come on."

"Oh." Yancey thought that over, not sure whether or not he should be disappointed. "Is it hard?" he asked.

Zoe nodded, carefully watching Yancey's expression. "It's pretty hard, yes it is; takes a long time."

"You ever make any movies about baseball players, Cousin Zoe?"

Zoe made a face of intense concentration. "Let's see," she said while Yancey waited breathlessly for the answer.

"No, but I worked on a cowboy picture not too long ago."

"Yeah? Who was in it?"

"Clint Eastwood," Zoe said with a quick wink at Jim, who was listening with interest while he sipped his second stinger.

"Aw *right!* Lowieeee!" Yancey zoomed off to find his brother while Zoe started to laugh and looked over at Arthur, who was putting down his drink with one hand as Yancey, back again, yanked at his free arm, sneakers dug in the soft earth. Arthur, shooting a melodramatic look over his shoulder, allowed himself to be dragged into the house to help bring this exciting news to Lowie.

Zoe felt a quick sting of sentiment as her brother followed the wiry little boy across the yard. She saw how pleased and safe Arthur looked surrounded by these people, so different from the man who had visibly cringed under the doctor's crisp advice, Annabelle's bitter rebukes.

It was nearly one-thirty by the time they all sat down at the weathered redwood picnic table. Lowie surreptitiously scooted himself over close to Zoe, glancing up at her every so often with an enraptured little smile, then looking quickly down at his plate whenever she caught his eye.

Zoe was amazed at the amount of food and the almost magical speed with which it disappeared. There were grilled salmon steaks and a huge endive salad, complete down to the tiny radish disks and scallions, which the boys would not eat no matter what, knowing their mother's threats of "no cake" to be hollow. While Eddie served the fish, Claudia passed around huge bowls of chilled macaroni and potato salad with pared tomatoes and bright bits of carrot, meticulously diced, fancy gherkins and sliced avocado in a pretty dish, and a lovely vegetable soufflé with mushrooms and broccoli florets. Baskets of fresh sourdough rolls were passed up and down the table, followed by jars and saucers filled with an endless variety of condiments.

Eddie had just begun to open Arthur's bottle of Australian wine when all at once Claudia gave a little shriek and ran back into the house, returning moments later with a large cut-glass dish filled with enormous pimento-stuffed olives, which she set down directly in front of Arthur. He laughed aloud with pleasure and popped two in his mouth at once.

And though everyone ate with relish, they didn't stop talking for a second. Zoe was quiet but attentive, letting the streams of conversation sluice over her. As they had on Friday night, the family left her to contribute as she wished, to volunteer a comment, a story of her own, only if she chose to.

At last Uncle Jim groaned theatrically and patted his taut little paunch. "Well, I'm stuffed full as a Christmas goose!" He took a long swallow of iced tea and leaned toward Zoe and Arthur, who sat side by side across from him.

"Now, you youngsters won't remember, I guess, most of it's well before your time, but we sure had some marvelous meals over at Mrs. Hillyard's place on Comm Ave. In the old days I'm talking about now— days of yore! Great victuals. . . . Let's see, Vinnie was it? Verbena? Your great-grandmother's cook—what the devil was her name now? Veronica! *Veronica!* Heavens to Betsy, that woman could cook! Did a crown roast with sweet basil . . . well, Augusta Hillyard always set a fine table, a fine, fine table . . . just like my Claudia here." He reached for another gherkin, but Claudia gently slapped his hand away and got up to start clearing the table. Zoe moved quickly to help her, gathering the plates and silverware, making a pyramid of the empty bowls and casseroles, and carrying it all into the house.

Eddie looked up into the whitening sky, across which pale, flattened clouds had begun to arrange themselves. "I think we better move the party indoors, folks," he said, dragging a big plastic trash can over to the table.

Zoe had just finished rinsing the glass salad bowl when Claudia came up behind her with a large bib apron and slipped it over her head to protect her white silk shirt.

"This is a beautiful party, Claudia," Zoe said. "Just lovely. Your boys are terrific."

Claudia began setting out clean forks and cake plates. She reached up into the cupboard for the package of birthday napkins before she answered.

"They're definitely a handful," she said, smiling in a private way. "Especially Yancey." She put the napkins on the table and peered into the freezer, pulling a half-gallon carton of strawberry ice cream toward the front.

"And Arthur just adores them," Zoe said with a chuckle. "And they him."

"Zoe, he's like a kid himself when he's with them. It's so nice to see it; he's relaxed, silly . . ."

Zoe nodded and, without thinking to ask, opened the cupboard under the sink for a can of Comet, just as if she'd washed dishes in Claudia's kitchen all her life.

"The last few years have been rough on him, Zo. There isn't too much enjoyment in his life, as far as I can tell. Remember how he always loved a party?"

Zoe was scrubbing dried cheese off the casserole. "Sure I do," she said softly. She put the dripping dish in the drainer, turned off the water, and dried her hands on the dish towel.

"Yeah, well, I don't think there's been too much of that for him, not lately," Claudia said. She paused and touched Zoe's hand, squinting up into her face. "I imagine you thought I was exaggerating . . . when I called you in L.A., I mean. But if anything, I didn't say enough, huh? You've seen the house, the way they live . . . the place is absolutely disgusting, isn't it?"

Zoe nodded again, her throat suddenly dry and tight. She had stepped into the downstairs bathroom just that morning and looked with regret at the chipped sink, the clean but stained tile floor, the frayed though freshly laundered towels.

"It's a shame you have to go back so soon, Zo," Claudia said in a quiet tone. "It's really too bad."

"Well . . . you know, maybe I don't," Zoe said.

"Oh, Zoe! Do you think you could stay? A day or so?"

"Probably," Zoe answered, realizing that those unregretted words had burst out of her with complete spontaneity. "I don't see why not, but frankly, Claud, I want to ask Arthur first. I don't want to assume that . . ."

Claudia sighed and leaned against the refrigerator, looking at Zoe's profile. "No, you're right," she said, nodding. "You know, there are two things Arthur never talks about: his feelings and his money. In some ways, poor guy, his feelings are absolutely transparent—I mean, I can tell things didn't go that well yesterday. But money? I'm sure you noticed that display he puts on . . . the gifts, the wine, the fancy food . . . all the expensive new stuff in the house. I know he's always been terrifically generous, Zo, but I'm starting to wonder whether he can afford all that. I'm not sure *why* I wonder, but I do."

Zoe listened to that with a frown. Yesterday, on the way home from the hospital, Arthur had insisted that they stop in a fancy little market on Newbury Street and in no time at all he had filled two bags with groceries for Claudia's party—out-of-season fruits, the imported gherkins in brine, a special new tea for Eddie, two bottles of wine, and a box of chocolates shaped like shells. Watching him, Zoe had the sudden thought that Arthur might not be able to afford it. She had no idea where such a suspicion had come from, but it was strong and clear, even more so when he refused to let her share the cost, tucking the twenty-dollar bill she offered him back in her pocket.

Zoe glanced up into Claudia's serious blue eyes for a second and then began folding the stack of astronaut paper napkins into triangles. She felt disloyal talking about her brother this way, even with someone who obviously cared so much for him, somebody who probably didn't want to talk about him behind his back any more than she did.

"Well," she said, "I'll mention it tonight. I don't think I can manage more than a day, Claud. Preproduction's just starting and I've got a ton of work to do, but maybe, in one day, there might be something . . ." She trailed off as a vision of Julian Frye in the dark parking lot on La Cienega crossed her mind.

"Dammit, I'm glad you're here, Zoe," Claudia said, giving her a quick hug, "and so's Arthur, even if he can't quite bring himself to . . . Shoot. Of course you have to go back. I mean, who can leave their life, right?"

She kissed Zoe lightly on the cheek, then turned away, sniffing loudly. She took a Kleenex from a box on the counter and, using the shiny side of the toaster as a mirror, wiped off the little smears of eye makeup on her cheeks.

Just then Lowie came into the kitchen, looking shyly at his mother and then at the floor.

"Hi, Lowie," Zoe said, smiling at him, glad of the interruption yet vaguely regretting it at the same time.

"Cousin Zoe," he burst out, "you want to see my collection? It's pretty nice."

"Sure I do. Collection of what?"

Lowie looked at his mother, who smiled and nodded while she blew her nose on another tissue.

"I have some, uh, shells and stuff, and . . ."

"My goodness."

"I have three yellow cowries and a Triton's trumpet Uncle Jim got me in Florida and some whelks . . ."

"Well, I would love to see them."

"Really?"

"You bet."

The sunshine broke out in his blue eyes and he clasped her proffered hand and led her off to his sanctuary.

Claudia watched them disappear up the stairs and paused, just as she was, the little birthday candles forgotten in her hand, stymied by a weave of feelings that came and went in a moment. She found herself, as so often lately, silenced by events, snagged on the realization that she was, at forty, starting to want things she had never wanted before because she hadn't known they were out there.

Large pieces of ripped-up gift wrap and discarded ribbon from Yancey's birthday presents littered the family room. Uncle Jim plunked himself down next to Zoe on the overstuffed couch, pushing aside the embroidered pillows. She slid over to make room and put her arm along the back of the sofa behind him. Eddie had lit a fire and sat cross-legged on the stone hearth, poking at the spitting logs with a piece of kindling. Edwina, exhausted from all the ice cream and cake she had eaten, was asleep at Eddie's side.

"Yessir, we're due for a blackberry winter," said Jim, looking thoughtfully at the crackling fire and then out the window at the gloomy sky. "Often happens, you know," he said to Arthur. "Snow on the croci, seen it more than once. I remember a time, must have been '34 or so, '35? I'd gone over to Augusta Hillyard's for dinner with Paulette and Henry. They were just engaged, I think. My baby sister was mighty fond of old Mrs. Hillyard, so . . . We're talking about your dear mother, Claud," he called out as Claudia, a relentless hostess, came in with a fresh pot of coffee and a big ceramic bowl filled with Arthur's exotic fruits.

"Uncle, are you telling ancient stories again? I keep telling you to look ahead, darling, not back."

"Anyway, we all had to stay overnight, it snowed so hard," Jim said, undaunted by the look she gave him. "Must have been mid-April at least."

Claudia set the fruit bowl on the coffee table in front of Zoe and started gathering up the debris from Yancey's birthday loot. She stacked all his presents on a table by the door, including a shiny yellow boom box radio with every imaginable feature and attachment.

"That's from me and Zoe, kiddo," Arthur had said, beaming, when Yancey tore the paper off. "Just don't play it too loud," he added, laughing at the futility of such instructions. Zoe had stared at him with embarrassed astonishment just as Yancey threw his strong skinny arms around her neck and gave her a big, wet kiss.

" 'Course when you all were kids, Claudia, you didn't have such fancy toys," Jim said with a chuckle, watching her straighten up.

"Half of it hadn't been invented yet," Zoe said, winking at Claudia, "but we had fun all the same, didn't we?"

"Well, yes, you surely did," Jim said, "and I found a little something the other day that I thought might bring back a memory or two." He reached into his shirt pocket and withdrew a cracked old photograph with the crimped edges that snapshots used to have, years and years ago.

"Clean forgot I still had it," he said to Zoe, holding the picture out to her.

"Oh, will you look at this! Claudia, it's you and me, and wait a minute—who's this? Your brother Malcolm! And Sue . . . my goodness, look how little she was. . . ."

"For heaven's sake, and Mother and you, Uncle Jim, with a *mustache?*" Claudia knelt on the rug beside Zoe and screamed with delight. "*Look* at this!"

"Nahant, 1948. Yup, grew it in the army. Didn't shave it off until 1952, either."

"Where's Daddy?" Claudia said, grinning over at Jim.

"Taking the picture."

"Oh, my goodness—Arthur, come *look*. . . . Uncle, how marvelous!"

"We surely had some wonderful times up there," Jim said. "I was just overcome when I found it."

Zoe looked intently at the photograph, at the children lined up by height, standing at the ornately carved porch railing with Aunt Paulette just behind Arthur, her curly silver hair shining in the sun, and a jaunty young Uncle Jim, sporting a dark Ronald Colman mustache, holding little Sue in the crook of his arm. All of them were framed by the drooping runners of the wisteria vines that grew in profusion over the pillars of the veranda. And behind everyone, sitting in a large curved wicker chair, deep in the shadows of the porch, was a long-legged old man with hollowed black eyes, a big Panama hat tilted slightly over his face, a cigar in his hand.

"Jim," Zoe said, interrupting Claudia's squeals, "Jim, I just noticed this man in the picture . . . in the back, look, who is that?"

Jim looked up at her and took a sip of his coffee, smiling in a vague, ironic way.

"Zoe, that's Anthony Hillyard—your grandfather."

"My God." Zoe strained her eyes into the shadows of the photograph. Her own eyes seemed to look back at her from under the wide brim of the hat.

"As I recall, he never did care too much for having his picture taken. Henry must have just caught him by accident." Jim snorted with laughter and put his penny loafers up on the edge of the coffee table.

"This particular day, let me see . . . this was fairly early on; must have been shortly after Henry was able to get that house back into the family."

"What was he doing there?" Zoe said, turning to Jim. "Did he live there?"

"Oh, no, honey, no. Anthony lived in New York in those days after the war. Um, look at that face. No, he was just visiting. Came up for a day or so on one of his mysterious little trips. Too bad about the house, though, Zoe," he said, settling back into his reminiscent mood. "It was a real shame, but just one of those unfortunate things."

He turned to smile at her with his kindly elegance. Zoe looked back at him, her eyes bright with the beginning of what she thought might be a memory of that very day.

"What do you mean?" she said. "Shame about what?"

"Well now, that was the Hillyard summer place for years and years, until old Eugene, your great-grandfather, my dear, sold it just prior to the First War. Well, let me tell you, when Claudia's dad heard that . . . !"

"Uncle Jim, lambie-pie," said Claudia, "I don't know if Zoe wants to hear all this."

"Yes, she does," Zoe said, winking at Jim and resting her wrist lightly on his shoulder.

"Just hang on there half a minute, Claudie, I'm getting to it," he said, turning back to Zoe, who was starting to remember afternoons on the warm sand, sunny rooms full of wicker furniture, Lorna Doones and peaches for dessert.

"Well, what happened was Henry, who was a sentimental fellow, had the titles searched and whatnot and finally, well, damned if he didn't find a way to *buy* it! Back in the family at last!"

Jim slipped the photograph back into his pocket. "Too bad Augusta Hillyard wasn't alive to see that day. Her Zachary was buried on the property, you know, in a little garden," he said, sitting back and taking another sip of coffee. " 'Course, Paulette had to sell the place when Henry took sick, but we all had a lot of fun up there in the old days. Sure did."

He paused and winked at Zoe as he stole a glance at Claudia's look of fake exasperation. "Yep, I'm an absolute *repository* of antique information," he said, grinning. "Yes, indeed."

Zoe laughed and gave him a tiny, unpremeditated hug. "I think it's wonderful," she said. "I love hearing about it."

"Well, I confess I never turn down a chance to talk about those fine old days," Jim said, looking fondly around the room. "You know, Zoe dear, I would be absolutely charmed if you'd have lunch with me at my club, sometime this week if you could. Claudia here can come along as your duenna . . . wouldn't that be nice, Claud?"

Claudia tilted her head and looked at Zoe with arched eyebrows. Arthur looked up from his second piece of birthday cake to glance at her with an expectancy he quickly smothered.

"Well, I'd love to," Zoe said, turning to Jim with a small frown, "but I might not be here too much past tomorrow, you see."

"It'd be a shame for you to miss it, dear. I thought you might like to see it, because it's real authentic. Been refurbished a time or two, naturally, but it goes all the way back to the early nineteenth century. It's the genuine article."

"Really?" said Zoe in a clear voice, sitting up straighter.

"I've been a member for years," Jim said with a sly grin. "Fortunately, they don't charge me dues anymore, couldn't afford it. Happy to pay for my food and drink, though."

"What are you talking about?" asked Claudia, not liking to be left out.

"You just haven't had a chance to hear all about Zoe's movie, Claud," said Jim, waving his hand at her and turning back to Zoe.

"Now, Arthur told me that this motion picture of yours is about Victorian art thieves. . . . Let me guess—rich insiders?"

Zoe chuckled and sat forward on the edge of the sofa. She put her coffee down. "That's right," she said with a quick glance at Arthur, whose eyes were on his plate. "It's set in the 1890s. In New York."

"Yep, Arthur told me. *The Gilded Affair*—jim-dandy title. And some of the scenes take place in a highfalutin gents' club?"

"Yes," whispered Zoe, unable to decide how she felt. "Yes. One of the characters . . . well, they plan their crime there."

"Seems to me there'd be quite a bit for you folks to consider here in Boston, even though your story takes place mainly in New York," Jim said in a voice filled with disingenuous speculation. "Who'd know? Anyways, I don't imagine you can do historical films in Manhattan these days. . . . Now that place over on Comm Ave," he went on, warming to his topic, "I'd say it's about the same period as your movie. Ain't that interesting? Arthur, about how old would you say that house is—hundred years?"

Arthur, who had been pretending to look with concentration at one of Yancey's birthday books, even as he had missed not one word of the conversation, looked up with feigned distraction.

"Huh? Oh, yes . . . yes, about that, um-hmm." He looked back at the page, somewhat flushed, but Zoe saw that his teeth were clenched inside his pink cheeks.

"Hundred years. Isn't that something? I didn't meet up with the Hillyards, of course, until the thirties, but even then it was quite a show-place, though I'm sure not what it was back when Augusta was a young woman. You surely wouldn't ever consider selling the old place, would you, Arthur?"

"Uncle Jim . . ." Claudia began, not quite sure where he was going with this. She glanced over at Arthur to check his reaction, but his eyes were glued to Yancey's book.

" 'Course you wouldn't. Goodness me, I remember how Augusta Hillyard loved that house. It'd sure be a shame to have it out of the family . . . sure would . . . a shame."

Then, realizing that not even the solid warmth of the atmosphere could withstand pursuit of such a topic, Jim patted Zoe's knee and stood up.

"Anyhow, the invitation stands—lunch at the club anytime you say!"

"I'll remember," she said, and rose to kiss his cheek. "Thank you, Uncle Jim."

"Yessir, we'd sure have a lot to talk about," he said, rattling on, linking arms with Zoe and moving toward the doorway. "I could 'reminisce' to my heart's content. Isn't that right, Claudie?" Jim said with a sneaky look in her direction. "Zoe's a kindhearted woman. She'll let me talk about the old days till I'm blue in the face—till I keel over dead from talking!"

Zoe laughed out loud and squeezed him to her. "Maybe I *can* come," she whispered in his ear as they made their way slowly to the front hall. "Maybe I can stay."

NINETEEN

*W*hen they got home, Arthur made a beeline for the phone. He had called the hospital once in the morning and again in midafternoon from Newton, and they had told him then, as now, that Miss Hillyard was sleeping a good deal, not eating at all, but holding her own. The translation—"not yet dead"—was not supplied.

Zoe went upstairs to change into her robe and came back down to fix herself a cup of Decaf, and the two of them sat in the dining room, Arthur working on the bottle of grappa, the level of which, Zoe noticed, had fallen dramatically since the seal was broken Friday night. A huge spray of barely budded lilac branches, a parting gift from Claudia, who had cut them from her garden for Zoe to force, was arranged in a tall pewter vase that Zoe had placed in the very center of the table; the lilacs threw mysterious, almost Asian shadows on the wall.

"It was a good party, wasn't it?" Zoe said, pulling her heels up on the broad seat of the mahogany chair. "Claudia's a sensational hostess."

"Isn't she amazing? Nothing's too much for her—she exhausts me with all that energy." Arthur smiled and took a sip of his grappa. "You got a kick out of the kids, didn't you?"

"Yes, it was fun to see them at last. That Yancey's a trip. Any possibility he's a little bit spoiled?"

Arthur laughed out loud. "It kills me, the stuff that little con artist gets away with, but it's interesting that he's turned out to be such a brat when Lowie's so . . . so different, so quiet for a kid his age."

"He's what? Thirteen?"

Arthur nodded. "Next summer."

"He's a lovely child. Maybe a little too shy, but . . ."

"Well, God knows he's a little brain," Arthur said. "He even won the science fair at his school for those famous shells of his. Claudia told me he showed them to you."

"He did. And he's so serious about it, too, like a little old scientist. But it's really a marvelous collection. I wonder, though, you know, shells . . . ?" Zoe made a shell-like shape with her hands. "A symbol of . . . ? I don't know, it's too pop-psychy for me. I think I'll send him one from L.A., though, a nice California shell, or maybe something from Hawaii."

She paused and slowly unfolded her hands, sipped her coffee. "By the way, Arthur, I want you to let me give you some money for that radio. No, I mean it. It was sweet of you to say it was from the both of us, but really . . ."

Arthur was waving his hand in shooing movements. "Forget it. Got it on sale." He smiled at her with a sudden gushing warmth. Zoe smiled, too, but not without remembering what Claudia had said earlier in the day about Arthur's extravagance.

"And Uncle Jim is just a darling man." Zoe reached up to rearrange one of the lilac stems, tilted in the water. "I remembered him more and more as the day went by."

Arthur grinned and took a sip of his grappa. "He certainly took a shine to you, didn't he?"

"You know," Zoe said, straightening her legs, "it would be a lot of fun to have lunch with him, listen to him tell his stories about the 'days of yore' . . . see the club. Listen, Arthur, I was thinking, maybe I could get a later plane. I mean, if you'd . . ."

Arthur looked up more quickly than he meant to; his eyes were bright behind his glasses. "You think you could change your flight, what with school vacation week and Easter and all?" He took in a shallow breath and lit a cigarette.

"Well, I could at least call, maybe look at something later on Tuesday, see what's open. Might be a cancellation."

"That would be fine, Zoe, just fine," he said, looking into his glass, not into her eyes.

"I'm here to do what I can, Arthur, get a little bit organized, you know . . . whatever."

When Arthur didn't say anything, Zoe got up and went to the fireplace, touching the edges of the Piranesi drawings above the mantel, waiting to see what he would offer into the silence.

"I guess I could probably work it out, you know," she said. "A day or two. I . . ."

"Zoe, I understand how much that movie means to you. If you have to get back, that's okay, really."

"Arthur, answer one question, please. Do you want me to stay? I want to help you if I can. Look, there must be things to gather . . . papers . . ."

Zoe wet her lips, took a deep breath. "And the social worker; I think we have to at least try to see her tomorrow, make some kind of decision. I want to do whatever—"

"Zoe, I told you before—Annabelle's coming home. There's no reason to talk to a social worker or anybody else. I've already *made* the decision, so . . ."

Zoe felt a warm flash of annoyance that she tried, with only marginal success, to hide. "Mainwaring says she can't *come* home, that it's not the best thing for her. . . . Arthur? . . . Arthur, look at me. I know how hard . . ."

But when Arthur refused to respond, Zoe retreated, sorry she'd been sharp with him.

"Well," she said, "it's getting late . . . almost ten. I guess we can talk about it in the morning, okay?"

As if startled, Arthur looked quickly up at the mantel clock. He stood up and looked at her with an unreadable expression that could have been regret at his small outburst.

"I think I'll take a little walk," he said. "Go over to Boylston and get some cigarettes. I'm almost out."

Without another word he took his jacket from the back of the chair and left the house. Zoe stood by the ragged velvet drapes in the dining room, biting her lips, and watched him out of sight around the corner of Exeter Street.

Half an hour later, Zoe came slowly down the stairs, enervated by a shower in which she had stood until the hot water gave out. Edwina waddled along behind her, her nails clicking on the bare marble floor. As Zoe rounded the banister toward the kitchen, the old-fashioned turn-knob doorbell rang—a long "brinnnngggg" of sound—and then again. She tiptoed to the door and peeked out the frosted side panel to the stoop, where she could barely see, in the light from the street lamp, the outline of a man. He was medium in height and stocky, an air of arrogance apparent even through the distortion of the hundred-year-old glass. It was obviously not Arthur having forgotten his key.

"Who is it?" Zoe said, her mouth two inches from the dead bolt. It was already locked, but she held it horizontal with firm fingers.

"Artie home?" A soft, calm voice, drenched in Boston. "Aahtie home?" he said again.

"Come back tomorrow." Edwina was stiff and growling behind her, edging backward. "He's in bed," Zoe said, in a voice she thought might sound assertive to him.

"Wake him up."

"I said come back tomorrow!"

She spoke more forcefully, feeling wide awake now, but her heart lurched a little when the doorknob rattled once, and then a white envelope slid under the door. Zoe pressed her ear against the jamb and thought she could hear footsteps—retreating? She hiked up her long nightgown and ran on tiptoe to the parlor window. She saw the man, now fully in the shine of the street lamp, swing himself into the front seat of a white Cadillac and pull carefully away into the street.

Zoe went back to the hallway and picked up the thin envelope. It was unaddressed but had "B&G Finance" and a Boston address stamped crookedly in the corner. She wrote a short note to Arthur, which she folded around the envelope, propping them on the hall radiator. She turned off all but the front hall lights and climbed back up the stairs to her bedroom.

"Well, you're certainly a tiger, aren't you?" Zoe said in a dry tone, looking over her shoulder at Edwina, who was strutting along behind her. "Scared him off. If not for you I'm sure he would have broken in and murdered us all." Edwina barked and pranced into Zoe's room, her tail wagging furiously.

Feeling suddenly too warm, flushed, Zoe opened the window just a crack, standing for a moment with her arms open to the flow of chilly air before she sat lengthwise on the window seat, hunched over her bent knees. Edwina, irked at being so suddenly ignored, turned around a few times to get her bearings, collapsed in the middle of the crewel rug, and promptly went to sleep.

Zoe's mind sifted through the events of the last two days, trying to sort out what had happened from what only *seemed* to have happened. She thought of her first view of her brother standing in Grandmère's entrance hall, of the bizarre, one-sided conversation in the hospital with Annabelle, of Anthony Hillyard's face in the shadows of the veranda at Nahant. She thought again of Jim's invitation to lunch and his suggestion that there might be "quite a lot for you to consider here in Boston." And then the envelope, thin and rustling, sliding under the door. "Oh, Arthur," she whispered to herself. "Arthur, what's with the envelopes and the white Cadillacs in the middle of the night?"

Last week Roger had said, "See what happens . . . see how it is, how it goes." Well, Zoe thought, staring out at the trees on the Mall and the elegant street lamps that threw fans of light across the sidewalks, how is it going? What do I see?

"But if I stay," Zoe said aloud, and was jolted out of her reverie by the sound of her own voice, "if I *stay* here . . . then what?"

She took her credit card out of her purse and went along the hall to the antique bridal chest, where, incongruously, a powder-blue Princess phone sat on top of a five-year-old Boston Yellow Pages. She gave the operator Roger's number and listened to the hollow ringing. And then:

"Hello-oo?"

"Hello yourself."

"Oh, Zoe! Wonderful! I just walked in the door. How are you, sweetheart?"

"Okay. I'm fine."

"Really?"

"Um-hmm. You certainly sound cheerful."

Roger laughed, delighted to hear her voice. "I am indeed a cheerful guy," he said. "Just had a sensational dinner—and a snootful. Sidney paid."

"Well, that's remarkable."

"Isn't it? I guess I have no principles. Funny, though, I told him I was going to call you tonight, and here you are. Must be ESP."

"It must be." Zoe held her mouth close to the phone. "So how are things? How're you, my friend? Aside from being full of Sidney's booze?"

"Fine, fine. I've been thinking about you all day. How's it going? Everything okay?"

Zoe swallowed and cleared her throat. "Oh, Rog . . ."

"What's happening there, Zo?"

"Roger . . . I . . ."

"What? Things going worse than you thought? Better?"

Zoe took a big breath and considered that. "Not worse, no . . . not worse. Um . . . different."

"Ah. You mean not quite like you imagined? Like you think you re-member?"

"It's hard to be sure," Zoe said. "At the party today—"

"Party? My goodness."

"Well, it was for Yancey—Claudia's son's birthday. But, Rog, her Uncle Jim was there. I knew him years and years ago, and . . . oh, he knows so much about the history of the family, and we talked about Grandmère and the old times, and then of course yesterday Arthur and I went to the hospital to see Annabelle, and she . . ."

Relieved to be talking about it, Zoe spoke in a rapid, hushed voice, telling Roger about the picnic and then about Annabelle's obvious de-mentia and Arthur's absolute unwillingness to face it. When she stopped to take a breath, silence whistled on the line for a moment.

"You're not coming back tomorrow, are you?" Roger said.

"I don't see how I can leave Arthur. There's so much he's not telling me, and there's so much to *do*. I'm not even sure what it is yet, but I have to stay here, Rog. I have to."

"I know."

"You were right. Last Saturday? God, I can't believe that was only a week ago. But I definitely can't leave things as they are. Like tonight, for example, I thought Arthur was going to ask me to stay, but . . ."

"But he didn't."

"No."

"You offered."

"That's right."

"How's he doing?"

"Well . . . I know he really tries, he does, but he's not doing a particularly good job of pretending."

"Pretending what?"

"Oh, that he's not . . . miserable, confused, everything Claudia said he was. And you know, being with him again after so long makes me remember that he always used to do that, pretend everything was just dandy. And it's not, of course."

Zoe took another deep breath. She thought of telling Roger about the man at the door, the envelope, her suspicions that Arthur was having problems that had nothing to do with Annabelle, but almost as soon as she considered it she realized that she wouldn't know what to say, that she had talked about Arthur and his private torments far too much already.

"So you're coming Tuesday instead?"

"Probably more like Wednesday."

"Well, in that case, darling, I think you'd better call Frye and let him know," Roger said in a quiet voice. "I mean, I'd be happy to, but Sidney told me tonight that there's some big production meeting Tuesday, supposed to last all day, he said, so . . ."

"Oh? That wasn't scheduled. When I left Julian Friday morning—before you and I went on to the airport—he said he was going to be out of town himself until I forget when . . . Thursday?"

"Well, the plans are obviously changed. Sidney was practically foaming at the mouth—you know how he gets when he's not fully up to date." Roger's deep dislike of Sidney showed plainly in his voice, in the uncharacteristic sarcasm.

"Up to date on what? He doesn't even know what the problem is?"

"No, he knows a little bit. He says that apparently Frye's first choice for Beatrice Holland has a commitment and her agent's giving Frye fits right now, wants billing above the title in exchange for getting out of the commitment—if there *is* one, of course."

"Oh, my."

"Sidney just loves giving me his analysis of all this whoop-de-do."

"Insider intrigue." Zoe was smiling, imagining Sidney's usual "dirt-dishing" expression, the narrowed eyes, the pursed lips.

"But at any rate," Roger went on, "something's obviously up, and

Sidney thought Frye was in an especially shitty mood when he saw him this morning. So if you can't be at the meeting Tuesday, it's probably a good idea if he hears it directly from you."

Zoe hesitated for a second, swamped with an odd, dizzying confusion. Of course, she should be in L.A. working on the movie, going to the meeting, not here. But what about Jim's club, Victorian Boston, Grandmère's house, the social worker, the man in the Cadillac? She realized she had told Roger very little after all.

"That's all right," she said. "I'll call him in the morning."

"Good. . . . Zoe?"

"Hmm?"

"Do you miss me?" he said in a playful, husky stage whisper.

"Oh? Did I forget to mention that?"

"Want to tell me *exactly* how much?" he asked in the same low, intimate tone.

"What do you . . . ? Oh!" All at once, Zoe realized that this was an invitation to a little lighthearted phone sex and she tried to smother her laughter, to play the game with him, but she couldn't quite do it. "Oh, Roger, I can't . . . oh, don't make me! Not on the *phone!* No fair," she whined melodramatically. "Oh, Roger, that is *not* fair!"

"I know, but at least it would have the beauty of not being fair to me, either," he said, laughing. "So I guess this means I must confine myself to, uh, *recollection*, as some poet must have said?"

"I guess it must."

"But just till you come back."

"Rog?"

"Ummm?"

"Roger . . ."

"What, darling? What, Zo?"

"You would have loved the party today. It was . . . it was wonderful. I wished you were there with everybody." Zoe inhaled and waited, but Roger didn't say a word.

"Good night, sweetheart."

"Night, Zo."

TWENTY

(FROM THE DIARIES OF AUGUSTA HILLYARD: 1919 TO 1921)

Saturday, March 22, 1919

In the months since the shipyards closed, Eugene has seemed very much at loose ends, but some instinctive caution keeps me from asking him directly. Yesterday, when I tried to pry something out of brother Alex, who has been flustered and evasive for many months, he merely patted my shoulder in that way he has as if to say: "The poor feebleminded little female is not to know what the big strong men are having these days in the way of problems." I find that sort of thing so irritating, but one look at Alex's worried face and I haven't the heart to press him.

I do understand that Trefoyle has a new project of some sort, something that he has no doubt created out of his patronage from Mr. Curley, but although Eugene is out and about early each morning, just as usual, it is very hard to understand his role. I think he should undertake to revive his construction business as before, and on his own, but I have said nothing. Keeping my own counsel seems wise to me just now.

Monday, May 26, 1919

I read in the *Times* this morning that stocks continue up; there was a long report about it. It would appear that the Armistice has given renewed vigor to the market, and the railroads in particular are all the rage right now. As far as I can tell, however, Eugene—who has never trusted the stock market—is not taking advantage of what seems a genuine opportunity. I think it might be rather clever to put at least a portion of the Nahant money (which I feel must have been handsome) into steel or coal or railroads, and yet I find that I cannot suggest it, even though Frances said something the other day that makes me suspect that Anthony has put some tidy sum of his own into this "bull market." Thursday afternoon, when we took tea with Celia Wheelwright on Bay State Road, Frances, who surely knows less than any other woman in the world about these matters, remarked that she saw stock brochures and documents spread out all over Anthony's desk when she went in with some fresh flowers.

I hardly know what to think about Eugene. He seems to have a faith in Trefoyle that captures both his spirit and his purse. There is more to all this than meets the eye, and it is my duty to find a way to understand it. Perhaps if Eugene did embark upon his own enterprise again Trefoyle and Curley would sabotage his efforts. Does he fear this? Does he need *them* now?

Thursday, March 25, 1920

Although all Bostonians know it's much too early, spring seems to have crept upon us in the night. We awoke to a soft cerulean sky and tiny slivers of green which will soon be leaves. The crocuses that Veronica planted along the front walk several years ago are just now poking out, their prim little yellow shoots basking in the sun. As I have lived in Boston all my life and could wager that a blackberry winter will come upon us soon, perhaps within the week, I seized the opportunity to take myself out after luncheon and walked quite a distance up to Houghton & Dutton, where I bought a simply lovely pair of yellow gloves. As I paid the clerk I smiled to myself, thinking how utterly frivolous this was, as I shall surely *never* have an opportunity to wear them, and yet it seemed that I was paying homage to my crocuses!

Feeling quite self-satisfied, I strolled back home in the late afternoon under the frilly shadows of a million tiny leaves, only to be met at my own front door by a vigilant Potter standing tall and disapproving on the steps. He had been out in the alley fixing a chair for Veronica when I (as Potter views it) made good my escape earlier in the afternoon. Bless him, he still believes the mistress should not venture forth alone, even in spring sunshine, and was "horrified" (Veronica's word, not mine) when he learned that I have been behaving in this scandalous fashion for quite some time now. Poor Potter, so insulated as he is by Eugene's pretensions, has by some alchemy become the greater snob.

Saturday, May 22, 1920

I've just had a delightful birthday letter from Mathilde and was quite amused to find it arriving one week early this year instead of two weeks late! Mathilde herself commented very charmingly on that (she wrote, "Ha! I've flabbergasted you—haven't I?" in the margin), but she goes on to say—oh! I can barely write this from excitement—goes on to say that she has purchased a summerhouse in the Beauvais district north of Paris where her mother lived as a girl, long ago. She writes that the "chateau" is rather small ("really, Augusta dear, nothing so grand") but comfortable and beautifully situated near a small lake. She "implores" (her very word) me to be among the first to see it. She writes: "Now I don't see how you can refuse—not after all these years. How many *is* it since our last satisfying gossip? We shall walk in the orchard and speak knowingly of art and music!" She tempts me with her wonderful descriptions of the garden pond and roses—even an apple orchard! How lovely it does sound. (If I go, I will definitely take along those silly yellow gloves!)

Friday, May 28, 1920

I must confess that when I broached the subject of a journey to Eugene, I did experience some stabs of guilt, as Mathilde's invitation arrived only a month after he was finally up and about after his indisposition. To my amazement, however, he acquiesced at once and proposed the journey to me as a birthday gift! Is he back to his old trick of plying me with what I most desire when he is at his most inauspicious? A gift horse for fair! . . . into whose mouth I have no intention of looking, however, because (oh! *Oh!* I am just beside myself!) the tickets are definitely purchased for my passage on the *Mauritania* and Eugene dispatched Potter not fifteen minutes ago to collect them from the agent at White Star! I shall confront my "guilt" at some more suitable time. Actually, I am somewhat peeved with myself for feeling any twinge of guilt at all, and as a consequence I have been in something of a dither all morning, only now pausing for a cup of tea. I've been rummaging about in my drawers and cupboards for days, trying to plan a wardrobe suitable for sophisticated French country in the spring! The dressmaker is coming tomorrow morning, bright and early, but, my goodness, we've only two weeks!

Monday, June 14, 1920, the Mauritania

Our first two days out have featured less than ideal weather for June. Many of the passengers are keeping to their cabins, I among them. Although I enjoy walking on deck, even in the harsh weather, one of the stewards hurried over to me yesterday, all solicitude, to say that the captain prefers that the first-class passengers not frequent the deck during rough seas. (Presumably the third-class voyagers may be swept into the sea at their pleasure.)

But I realize how impatient I am for our ocean passage to be over. I am distressed to find myself clutching at this trip as some *treat* that will soon be consumed; I fear that I have allowed my anticipation of the splendors Mathilde has described to run away with the quiet savor I should feel. I am alternately amused and irked at myself for this and yet I find I cannot help it. I have yearned so long to make this journey, and here I am, like a foolish girl, awaiting culmination. In days of old, my mother used to spy me sitting by the casement window in my bedroom, daydreaming, my book or sewing fallen into my lap, gazing out at nothing. "Don't you be wishing your life away, my girl," she used to say. "Don't you do it!"

Saturday, November 13, 1920

I am becoming more and more upset at the tremendous disorder into which my household has been flung. Am I becoming so set in my ways that I can't tolerate a little disarray? Or is it more likely that I am sincerely concerned about my husband's illness and not quite willing to admit it? Eugene, of course, denies that he is ill at all. He claims merely to be "resting," but he has barely stirred since he took to his bed nearly three weeks ago. He keeps Veronica hopping, as I overheard her complain to Flora the other morning, running in and out with tea, with brandy, with small exotic meals that he doesn't eat. The baker's boy was sent back three times last week to fetch a different kind of bread!

I wonder if it's possible that Eugene has lost his spirit. Yet I can't credit that, not really. Whatever Eugene's faults (and they are legion), he survived on arrogance and charm for decades, sustained by what I know to be a deep-seated belief in his own ability to carry on and to prevail. It was this quality in him that drew me to him in the earliest days. And yet he has lain for almost a month either in his bed or on that dreadful blue leather chaise, and seems to be feeling very sorry for himself.

Wednesday, November 17, 1920

He is still on the chaise in the library. In spite of what he claims to be some mysterious, unnamable "affliction," Eugene sees no physician that I know about, only Anthony and Alex, who are received daily, alone or in tandem. The three of them are in there this very minute, plotting and scheming as usual, but to what end?

Eugene's clever plan last spring to return to contracting "in a big way," as he said, to involve himself in remodeling some of these great houses on Commonwealth Avenue, evidently died aborning. There is no space left to build on the Avenue, but many of the homes, of course, go back to Reconstruction days and could do with a little reconstructing now. When I asked Alex about this some weeks ago he did confess to me (and unfortunately this was in the tone of a confession) that they had indeed thought to do remodeling and fine finishing, consolidating a group of tradesmen and working with the preformed decorations which are now so popular—lintels, ceiling medallions, dadoes. They actually purchased a great many board feet of cornices, now rotting I suppose in some warehouse in South Boston. But this great plan "did not come to fruition," Alex said, and they are obliged to begin again. When I pressed for details, he did say that he and Eugene are "temporarily" out of favor with the Irish elements in a way that may be more significant than they anticipated. He tried to make light of it, but Alex's indefatigable cheerfulness, which he inherits from our papa, did not put my mind at rest.

Friday, December 10, 1920

It must have been close to five o'clock when I saw Alex on the turning of the stairs. I watched him as he lumbered down the staircase and then I tiptoed back to Eugene's door and looked in, expecting to find him asleep, exhausted by Alex's long visit.

He lay awake, however, reclining once again on the blue chaise, and reached out his hand to me. I very quietly closed the door behind me and went to sit on the edge of the chaise. Eugene looked at me in that odd, inquiring way he has developed, as if he scarcely knows if I be fish or fowl, and taking my hand in both of his, and pressing it flat against his chest (whereupon I could feel the very beating of his heart), he told me that he wanted me to know (and this with a formality that can be *so* like him) that in spite of what I may ever have thought, he has without exception found me to be the most admirable of women and a superb wife in every way, and that I must excuse this show in him but he wanted me to know it.

I felt that a response of some sort was required of me, but stunned to speechlessness as I was, all I could do was to put my hand to his un-shaven cheek and look deep into his black eyes. We stayed thus, my hand still upon his face, until, some minutes later, he sank back against his pillows, closed his eyes, and fell asleep.

Saturday, February 19, 1921

I am at last a widow.

Eugene Hillyard departed the hurly-burly of his life last Monday af-ternoon; he would have been sixty-six in May. We had the funeral today at Trinity, and the preparations occupied the week. It has been bitterly, bitterly cold, and it pains me to think that Eugene, who so loved sum-mertime, has gone into his tomb on a day rimed with frost, the leaden sky touching the top of the stone angel in the graveyard. We have not buried him out in Lincoln, next to his parents, as he may have wished, but I was not aware of his wishes. Eugene, in character to the end, never saw fit to discuss his plans with me.

I made some effort early in the week to contact Eugene's brother, Baxter Hillyard, who was present at our wedding, leaving, as I recall, before the champagne had ceased fizzing in the glasses. We have heard of him but rarely through the years—at one time he was thought to be in Oregon, or perhaps Alaska—and I'm not actually sure he's still alive. However, although there was scant love between him and Eugene, I felt a great upsurging of sentiment that I had no thought to deny and made the effort, though in vain.

Although I thought it not entirely proper to read Eugene's will before his remains were in the ground, Anthony felt it was important to do as his father had specified (apparently to him alone), and we were a somber group in Mr. Ford's office Thursday afternoon. The details were not entirely clear to me, but it appears that Eugene left almost everything he had—almost EVERYTHING—to Anthony! I realize I am now at Anthony's mercy. (I see that I have written "mercy"—the last word perhaps to couple in a sentence with his name—and thought for a moment just now to scratch it out, even in this utter privacy, and substitute another, and yet no other word will do.)

Nevertheless, I am gratified to be able to report, on this otherwise dark and unhappy day, that Eugene did right by Potter and Veronica. He left small bequests to each, in trust for their old age, quite wisely naming me trustee. I think this was very handsome of Eugene and possibly more than they anticipated. They had been summoned by Mr. Ford to be present at the reading, and Veronica, who is much given to tears at the death of a caterpillar, was silent and dry-eyed. Potter, standing massively in the rear of the chamber, clutching his cap, looked rather fixedly at the pattern in the Persian carpet, although I caught his eye as we arose to go and found there a look of lost affection and regret. Whatever may be said in eulogy of Eugene Hillyard, he commanded Potter's respect and affection for nearly forty years. No small thing.

And so today we put him in the ground with just a smattering of ceremony and only the remains of his family and a few old friends to see him to his reward, if such there be. Hortense, who had so recently been here for her customary New Year's visit, came back again, Eliot beside her. Annabelle wept before her father's grave, quietly but with a sincerity that both pleased and surprised me. With the exception of his devotion to Anthony, I never had, in all the years we were together, the sense that Eugene Hillyard valued or loved his children. Even Anthony was a possession to him, his fatherly sentiment composed more of mastery than of love. Although I stood dry-eyed myself, I had with me some clematis from Nahant that I had saved in a book, plucked in the early days when we used to run off there to make love of an afternoon. The thought having come upon me quite suddenly last night, I looked for it, and, sure enough, the poor dried sprigs were as I left them years ago, pressed between the pages of a book of verse, and before they closed the casket lid, I put the dried clematis in my husband's hand. I hardly know where that inspiration came from—a nostalgia now foreign to my feelings—and yet there was a rightness to it.

Eugene Hillyard strove so violently throughout his life toward goals both wise and foolish. Whether the contentment of his family was ever truly in his thoughts I do not know, and yet we stood there, his wife, his three living children, his brother Alex (for so Alex had become to him, much more than "brother-in-law"), and his little grandson and namesake, who wept only in imitation of his mother. Ah, yes, there was *one* Trefoyle in evidence today, dear little Frances, to whom Eugene was always very cordial, even kind . . . only *one* Trefoyle.

Eugene has thus left me a widow without legacy. He has left me with my passion spent and my hair silvered over. But there were years when he was more to me than my own life, although I have no wish now to be the Alcestis of my time. No Viking this, no Pharaoh. Just an old man whose heart emptied itself of its last gulp of blood on a cold winter's day. I was wife, lover, and adversary to this man for decades, and though I shall miss him, I do not expect to mourn.

Tuesday, March 8, 1921

I have had a series of singularly unsatisfying conversations with Alex, for one of which the referee was Mr. George Ford, who I have learned is Trefoyle's attorney also! This definitely will not do, and I shall naturally make other arrangements at the earliest possible time. But I have been given at least a hint of the state of Eugene's once-handsome fortune, and following a few private but very crisp words to brother Alex, I took myself downtown this morning to the Columbia Trust Company, where Eugene's accounts were chiefly kept.

A Mr. Grayson, a very punctilious sort, took me practically step by step through these accounts, and yet I soon lost my taste, and my nerve, for it. There is indeed a pittance for Annabelle, the income of which promises to be quite microscopic (she shall not have her ribbons of it), a scrap for Hortense, and a somewhat larger scrap for me. I imagine I shall have all I can do to keep the house on this amount, but at least I have now some slim hope of being able to elude Anthony's "mercies," though not for long.

I suppose Eugene must have believed that there would always be a swindle, or a "deal," or patronage, or an "arrangement." I'm sure he never thought that old Trefoyle, dipping into the barrel of Eugene Hillyard and his Back Bay friends, would ever scrape bottom, but he did— and threw the cask away. Evidently Eugene did not have the foresight to set up the "spendthrift" trusts which the Commonwealth has had cause to regret, but which remain legal to this day. Certainly, many families have benefited from these ancient laws, but ours is not among them. The word "spendthrift" came into Eugene Hillyard's lexicon only in reference to his love of making a grand show. Since the Hillyard trusts were always fully accessible, and as Eugene was the self-appointed trustee, he felt free to dip into them time and time again, and in so doing he has revoked the birthrights of his children—a situation which I must now try to rectify with as much haste as I can summon up.

Mr. Grayson volunteered to prepare a summary accounting of these funds, which he will have delivered to the house sometime within the next two weeks. When he then rose to indicate the end of our interview, I took my leave as graciously as I could and went into a small tearoom down near Milk Street, where I sought to soothe my nerves and collect what passes for my "thoughts." When I felt I had done so, I took myself further down the street to the offices of Lee, Higginson, who have handled Lattimore money from my father's time. What I learned there need consume but a line of these pages:

There is nothing.

A Mr. Joyner brought me to his office, closed the door, cleared his throat quite magnificently, and said, all too plainly: "Mrs. Hillyard, there is next to nothing. The Lattimore Family Trust is down to a shred of its original principal. Surely you were aware of this?" His tiny chocolate-brown eyes looked with what I imagined to be some disdain into mine. "Surely Mr. Alexander Lattimore, as trustee, has apprised you and Miss Sarah Lattimore of these withdrawals?"

I was at pains to recover myself, but did the best I could and said that I was aware, of course, that these funds had been used for private investments, et cetera, et cetera, and burbled on in that fashion for some minutes, but I could see that I was boring him to death and, more to the point, that he did not believe me. The Lattimores have clearly ceased to be a source of income for his firm. If there is a saving grace in all of this, it is that Papa never knew that the Padraic Trefoyle would get it all.

In the end, Mr. Joyner did agree to send over an accounting, and I swept out with what dignity I could muster and made my way to Commonwealth Avenue on foot, hardly knowing where I went, reluctant to spend a dollar on a cab, and gained my own front door and went to bed.

Sunday, April 3, 1921

I have spent the last three weeks nearly alone. I am trying to absorb the truths that I have learned since I put my husband in the ground, and to find a way to go forward through what may be left of my life, be it an hour or another quarter century, for once in full control of my fortunes. The accounts arrived from Columbia Trust and from Lee, Higginson as promised. I have some skill in figures from all my years of managing a large household, and locked myself in Eugene's library to study the remarkable sheaves of paper in detail.

The splendor of the Hillyard style (and quite dazzling it was, of course, for many years, my constant bickering with Eugene notwithstanding) will clearly have to change at once. I see now that we lived day to day, that our position—such as it was—was bought with daily funds. Eugene dipped into principal at every turn. Indeed, funds were barely allowed to cool in the deposit box before being withdrawn again. I have not yet confronted Alex, though I shall, and with the detail to defy his usual bombast. It was all for Trefoyle! Draft after draft made out to "Trefoyle-Hillyard & Sons" (now "Trefoyle & Company," I understand, just by the bye).

We shall be playing our financial cards rather close to our (frayed) vests here, but I do believe we'll manage. We must gird ourselves now to make transition from opulence to mere decency.

Wednesday, May 18, 1921

I have gone downtown once again and retained another attorney, known only to me. I have withdrawn (with Hortense's signature and Annabelle's) what funds I can and have consolidated these into an account in the Merchant's National Bank which shall go to help us live. I have protected Hortense and Annabelle from the deepest knowledge of these matters; I blush to think that I am doing what was done "for" me for many years, but do it I shall.

Friday, May 20, 1921

There is a joke on me in all of this. This afternoon Mr. Joyner sent one further document, which I read with great attention. It seems that my wonderful diamond earrings, which lie before me now in their blue box, were bought for me with my own money. Is that not exceedingly humorous? Is that not reason for great peals of laughter? (As, indeed, I laughed when I read of it in Mr. Joyner's report!)

My Tiffany diamonds: ha! Bought twenty years ago with income from the Lattimore Trust. Ah, Eugene, you poor, dead, extravagant fool. Did you think that I would never know?

I am done laughing now. After I wrote the words above, I lay myself, Camille-like, on the chaise and held my earrings in the tips of my fingers, twisting them this way and that to catch the evening light. But soon tiring of this foolish sport, I clasped the earrings in my fist and closed my eyes and thought:

At least this house is mine!

TWENTY-ONE

*O*n Commonwealth Avenue that Monday morning, while the budding purple lilacs waited in the shadows of the dining room, Zoe sat at the kitchen table, drinking instant coffee, looking out the window at the misty rain. She was thinking about risk and symbols, and of other things, too, like corners turned, and time. She wondered from what deep ground she had dug the words to tell Roger that she would not be back just yet. Where had it really come from, this understanding that she could not leave?

"What am I doing here?" she whispered. "Why am I staying?" She thought it entirely possible she was being too melodramatic about what was really nothing more than a simple duty that decency demanded. A famously "disputatious" woman was coming closer and closer to the end of her long life, and then arrangements would be made. There was no drama here—no symbolism, no big deal; this was not a Greek play, after all . . . just regular life.

She dawdled in the kitchen, putting off her call to Julian Frye in California, telling herself (as she polished Arthur's fancy German coffeemaker) that he would be so preoccupied with casting the role of Beatrice Holland that he would never miss her. She opened the kitchen door and watched the drizzle in the alley for a while, and then finally dragged herself to the telephone.

Frye grumbled and rumbled, unmoved by claims of "family matters."

When Zoe explained she would be using the time to work out the final splendid dinner scene—the betrothal party that signaled Laurence Thane's escape—and would send the sketches to him Air Express, he was unimpressed. He reminded her of their conversation on La Cienega the week before, of the "imperatives," as he called them.

"You told me just a weekend, dammit! So, by Wednesday? Yeah? Yeah? By Wednesday? Not that that makes a helluva lot of difference—we got a monster production meeting coming up Tuesday—hey, tomorrow—goddam *Tuesday!*"

"I know."

"So? You expect me to do preproduction without the production designer? That make sense to you?" He still wasn't threatening, hadn't actually brought his voice to the astounding levels of which she knew him capable.

"So, Wednesday, yes?"

"Julian, I don't know, I think so, but, well, I can't be sure. I'm sorry, but my family—"

"Shit. I didn't even know you *had* a family, for crissakes."

Zoe hung up the phone with a sour face, mumbled "bastard" under her breath, and went upstairs, dimly astonished that at no time during the conversation had she felt defensive or intimidated. It had been almost an errand, a minor task easily dispatched.

Musing over this, she sat on the top riser of the sweeping staircase, staring down at the wainscoted symmetry of the stair hall and the foyer, noting the fine detailing, the handsome proportions, barely aware of the stains, the chipping, the warping. The diffuse, watery beams that came through the fanlight, casting its pattern on the marble floor, seemed to wash away the years of neglect. Zoe's mind drifted to a small fantasy of a tall, gaunt butler opening the heavy front door for two ladies in long, lacy dresses, laughing and gossiping together as they entered, their enormous flower-laden hats making whispering impossible. They flowed through the sparkling foyer, banked with large bouquets of lilacs and ferns arranged in stone vases set on the carved pedestals that lined the hall, gliding through a sudden beam of blazing sunshine just as . . . the phone rang.

Zoe yanked herself back to reality and ran down the stairs, two at a time, to the kitchen. It was the social worker, offering to squeeze the

Hillyards in at four. Zoe agreed, looked at her watch, and ran to her room to get her bag.

She walked all the way to the Common, watching as Boston's spring roused itself from the beaten dirt, just giving way to grass. Back Bay spread itself out under a pale, clearing sky, the low clouds casting green shadows on the plantings of the Public Garden; yellow waves of forsythia splashed against wrought-iron fences. As she wandered along the twisting, crisscrossed paths, Zoe found herself thinking of the complex and erotic labyrinth scene in *The Gilded Affair*. There, at the deserted country house where the stolen paintings and art objects have been hidden, under a shimmering rain-filled sky, the lovers, unaware of Mortlake's treachery, have their first intensely sexual encounter. She knew Frye had not yet decided exactly how to film it.

Zoe sat on a bench on the Common and took out her sketch pad, using the random patterns of the meandering paths to try to define the scene and the way in which the beautifully tended maze might be made to form a metaphor for the lovers' feelings. When she looked up from the page, Zoe fancied that Laurence and Beatrice were standing under the tree across from her, a gray umbrella shielding Beatrice's eyes. She drew them as they stood, close together, their fingers intertwined. Then she drew Beatrice reaching into the low, wet branches of the tree, and then, quickly, a sketch of Laurence Thane encircling her with his arms, plucking the small leaf she wanted.

Just then—in Zoe's mind—Beatrice turned and touched Laurence's gentle face with the finger of her glove and waited while he smiled. Zoe held her breath as she quickly sketched them walking arm in arm around a large bush of yellow forsythia, curving away into the labyrinth. Sighing faintly, Zoe put her pad away and went slowly toward the State House at the top of Beacon Hill. A few minutes later, still deep in thought, she turned on to Mt. Vernon Street and came to rest leaning against a budding maple tree in Louisburg Square, watching while a young woman who looked—to Zoe's painterly eyes—exactly like Beatrice Holland stood at the door of what could have been her family's town house in New York, searching in a Filene's tote bag for her keys.

Midafternoon, Zoe took a cab from the side entrance of the Ritz Carlton Hotel to the hospital. She found Arthur behind the glass wall of the lounge on Annabelle's floor, smoking and staring into space. When she spoke to him he seemed almost frightened, but after the briefest conversation he came with her to the social worker's office, tense and unwilling, looking awful.

The woman was haute Cambridge to her fingertips. Zoe looked with instant distaste at her ankle-length skirt and fish-shaped beaded earrings. A wide barrette, fashioned of some sort of bone, held back a long gray ponytail.

Zoe greeted her with a terse politeness, but Arthur chose to sulk, his courteous soul well veiled for the occasion. The woman crossed her legs, dangling a handmade sandal from a toe.

She asked immediately about Annabelle's finances, explaining that the bill was mounting—three CAT scans, private room, no Medicare. "We may want to consider Title Nineteen," she said in a simpery, educated voice.

"What is that, please?" Zoe asked.

"Welfare."

Arthur got up and leaned against the cold windowpane.

"Of course, her house will have to be sold before Welfare can be considered," the woman said, her eyes on her paperwork. "Her assets have to be spent down completely."

"I beg your pardon?"

"Exhausted, spent, depleted . . . you understand. She can't have anything. Now. We've located a nursing home in Framingham that will take her if they can have a deposit—will that be a problem? We'll need financial reports, of course, twenty-four months of bank statements, all her stock certificates; you'll want to get her lawyers to help."

Zoe glanced over at Arthur, expecting fireworks, expecting him to say that he had plenty of money—that there was no need to beg, borrow, or steal for Annabelle, no need to sell off Grandmère's precious house—and, so saying, to stalk out, throwing a scornful look over his aristocratic shoulder.

But he didn't. He stood staring out the window, his shoulders hunched up, his forehead pressed against the glass.

Zoe looked back at the social worker, who was now peering at her over the rims of her granny glasses. But Zoe said nothing, and the woman seemed to take her defiant, appalled silence for despair.

"Oh yes, these things are always *so* difficult," she said with a tight smile. "We try to reach out to these people, naturally. We like to address their issues, work through their rage with them, help them get in touch with their feelings. But Dr. Mainwaring says she's not doing that well—she'll never know she's not in her own home."

Zoe took a large brown envelope filled with papers, forms, instructions, nursing home brochures, and rules for signing everything away and led her silent brother back upstairs.

After a moment spent swaying in the doorway of Annabelle's room, Arthur went away to smoke and Zoe sank onto the chair at the foot of the bed and stared at Annabelle, who lay motionless under fresh white sheets. A nasogastric tube was anchored with two strips of surgical tape, and her wrists, once corsaged with baby roses and braceleted with gold and peridots, were fastened with strong straps to the raised side rails of the bed. Could this be the same Miss Annabelle Hillyard who was once the dancing partner of mustachioed gentlemen who drove Hispano-Suizas and shot birds with dukes?

Zoe wondered where she had first absorbed the knowledge that selling the house was out of the question. A sudden flash of engulfing anger at the social worker brought her to her feet. How could that woman possibly not know that selling Grandmère's house was unthinkable? How did Zoe know it? Uncle Jim's remark yesterday had at first gone over her head, the assumption was so strong. "It would be a shame," he'd said, to have the house out of the family. A *shame*. But Zoe realized she had not reacted because she'd always known it.

But were there perhaps no alternatives to the unthinkable? . . . to shame? Shall I run back to Commonwealth Avenue, Zoe thought, and pack it all up—shove a century in cartons, sweep it out, burn the trash, gut it of pictures, portieres, and leather books, strip the dadoes from all the fireplaces, roll the Kermans, Sarouks, and the Hunting Tabriz in the library into tight cylinders, roped against the locked breakfronts and bridal chests—and put it all out in the street?

She sank back onto the hard chair, staring again at the slow, shuddering rise and fall of Annabelle's chest, listening to the soft whistle of her breath.

"Is that what I'm doing here?" Zoe whispered to herself. "Did I come back for *this*? To sell my Grandmère's house?"

It was almost suppertime when Zoe pulled herself up by the footboard of Annabelle's bed and went looking in the lounge for Arthur.

"I'm going to stay here tonight, Zo. I'll get something in the employee cafeteria; the nurses get me in."

"Are you sure?" she said, with a hand on his sleeve.

"Don't worry about it," he said, walking her to the elevator. When the doors slid open he leaned down and kissed her quickly on the forehead. Zoe rode down to the lobby with her hand pressed to her face.

She walked all the way home through the chilly dusk, glad of her jacket. As she passed the large supermarket on Boylston Street, thinking she ought to pick something up for her own dinner, she remembered what she'd seen on the cupboard shelf that morning, the sad jumble of cheap groceries, boxed, canned, laden with chemicals. Suddenly she wanted to buy as much real food as she could carry.

She stuffed her cart with packages of boned chicken breasts and perfect steaks, two large, pale wheels of French cheese, several loaves of whole-grain bread, and a foil bag of elegant homemade oatmeal cookies. She chose fat carrots, one at a time, long perfect runner beans and smooth white mushrooms, and a head of garlic. She bought a large package of fresh, limp pasta and two cartons of sweet cream. She gathered half a dozen Bosc pears and three limes, red grapes and green apples, and oranges without seeds . . . but standing still in the aisle with the fruit held in her fingertips, Zoe wondered how such a thing could be. How can there be a living thing without a seed, a pit, a kernel, a stone of being in the middle?

TWENTY-TWO

*Z*oe spent the rainswept early hours of Tuesday morning walking through the Back Bay neighborhoods west to Kenmore Square, and north to the riverbanks. Arthur had indeed not come back from the hospital Monday night, even to change his clothes, and she had a miserable, damp Edwina whining and snuffling at the end of her sequined leash, but glad of the attention.

On the corner of Raleigh Street and Bay State Road she stopped to wrap her wet fingers around the ornate iron rail that enclosed a small handkerchief of lawn and gazed for a long time at her grandmother Celia Wheelwright's ancient dogwood, gnarled but still alive. She reached over the railing to touch a drooping branch and then shuddered a little when she realized what she was feeling.

She went back home and spent an hour at the dining-room table with the papers from the social worker, struggling to read them all. Of course, she did not have the information to fill out the forms, only Arthur did (*if* he did), but it was clear to her that he would never do it. It almost amused her to see that her brother had remained capable of the most inventive elusiveness; it was impossible to engage Arthur once he'd taken flight, in his mind, from what he would not confront, and it always had been. His dismissal of her questions about the envelope that had been slid under the door Sunday night was utterly in character. She knew that he would evade the social worker and her many forms and lists and questionnaires with the same irresistible clumsiness.

At last she piled everything up and left it stacked on the corner of the vinyl tablecloth. Zoe knew she was as unwilling as her brother to take so much as the first step toward getting rid of Grandmère's house. Even the small effort she had made, reading the papers under the thin light of the dingy chandelier, seemed disloyal.

At noon she went outside with a cheese sandwich and a bunch of grapes and sat on the Hillyard bench in the damp but clearing air. With the departure of the rain had come a cooler, stronger wind, and there were few passersby to mar her solitude. She sat eating the sandwich, gazing idly at the tall facade of the house. A scene from the script of *The Gilded Affair* drifted into her mind, and she imagined DuBose Mortlake's matched grays drawing a lacquered calèche to a stop before that very door. Zoe squinted from across the street as Beatrice Holland, swathed in furs and velvet, was handed down. She seemed to pause, one hand on the carriage door, looking furtive and uncertain.

She jumped up, ran back into the house, and dashed upstairs, almost out of breath, to lean into the doorway of Eugene Hillyard's paneled library. She saw Laurence Thane, limp with longing for Beatrice, lying on the cracked leather chaise by the fire, the mirrored entablatures reflecting his sad, handsome face.

"No . . ." Zoe whispered to herself. Then: "But could I? Maybe . . . ?"

She hesitated only a second before running back to her room to get the sketches she had done the day before. Moments later she was sitting cross-legged on the worn loveseat in the back parlor with her pad propped on her knees; the pencil sketches of Thane and Holland that she'd done on the Boston Common and the quick line drawing of the woman in Louisburg Square were fanned out in a semicircle at her feet. Her bound copy of the script was on a table beside her, flattened open to a scene in Mrs. Van Riis-Griffith's mansion on Fifth Avenue.

Zoe had already done at least a dozen sketches of that small parlor, and she and Frye had agreed that it was to be an informal family room, furnished with slender tables of dark wood, and on the mantelpiece several of the valuable old Greek bronzes that Mortlake later steals. Zoe went upstairs and found a small statuette in one of the breakfronts in the third-floor hall—a porcelain demoiselle actually, hardly Greek, but she brought it down and placed it near the single candelabrum on the marble mantel shelf, where it seemed quite at home.

She sketched the effect quickly at first, even adding the tall wicker vase of pampas grass in a dark corner as she had before; but now, redrawn, the scene seemed different to her, clearer, more alive. The Italian-looking pictures in old frames that she had originally thought of were already hanging on the narrow wall beside the single window. These were Grandmère's pictures, no doubt chosen and placed with her own hands, and Zoe drew them as they were, not making anything up, as she had the first time. She added the figures of a man and woman against the fireplace, wrapped in an aching embrace, Beatrice Holland's dark eyes wide with anguish over the curve of the man's shoulder. Then she carefully tore the page from its pad, leaning over to place it beside the pictures she'd done the day before.

After a while, she carried everything to her room, where she sat, feeling dazed, with her hands folded limply in her lap.

"What the hell is going on here?" she asked Edwina, who, grumpy but loyal, had followed her up the stairs. "What's the matter with me?" But, of course, she knew.

For more than half an hour, thinking constantly of the many childhood years when entrance had been explicitly forbidden, Zoe paced up and down the long, gloomy hallway in front of Grandmère's door. But finally, with a deep breath, she leaned her weight against the paneled wood and pushed. The heavy door strained inward against its expanded frame and, rocking against Zoe's steady shoulder, opened in a cloud of powdery splinters.

The room was dim, cool. The rainy afternoon light from the Mall swam through the curtains and over the maroon velvet lining of the ancient ribbon-striped portieres, which had faded into streaks of cerise and mauve. Even the jacquard embossing of the silk-covered walls seemed flattened with time, as if the air that made the pattern had somehow been *exhaled* into the room. The very figure in the carpet appeared to have vanished into a mere blur of soft color as it lay for decades in that almost magical pink air.

The long west wall was faced with ornamental plasterwork which rose in a series of arches to the ornate cornices and outlined the wide fireplace with its carved mantel. Above the fireplace was a rustic mill-house scene with poplars and a field of copper flowers, shimmering under an autumnal sky. To each side of the picture were rose crystal sconces with stubby, unevenly burned white candles still inserted into the waxy glass bobeches.

Zoe cautiously pushed the door shut behind her and stood for a minute in almost reverent silence, just on the edge of the carpet. When at last she moved slowly toward the middle of the room, her eye was caught by a small rosewood table by the bed. Bending over, she lifted one of the silver-gilt frames arranged on its dark surface, a photograph of a young boy, and was surprised to find only a thin scar in the dust on the table. There were several other pictures, too—a daguerreotype of a man in Civil War uniform, a young woman with little curls frosting her forehead and a book open in her lap, and another of the same boy, set in a crystal frame into which scallop shells had been meticulously etched. He was now obviously older, his fine nose lengthened, his eyes more knowing. On the table also was a huge conch shell, still somewhat crusty from the sea, the inner lip still glowing with color.

Zoe set the boy's picture down and went to a slim-legged French writing table set squarely in front of the windows. On the top lay a book of Shelley's poems bound in dull morocco, a stiff linen handkerchief, and several loose pen nibs. As her hand smoothed the leather desktop, a thin layer of dust formed swirls with the gentle motion of her fingers.

In the corner of the room stood an old dark wood armoire, carved at its edges with intaglio-like vines and flowers, the panels made of perfectly mitered crotch mahogany veneers. One of the tall upper doors stood slightly open, and Zoe peeked inside, inhaling the deep sweet odor that rose, even now, from the dresses still lined up inside on velvet hangers. As she reached up to open the door, intending to move it just an inch or two, the skirt of one of the dresses, evidently caught somehow on the inner hardware of the door, came with it, threatening to tear. But then, as Zoe held her breath and brought her other hand forward to free it, the dry silk seemed to loose itself and fell against her face in a shower of pink beads and yellowed seed pearls; the warm, still-pungent scent of Nuit de Noël escaped from the silk folds.

Zoe sat on the edge of the brocade-covered bed, holding the pink dress in her lap, unmindful of the sharpness of the crusty beading against her face, breathing the sweet flowery perfume through her open mouth. She sat there, curled over the dress, for quite a while.

She phoned Claudia late in the day, happy to find her home, just starting dinner. Claudia had made a quick trip to the hospital, early in the afternoon.

"Annabelle's the same, Zo," she reported, "but your brother looked pretty ghastly, all clammed up and miserable. He alternates between sitting by Annabelle's bed with his head in his hands and pacing in that smelly lounge smoking one cigarette after another. He stayed there last night, he told me. Slept in a chair."

"I know," Zoe said. "I wanted him to come home, but . . . well, maybe he'll come tonight. I have plenty of food."

"You shopped?" Claudia sounded insulted. "Oh, Zoe, why didn't you let me *drive* you? I could have—"

"No big deal, dear. I stopped on the way back from the hospital last night."

"Well, let me know next time. For heaven's sake."

Zoe smiled. "Okay."

She told Claudia about her day, giving Claudia a chuckle as she described her walk through Back Bay and along the Charles River, reminiscing about how they used to do that when they were in school together.

"Ha!" Claudia chortled. "You always wanted to collect leaves and stuff to decorate your room, and—"

"—and all you could think about was throwing rocks at the Harvard crew team," Zoe reminded her, grinning into the phone.

When Zoe asked if the invitation to lunch with Uncle Jim might still be on, Claudia responded with a spontaneous outburst of enthusiasm that actually made Zoe laugh.

"Oh! Jim will be thrilled to death. Great news, Zo. But I'm afraid it might have to wait until Thursday, if that's all right. He's down in Providence for a couple of days."

"Sounds fine," Zoe agreed, getting directions to the club. "See you then, Claud."

After she hung up, though the setting sun was obscured by pearly clouds that threatened rain again, Zoe went out to buy four rolls of thousand-speed film and wandered back in the misting air, looking at the housefronts on Commonwealth Avenue through the viewfinder of her camera. She turned down to Marlborough Street and paused, leaning against the brick facing of the old Crowninshield house on the corner of Dartmouth to watch the soft, light rain for a while, and then moved on. Despite the gathering darkness, she took a full roll of pictures of arched doorways, crenellated balconies, and ornate door knockers, stooping for interesting shots of the opulent leaded fanlights, and then climbing up a steep flight of stone steps to focus on a spray of staunch forsythia that dripped against a wrought-iron railing, thinking about some of the exteriors in *The Gilded Affair,* wondering if they could perhaps shoot them day-for-night.

At last she went home and opened a can of fancy dog food for Edwina, who leapt around her feet, whining with anticipation, her paws scraping against Zoe's jeans.

"Take it easy, my cupcake," Zoe said, laughing down at her. "Take it easy. Okay, here."

While Edwina gobbled up her supper, Zoe called Arthur at the hospital and told him that dinner could be ready whenever he was. But he was more expert at evasion than she had given him credit for.

"I'll be late, Zoe, very late," he croaked. "I'll be there, but . . . it'll be real late."

"How is she?" Zoe asked him. "Shall I come?"

"She's about the same, I guess. Well, I don't know, maybe worse. You don't have to come, though, no need . . ."

"Arthur." Zoe spoke with her eyes closed.

"Don't wait up, Zo."

After she hung up the phone, Zoe scrambled some eggs for herself and nibbled at a piece of toast while she prowled the large front parlor, looking with fascinated distaste at Annabelle's things. On a whim she made no attempt to understand, she gathered up a large trayful of porcelain and crystal knickknacks and carried them into the butler's pantry. She soaked them in the deep sink, then washed them all under hot running water, polishing each piece with a dry linen towel, holding the crystal flower baskets and bonbonnières up to the light to catch the rainbows. Then she put everything back on surfaces that she had already wiped off with a damp cloth. When she was done, she stood for a long time holding one of the heavy tarnished silver frames from Annabelle's chairside table, staring into Spencer Trefoyle's dark eyes.

She finally went upstairs to her own room and opened her bound script of *The Gilded Affair*. She sat on the bed and reread the dinner scene, the splendid party intended as a betrothal celebration. But of course no one knew that poor Laurence Thane, duped by the brilliant Mortlake, would be fleeing out the back door after the final toast, his beloved Beatrice complicit in his escape. And though Beatrice had agreed to run away with him, seeming to choose a romantic exile over solitude, not even Laurence knew that the ties of custom and family were the more compelling, that not even her passion for Laurence himself could withstand the force of that stifling power. Beatrice would not be joining him in England, and only Beatrice knew it. Zoe closed the script over her finger and lay back against her pillows thinking of the lovers' sacrifice, wondering how best to mirror all their pain and loss, set against the glitter of the dining room and the elegant forces that had flattened and destroyed them.

It was getting very late, and Zoe could feel herself sliding in and out of wakefulness. Images of Laurence and Roger, of Arthur and the boy in the etched frame in Grandmère's room, of Beatrice and the conch shell—all swimming in a dusty, reddish light—floated in and through her mind. The digital numbers of her little travel clock had just clicked midnight when she heard Arthur come in. He climbed with a heavy, slow tread up to his room, and Edwina roused herself from the rug by Zoe's bed and waddled off to find him.

When all was silence, maybe twenty minutes later, Zoe went slowly down the staircase to the kitchen to call Roger.

TWENTY-THREE

(FROM THE DIARIES OF AUGUSTA HILLYARD: 1922 TO 1925)

Monday, June 5, 1922

Anthony, a year after his father's death, is behaving in such a ragingly undisciplined fashion that one might almost imagine he was disciplined before! Whatever influence Eugene might have had over Anthony and his harsh, demanding nature is now, of course, as dead as Eugene himself, and Anthony has just plunged on, completely unrestrained. I think what has elicited such bitter and angry thoughts this afternoon is that Potter has informed me (once again I am getting my news from my servants!) that Anthony has removed Papa's port from the cellar, no doubt in aid of new enterprises in South Boston with the Trefoyle gang.

I consider the removal of the port to be theft, plain and simple, but of course I pretended to Potter that I had given Anthony permission to take it. Dear me! Whatever shall I do for port myself? But damn him! He is shortsighted and greedy, just like his father! He goes regularly to Canada to fetch illegal whisky, diamond studs firmly in place on his ever-expanding shirtfront, and devil take the hindmost! He seems to have no concern whatever for the future of his family.

Frances joined me for luncheon yesterday, along with that drab little Eugene. After dessert, sending the child out to the Mall to play with his new terrier, she wept to me that she believes Anthony has a "mistress" (the very word she used!). Of course, I commiserated; I gave her a small glass of whatever Madeira is left, and assured her that he cares very deeply for her and little Eugene. I suggested that she take her cue from me and revel as I did in the thought of a powerful and vigorous husband.

Oh, upon my word, how I dissembled! But *of course* Anthony has a mistress—it hardly bears mention! And where was our poor trusting Frances when he had the last one, and the one before that? (But let me not claim too much credit for sang-froid . . . not when I was young. Had I, as a young wife, reflected on the possibility that Eugene had such relationships, I'm sure I would have gone quite mad myself.)

J.S. has just left, and I find it very difficult to tell if I am more numb before he comes or after he has gone—in contemplation of or in reflection upon his so-infrequent visits here. . . . He has been in Boston to do yet another portrait of Belle Gardner, whom I have not seen, of course, for quite some time. John describes this one as a stark contrast to the "Pearl and Shoulder" picture he did back before Jack Gardner died. It is more somber, he tells me, the subject all veiled in white, with only her homely, aging face peeking out (the adjectives are mine). This is his only portrait in nearly fifteen years, and for her: his "patroness." As he spoke, I thought of my own painting, and the memories of that early time shuddered through the decades to my heart. Am I jealous of that dying, dried-up old woman in her fake palazzo on the Fenway because she can command another portrait of this man? I cringe to tell it, but I am. Ah, the flashes of anger that come to me these days! It seems that I have kept what I most anticipated losing: whatever fuel there is in me to kindle anger and its surrogates is obviously not yet depleted.

We spoke of his travels, of England in the summer, and all the excitement of his life in the three years since last he came to see me. But even as I laughed and gaily offered him another finger sandwich, I felt so diminished, so small and weakened, that even his dear presence could not drive it out, and my joy in his visit was a poor thing at best.

Yet I somehow managed to see him to the door as if he were just another glamorous caller in a life lavished with tea parties and fine conversation. . . . And now he is gone, his empty teacup itself a secret from all save Veronica.

We have had the first satisfactory snowfall of the season, just in time for Christmas. My holiday shopping is not quite complete, as I have determined that Veronica *will* have those cashmere gloves I heard her remark upon to Flora just the other morning. However, I have decided to put that final errand off until tomorrow and to spend this snowy afternoon finishing my book.

Last summer I drowned myself in the novels of Mrs. Austen and the poems of Lord Tennyson, and even translations of Turgenev and Flaubert, but I am back to the more fashionable "mainstream." I have occupied a good part of the last four days reading Mrs. Wharton's latest effort, *The Age of Innocence,* reflecting somewhat dispiritedly on her story of a failed romance and the great power of families to consolidate themselves toward fulfillment of a common goal. The unhappy lovers notwithstanding, the book is in so many ways a discourse on the strength of The Family that it should be the inspiration that I yearn for, but somehow it is not. The "matriarch figure" appeals to me in an odd and perhaps too self-regarding way, but I do not seem able to emulate the steely insouciance with which she wields her power. . . . All in all, apart from the interest of the story, this book is about a vanished world, a dead world. The war took care of much of it, and solitude more or less takes care of the rest. . . . As I lie here tonight, drowsy and out of sorts, I feel a dwindling that I seem powerless to stop. It's as if someone has run off with the ball of yarn that is myself and though I stretch out my arms to stop the runner, they unravel with the gesture.

Not fifteen minutes ago, Flora shut the front door on one of my increasingly frequent visits from Frances. Now that she is feeling a trifle stronger, having lain abed all summer with an ailment for which the doctors could do nothing but throw up their hands, she calls on us at least three times a week, and I cannot bring myself to be impatient with her. She tells me that Anthony and her precious papa have had words over the nature of Anthony's investments. I hardly know whether his latest encounter with the almighty dollar is to his ultimate advantage or not, but evidently this business of "importing" scotch whisky from Canada has proved remunerative indeed, and he has taken the profits thereof out of Trefoyle's hands. Trefoyle, or so Frances reports, has thrown him out with enthusiasm, and Anthony, in turn, has chuckled all the way to the stock exchange, where he has used this money to purchase shares under some strange arrangement that Alex tells me is called "on margin."

I have been perusing the *Times* to try to understand this concept. It sounds foolish and risky to me to put down a fraction of the price of the stock. If the shares fell in value, one would need to scramble rather furiously to come up with the rest of the money! But this arrangement seems to suit Anthony just fine; the notion of something for nothing has always appealed to him—he finds restraint a bore.

He has thus abandoned the Trefoyle connection, apparently without a backward glance, seeming to believe that the opulent style of life to which he so heartily subscribes will never fade. His old mother could certainly tell him that nothing is forever, but I suppose he will have to learn that for himself. This may or may not become my problem. Time will tell.

Monday, July 21, 1924

Mere hours ago I returned alone and on foot from Belle Gardner's funeral at the Church of the Advent over on Brimer Street. As I approached, I saw the grandees going into the church, and I had fully expected to join them myself, but when I reached the police barricade, although I was at the very front of the huddled masses, I knew at once that I lacked the assurance to push my way inside, to declare myself of the proper caste to do so.

I saw Pickmans, Snells, Ameses, the odd Cabot going in, as well as little Fannie Mason, haunches twitching with importance, claiming a place, I shouldn't wonder, very much toward the front pews. I saw Anne Lowell, also, though she did not notice me. I stood there, transfixed behind the police lines, at the foot of Beacon Hill, where I spent my happy childhood, and suddenly my thoughts were of myself and not of

Belle. Ought the hoi polloi, I wondered, the outsiders (the Widow Hillyard among them), be permitted to catch a beam of reflected glory from Mrs. Jack's cortège? . . . I shrank back, all at once fearing to be seen, and left before the crowd dispersed. I made my way back home, where I gained my room before my own trembling began.

Though I will surely not miss Belle, and do not grieve for her, ironically enough I do have something to remember her by, and I gaze upon my portrait even now, looking over my shoulder at it as I pause in my writing. In the three or four years that it has been back in its spot beside the fireplace I have occasionally wondered if it is too large for this room and whether it might not be such a bad idea to move it back to the drawing room, where the proportions are so much more congenial and where, the truth be known, I might be looking at it less. Every time I look at that youthful, smiling face, I am refreshed somehow, and yet I seem to shun those feelings—I seem to turn my back on memories of the remembered joy it brings, for it is remembered only and thus twice removed.

Is this the same Augusta Hillyard? This somewhat stout and silver-haired old dear who sits here now, scribbling away? And yet if I put the painting back downstairs, won't everyone look at it and remark: "Oh, my, my . . . Augusta Hillyard is not what she was."

Thursday, April 23, 1925

It distresses me that I have not been feeling well of late. I think I have always taken a robust constitution too much for granted, and as I approach my sixty-third year, such an assumption probably shows some failure to have achieved a concomitant wisdom. Things that I imagined I would do once liberated by the passing of Mr. Eugene Hillyard no longer appeal to me, and I am forced, as I sit without occupation in my room on this wet spring day, to wonder if perchance I miss him. Isn't that remarkable? I might be missing Eugene! Whatever lack of cordiality we experienced in our last years together, he gave me, by his very existence, some sense of my place in the scheme of things, and now I see that I must seek out my own. . . . A tricky business, this widowhood. I find myself looking to Anne, who has now borne her widowhood for decades, for inspiration, but find none in her example: simple endurance is not my wish, however it may be my lot.

Thursday, October 1, 1925

The Trefoyles have this morning taken their daughter to the Irish graveyard in South Boston. I would not have thought that I would mourn the
passing of our Frances as I do. In the twelve years that Frances was a
Hillyard, I think she came to look to me as her only source of friendship. This was a burden that I did not shoulder with any pleasure, but
because her husband is my eldest child, and a fearsome one at that, I
made the effort. I suppose I gave her some small comforts and she clung
to that slim giving, having little else. I hope I did . . . but, oh!—how
could I have known that any crumb that fell from my table was a loaf
to Frances? I treated her as I did, and that inadequately, because—or
in spite of—the fact that she was a Trefoyle. That is my sin to bear.

I think what saddens me most is that her little life was just so pale,
so passionless! Thirty-four meager years undistinguished by any passion
aroused in any mortal on this earth, even herself. Our dear, poor
Frances had all of the superficial advantages and nothing of the inner fire
that makes it possible to live. And what can kindle such a blaze? Possibly the feeling that one is loved, if only by oneself?

It has never been my wont to speak (or write, even here) of "Love":
I have not been a sentimental girl for half a century. And yet, I did not
truly love her either. I might have learned to; I don't know. And now
whatever was eating at her bones has done its work and I will never
know. Mere fondness is never enough, I think—only consuming passion gives humanity.

We gathered this morning in the church where she and Anthony
were married twelve years ago and lined up on either side of the aisle
as we did then: Annabelle, Alex, and I on the "groom's" side. Anthony
sat with us because he is still the "robber bridegroom," still deeply out
of favor (at his own devising) with his wife's hoary progenitor. The Trefoyles had somewhat more impressive representation, since the old
man brought his many hangers-on to make a show—I'm sure for his
own satisfaction and not for Frances.

I had roses for her, and Annabelle sent a lovely spray of asters and
chrysanthemums, and there were hothouse lilies by the score. Little Eugene sat next to Mary Trefoyle, dry of eye and staring straight ahead.
But as I glanced around the church I noticed a face among the Trefoyle
family circle that I had not seen before. I learned later from Anthony

that this is the shadowy and mysterious Spencer, eldest child and scion, who has traveled back from his affairs in New Mexico, where Anthony says he has been for many years—presumably come back out of affection for his sister.

I thought that quite strange, as in my growing relationship with poor Frances over the last number of years I never heard her mention him nor any message from him. And yet he was there—looking very prepossessing, rather like what I imagine Padraic Trefoyle, the old devil, may have looked like in his youth. In figure, too, he is very like his father—a large man, not conventionally handsome—yet, unlike his father, silent beyond respect for death or priest. Silent, I suspect, deep into his nature. Alex told me later that he, Spencer, is here to stay for a while. Whether it is indeed his sister's funeral that occasions his return, or whether he has been summoned pursuant to Anthony's defection from Trefoyle's embrace, who can say?

All in all, a fairly exotic creature, yet one I doubt that we shall see again.

Thursday, November 19, 1925

My walk along the river was a somber one today. We have had a week of leaden weather, and all the autumn glory is now gone. Even the broad, honey-colored leaves I look forward to each year are now too dry to cling another day to the branches of the tree across the way— they have fallen at last, blowing in great swirls even as I paused to watch. In doing so, they have exposed our brave and stalwart bough, the one that survived that lightning storm some years ago. Each fall as the leaves blow away, I watch for it to reappear, taking heart at this symbol (for so I must call it) that Nature's other fire gave us as a gift. It seems to me that if that dead bough can stand fast amidst green glory in the spring and in the flames of autumn, so can I. . . .

I wended my way home along the embankment, vaguely planning to amuse myself a bit by a visit with Annabelle (who has been keeping very much to her room these days) and to liven us both up with a glass of sherry (safely hidden by dear Potter!). I climbed slowly up the stairs and entered, as I thought, an empty house, it lacking still more than an hour to dinnertime. As it had been thought that I would take an informal tea with the Wheelwrights, I was not expected, and both Veronica and Potter, as well as the girls, had been given the afternoon to their own devices.

But I had scarcely taken off my hat when I thought I heard noises from upstairs. Thinking perhaps that Annabelle had one of her old chums in to visit, I went to join them. As has been my custom for all the thirty-five years of my daughter's life, I rapped lightly on the door of her room and immediately entered, amazed to find, at this late hour of the afternoon, the bedclothes in violent disarray, unmistakable articles of masculine attire strewn on the floor, on the armchair, and on the bed itself . . . and through the slightly open door to the dressing room, the even more unmistakable sound of murmurings, the aftermath of passion spent, perchance reviving.

I can write this now at midnight, many dark hours having passed. I crept off like an intruder to my own room, where I locked the door and sat on the edge of the bed for I don't know how long, still in my coat and overshoes.

I hear my daughter's voice even now—that harsh and breathy sound I can remember in my own throat—"Spencer . . . please, please . . ." I cannot gauge the magnitude of the embrace I almost interrupted.

I should be resigned, I suppose, to the attacks of the Trefoyles upon my family; surely after all these years I might have grown more used to that. And yet my sense of humor flees this scene. I rather thought that once the break was effected between Anthony and Padraic and once poor Frances found her grave, we would have no more Trefoyles in our lives, in our thoughts, in our pocketbooks, and surely not in our bedrooms! It seems I was mistaken. But damn it! *Not in my house!*

Friday, November 20, 1925

I am appalled at Annabelle's defense of her indefensible behavior and the horrid, disrespectful way she screamed at me to mind my own business. It is damn well my business what goes on beneath my roof! If Annabelle wishes to play the slut, she must do it elsewhere. I have turned the other way for years . . . I have winked at "house parties," at staying out all night, at balls in New York and late suppers in Providence, but I do not think that I can wink at Spencer Trefoyle naked in my daughter's bedroom. That there may be solace, advantage, happiness there for my Annabelle is, of course, impossible. I can comfort myself at least in knowing she did not realize that I had seen her tumbled sheets—she believes that I am aware merely of his presence in my house. Whatever I will do about this, I just don't know.

$\mathcal{B}$y Wednesday morning the buds of the lilacs on the dining-room table were plump almost to bursting; the antler-like branches yearned toward the light that seemed to bounce off the housefronts on the "sunny side," two hundred feet across the Mall, where the famous magnolias that lined Commonwealth Avenue from the Public Garden to Kenmore Square were a blur of color in the sun beyond the window.

But Zoe was not interested in magnolias. She stood in the arched doorway to the dining room, frowning at the dusty furniture, at the pallor of the light shed by the crusted chandelier, and tried to imagine the characters from *The Gilded Affair* toasting Laurence and Beatrice around her Grandmère's table.

She moved across to the kitchen doorway and regarded the room more critically from that long angle. It showed to such disadvantage in the morning light; she wished she could rip down the velvet drapes, fringe and all, scrub the lacework sheers behind them, paint the ornate cornices, strip away the greasy wallpaper, make it all new, make it as it surely once had been. It occurred to her that with the exception of Annabelle, and possibly Jim Forbes, no one now living had ever seen the room as it was meant to be, set with Grandmère's crystal and china, the chandelier blazing with light.

She went into the butler's pantry off the kitchen and opened the ceiling-high cupboard doors. When she'd looked for a vase for the lilacs Sunday night, she'd been amazed to see, stored in newspapers that told of the deaths of reigning princes, stack after stack of Grandmère's precious china—service for twenty-four of antique Coalport, rimmed nearly to their centers in gold leaf. There were dinner plates, platters, and service pieces, as well as three sizes of bread and butter, salad and dessert, soup plates and small fruit dishes with matching saucers— even bone dishes and finger bowls—all wrapped in paper that had been folded only once.

The good crystal was in the lower section, packed in pale blue tissue—twenty-four each of goblets, hock wine, white wine, champagnes, cordials—rimmed in gold just like the china, a thin, perfect stripe around each spotless, unchipped edge. Zoe paused to wonder who had packed all this away as if no further use was dreamed of.

The silver was a problem. The chests that held it all were constructed into the paneled cupboards under the long pantry table. There were two services for twenty-four; one was rather plain except for a thin, elegant "L" monogram, but the other, as if in deliberate contrast, was extravagantly ornate, each piece tipped with a deep scallop shell. The bowls of the fluted dessert spoons were gilded with vermeil. But every single piece was so tarnished that the designs were blackened into ambiguity, only the powerful shell forms were resistant to the years that separated Zoe's hand from the last that held each fork.

"I'll have to make it up," she muttered to herself, placing the silver carefully back into the velvet-lined compartments. "I guess I'll just make it up. . . ."

When the table was all set, crystal and Coalport placed in perfect alignment down the long mahogany table on the sheet Zoe took from her own bed for a cloth, each place marked off by the oddments of scarred silver Arthur and Annabelle used every day, there was a grotesquerie to it that made Zoe furious with herself because she knew better. Though the dishes and glasses were clean, the ugly flatware and the flowered bedsheet looked foolish and out of place. It was ridiculous— a mistake and a waste of time.

Zoe leaned against the molding of the doorway and then slid down to the floor, her knees touching her chin. "Shit, it looks just awful," she whispered to herself, pushing her hair back. From floor level it looked

2 3 7

like a random collection for a flea market. Despite the gleam of the clean goblets and the gold-bordered plates, it was completely without magic.

"Do it *right,* bean-brain," Zoe said aloud through her teeth and got up again, knees creaking. She went back to the silver chests and took out twenty each of the scallop-shell pieces—even pickle forks and serving spoons—and placed all she could carry on a towel laid in the bottom of the kitchen sink. She went back and got the rest, including twenty fish knives she found in the bottom drawer, the sugar tongs, and twenty of the ornate butter spreaders, and went to work.

It took more than an hour of intense, unbroken activity to polish it all. Once started, she felt compelled to do a perfect job and went through three or four sponges, using nearly half of the almost new jar of Wright's Silver Cream she found, taking its very presence under the sink as an omen.

She went back into the dining room, stripped the table, and then ran upstairs to the linen closet, where, under piles of unmatched bedsheets and frayed towels, she found several dozen ecru damask tablecloths and napkins. All were yellowed at their creases, many were frayed or torn, but she chose the best ones and set the table again, replacing the plates and crystal and adding serving pieces and all the silver she had polished, laying out the guests' places to the fourth fork.

Then she set the budding lilacs in the center of the table. On each side she placed the matching sterling silver vases, now brilliantly polished, that she'd found in the cupboard under the pantry sink. As Zoe moved back to make sure they were precisely centered, magically, they began to fill with pink tea roses and maidenhair. Even Claudia's lilacs seemed to blossom out, the thick purple cones of the flowers casting shadows on the damask cloths, whose discolorations had all, somehow, disappeared.

Zoe stood back, wide-eyed, exhilarated, knowing that much of this was only her imagination. But even as she thought that, a large basket of white orchids from the Van Riis conservatory appeared on the buffet next to the old Hillyard majolica tureen. Gasping, she ran through the house, collecting all the candleholders she could find—cut crystal, silver filigree, gilt vermeil—and brought them to the table, imagining that perhaps Beatrice Holland herself would light the candles.

When all was perfection, just as Laurence Thane was about to escort his beloved to the table, Zoe began to sketch the scene she had created. As her pencil sped across the heavy paper, the guests took their places in Augusta Hillyard's deep mahogany chairs and raised her sparkling goblets to Beatrice, who sat to the right of her betrothed. The multiple strands of the Holland family pearls shone against her throat.

Zoe moved urgently around the table, leaning over shoulders, inhaling the deep perfume that surrounded the ladies, at one point standing on a spare chair for perspective, then falling to her knees, seeking a new angle for Frye's camera. The warm candlelight of Mrs. Van Riis-Griffith's dining room replaced the shadows cast by the filthy Hillyard chandelier. Zoe, her thighs pressed against the table rim, drew Beatrice's face behind the pink tea roses, framed by the gleaming bared shoulders of the ladies and the smooth beards of the gentlemen.

She moved to the far wall for a moment and looked at her sketch pad, overwhelmed by what she saw there; she barely remembered doing it, but it was wonderful: crisp, evocative, the angles and perspectives absolutely right. Though the drawings were, of course, in pencil, Zoe could almost see the colors that would someday come—the ladies' satin décolletage, the blushing flowers, the fine gold borders of the china plates. Almost breathless, she leaned against the wall, her hand over her mouth, entranced by her own inspiration.

She left the image of the dinner guests frozen at the table—Grandmère's hock wines inches from their lips—and ran into the drawing room, where she stood in the middle of the huge, dusty Sarouk, her heart thudding in her chest. Ignoring Annabelle's bed, the television, and the shabby velvet chair, Zoe turned her attention toward the window, her eyes taking in everything at once, one pencil in her teeth, another in her hand.

Suddenly, in the wide sweep of the bay window she saw a gilt bamboo jardiniere filled with primulas and camellias. Zoe imagined that eccentric old Lavinia Van Riis-Griffith sat beside it, her book of verses facedown in her lap, and quickly drew some close-ups of the old lady and her granddaughter, Beatrice, and of Laurence Thane beside her, flirting with a handsome smile as he accepted a chocolate from a silver candy dish (the one Zoe had polished only yesterday!), his dove-gray gloves across his thigh. She framed the trio with yellow silk portieres, and added potted palms and Boston ferns in immense chinoiserie pots.

Leaving those drawings on the parlor floor, Zoe took the pad back to the dining room. She imagined that the dessert had been served while she was sketching in the parlor and the tall silver compote of strawberries and *framboises* gleamed in the candlelight. As Zoe drew them in, her eyes leaping constantly from the page, Laurence Thane, mindful of his role as bridegroom, rose to propose a toast to his intended, his champagne glass trembling in his hand, his eyes glistening with the knowledge that the carriage that would spirit him away to safety was even then arriving at the door.

And finally, she drew Beatrice Holland with her white hand on Laurence's sleeve, looking with such love into his eyes, knowing, of course, that fulfillment of that love would have to wait, perhaps forever.

Moving backward, Zoe realized that the *mise-en-scène* she had created had somehow formed itself into concentric circles—she had been too close before to see it. Each guest and table setting formed a circle around Laurence and Beatrice as they stood at the head of the table, embraced, as it were, by the context. Zoe, feeling almost like a guest herself, stood in the arch of the doorway while Laurence completed his toast, seeing that concentricity for the first time—perhaps at the very moment when Laurence himself began to see it—understanding as she never had before that *The Gilded Affair* was not just an adventure, or a crime story with fancy Victorian trappings, nor even a tale of sad young lovers doomed to part. It was also about the family—its order, its endurance, and its strength.

It was full afternoon by the time Zoe had put everything back as she had found it, left her sketchbooks in her room, and bounded down the steps to the sidewalk. Inspired by an intuition she never questioned, she ran to the hospital, convinced that Annabelle was a last indispensable link between Zoe herself and what had happened in the dining room.

Sitting again at the foot of the bed, Zoe took her small sketch pad from her bag and drew her great-aunt as she once had been—full of color, definition, shine. She sketched a face recalled from photographs unseen for years: the coquette's glance, the debutante's brilliant, laughing eyes. And then, in another corner of the page, the uncertain smile of the woman who had loved Spencer Trefoyle to such distraction; it was a face seamed with lost love and regret. Finally, she turned another page and drew Annabelle Hillyard as she was right then—mere hours from her death.

But as the pencil moved, other shapes gathered into Zoe's drawing and a new concentricity began to form. Looking up, astonished, she saw them arrange themselves behind the bed—at first only as shadows, wandering in as had the guests at the betrothal banquet. And suddenly, although their faces were obscured, Zoe knew them for what they were: all the dead Hillyards, and one irresistible Trefoyle, the infrastructure of Annabelle's long life, not well lived, now ending.

Annabelle seemed to rise in her bed to welcome them. Under Zoe's resurrecting fingers the faintest blush returned to those pale cheeks; the platinum eyes danced with their familiar malicious sparkle. Great rings flashed on her plump hands; her silver bracelets were crusty with amethysts and fire opals.

Then the striped hospital curtains on their aluminum rails swept back to become the fringed portieres from the drawing room on Commonwealth Avenue. Their color was deep and fresh, the velvet new and smooth, and as they parted, the circle of ghosts widened, and yet another shape came forth. It was Grandmère, regal in her pink beaded gown, benevolent and calm, looking with eyes of infinite depth into Zoe's face, the silk of her gown rustling in the winds from Zoe's mind.

Zoe got up from her chair and moved toward the window, hoping to illuminate herself in the backlighting of the April evening. Though she was perfectly aware she'd made it all up and that Annabelle still lay there, her glamour silenced forever, Zoe knew this for the inspired recognition that it was—no bold scenarios, no daydreams . . . only truth:

You cannot leave us out! she cried to her vision of Grandmère. There are just Arthur and Zoe now. We are what's left of you.

TWENTY-FIVE

Z oe persuaded Arthur to come back for the night, and they walked through the dusky streets all the way home. Arthur took a shower and then stood in his fresh clothes leaning against the refrigerator with a glass of wine while Zoe made their dinner, silently watching as she crushed tarragon leaves against her palm.

They carried their food into the dining room and moved the lilacs, edging closer to their flooding bloom, down to the end of the table. Zoe noticed that for some reason, when she put Grandmère's things away early in the afternoon, she had missed two of the heavy lead crystal wineglasses and some pieces of the silver, too. Obviously a slight Freudian lapse, she thought wryly as she set the table with the beautiful shell-tipped forks and knives that she had "forgotten" to store away. If Arthur noticed, he made no comment, but she saw him balance his gleaming fork in both hands for a moment before he used it, touching the strong carving of the shell forms with his fingertips.

Arthur ate with a businesslike attention that seemed more self-preserving, instinctual, than indicative of any pleasure in the meal. She knew that these were foods he liked, had added the water chestnuts to her basket the other evening at the market remembering how much he loved them. He had once told her that he enjoyed foods as much for the way they felt in his teeth as for the way they tasted, but now he chewed his dinner, washed down with unsavored swallows of the warming wine, as if it were nothing more than cardboard.

They sat there, eating mechanically, the conversation desultory and boring, focused on nonsense like cooking and some pointless gossip about one of the nurses whom Zoe didn't know and surely didn't care about.

How can he resist me? she thought, and felt a rising in her that she could not name. She had been in Boston more than five days and they had barely been alone. So much to talk about, and so far nothing had been said. She realized that if the plunge into the unspoken were to be taken, she would have to be the one to do it. She thought of Claudia's words last Sunday: in some ways, she had said, Arthur's feelings are absolutely transparent, but he never talks about them.

Zoe felt a sudden flood of something similar to anger, though so mixed with other feelings she could not identify the parts for what they were. It's happening again, she thought. This is just exactly the way it was ten years ago! This is how that started! And as always, it was Annabelle who came between them. Now, even with death approaching, it was as if a part of Annabelle's self remained alert, able to make use of any opportunity at all, up to and including her own death, to keep Zoe and Arthur apart.

That afternoon at the hospital, Zoe had been standing with her back against the window, still trying to catch her breath, when Jack Mainwaring had stuck his head in the door and motioned her into the hall.

"Where's Arthur?"

"In the lounge, I guess."

"Good, let him stay there; it's you I want. How are you guys doing with the social worker?" Zoe blinked; not even movie producers were so blunt.

"We're not," she answered, trying to come back to the here and now. "In fact, we haven't even gone over the papers together. I looked through them the other morning, but I can't fill them out by myself."

"Arthur needs a good swift kick from somebody," Mainwaring said. "He's dropped out of all this a little soon. After all, he has her power of attorney, and he's the one's got to make some decisions here." He looked peeved and affronted, as if Annabelle were not dying on his schedule.

Zoe looked up and down the hall and pulled him by his sleeve around the corner. "I don't actually see why we have to go through this routine with the social worker, anyway," she said in a low voice. "Annabelle's going to *die,* Dr. Mainwaring. Why does she need a nursing home?"

Mainwaring shrugged, not especially annoyed at the question. "Averages. As I said the other day, there's lots of odds-making in medicine. She could linger on. I've seen it time and again—not get better, you understand, just linger. Or not. And if not, a power of attorney, as I'm sure you know, ends with death, so Arthur'd better get on the stick."

He looked at his watch and made a gesture toward a closing elevator down the hall as if Zoe had made him miss something more important.

"I think you'd better talk to him regardless," he said, "and get those papers filled out and back to the girls downstairs toot sweet."

"What if we refuse?" Zoe said. "What if we decide we just want her to stay here until she dies?"

Mainwaring frowned, not sure how to respond. People did not generally talk back to him.

"Uh, you can't." His hard blue eyes fogged a bit.

It was Zoe's turn to shrug. "Sure we can. We'll just pay—isn't that the issue, after all? Paying for all this . . . splendor?"

"Can you kids afford it?"

"I think that's our business," Zoe said softly.

"Miss Hillyard!"

"Listen, do you really think my brother and I believe that anyone in this whole place gives a rat's ass what happens to our aunt as long as you people get your money?"

"It's not that simple," Mainwaring said, looking over his shoulder and drawing her into the nearby stairwell. "You have to understand, Zoe— may I call you Zoe?—she could go on and on, believe me." He smiled, showing perfect teeth; his silver hair gleamed in the harsh fluorescent light. Zoe was uncharmed.

"Yes. Well, I've been in there all afternoon," she said, "and I don't think she can last the night—not *two* nights, anyhow. You're her doctor, for God's sake."

Mainwaring passed a hand over his face and leaned against the iron stair rail.

"All right," he said slowly, taking a box of Newports from his lab coat pocket. "How do you think Arthur would feel about a no-code order?'

"What's that?" Zoe folded her arms and stood up as straight as she could. Their eyes were level.

"It means 'do not resuscitate' . . . so if she codes—goes into cardiac arrest, pulmonary arrest, strokes out—they will not revive her." He looked at her carefully through the curling smoke. "Think Arthur would sign off on that?"

"No monitors? No tubes?"

"I'll take the NG tube out, but I can't disconnect the IV."

"What's in there, anyway?"

"Just fluid—hydration. That has to stay."

Zoe considered, making him wait.

Mainwaring sighed and put the cigarette out on the cement floor of the stairwell. "Zoe, she's ninety-one years old. She's about a hundred pounds overweight. She's had at least three strokes and I don't know how many TIAs. Her kidney function is badly compromised, as I told you the other day."

"So there's nothing left for her? No miracle?"

He shook his head. "No."

Vividly remembering that conversation, Zoe took some wine into her mouth and let it sit there for a second, stinging her tongue. She consciously kept her eyes on her plate, knowing she had to pull herself together before she spoke. She swallowed the wine, took another sip, and looked across the table at her brother.

"Arthur," she began, laying down her fork, holding her hands together in her lap. "Arthur, I had a talk with Dr. Mainwaring today. . . . Arthur?"

His blue eyes flicked up once from the water chestnut speared on his fork, and down again. "Yeah?"

"We talked about something called a no-code order. He said it means—"

"I know what it means, Zoe," Arthur said softly.

"Well, maybe you . . . we . . . should . . ."

"Zoe, I told you the other night that I've decided that she's coming back here just as soon as she—"

Zoe's hands came up from her lap as of their own accord and reached toward him.

"Arthur, please. We have to have some sort of common sense here, some sort of plan. He told me she can't; he said that when she . . ."

Arthur had put his fork down, and his hands were in fists on either side of his plate; a fine mottling suffused his face as he spoke. "I'm going to bring her home, and—"

"Oh, Arthur, darling, don't you see, she not going to make it through the weekend!"

"She's not dead yet!" Arthur rose from his chair, which rocked but did not quite fall; his face flushed with uneven dark colors. "You come back here after ten years . . . and then you . . . you come right in here just like—"

"Arthur!" Zoe stood up in a single movement as if her body had been yanked up by the word itself.

"I can take care of her—I always have and I always *will!* She took care of *us,* or don't you remember, for years and years! She was—"

"Arthur! *Jesus!*"

"You don't care one bit, you—"

"That's *not true!*"

"I love her and you don't!"

All at once, from one second to the next, Arthur burst into loud, hiccoughing sobs; tears covered his cheeks, adding shine and dimension to the livid blotchiness that faded as suddenly as it had come. He nearly fell back into the chair, his head down, his hands over his face.

Zoe knelt beside him, his half-full wineglass in her hand. He wept with heaving breathless sobs, his face reddening with the blood now flowing back down into his head.

"Have a sip," she whispered, one hand on his shoulder. "Just a sip, come on . . ."

He inhaled and swallowed some of the wine.

"Oh, God, I don't want her to die, she's so . . . Here we are having such a nice dinner . . . and the birthday party and everything . . . and she's . . . she's . . ."

"Shhh. Have another sip." Zoe kept her hand on his shoulder while he finished the wine and then bent over him and took two wrinkled tissues from the pocket of her slacks.

"Blow."

Arthur blew his nose and wiped his wet face. "I'm sorry, Zo. I'm sorry, but I'm . . ." He got up and went into the kitchen to get more tissues from the box on the counter. Zoe followed him and stood in the doorway, terrified that it had happened so fast—just as it had ten years before.

"Tell me why you love her so much," she said suddenly in a strange, raspy voice. "Why did you choose her over me?"

Arthur turned around with a glass of water in his hand and looked straight at her as if this was the first moment in his life he had ever understood who his sister really was.

"How could you love her more than me?" Zoe whispered again, and shivered at his answer.

"I didn't, Zoe. I don't now," he said, looking at her down the length of the kitchen with a clarity she had never seen in him before. "I didn't 'choose' her, Zo. It was only that she needed me so much more than you did. You were so strong, so sure of what you wanted—I never thought you needed anything from me."

He moved a few feet toward her and then stopped again, his myopic wet eyes staring into hers. They stood in tableau facing each other across a yard of empty space.

"She had nowhere else to turn to for it, but to me," Arthur said softly. "Can you see that, Zoe? Can you? I don't think Spencer ever loved her, and I believe she came to realize that, in a part of her mind, anyway. Zoe, I never asked myself if she loved me back; it didn't seem to matter particularly. When I lost you ten years ago I think I just gave up somehow, holed up here with her. Annabelle became all there was for me to love, so I gave her all I had."

He put down the glass of water and leaned toward her, his eyes full behind his spectacles, magnified by fresh, waiting tears.

"Zoe, I wanted so much to go to L.A. ten years ago—to come with you, follow you there, to tell you how sorry I was that I let you . . . made you . . . My God, when you got in that taxi, I thought for a while that I'd died. Literally. I didn't leave the house for days after that, I just . . ."

"I begged you," Zoe said finally. She had stood listening to him, struck dumb by what he had said. "I begged you to try to pull away, to help yourself, Arthur . . . just to help yourself." She imagined her voice rising with the words; it seemed she was shouting them across the room to him, though she could do no more than whisper.

"I know. I knew it then, too, but I couldn't, Zo, I just couldn't . . . care about myself, somehow. I was just too full of feelings to explain it, even to myself. When you came from Italy that day I knew right away that you were frightened, exhausted, needing so much, and I couldn't stand it—I didn't want to see it. I needed you to be as strong as you always had been. Oh, Zoe, even now I don't . . ."

Arthur threw his arms out in a gesture of anger and pain and then sat down at the table, his face in his hands again.

"There wasn't anybody else to love her—nobody else, do you see? Nobody to feel as sorry for her as I did, to regret her shallow, empty life. Don't you think I know she's a bitter, self-centered, frivolous old bitch? Of course I know that. But in a way she almost couldn't help it. What did she ever have, after all? Spencer? That bastard? After a while she couldn't even dine out on being a Hillyard anymore—nobody cared about the fancy Hillyards. But that was all she ever really had—being a Hillyard. My God, she was behaving like this season's debutante until two weeks ago, Zo."

Zoe thought of the bracelet of fire opals she had drawn on those fat, blue wrists, so bruised by the IV line. "You could have taken care of her, Arthur. I never said you should abandon her. I only meant . . . your own life, your music . . . the life we used to scheme about when we were kids . . ." Zoe wrapped her arms tight around herself. "I so much wanted you to have a life, Arthur. A real life."

Arthur looked up at her, squinting, and took a deep, ragged breath. "I knew that," he said, "but I couldn't seem to . . ."

He gulped and looked down at his open hands. "Zoe, she lost everybody. Don't you see? There had to be someone left to be all hers."

Arthur got up and went into the dining room and carried their dinner plates back to the kitchen, where he set them on the floor for Edwina, who came running. Zoe followed him and cleared the rest of the things off the table, leaning around him to put them in the kitchen sink, except for the two beautiful wineglasses. She set them carefully on the counter and turned to him.

"Did you understand all this then? Ten years ago? In these terms?" Zoe's black eyes were on his face, and Arthur looked down at her a moment before he answered.

"No . . . no. It kills me to say it, but I don't actually think I began to see *any* of it until she had the stroke and I knew she was going to die at last."

Arthur shook his head slowly, his eyes on the floor. "Zoe, I've only loved a few people in my whole life, only just a few, not many more than I can count on the fingers of one hand, and when Claudia told me you were coming back, I started to think . . ."

Arthur broke off and looked up at the ceiling light, his lips pressed hard against his teeth. "You have to go back to California soon, don't you?"

Zoe remembered the magical scene at the dining-room table, and for a second she thought she could smell the imaginary orchids in their overflowing basket. Finally she said, "Yes, I do."

Zoe told him then about the conversation she'd had with Mainwaring in the stairwell outside Annabelle's room. Arthur did not interrupt her as she spoke, her hands on his arms, smoothing the soft fabric of his sleeves.

"So if she has a heart attack or something, they won't, uh . . . revive her, or whatever?"

"That's right." Zoe reached up and put her arms around her brother's sloping shoulders. She could smell him, a spicy scent made of wine, cigarettes, woody aftershave.

"It's time for her to die, dear," she said. "I think she's ready. Why don't you do this last thing for her and let her go?"

"Oh, Zoe, I don't want her to suffer," Arthur said, his words muffled by her sweater. "I couldn't stand to think that she was suffering . . . in pain."

Zoe leaned back and put her hands on the sides of his wet face and wiped his tears away with her thumbs.

"Arthur, I promise you she is not suffering," she said.

Arthur took a deep breath and exhaled it through his mouth. "Could you possibly stay until . . . until she dies?"

Zoe thought of the Hillyards gathered around Annabelle's bed, of Grandmère come to get her daughter.

"Yes," she said. "Yes, I will."

TWENTY-SIX

*I*t was fairly late when Arthur took Edwina out for an extended walk. While he was gone, Zoe finished up the dishes and then sat alone in the murky light of the dining room. A single shell-tipped spoon was still on the tabletop, forgotten, and she sat rubbing the end between two fingers. She couldn't get over what Arthur had said about having loved so little in his life—or so few people, as he'd put it, for there was a difference, and Zoe knew he realized that. She was heartsick at a loneliness so intense that one might feel a need to comfort oneself with such a list, and then be desolate to find it short indeed.

After a while, Zoe turned off the lights in the kitchen and the dining room and went slowly up the stairs. In her room she dug inside her bag for the old snapshot of herself and Arthur and stared fixedly at it until, on an impulse she had no desire to identify or curb, she jumped up and ran to Grandmère's room, pausing in the doorway, leaning for a second on the frame.

None of the lightbulbs worked, so she lit the stubby candle ends still in their sconces. She looked carefully, as she had not the day before, at the objects on the mantel—a pretty inlaid orangewood clock, and a collection of small porcelain hinged boxes among which were placed old photographs in tarnished silver frames. Zoe reached for one that was the same size as her snapshot and with only the slightest hesitation removed the thin cardboard backing and the blurry photo of a lady. She tapped the picture of the children into place, swiveling the little tabs to hold it in. For a moment she thought she should put the lady back, believing that she was without prerogative here, without entitlement to snoop, to rearrange. But such scruples were silenced somehow by the comfort of finding her own face on Grandmère's mantel.

Just then, one of the candle ends sputtered and went out. Zoe sat for a few moments on the foot of the bed, staring thoughtfully into the gloom, and then went downstairs to the kitchen, where, earlier, she had noticed some spare lightbulbs in a cupboard. Back in Grandmère's room, she screwed them into the lamps on either side of the bed and on the writing table. Then she went to the wall switch near the door and flipped it on, waiting with clenched teeth for fuses to blow all the way to Philadelphia.

But, no. A rosy glow came through the fringed silk shades, bringing even the deflated wallpaper back to life. Zoe stood and looked a minute, blinking slowly, then blew out the one remaining candle, turned the switch off, and closed the door behind her.

She went to the tall, narrow window at the end of the hall and parted the ragged lace curtains to stare out onto the Mall, her thoughts inevitably sliding from Arthur's list to Roger and how much she was missing him. When she'd called him late last night, eager to talk, there had been no answer either at the gallery or the apartment, and as she stood by the window, the bright glow of the street lamps blurring slightly, the need to hear his voice surged up again. But just then, as if in response to her thoughts, she heard the burring of the phone on the bridal chest, and, suddenly elated, knowing absolutely who it was, she ran to answer.

But Roger was somber in his greeting.

"How you doing, Zo?"

"Okay. I'm okay . . . but you sure sound down in the dumps. What's the matter?"

"Oh, nothing. I've had a dull headache all day, that's all. I tried to call you about three o'clock your time, but there was no answer."

"I was at the hospital."

"I figured that."

"Actually, I called you, too, last night, but—"

"Yeah. I was up in Santa Barbara to see if that Fragonard might be available."

"Oh, good for you. Are they going to let you use it? You know, maybe you could get . . ." She broke off when she realized he wasn't listening to her. "Roger, what is it? What's wrong?"

"Zo, look, I had lunch with Sidney and Julian Frye today."

Zoe chuckled. "Oh? That must have been a thrill. No wonder you have a headache. How'd that happen?" Her voice was ironic, but truly amused.

"Well, Sidney called the gallery in the morning, all in a panic, to say Frye was freaking out and could I meet them both at the Polo, so I did, and . . . well, he was pretty upset."

"Oh? Because . . . ?"

"Because you're still in Boston. He was really pissed."

"Oh, I know. He was in a lousy mood when I called him Monday— just like you said. I had to listen to a lot of crap about my being gone, about how much work we have to do, blah, blah. But I told him I'm sending him a whole portfolio of stuff. In fact, I'm going over to Air Express in the morning with—"

"Zoe . . . I'm afraid there's a problem."

"Roger, *what* is going on?"

"He's threatening to replace you." Damn, Roger thought. He'd never meant to do it like that—to spit it all out so abruptly.

"Well, isn't that stupid," Zoe said, sounding almost more annoyed than angry. "Oh, he's such a baby sometimes. That is really stupid."

"As a matter of fact, that was the very word I used when he said it, but I doubt he heard me. He was really cooking—you know how he gets."

"But it's just ridiculous! So who is it? Anybody in particular, or is he planning to put an ad in the paper?"

"Well, he's gone down to Mexico to see about getting Gianfranco Sessa. Evidently some shoot down there is wrapping this week, and—"

"Frank Sessa?"

Roger couldn't understand Zoe's reaction; she sounded a little sarcastic, but not really angry at all.

"What in the world does he want with Frank Sessa? He can't do Victorian, Rog; everybody knows that. God, he can't do *interiors* at all. It's nonsense."

Zoe thought of the dinner-party scene she had created—the champagne goblets, the silver vases and the candlelight, and Beatrice Holland's brimming eyes—and knew that Gianfranco Sessa couldn't come within a million miles of such a setting. But he was a big name, and vastly experienced, even if he wasn't all that talented. All of a sudden, Zoe was not quite so amused.

"What about Alan, by the way?" she asked. "Julian fire him yet?"

"As a matter of fact, he did," Roger said with a sigh; he'd been hoping she wouldn't ask. "Fired him, according to Sidney, in front of half the world. And he's talking about letting the cinematographer go, too . . . Niels something? Sidney says he and Frye have been bitching at each other for days."

"Fire Niels?"

"Sidney says he will," Roger replied.

Zoe had a sudden image of a raving Julian Frye, his puffy outraged face, his flashing, beady little eyes. Yes, she certainly did know how he could get. She held the phone closer to her mouth and pulled the receiver on its curly cord over to the banister, peering down into the gloom of the entrance hall. She didn't want Arthur to come in and hear this.

"So what about the locations?" she said. "If he fired Alan he'll have to more or less start over, which will take a lot more time. Alan was out looking way back in January, for heaven's sake."

"Well, speaking of time, I also heard from Sidney that Frye's moving up the schedule. He's talking about starting principal photography somewhere around the first of June."

"June? Well, that does it. The poor slob has lost his mind," she said, the irony back in her voice.

"Apparently he told Sidney June fifteenth at the latest."

Silenced by that news, Zoe thought about Frye's famous unpredictability, his vicious, capricious temper. The first rule of moviemaking, which Frye certainly knew, was that you don't start until you're completely ready. But Zoe knew, from her own experience, how important it was to him to be the boss. He'd had to go with private financing because the studios all knew he would demand complete control of every detail. None of them would so much as touch *The Gilded Affair* because they didn't want to have to deal with Julian Frye.

"I can't believe this!" she said, her voice strained and tense. "What the hell's the matter with him?"

"Sidney told me he's sent one of his lackeys to look for some locations that—"

"Roger, Roger, the locations are *here*," Zoe said in a hissing whisper.

"What?"

"We could do it *here*! Right in my Grandmère's house. That's what I wanted to tell you last night! If we bring the whole production east, which is what that son of a gun *should* do, for God's sake, we'll have our choice! And by the time we get to the winter scenes, there'll be snow up in—"

"Zoe, honey . . . he's talking about that nonperformance clause in your contract. At lunch he—"

"Nonperformance! Wait'll you see what I've been doing! No, listen to me, Roger . . . I practically storyboarded the whole final dinner party in Grandmère's dining room. This morning! Just wait'll Frye sees the stuff I'm sending him. He's nuts if he thinks he can manipulate me with that stupid nonperformance business!"

"Zoe . . ."

"And last night I took a long walk around Back Bay. It was drizzling, and a little too dark maybe, but I shot two rolls of door knockers, fan-lights, ironwork—the kind of thing he can cut away to—"

"Zoe . . ."

"You know, Rog, maybe it wouldn't be such a bad idea for me to call him back, right now, tell him myself about—"

"He's gone, Zo. When he left the restaurant he was going straight to the airport. Sidney said he had a two-o'clock flight to Guadalajara."

With that, Zoe finally absorbed it. "Dammit! He's really going to do this? Frank *Sessa*? I deserve better than this crap from him! I should be able to take a few days of my life to deal with my family, to—"

"I know, Zo, I do," Roger said, as calmly as he could, "but I think you need to try to get back here as soon as possible. Tomorrow, you think?"

Zoe paused before she answered, pulling the phone into the crook of her shoulder. "Roger, I can't. Tonight I promised Arthur I'd stay until Annabelle dies. I promised him. I don't think it'll be all that long, but I'm staying."

"Zoe . . ."

"I have to. I can't leave him . . . and I won't."

"Zoe, shall I come? I could get a plane in the——"

"Oh, Roger, if you . . ." Zoe looked up into the shadows of the hall-way, at the large, dark paintings of birds of prey in their filthy, ornate frames.

"You only have to say the word, Zo."

Just then Zoe heard the front door click and the sound of Edwina whining for a treat. "I have to go," she whispered into the phone. "Arthur just came in. I'll call you back, I promise . . . soon."

Roger waited until she hung up to tell her that he loved her.

Later, Zoe lay on the floor of the music room and listened to Arthur playing Chopin. He warmed up at first with elaborate scales and complex arpeggios, but his movement to the first *ballade* was so smooth that it took her several seconds to recognize the plaintive, distant sound of the opening main theme.

Arthur, who loved all Chopin, loved the *ballades* best. He had explained their structure to her once, the narrative line of the sparkling, sad, self-generating music. She had not heard Chopin's first *ballade* since the last time Arthur played it for her, one night ages ago in the near-dark of this very room.

As he played, the music shimmered as if a stick were being swept across a long fence made of crystal, evoking a spirit of old, unhappy, far-off things. Zoe, who had lived for so many years in a world of color and shape, and very little music, knew that the *con fuoco* of movie themes was not like this—not like a message, not like memory.

Arthur moved subtly to the second theme, and Zoe smiled at a fantasy she knew was really *his*—an image of himself that Arthur had confided to her years before. And suddenly, in her mind's eye, Zoe could see her brother as he was to himself, handsome and slim in a perfectly tailored tuxedo, bowing to roaring audiences in New York, London, and Vienna, smiting them all with sizzling polonaises and perfect phrasing—his scherzi fierce, the *largo* portions plangent and tearful, rising like cresting water over the thunder of applause.

And then the coda—crystalline smithereens of sound, ice chips falling, as if in accompaniment to the splitting of the shell that had enclosed her for so long.

TWENTY-SEVEN

(FROM THE DIARIES OF AUGUSTA HILLYARD: 1926 TO 1930)

Sunday, September 19, 1926

We have had a drizzly time of it since the end of last month, but I think I see a bit of Indian summer inching toward us with October just around the corner. I was sitting this morning in the big parlor in a beam of very welcome sunshine, enjoying my coffee and some lovely scones, just about to open the theater section of the *Times,* when I looked up to see Mr. Alexander Lattimore standing in the doorway, looking rather more chipper than I have seen him in some time. When he was here for supper last week he seemed so dreadfully weary; Veronica had prepared a delicious cold collation, and everyone was feeling quite merry and satisfied, except for Alex, appearing on that occasion quite diminished by his recent trip abroad. No doubt that was because his itinerary included some weeks in Belgium to see after Sarah's affairs.

When our sister died last July, on Independence Day, we both thought how terribly ironic it was that Sarah's end had come on the birthday of the nation on which she (perhaps reluctantly?) turned her back more than a quarter century ago. When Alex offered to go to the village where she made her home for so many years, for one fleeting second I thought to join him, imagining myself a pilgrim, perhaps laying a wreath of flowers on her grave. But all the practicalities aside, I felt that would hardly be becoming.

Nevertheless, I cannot, will not, judge her. I am better advised to care as best I can for the one brother who is left. Poor Alex, he is an old man at sixty-five. I see from his color and the drooping of his famous jowls that he is not at his best. He is a lonely, vain old man, and that he is now our father's eldest living child seems to prey on him in a way that it certainly needn't. He feels responsible for me . . . belatedly, to say the least.

He very cheerfully took a cup of coffee from Veronica and gobbled up some scones as we chatted idly about the week's events, soon falling into silence with the *Times* before our faces, shielding the sunlight. Then, all at once, I happened to look up and noticed that Alex had gone quite pale and choked in fact on his bit of scone, tucked in his cheek at the time. I jumped up to pound him on the back, and Veronica bustled in with a glass of water, and at last he settled down, still breathing fairly hard but with the spasm ended. The shadow of an explanation followed.

It seems that Anthony (with his uncle's blessing and participation?) has invested fairly heavily in this new land speculation fever down in Florida and has apparently, or so Alex feared this morning, lost a good bit of it in a tornado which spread destruction across the state just yesterday afternoon!

"What does this mean?" I asked. "Wiped out? How much land?"

"The investors lost tens of millions of dollars altogether," Alex said, coughing again as he told me, pointing to the page. But when I pressed him for details, scanning the newspaper spread upon the table in the sunlight, he ran off while my back was turned, no doubt to bring this dour intelligence to Anthony.

Wednesday, September 22, 1926

Although Alex reports that Anthony has taken himself, with all expedient haste, down to Florida to review his losses, I wonder if Anthony even acknowledges the existence of setbacks in a world grown increasingly (or so he must believe) laid on a plate for his taking. He left poor little Eugene alone on Clarendon Street with the "housekeeper" (I believe there is a euphemism hiding there, but it's difficult to be certain, as Anthony is so secretive!) and dashed away to see if something to his own advantage may be salvaged from the wreckage made of other people's lives. We had young Eugene here for a nice fish dinner tonight, perhaps his first proper meal in several days, and he seemed glad enough to come, though he picks at his food and is possessed of the most unattractive table manners. Keeping my own counsel in the face of his spotty, sour puss is a challenge indeed. All the same, as I reflect tonight on Anthony's fortunes, it is clear to me that even if this investment of his has met with complete disaster, he will not be offering the details to his mother.

Wednesday, August 10, 1927, Lark's Neck, Maine

My friendship with Anne Higgins Lowell, stretched over all the years since our shared childhood, seems rather comfortably to have survived the vicissitudes which, I suppose, from the perspective of my age, are but to be expected between mortals. The two of us have had a splendid visit, enhanced by the invigorating weather that Anne promised when she begged me to come up and stay with her awhile. Anne extended her invitation to Annabelle and young Master Eugene as well (the dregs of the Hillyards, what with Anthony traveling constantly these days between Canada and Florida), but the boy has been sent off for the summer to a ranch in the Rocky Mountains, there to break his little neck, I suppose, out of earshot of his father, and Miss Annabelle prefers to remain on Commonwealth Avenue, languishing in the absence of Mr. Spencer Trefoyle, off in the desert these last two months.

It is an indication to me of how relaxed and mellow my mood must be that these are the first words I have written since my arrival. I came well supplied with paper and pen, somewhat mean-spiritedly suspecting that quietude would soon translate to boredom, and yet it hasn't, for we have been joined by the Wheelwrights! Just this past Monday afternoon we heard the rollicking noises of arrival, and there indeed were Celia, James, and the children, come to stay with Gran. All three of Celia's youngsters are now definitely "adolescents"—sap rising in every one of them and all the rocky coast of Maine to cool it off.

Henry, Celia's eldest, is a strapping lad whose fourteenth birthday we are to celebrate tonight. My goodness! I remember the day he was born. Horace, at twelve, is somewhat noisy and a "sportsman" (to his father's clear delight), and gregarious as they come. Celia's boys have always been extremely jolly, and yet Laura, the only daughter, who is a cheeky little belle at thirteen, fancies herself rather more than I enjoy seeing in a young lady; in my experience, a demure demeanor is far more suitable for girls her age. Laura seems not too much at all like her gentle, quiet, and kindhearted mother. How well I remember Celia standing on Mlle. Roulleau's footstool to have Anne's wedding dress fitted down for her, worried lest Mr. Wheelwright find her a disappointment, and now here they are, many years later, Celia *bloomed* to a fare-thee-well, welcoming the adoring attentions of her husband with a full-hearted and most womanly smile upon her lips I wish I could remember in myself.

Saturday, August 13, 1927, Lark's Neck, Maine

We have made a very cheerful party here all the week, and I do confess it has been my pleasure to watch dear Anne beaming in the presence of her offspring. It hurts me less than I would have thought that my own progeny are not here to mirror hers (and to suffer in the comparison?). I have not spoken to Anne of the increasing coldness between me and my younger daughter. I thought Annabelle showed a certain grace, oddly enough, in declining Anne's invitation, though perhaps I am completely mistaken. It may be only cowardice . . . or a disinclination to endure my society.

Whether or not Annabelle has heard from Spencer Trefoyle since he took himself off late in June, I have not the faintest idea, and although I admit to curiosity, there is all the same a part of me that does not wish to know. Early on, I considered asking Annabelle to leave the house, but I will not. My former outrage has given way to pity for my child's obvious suffering.

My poor Annabelle seems quite incapable of withstanding the assault of Spencer Trefoyle upon her life and senses. He has managed to do what none of his frail predecessors ever could: he has made Annabelle forget, nay, *lose* herself. I would almost wish that narcissistic vixen back again, so dim a representation of her old self has Annabelle become. When Trefoyle goes away, and he does so more and more frequently of late, she takes to her bed, reading foolish magazines, stuffing herself with foods she never touched before, and grows somewhat stout in the process. I have told her that at her age she can ill afford to ignore her appearance, but she gazes at me with uncomprehending eyes and waits in silence for his return.

I am grown quite inured to what others might call the shame of it. "Shame" does not do this justice—indeed, the word "tragedy," which quickly comes to mind, is imprecise as well. Annabelle is helpless, *helpless*. She listens to no one, not even to Anthony, of whom she has been always rather fond, and who knows best what vipers the Trefoyles are. My gloom over this comes from the simplest sadness for my child, and all the more because I know myself to be powerless to straighten what Trefoyle has so cruelly bent. But as I watch Anne and Celia, strolling, even as I write these words, arm in arm down along the ocean's rim, it saddens me most of all that my daughter does not know (or at any rate would profess to disbelieve) that I do love her and am glad to have her with me in our home in spite of everything.

*   *   *

As the stock prices rise (which I note in my daily perusal of the *Times*) into the empyrean beyond the farthest planets, Anthony (his Uncle Alex tells me) is daily at his broker's establishment continuing his spree. The source of his funds, aside, of course, from his dealings in illegal spirits, is hard to understand since his losses in Florida, but I am not to know the details. Perhaps scotch whisky *is* as good as gold these days.

If I ever wondered when I held that black-haired little boy to my breast if he would grow to be his father's son, I cannot doubt it now. And yet there was (ah, hindsight!) a sensibility in Eugene, even in his most extravagant moments, that I cannot find in Anthony. Alex has confided his fears to me, on more than one occasion of late, although Alex's own business ventures would not, I warrant, bear much scrutiny by the government or by the gods. This business of buying stocks "on margin," as they say, with borrowed money, has now been illegal for some months, but Anthony has apparently found the broker of his dreams, according to Alex, and continues high, wide, and handsome—spending as before.

As I reread what I have written, I note that I have substituted irony for worry. I think I do that with increasing frequency. My fears and trepidations for my children express themselves in a manner unworthy of the love I bear them, in a sarcasm I do not truly feel. But oh!—they cling to the disordered lives they have made for themselves with white and clutching fingers.

Tuesday, August 6, 1929

There has clearly been an ebbing of the tide of Anthony's fortunes. After negotiations worthy of the Treaty of Paris, he and young Master Eu-. gene have moved into Grandmère's house. I have turned most of the second floor over to the two of them, and although I am far from happy about this, it is unthinkable to refuse. This is their home as well as mine. My father would not have had it otherwise. Of course, Anthony came bearing baroque arguments about the wisdom of consolidating our households, about the bundles of money he would be giving me to keep the table and maintain the house, and yet even though he does help out a bit with the expenses, he certainly makes small contribution to the atmosphere.

The saving grace in all this is that young Eugene will be off, in just a few weeks, to a boarding school as yet to be determined. The great institutions of New England have not vied with any passion whatsoever to claim his scholarly hide for their own, and Anthony will no doubt have to endow a chapel at the very least to get him into one of them.

. . . And so we are all back together—all living Hillyards under one roof as of old, with the exception of sweet Hortense, who sends a weekly letter to her mama. I bless her "in absentia," fully realizing that Eliot Duke is the greatest blessing my dear girl could ever hope to have. Who would have thought that poor, bashful, self-effacing Hortense would know far greater joy than all the other Hillyards put together?

Monday, November 4, 1929

Anthony has locked himself in his father's library with Alex and old Mr. Ford, Eugene's erstwhile lawyer, of whom we have seen very little in recent years. This morning he minced in his pretty fashion through the door, which I opened myself, quite surprised to see him.

Stunned as they are by the news that sixteen million shares sold low on the stock exchange last Tuesday, Alex and Anthony feel the need of solace and lawyerly advice. Though Anthony, I do believe, has dealt exclusively with Ford *fils* since Eugene's death eight years ago, he must feel that more powerful remedies are now called for. Ford *père* is well into his eighties and, I am told, but rarely leaves his estate in Brookline (a fortress toward which I am quite sure Eugene Hillyard the First contributed handsomely in days gone by). The magnitude of Tuesday's catastrophe must be very great indeed to bring him here.

Many hours have passed since they closed themselves inside the library, allowing no interruptions except for Potter, bearing a variety of refreshments on large trays. It is impossible to tell what this may mean. . . . I hear coughing, bellowing, and worse from behind those locked double doors.

Tuesday, November 5, 1929

Hoping to escape the mood of near hysteria on Commonwealth Avenue, I walked almost to Cambridge today. I turned off over the bridge and made my way along the river. The air is somewhat cooler there and leaves are beginning to fall, having turned their colors round some weeks ago. I sat on a bench by the shoreline and smoked a cigarette and thought about my Zachary. He would have been thirty-nine years of age today. I cannot help but wonder what he would have to say about his big brother if he could see him now. . . . I think if he had been sitting there beside me, he would have leaned against the bench and spread his arms wide across the back and told me all about the golden dome of Mr. Bulfinch's State House, shining in the sun across from where we sat. I'm sure he would have laughed and hugged my shoulder to him, whispering: "Mama, Mama, look at that duck . . . shhh, so close to shore . . . how *brave* he is, hmmm? All the wild brown leaves blowing past the bank and he paddling as fast as his little webbed feet can go, through all that cold, cold water. Watch! Mama . . ."

Oh! How I loved my boy . . . how I miss him. . . .

Wednesday, November 13, 1929

Alex has come to me looking absolutely dreadful, yellow and thin. My exhortations on behalf of his health have fallen on ears that are deaf to everything but more disaster. Apparently the immense black headlines in the newspapers, of which we have piles enough in the library and on the dining-room window seat to start a conflagration, mean simply that the wealth of our nation has been built on paper—a foundation far less substantial than sand. The ranks of the rich and powerful are much diminished. Anthony's famous ability to land on his feet, whatever the circumstances, will be sorely tested now.

Friday, November 15, 1929

Anthony and I have "had some words" (as my dear mother would say). Last evening when I asked him to explain what has been happening, what it all might mean (my avid reading of the *Times* being no substitute for being bloodied in the fray), he was quite beside himself and actually raised his voice to me. That, and the language which accompanied his outburst, I am prepared to overlook, but not to forget. Such heat from our icy Anthony bodes no good.

Monday, December 2, 1929

Hugh Alexander Lattimore's will was read today. In the week since his funeral, we have had the most morbid of circuses here on Commonwealth Avenue. Alex was in many ways a quiet man, and I would have hoped that his obsequies might have more truly reflected his innermost nature. Unfortunately, the circumstances of his death, and the time at which he chose to die, did not permit.

Potter and I returned an hour ago from Back Bay Station, having put our darling Hortense, who so sweetly came to be with me, on the late train to New York, Washington, and points south, and reunion with her Eliot. Annabelle has slunk off exhausted to her room, having made a really rather valiant effort to participate in the rituals of mourning (if not the substance, though Alex was, after all, her only uncle). Anthony, who has taken to sleeping in the library, is locked in there once again, trying to accustom himself to the rather bald fact that Alex, now safely in his grave, could pretend no more and left only five thousand dollars (discovered in cash under the socks in his chiffonnier), and our mother's wedding ring—and all to me.

Of the once munificent Lattimore Trust we have only Alex's poor hoard of money and the ring, which is in the little velvet box where it has lain for years. I have put it in the drawer where I keep my trinkets, where, I am sure, it will remain until I myself am buried. Whatever that gold circlet may signify is gone with the passing of my brother. There are now only Hillyards to carry whatever flags there are, and only Augusta to bear the name. I did not even give my own family name to any of my children, hoping "Hillyard" would do well enough for them.

And so it has fallen midnight. Annabelle weeps in her room, Anthony rages in his lair, Hortense dozes in her compartment on the night train to Washington, and my transition from mere Dowager to Matriarch appears complete.

Friday, May 2, 1930

We enjoyed the most delightful afternoon of Brahms and Massenet at the Symphony—after a charming luncheon at the Vendôme—rare treats in these dismal times. Anne and Celia were with me, and young Laura favored us with her companionship, looking quite lovely in a frock that much became her, matching her sky-blue eyes. She is turning out to be very pretty, though no less pert than usual. She reminds me remarkably of my Annabelle at that age; there is a predatory post-debutante sparkle in her eyes that I remember well in my own younger daughter, though Miss Laura will have no actual debut, Celia not finding such display appropriate to the times. She is quite right, of course, although Anne is being a goose about it. Where Anne Lowell ever got the notion that only a debutante can find a proper husband, I'm sure I have no idea.

Tuesday, May 13, 1930

I don't much like having Anthony in the house, though to be fair, he's not here very much, dashing off hither and yon as he does with what seems but the slightest provocation. Remarkably, however, he has taken to coming to me for advice, which he never used to do, and I find I am amused as well as mystified; he certainly did not care for my opinions in the past—he just barged on. I give him what counsel I can, and that free-heartedly, but I know quite well that he comes to me from desperation: there is simply no one else to ask! There is no Eugene, no Alex, no Trefoyle, and he is thrown upon an elder of a somewhat different stripe.

I have always imagined that Anthony would forever rage against the elements (both man-made and "divine"), falling back with glee upon his more devious talents in time of trouble. Yet when he appeared this morning and asked me for my diamond earrings (which naturally I didn't consider giving him even for a moment), I realized with a shock that my bold Anthony has, at forty-six, become a somewhat pathetic figure. He is drawn and thin and shows a petulance and doubt I never saw in him before.

Nevertheless, after some discussion (little of it pleasant), he did depart at last, and with my citrines and the amethyst brooch with the pearl cabochon tucked into his pocket, though he was stinging from my steadfast refusal of the diamonds. Watching the back of his shoulders as he hurried down the stairs (as if fearing I would take the items back), I realized that I will not miss my jewelry at all. I have thought far too often in recent months about a damnable sense of *loss* that has crept upon me unawares, instead of concentrating on what *remains*. It is remarkable that I have Anthony Hillyard—of all people—to thank for these reflections.

Saturday, August 23, 1930

I have spent the best part of this sultry afternoon sitting at my window, which Potter has thrown wide open to try to catch just a breath of fresher air from the Mall. It has been so oppressive that I have been quite tame and quiet, letting my new book lie facedown on my lap, drinking lemonade, and thinking of the olden days—scarcely a healthy turn of mind for a lady who has taken increasingly to "watching the world go by from her front porch."

Yet I find myself responding to the dreadful state of our nation as a renewed challenge to my spirit after what has been, at least for me, a decade of black years, filled with loss, decay, diminishment. I have before me the example of my old friend Anne Lowell, who has gotten through her life by endurance of her losses, but in my heart I know it is much better to confront the trials of life . . . look them in the face! *That* is the better way!

I don't pretend to know why we were scattered here like seeds from some gigantic apple (unless it is a "divine" apple, *His* apple, which certainly would explain everything), but I doubt it was to weep and moan and enumerate our losses and lament our daily pain. I think what

I am feeling now is not so much false hope as shrill refusal to be sub-merged by lack of hope! I know I must not look at these dispirited shards of family, of society, with dismay. The old saw "This too shall pass" gives the comfort not of cliché, but of hope. The ebbing tide exposes the de-bris, the dead, the hollowed-out, but ah! the flood—the sparkle of it, the movement, the renascence! Were I to look for comfort I would look no farther than the world of nature. I hark back to the hours I spent on our veranda at Nahant watching the ocean surging, watching the flow-ers bloom, and know that regeneration is the truest, most natural phe-nomenon there is.

To watch the generations, one by one, rowing out upon green, frothing waves in a new boat while one stands safe on shore, waving one's handkerchief, is still a blessing, however Fortune sometimes brings unwelcome surprises. One likes to think that there is more to come—that one's line has not died out. Perhaps it is the triumph of hope over experience (as I believe that dreadful old man remarked in quite another context), but that in itself is proof enough that what was bitter sweetens with time.

As I contemplate the end of summer, the withering of the year, my children's pain, I choose to remind myself that the cycle will come round again—if not in our lifetimes, then in others. There are sure to be new leaves, new life, new reasons for joy . . . and, yes, new "matriarchs" to sit in the window of this precious house and think a regenerated, future version of these thoughts.

TWENTY-EIGHT

*T*hursday's warmth, called "unseasonable" by chagrined New England weathermen, became, by noon, an imitation of summer. Leaving the Air Express office, Zoe made a point of walking up the middle of the Mall, just to give herself a good look at the famous magnolias on the north side of Commonwealth Avenue, now at their peak. In the brilliant sunshine, the heavy flowers seemed to have sprung from their velvety pods almost overnight, and Zoe, unable to resist, ran across the street to touch the huge, smooth petals.

She felt the odd sense of completion sometimes inherent in a job barely begun. Her sketches, photographs, and sheaves of notes, all packed up in a large cushioned envelope, were finally en route to Frye—promised for tomorrow. It's in the lap of the gods now, she thought as she leaned into the steep slope of Beacon Hill. Maybe that's exactly where it all belongs.

Claudia and Uncle Jim were waiting for her on the sidewalk in front of the club, nearly at the crest of the hill.

"Aren't those daffodils a sight!" said Jim, kissing her cheek and smiling into the sunlit Common, while Claudia, looking wonderful in a blue linen dress that matched her eyes, hugged Zoe and linked arms.

"Headquarters of male chauvinism," she whispered into Zoe's ear, as they looked up with fascination at the massive pearl-gray facade, protected by high, bowed-out balustrades. Zoe laughed and winked at Jim, who led them up the tall stone steps to the door.

The interior of the club was hushed and cool. The lines of the main salon drew the eye toward an immense mantelpiece with marble entablatures, rising to a museum-quality model of a full-rigged four-masted sailing ship.

"Isn't that fabulous," Zoe said, looking wide-eyed at the ship.

"China Trade," Jim said. "That's where a lot of these old boys made their money, or their great-grand-daddies did. Lots of coupon cutters here now, though. Wonder how they ever came to let me in," he laughed as they walked into a smaller room behind the salon, where French doors gave onto a small shaded garden. Jim put his arm around Zoe's shoulders.

"Now this used to be called 'the writing room'—pretty damn civilized, isn't it? Take a look at this furniture, honey," he said, pointing to a tall cabinet with lacquered panels. "All bona fide anti-cues. I'm told some of these pieces are worth a mint."

Claudia was staring at the heavy, elegant furnishings with preoccupied amusement. "This is terrific," she said.

"Well, we'll look around a little more after lunch."

They were seated at a table by a sunny window, the white linen weighted down with old heavy silver with a crest and initial engraved into each piece.

"How's Arthur holding up?" asked Jim, wiping off his fork with a thick napkin.

"Well enough, I guess," Zoe said, sighing, looking into Jim's eyes. "He's determined to see it through. He was gone this morning before I even got up, and that was early—off to the hospital."

"He would have been entirely welcome to join us," Jim said with a hostly little expression of worry as if that had not been clear.

"Oh, he knows that—in fact, I mentioned it to him specifically—but he insists he wants to be there when she dies . . . whenever that turns out to be," Zoe said, ducking her chin to slurp at the top of her overflowing whisky sour, which had just arrived.

"He's such a precious person," Claudia said, sipping a wine spritzer through a straw, looking away toward the small field of daffodils beyond the window. "Zoe, I'm so sorry to say it, but I think in some ways you've missed the best of Arthur. All that seems to be left of the old enthusiasm is that insane generosity of his."

Jim was nodding over his stinger as she spoke. "That's a fact," he said thoughtfully, looking at Claudia. "Arthur's always been generous to a fault, no doubt about it. But you know, he seems to have trouble accepting the generosity of others, even from folks who care a lot about him. Runs in the family, is my belief," he said, turning to Zoe with a gentle smile. "Generosity *and* pride."

"He's locked himself into a kind of, I don't know, 'vigil mentality,' I guess you could call it," Zoe said. "He slept at the hospital Tuesday night, and even though I did get him to come home yesterday, as I said, he was out again this morning at the crack of dawn. He just doesn't have anything else on his mind."

She wondered if that was actually the truth. She said nothing of the conversations with the doctor or the social worker, of Arthur's sobbing fit in the dining room last night as he spoke of his love for Annabelle . . . of how little he'd loved in his life. He was too bereft to bear the telling of it to someone else.

"But I know he gets comfort just from being there with her, even though she's . . . well . . . 'comatose' I guess is the word."

Claudia reached out impulsively and stroked Zoe's sleeve. "Well, I was just so pleased that he came Sunday," she said. "I was afraid he might not, at the last minute . . . you know."

"It was a mighty fine party, wasn't it?" said Jim, coming up out of his stinger. "Zoe, young Lowell confided to me later that he showed you his shell collection. Means a lot to him—you must really rate."

Zoe smiled broadly and put down her glass. "He's a sweetheart." She thought of the crusted conch in Grandmère's room, of giving it to Lowie with ceremony, with instructions to treasure it, to keep it for *his* children, to . . . but where had it come from? Whose hand? What shore? How could it be that she, who had endured for twenty years without so much as a china figurine, had begun to feel such a powerful need of heirlooms, received and given?

A snooty waiter arrived to take their order. "All right, then!" said Jim, slapping his menu closed. "Who's for the Clams Casino? Claud?"

"Oh, no, not me. I'm having only salad this week after that party. Oil and vinegar on the side, please," she said piously to the waiter, who looked at Jim for approval.

"Fine. Salad for the lady in blue. Zoe, honey? Try the clams?"

"Sure. Why not?" Zoe hadn't had fresh clams in years. It seemed that people in California ate only things like quiche and mako shark . . . and the brains of their enemies.

"Double order of clams for the lady in white, and I'll have the beef tips, my friend," Jim said to the waiter. "Rare—mooing!—and the white 'sparagrass, and another one o' these, if you'd be so kindly."

"Uncle . . ." Claudia was poised on the brink of a nutritional lecture, but Jim never let her get started.

"Now Claudie, this is a special lunch, and we can all have anything we want—even rabbit food." He leaned toward Zoe and stage-whispered at her, "She's worried about my cholesterol. But it's a little-known true medical fact that vodka actually breaks down the fat particles in beef. Ain't that something? True fact. Read it in the *New England Journal of Medicine.*"

He smirked benevolently at their laughing faces and sipped at his fresh stinger while he pointed out some of the architectural features of the dining room to Zoe, who looked up appreciatively at the vaulted ceiling and the fine paintings on the paneled walls.

"I do believe that's a Copley," Jim said, holding his glass out toward a portrait of a gentleman in a satin waistcoat with a long spyglass in his hands. "Everyone's extra special proud of the fact that this building is on the original site of his home. One of these days, Zoe dear, you might like to pop over to the Museum of Fine Arts and take a look at some of their nice Copleys. . . . Oh, my, my, *my,* will you look at this!"

The three of them ate with silent relish for a few minutes. The meal, beautifully presented, was really quite plain, Zoe thought, but fresh and tasty, the ingredients all the absolute finest of their kind.

"Yep, generosity definitely runs in the family," Jim said again, harking back to the earlier topic, obviously still very much on his mind. "Been my experience such qualities do."

He put down his fork for a moment and wiped his lips with a fastidious gesture. "Now, Zoe, here's an example. Your great-grandma, old Mrs. Hillyard—well now, she was generous to a fault, just like Arthur. Always determined to take care of everybody, her kids, her friends, servants. Everybody. Considered it her duty. Paulette told me once that the dear old lady paid—in full, so I understand—for several operations for old Eugene's driver and handyman . . . hundred percent.

Now people didn't know about that kind of thing, she just did it. Matter of fact, I can't imagine how Paulette knew. I suppose the mean-spirited would say, 'It's easy if you've got it.' " His lips pursed with disapproval.

"But *did* she have it?" Claudia asked, her eyes focused on a cherry tomato that kept bouncing away from her fork. "Were they really as rich as everybody always thought?"

"Hard to say. Hell, it's hard to imagine that Anthony didn't throw it all away, bit by bit. Everything except the house, o' course."

Jim put down his fork again and looked out at the small garden before he spoke. "Zoe, Anthony took the Hillyards like Grant took Richmond."

"Anthony? My grandfather?" Zoe took a sip of water and looked intently at Jim.

"Interesting man, I always thought," Jim said with a droll flicker of his eyebrows, "for all his faults, but driven, driven . . . though just what it was that made him that way, competition with his daddy or what, I couldn't say. You're entitled to hear this, Zoe. What's past is past, after all, but he was crooked as hell, any way you slice it. Good thing your dad couldn't afford to hook up with old Anthony, Claud. Too rich for his blood, he used to say . . . too *shady,* you ask me. I have a feeling that not too much of Anthony's wheeling and dealing could stand a lot of scrutiny."

"Did people know that about him?" Zoe asked. "Realize how he was making his money?" She was trying to understand what Jim was saying, realizing afresh how little she knew of family history. "Did Grandmère know?"

"If she did, she didn't breathe a word; not to me, certainly, and not to Paulette or anybody else that I can figure out. That just wasn't her way. I know it's hard to imagine, someone keeping so much inside. I mean, we all blow off steam, some more than others. But that amount of self-containment? Not much of it around anymore."

Jim chewed on a small piece of steak and thought for a minute about what he'd just said.

"Augusta Hillyard kept up appearances, though, whatever Anthony was doing with the money, whatever the problems were . . . absolutely. Had a real strong sense of the Hillyards' place in the community—civic responsibility, civic pride—all that was very important to her." Jim cut his asparagus stalks into inch-long wedges and concentrated on his plate.

Zoe ate her clams slowly, scooping them out with the tiny fork the waiter had slid beside her plate with a doubtful look, as if hoping she knew how to use it.

"Do you girls remember her at all?" Jim said, looking up. "Zoe, dear? You, Claud?"

They shook their heads slowly, as Jim sniffed and blew his nose on a large blue handkerchief.

"Well, you were both so little when she died. Shame you don't have her example to look back on. I'm sorry to say I think her fineness of character was unappreciated oftentimes because she always had such a grand manner. 'Matriarch to her fingertips'—I'm quoting Paulette now. . . . Um, *ummm* . . . try a piece of this beef, dear, I can't eat it all." He put a large slice of his steak on Zoe's plate.

"Oh, no—don't you give me any," said Claudia, putting her hands over her salad bowl as he reached toward her with his fork.

"I always did enjoy my food." Jim turned to Zoe and winked at her confidentially. "Got arthritis, aches and pains, said so long to my prostate eight years ago, and my hips seize up on me every now and again, but my stomach's holding up, for which I am damn grateful."

Zoe laughed and leaned over to pinch his taut pink cheek. "I think the rest of you's holding up just fine, too," she said.

Jim patted his mouth with his napkin again and settled back with the dregs of his stinger. "Yes, indeed, I was proud to know her," he said quietly. "Pity you girls can't remember her. Died on Christmas Day, nineteen and forty-five. Got a wire from Paulette about it—I was still way the hell and gone out in Guam. Broke my heart, but I just couldn't get to her funeral.

"You see, Zoe, she'd been very kind to me," he said, a sad look flickering for just a moment in his eyes. "When they sprung me out of Harvard Law . . . let's see, along about 1938, I guess it was . . . she hired me as her lawyer, wanted to give me my start. But then, first thing you know, I got drafted, and Mrs. Hillyard did her last will with some old feller down on State Street. Wrote me a letter and told me she was planning on it, too—didn't want to see my feelings hurt. Can you imagine? Damn fine woman. Damn fine."

Jim leaned toward Zoe and Claudia with a shine in his blue eyes that perhaps had not been there a moment before.

"It's nice to be able to talk about her, Zoe," he said. "There's no one else to tell, you see."

"What about my brother?" said Zoe. "Has he heard these stories, this . . . history?"

"Well, yes and no. He's been so tied to Annabelle, and now all this trouble with the old girl has knocked him for a loop. Things are going to be mighty different for Arthur. For better or worse," he added with a small frown.

"I just hope he's up to it," Claudia said. "He's too sweet and decent for his own good."

Jim nodded and pushed his empty plate away. "Arthur's got a whole cartful of fine qualities," he said with decision, "but I'm afraid that bright as he is, he's not particularly, well, devious." He scratched his neck in a thoughtful manner. "That's his problem. . . . And after all my years as an attorney you can bet your boots I've learned the difference. Arthur doesn't seem to know a great deal about how things *work*. You know what I mean? Like money—he doesn't understand it."

"How could he possibly understand money?" Claudia said, licking the tines of her fork. "After getting Annabelle anything she ever wanted— all that stuff he's bought the last few years—appliances, electronic junk, *Edwina,* for God's sake—how was he going to learn about money? Zoe, he's got this dinky little teaching job over in Cambridge—"

"He told me," Zoe said quietly.

"Well, he hardly ever goes over there; I can't imagine how they've lived on what he makes." Claudia dipped her fork in the salad dressing again and licked it off.

"Zoe, honey," Jim said, scooting his chair closer to the table, "you're entitled to know this, if you don't already. Back when I was lawyering for Mrs. Hillyard, there was a small trust, that much I knew—Hillyard money, Lattimore money, I couldn't say—maybe only the remains of the pile old Eugene made that Anthony managed to whittle down to just about a pair of cufflinks."

"How come she didn't confide in you?" Zoe's voice was quiet. "You were her lawyer, her friend."

"Yes, I was. But as I told you, it just wasn't her way—kept herself to herself, as they say. The jobs she had me work on were just little pissant things." Jim wiped his mouth again and signaled to the waiter.

"Anyway, there can't be too much of that old fortune left, and I hope you won't think I'm prying, Zoe, we sure don't get any pleasure from talking about your brother's affairs behind his back, but there's bound to be some terrific expenses coming up. . . ."

Zoe thought of Mainwaring's cold, dire warnings—no insurance, sky-high hospital bills . . . the filthy, broken house.

"And the funeral's going to cost the earth. I hope you don't mind my bringing it up, honey, but you seem like a real smart, levelheaded gal to me, and it's going to have to be dealt with."

"And undoubtedly not by Arthur," said Claudia, looking furtively at a dessert cart just passing their table.

When the waiter came over a conversation ensued in depth regarding the distinction of the Boston cream pie versus the lightness of the famous meringue tarts—Jim vigorously upholding both sides of the question. Finally, he ordered a selection of sweets and coffee all around and glanced over at Zoe, who had kept her eyes on the table during the fanfare over dessert.

"You know, Arthur was always like that," Zoe said with a fond smile, reaching out to touch the bouquet of little white flowers on the table. "Even when we were kids he had this amazing ability to ignore what he couldn't bear to face. Maybe he's doing something like that now," she said, looking up. She paused, feeling disloyal and unhappy to be talking about her brother this way, even with family.

"But it's true he hasn't said one word to me about money. Not one word." She realized that the subject had indeed been, perhaps too assiduously, avoided.

"Well, maybe you should make it your business to find out, my dear. Arthur's usually tighter than a tick on these things."

"Told you," said Claudia, cutting into a raspberry meringue ring with the side of a special fork. "Told you last Sunday."

"I didn't think it was really my place to ask," said Zoe. "After all, I've been . . ."

Jim put his hand on her arm, twisting her bracelet, just a little, with affection. "I know just what you mean, honey," he said. "I know just how it is. Went out to the Midwest myself, shortly after the war; made a life for myself out there. I was gone many years . . . many years. . . ."

He smiled and left his hand on her sleeve a moment longer before he went on.

"Your brother's not such a rare bird, after all," he said, cutting into his pie and popping one of the whole pecans that covered the top into his mouth. "The Hillyards never talked about money. They just made it and spent it. Now, here's another example, Christmas 1941. Lord, what a party! You were just barely three weeks old, Zoe; I always remember you were born the day after Pearl Harbor. . . . Well, Augusta must have said to herself, 'This is it.' I was shipping out, and your dad, and Henry. And what a shindig that was! A real send-off, and I'd say it's a good bet she couldn't really spare the money. But she saw a need and she filled it. She wanted to give everybody the memory of a special Christmas, war coming and all—and she did. It made wonderful memories for everyone in the family . . . wonderful."

Jim squinted thoughtfully at the daffodils, and then turned back to Zoe. "Interesting how all those proper, buttoned-up Hillyards liked a party. Annabelle surely did. Never quite got it figured out that she was getting older—kicked up her heels every chance she got. Whatever you want to say about Annabelle Hillyard, she had a lot of spirit, knew how to enjoy herself. That business with Spencer Trefoyle took it out of her, though. Not a party-goin' man, Spencer. Nossir. . . . Sexy son of a bitch, though, sort of mysterious. Wasn't a woman in all of South Boston *and* Back Bay wouldn't have liked a piece of that!"

So saying, and with an admirable bit of timing, Jim winked at Zoe and Claudia and went back to his pie.

Claudia burst out laughing. She knew her uncle's salty side well enough, but it always took her by surprise. Zoe bit her lips, laughing silently in delight at his style.

"Well, it's been my experience that women like a challenge. Like to work for it a little. Heh, heh. . . ." He winked again at Zoe, who thought with a warm rush of affection what a flirty old gent he was.

"I remember him," she said, "but only very slightly. He died in New Mexico or somewhere, didn't he?"

"That he did," Jim said, stirring more cream into his coffee. "Had a wife and four kids out there, too."

"No shit!" said Claudia, quickly covering her mouth with her napkin and glancing over her shoulder, as if such language were never heard within these walls.

"Yes, indeedy," Jim said, tasting his coffee. "Mrs. Hillyard asked me to have him investigated, and I did, too, must have been about 1939 or so, around there. Found out plenty, but I didn't have the heart to tell her. Paulette agreed with me, said it would kill her to know what a four-flusher he really was. All the same, even though she never did find out any of the actual facts, he just broke Annabelle's heart. In the forties, you see, he was out west a lot more than he was in Boston."

Jim poured a little more coffee into Zoe's cup from the silver carafe on the table, and then just an inch more into his own. "She never followed him, though, which I thought was interesting. Funny thing, too, now that I think about it."

"What was he like?" Zoe asked, her chin on her hand. "Was he really so fascinating?"

"Oh, yes. Yes, he was. Zoe, Spencer was probably something like that character of yours you were telling me about. . . ."

"DuBose Mortlake?"

"That's the one . . . same line of horsefeathers, same way with the ladies, dashing as all get-out."

"On the nose!" Zoe said, laughing.

"Who in the world is DuBose Mortlake?" asked Claudia, pushing away her tart. Virtuously, she had scooped out the fruit filling, leaving the meringue shell intact, as if the evil calories were there.

"He's the villain, Claud." Still chuckling, Zoe told her the basics of the plot of *The Gilded Affair,* of the elaborate scheme to steal the finest art objects from the homes of the naive, vulnerable New York aristocrats, the murder of the forger, and the exciting winter scenes at the country house where the paintings and statues are hidden by Mortlake and his accomplices—always just a step or two ahead of the police. She described the characters and added a few tidbits about some of the actors—those already engaged and those, like the female lead and her greedy agent, still wallowing in the delicious bargaining phase.

"And DuBose Mortlake, as I said, is the villain, the insider who plans the robberies that, ultimately, go badly awry." Zoe glanced at Jim and then into Claudia's wide eyes. "He's a vicious, brilliant, sexy con artist."

"Wow!" Claudia was delighted. "Who's going to play him?"

Zoe laughed. "I don't think it's cast yet," she said. "There's a rumor that the director might give himself the part, but I think he's also talking to Oliver Reed—Mortlake is English, by the way—who'd be fabulous. I don't know if he's interested, though, or available."

"Ooooooh." Claudia giggled and performed a fake little girlish shiver, at which her uncle and Zoe laughed together.

Zoe knew that Frye was also trying to get Gielgud to do a star-turn as Laurence's father, Clifton Thane, the arrogant old society lion, a part tailor-made for him. When she mentioned it, Jim slapped his knee in appreciation of such perfect casting, and Zoe treated herself to a little fantasy of Jim Forbes and Sir John Gielgud chatting together in this very room. She thought how wonderful it would be to have everyone out in Los Angeles for the opening—or doing it right there in Boston, at the Ritz Carlton. Oh, what a party *that* would be . . . if Julian Frye didn't fire her first. . . .

"We sure are proud of you, Zoe," Jim said. "You've worked hard, and you've got a fine opportunity in front of you. It's a shame we didn't have a chance to cheer you on over the years, but you're back now, that's what counts." He smiled candidly at her and sipped his coffee.

Zoe felt her mind seem to stop dead in its tracks. The authenticity of her welcome home had not fully impressed her before. Clearly, they accepted that she was, indeed, "back now"—they embraced her return, and she saw, not without a sting of shame, how subtle and kind they both were—Claudia and Jim—not to have alluded in any way to the trouble between her and Arthur. That Arthur had been exposed to the famously "disputatious" Annabelle Hillyard, hour after hour, years on end, while Zoe was nowhere to be seen was not even hinted at. Zoe looked at them with a mixture of gratitude and astonishment they could not have failed to notice.

Jim fell silent for a moment, but then suddenly laughed and spanked his hand soundly on the table. "So! What do you think? Film in here? I'm sure you'll need to use the smoking room, and how 'bout that fancy front? Oh, did I mention we've got a pool table? Zoe, it's a beaut—a *beaut!* Hand-carved! I'll just bet I could square it with the committee!"

Zoe burst out in a pealing laugh and looked around at the other diners, who had been watching the three of them with frank curiosity—and obvious forbearance. Glancing at their stony, patrician faces, Zoe was sure that a number of their fellow diners couldn't be much older than she and Claudia, but they seemed to have acquired that hawkish look of privilege long before their time.

"You guys have a movie committee?" she asked Jim, still grinning at her own thoughts.

"Well, not exactly, but they'd all get a kick out of it, no matter what they'd tell you. . . . What's your job now? Production designer?" He pronounced the words with exaggerated care. "You must be pretty proud of yourself."

Zoe raised her eyebrows. "It's a little early for that, Uncle Jim, believe me," she said, thinking of her conversation last night with Roger, even as she tried to push it from her mind. "There's a huge amount of work to do," she said. "It's unbelievable—sets, costumes, locations. Putting this picture together's going to take a good year. Believe it or not."

"That a fact? Sounds teed-jus."

"Is it?" said Claudia. "Tedious?"

Zoe smiled and leaned back in her chair. She put her dessert fork down, and the waiter took her plate away in a flash. "Well, it can be, yes. There's lots of hurry-up-and-wait in the movie business. In fact, it's the only thing I really don't like about it." She winked at Jim.

"Just like the army!" Jim snorted and recrossed his thin legs. He swallowed a last forkful of his pie and took another sip of coffee.

"Zoe, honey," Jim said, speaking softly, carefully setting his cup in its saucer, "I know this has been a real hard time for you—you itching to get back to your work and all—but we're hoping you'll find a way to stay a bit longer. I mean, until the funeral. Think you can manage that?"

"I already told Arthur I would," she said.

Jim nodded, not surprised. "That's good. He really needs you, needs not to feel alone. Not that we'd desert him, naturally, but . . ."

"But it's not exactly the same, Zo, you know?" Claudia broke in.

"I know," Zoe said, remembering their first phone call, Claudia's focus on Arthur's misery rather than Annabelle's impending death.

"I'm worried sick about what's going to happen with him," Claudia said, "all alone in that huge house. I mean, I guess he'll stay there, don't you think?"

Zoe shook her head. "Claudia, he doesn't talk about it, about after Annabelle dies. He barely acknowledges that she *will* die, even though he's constantly at the hospital. But when she finally goes . . ." Zoe clasped her hands on the tablecloth, shaking her head, thinking of last night.

"I know you'll do your level best to help him through it, honey, but I still think you owe it to yourself to get some facts." Jim looked at her in an appraising way that was uncomplicated by guile or maneuver. Zoe realized that there were no hidden agendas here. The byzantine mind games she was used to in Hollywood were foreign to these people. It was that rare thing—advice without treachery.

"Well, I'm sure Annabelle left everything to Arthur," Zoe said, "what there is, but it can't be much from what you're saying."

"Well, no, there's likely not too much more than just the house. And if that is the case, you could maybe consider a very small mortgage if you need something to help get Arthur back on his feet after the funeral and all the bills," Jim said, frowning at the thought. "I hate to suggest that, but you might need to help him with something along those lines. I'd be real careful, of course—Augusta Hillyard would turn over in her grave if anything happened to that house. Far's I know, Eugene bought it the day it was built. Nobody but Hillyards ever lived in it, that's for sure."

He sighed and put his hand on Zoe's arm again. "Zoe, she used to talk about it all the time—such and such happened in this room . . . here's where we did so and so . . . running her hand over the walls. Just loved that house. Doted on it. 'Our home,' she used to say . . . 'our home.' So, if it comes to that, using the house to help Arthur, you want to be real persnickety about how you do it."

Zoe thought again about Arthur's clumsy avoidance of all confrontation. "Uncle Jim, I'm not so sure he'll even let me help him," she said.

"He will," said Claudia, who had been sitting quietly with her hands folded over her stomach. "Believe me. I know Arthur can be terrifically aggravating, Zo—and these days he seems so overwhelmed by everything—but there's enormous integrity there, a real desire to do the right thing, and frankly, when push comes to shove, I've never known Arthur to fail to do it. Talk to him. You're just going to have to be a little slick about it, that's all."

Jim nodded. "Sure wish we could help you out with more than our big mouths, isn't that right, Claud?"

Zoe reached for their hands and covered them with her own. "I know that," she said. "Really I do. I'm grateful you said it."

"Zoe, the fact is you're Augusta Hillyard's only living female descendant, or you soon will be, and, well, as I say, I was proud to know her and I'm glad of a chance to tell you so. The woman had enormous generosity of spirit."

He looked at Zoe with what she realized was respect. "I'd guess you've more or less inherited a good deal of that, too," he said, "coming here as you did, what with your movie and all." Jim dug into his back pocket for the big blue handkerchief. "Shoot, our side of the family always was long on advice and short on cash!"

Claudia folded up her napkin and put it on the table. "I have to get going, boys and girls . . . got to pick Yancey up from Little League. Want a ride, Zo?"

"I don't think so; I want to walk awhile."

"Well, I'm planning to settle down in the lounge with the paper and work on my digestion," said Jim, getting up slowly. He glanced at Claudia with a quick, mischievous squint. "If I rest my eyes a bit in between sections, nobody's likely to accuse me of napping."

Beaming, Jim led them toward the foyer, catching the dour expressions of the other diners, those few remaining, who looked relieved to see the two women finally departing.

"Why don't you ladies take a short tour around before you go," Jim said, loud enough for most of the men to hear. Then, in a whisper, "Just as easy to ask for forgiveness as permission, I always say." With that, Jim put his arms around their shoulders and escorted them out of the dining room, laughing as he went.

TWENTY-NINE

*I*n the late afternoon, Zoe walked slowly home through the Public Garden and down the center of the Mall. When she reached the house, she sat down on Eugene Hillyard's stone bench, still thinking of the conversation at lunch and the warmth with which Jim had spoken of Grandmère, finding a sadness not so much in his recollections as in the image of a lonely, regal old woman that they conjured up. Zoe looked at the old brick-and-brownstone facade, the chipped steps, the rotting wreath-shaped moldings under the third-floor windows, and out of habit, she framed the house with her hands, moving the rectangle of her fingers from doorway to roof and down again to the ornate laurel wreaths under the windows.

When she went inside, almost an hour later, she was greeted by Edwina, whose little body twitched with joy. Zoe hiked up her skirt and sat on the bare marble floor of the foyer, rubbing Edwina's soft tummy and twirling her around and around on the smooth, slippery surface, laughing while Edwina playfully growled and yipped, her tail going a mile a minute. Whenever Zoe stopped wrestling with her, Edwina whined and bared her sharp little teeth, gently grabbing Zoe's wrist in her mouth to show she wanted more. At last, Zoe gathered her into her lap and rocked her back and forth until, just like a baby, she quieted down, her tongue lolling out of her mouth.

After she had taken Edwina for a little walk along the Mall, just up to Hereford Street and back, Zoe called the hospital, finally tracking Arthur to the lounge. She waited impatiently while an aide ran to bring him to the phone in the nurses' station.

"How's she doing?" Zoe held her mouth close to the phone. "Same?"

"Pretty much the same. Well, maybe worse . . . same . . . who knows?"

"Will you be back for supper?" Zoe said, aware that the conversation was an echo of the one they'd had the other night. "I can fix you something. We have plenty in the house."

"Uh, no. Thanks all the same, Zo. I'll get something from the vending machines, like I did before. . . . Whatever."

"You're not going to stay there all night again, are you?" Zoe asked, surprised that she'd said it, wondering why it mattered.

Arthur paused as if the question required contemplation. "Umm. Probably not. But I'll be real late—I don't know exactly."

"Well, whatever you decide, dear," Zoe said, concealing a sigh. "Just come ahead."

"Yeah." And with that, he hung up.

Zoe put the kettle on for some instant coffee and tidied up the kitchen while she waited for the water to boil, thinking that of course Jim was right, all the problems *did* need to be confronted, "dealt with," as he'd said. But with Arthur evading as he did with such graceless force, it seemed almost impossible.

She thought of the wan affection with which Claudia had spoken of Arthur. "A precious person," she'd called him, needing comfort, care, sustenance. As who didn't? But it was fascinating to Zoe that her brother elicited a concern from others that sometimes merely skirted pity, even as they looked with admiration at the stubborn solitude with which he endured the life he had.

She changed into jeans, drank her coffee, and wandered through the house, melancholy but alert, looking at it all again. She paused in the open doorway of the library and saw the old Christmas angel where Arthur had left it on the breakfront shelf the other night. She picked it up with both hands, smiling with pursed lips into the painted eyes. Holding it gently against her chest, mindful of the delicate tulle wings, she went back to her own room and sat in her window seat with the angel in her lap, watching the last faint streaks of color fade out of the western sky. Her attention drifted from the darkened sky to the lights twinkling on in windows far across the Mall, to the few strollers, hugging their sleeves against the chill of the evening, who were making their way slowly along the path down the middle of the Mall.

Just as Zoe was Augusta Hillyard's "only living female descendant," or, as Jim said, soon would be, it impressed her that he was the only living person who had known her, who remembered her as more than ghost or icon—or soon would be. What sort of woman had Augusta Hillyard been? Why had she aroused such affection, admiration, and remorse? There was acknowledgment from both Jim and Annabelle that each had somehow failed to understand her, regretting it only now that it was much too late. Was it tolerable that when Annabelle died—and someday Jim Forbes also, in his turn—Augusta Hillyard would pass from memory as well?

Jim took it for granted that Zoe had a right to know everything about the family, an entitlement to share all secrets. But this was balanced by a responsibility to bring to closure all the family's affairs—to preside, as it were, as chatelaine over the changes that were coming. It was as if the very phrase "only living female descendant" were a title, somehow—capable of being inherited—to be lived up to, and then passed on again.

Entitlement to what? Zoe thought, looking out the window again, not sure of which she was more aware—the darkness or the lights that pierced it. What strange privilege, she wondered, comes with the title?

Some time later, still holding the angel, Zoe pushed open the paneled door of Grandmère's room. She flipped on the lights and closed the door firmly behind her. She set the angel down and stood in front of the fireplace with her hands clasped together, feeling a calm, almost lethargic kind of peace. Her eyes moved slowly around the room from object to object. After several minutes, knowing she was not really sure what she was looking for, hoping for, Zoe moved to the huge bureau and slowly opened the top left-hand drawer, the gilded knob warm under her hand.

In the drawer was a cluster of small cardboard jewelry boxes in some disarray, a lid off here, a bit of cotton batting discarded there. But she saw only trinkets, thoughtless gifts for some forgotten occasion. There were brooches made to look like little animals and birds with fake ruby eyes, a little chain between two enameled posies meant to clip an old lady's sweater snug around her shoulders, a string of small, discolored pearls that looked as if they might have been real, inside a flat white velvet box.

In the right-hand drawer were several shallow piles of gloves wrapped in brittle tissue. One pair, a pale, buttery color, was wrapped separately in a piece of white lawn; even though they were badly soiled, smelling faintly of grass and something sweeter, roses perhaps, the fine leather was still smooth. Zoe sat on the edge of the bed and tried one on. The yellow glove fit perfectly, and she twirled her hand in a gesture of welcome, smiling, chin high.

From the corner of her eye she saw that the skirt of the pink-beaded evening dress was still splayed out of the armoire door. Frowning, Zoe put down the yellow gloves and went over to tuck the gown back in. She managed to close the door only with some effort—it had expanded and warped over the years and was no longer flush. Leaning her hip and shoulder against the heavy frame, Zoe turned the brass-work handle, hearing a faint click, but when she let go, it popped open again with a little sucking sound, and she stood back to examine it more closely.

The lower portion of the wardrobe was like a cupboard, meant perhaps for quilts and bulky blankets; the two doors were just like the tall top portion, but more squared, the crotch mahogany pattern more geometric and compact. In the center of each of the cupboard doors was a heavy rose-shaped brass knob, the design mimicking the wrought handles of the upper doors. She grasped one in each hand and pulled with firm, equal force. They opened easily.

Fitting perfectly within, on either side of the center stile, were two large dark green boxes. Zoe sat on the carpet, reached for the one on the left, and tilted it toward her, surprised at its weight as she pulled it carefully between her legs. Embossed on the lid in raised white letters were the words R. H. STEARNS & COMPANY, BOSTON. The box was slightly less than two feet cubed, its edges somewhat worn as if with frequent gentle use, but unbroken. She set the lid aside.

The box was filled with reams of dull white paper of an odd, not quite modern letter size, tied neatly into bundles an inch or two in thickness, some with string, some with narrow ribbons, others with lengths of lace. The edges of the sheets were precisely lined up, though a few seemed bent as if once folded and smoothed out again, and every page of every bundle was covered with a clear and finely pointed hand, the ink faded to purple in some portions, some still dull and black, some blue.

Zoe pulled her knees up to her chin and leaned back against the side of the bed, breathing through her mouth, staring fixedly at the open box. After a while, she reached forward into the right-hand side of the cupboard, grasped the other box, and pulled it down onto the carpet before her. It was less square, more oval, but as large, CHAPEAUX embossed on the lid in gold. This box, too, was filled to the top with bundles of paper, some faded to ivory or a pearly gray, some the palest tan.

Zoe turned to the first box and took out several bundles and placed them side by side on the floor. Each page was dated, and she soon determined the sequence, laying out the packets in order: 1889 . . . 1891 . . . 1904 . . . 1911 . . . 1914.

At first she read only the top sheets, scanning the words as quickly as she could, her eyes flickering from page to page:

(October 22, 1891) . . . My sweet babies celebrated with us, certainly not quite ready for the cake, but ice cream is now their favorite. . . . (Wednesday, November 9, 1904) . . . Our usual Wednesday afternoon at Sue Snell's was much enlivened today by a visit from a cousin of the Bigelows who has just returned from a long trip through the West. She fascinated us all with her many photographs and lantern slides; she spoke most wonderfully of great icy mountains and sweeping vistas covered with flowers and curly buffalo. The tea cooled in my cup . . . . (Nahant, July 20, Thursday) . . . I would never have thought to find such solace here. . . . The girls pursue their solitary entertainments while I sit on the veranda surrounded by my books and needlework and stare at the blue ocean in which I once thought to lose myself. . . . And so Professor Wilson has been elected in a landslide. His idealism strikes terror into the hearts of the robber barons past, present, and to be. . . . (Sunday, November 10, 1912) . . . Eugene favors "isolationism" and insists that the growing rumbles abroad do not concern us here. Our hemisphere, he says, is sacred ground.

Zoe leaned over and read without touching the pages, now taking in several lines at a time, her stinging eyes mere inches from the paper though the writing was clear and black. . . .

(Friday, November 13) . . . and took myself, quite alone, to the group exhibition of the Guild of Boston Artists at the Copley Society. A very decent sherry was served, and I strolled past all the paintings feeling surprisingly at home in the rather festive atmosphere. There was no one I knew well and yet many whom I knew slightly. Our illustrious Mr. Tarbell was represented, of course, as well as a woman called Marie Page, who had some very oddly sweet pictures of mothers and their children. . . .

Another packet, tied with a dark blue silk ribbon:

(Tuesday, December 30, 1919) . . . Annabelle is off to New York for the holiday with some friends of the Wheelwrights. My private judgment tells me that the less said about that the better, either by Mother or by darling daughter. We are not expecting her until Sunday, at the soonest. . . .

Zoe leaned back against the bed again, her elbows propped on her bent knees, staring at the piles of paper on the carpet. She felt a small grabbing pain in her chest and throat, and swallowed hard, trying to dispel it.

Some time later, she got up and went to the window, staring out into the blackness of the Mall, her fingers unconsciously making nervous tapping movements on the glass. She knew what they were, of course, those boxes, those pages, what they *had* to be. But although she concentrated as hard as she could, she could not recall ever having heard even the vaguest suggestion from anyone—Annabelle, Aunt Paulette, Claudia—to indicate they might have been aware of it. "She kept herself to herself," Jim had said that very afternoon.

There was a gouged-out flaw in one of the panes with small, spidery cracks radiating from the center—almost like a bullet hole—although whatever had scarred the glass had not broken it. Zoe rubbed her index finger around and around over the web of minute cracks, her mind drifting, feeling a little sick and dizzy at the possibility that no one, either living or dead, had ever realized that Augusta Hillyard kept a diary.

She went back and settled herself on the floor again, and sat smoothing the edges of the bundles of paper, running her fingers over the taut ribbons. She kept wiping her face with the dry flat of her palms, over and over, pushing her hair back, hooking it behind her ears.

She chose a bundle marked "1907–1910," for the first time untying a ribbon. She read about a luncheon party in 1908; all of Augusta's lady friends were gathered around a table that glowed with spring flowers and bright crystal. Flora, the new maid, broke one of the goblets and wept "inconsolably" on her mistress's shoulder. Several pages farther on there was a long entry about a quiet autumn afternoon spent looking through old photographs with Zachary and Hortense, who sat, "enraptured," on the love seat beside their mother. She read about Trefoyles, Snells, Pickmans, Gardners, Lattimores—and of Eugene, always Eugene. All the ghosts come back to life.

Zoe spread the remainder of the bundle in a fan across the carpet and leaned over the pages, her hands in her hair, staring at the writing, knowing that this could be a Rosetta stone by which to know the legend, to decipher her secrets, to untie, ribbon by ribbon, the weft and weave of her long life . . . wondering if she dared.

At length, still uncertain but unable to resist, Zoe struggled to her knees and took all the bundles out of the first box and spread them out by date across the pattern of the carpet. At the very bottom of the box she saw several loose sheets of pale pink paper, engraved with a small silver crown-and-feather emblem and the name of a hotel in London that was not familiar to her. Written in the same fine hand was *"January 15, 1882, Chestnut Street"*—the earliest date she'd seen so far. The entries on the pink paper told of the last days of Grandmère's wedding trip in 1881, and her return in dead of winter to Boston:

. . . darling Papa was so proud at dinner, smiling and kissing my cheek as he placed the key—tucked in a little drawstring pouch that Mama made from a bit of satin cut from the fitting of my wedding dress—into my hands. . . . Our home is to be in the new wilderness of Commonwealth Avenue, at the very border—the *frontier!*—near Exeter Street. Mama and Aunt Sallie Cabot spent the winter supervising the workmen and choosing many furnishings, though of course leaving the greater part for me to do, since Mama knows she does not share my taste. . . . It piques Eugene, I think, to know the house is really mine. Of course, what's mine is his, as the saying goes, though Papa was most specific.

Yet it is for both of us and for our children (joy to come!) and all the Hillyards after us.

This house . . . not left to Augusta by Eugene as Uncle Jim had implied at lunch, but hers alone?

Zoe flipped back through other sections, rereading pages in this new light, but not sure why it made a difference. As she read, she felt as if she were watching from behind a curtain, catching glimpses of musicales and tea parties and winter breakfasts with the children, the very preserves on the table made from the berries at Nahant. She saw Christmas receptions with French champagne and sparkling snow, and Thanksgiving feasts and birthday celebrations—a century lived in a house so well beloved, given to Augusta Hillyard by her precious father . . . *not* Eugene.

Zoe paused to catch her breath and held her limp hair out of her eyes with both hands, thinking of intrusion—and entitlement.

She had no idea how much time had passed when, finally, she roused herself and knelt to gather the sections she had strewn about and placed them neatly back into the first square box. She pulled her wrinkled blouse out of the waist of her jeans and, grimacing with the effort, lifted the box back into the armoire, shutting just the left-hand door.

Glancing at her watch, she realized she should stop. It was nearly midnight! Time to stop and reconsider. "Oh, Grandmère," she said aloud, looking up at the shadows of the ceiling. "What do you want me to do?"

Just then she noticed a bundle near the top of the second box that was tied with a pink ribbon as from a baby's gown; the stem of a little faded silk rosette was stuck through the knot. A small scrap of paper was tucked underneath with "1938 to 1941" written on it in the same decisive hand. Zoe pinched out the little floweret and carefully untied the pink ribbon, telling herself she could not let go so soon, would read only one more little bit:

(Tuesday, March 22, 1938) . . . a crisp and glowing early spring day— filled with crocuses, jonquils, and the arrival home of the newlyweds! When Celia was here to lunch last Friday with poor Anne (who is feeling not at all well these days), she reported that she'd had a letter from Paulette, postmarked Rome, just two weeks ago—and here they are returned! Celia called this morning to invite us all to dinner tonight to welcome her dear children back (and see their souvenirs!); Paulette herself got on the phone for a moment to tell me that she is delighted to be back in time to join in another welcome, as Celia evidently reminded her that Laura's new arrival is expected within the month. . . .

Zoe stopped abruptly and turned back to the date of the entry. Laura, she thought to herself, my mother—pregnant with *Arthur!*

. . . but Laura is somewhat out of sorts these days, and has declined to accompany the rest of us to Celia's dinner party. Of course, pregnancy in its last days can be a wearisome thing, but her ill temper does not seem to be much brightened by the joy to come and Laura will not be swayed from her unsocial course. . . . (Thursday, April 28) . . . Arthur John Hillyard presented himself to his expectant family very much on schedule. Old Dr. Thayer, buttoning his cuffs as he came down the front stairs of their little place in Brookline, was surprised, I think, that Laura brought Baby Arthur all the way to term, since she was so peevish toward the end, but here he is—not a large infant, but rosy and stout of lung all the same. That little Arthur has been named for John Arthur, my eldest brother, seemed, at first blush, to be a handsome compliment on Laura's part, and one imagined (for a moment!) that young Eugene himself had insisted that an old Lattimore name be carried through. But in retrospect, having had some time to mull this over, I think perhaps Laura and Eugene have given the child this name out of indifference, turning the two names around in fact from a failure either of memory or of interest, as if it were so much easier to hark back to the early generation, pick out any old name, and have done with it. . . . Annabelle, however, has taken quite a fancy to the child, for reasons which are not really a mystery to me. In the two days that the little man has been upon this earth, his great-aunt Annabelle has coddled and cosseted him far more than his own mother now seems likely to do.

Zoe put the page down and thought of Arthur, who was even at that moment at Annabelle's bedside, "coddling and cosseting" her with the same devotion she had shown to him, forty-four years before. She found it ironic that Grandmère could not have foreseen the symmetry with which that fierce attachment would draw to its conclusion.

The next page was covered with a series of scribbled numbers and small calculations, all of which had been vigorously scratched out, almost in anger, some by the very splatters of ink caused by the motion of the pen. Zoe wondered why Augusta had saved the sheet; perhaps she'd merely forgotten it was there? But the next entry seemed to provide some explanation:

(Monday, May 30, 1938) . . . I have taken myself off to see young Jimmie Forbes, who has set up shop as a lawyer. He's rented a small chamber down on Batterymarch Street, not very impressive if he wishes to build a practice on the backs of the self-styled aristocrats hereabouts, but that's not important now. Our Jim has two qualities I've learned to value, possibly too late in my elongated life: he is honest and he has a sense of humor—exactly like his sister, dear Paulette. I traveled into town this morning and spent two pleasant hours with him. His cheerful disposition may or may not stand him in good stead with his dour clients-to-be, but those twinkling eyes suit me very well. Naturally, there's a great deal that young Jim has no need to know, but I do have a few pennies put aside, and these we have arranged in trust for little Arthur, who may find himself glad of Grandmère's small nest egg in the future. . . .

Zoe paused again as she imagined Uncle Jim smiling at Grandmère in his courtly way—just as he had looked at her that very afternoon.

The next entries were scattered, as if Grandmère had had a busy summer; there were just a few notes for a week in July, and a Monday afternoon in August when there was some sort of spat between Laura and Annabelle that Grandmère wrote about at great length, her annoyance with them both perfectly clear.

Then there was nothing until September 22. Glancing down the page, Zoe realized that this was about the great hurricane of 1938, and, intrigued, she went back and read more carefully:

. . . and the trees on the Mall are still blowing nearly double! Though the hurricane has now moved well offshore, or so they told us on the radio this morning, it has taken with it, I fear, a good part of the Hillyard roof, as well as trees and bushes by the score and more than seven hundred lives here in Massachusetts and down the eastern seaboard. . . .

There is no question of not repairing the house, and I said as much to Anthony in no uncertain terms, but he is entirely concerned with his own losses, although what he has left to lose, I'm sure I've no idea. . . . (Saturday, September 24) . . . This morning I was paid a visit by Mr. Spencer Trefoyle (whose sulking paramour lounged in the doorway behind him as we spoke). He asked to be allowed to help with the repairs to the house. Although my first reaction was to throw him out, I held my tongue and thought: Well, Augusta! "Pride goeth before destruction and a haughty spirit" and all the rest of it, and if he's offering to help me fix my house, whyever not? It is rather too late for "pride," after all, as the "destruction" has occurred already! . . . There will be quite a bit of work to do, particularly on the roof and in the front yard, and we are anticipating, I believe, a very large expenditure. Although I despise the circumstances, I may permit myself a small metaphor and say "any port in a storm!" Since Anthony Hillyard is not to be a port in this crisis, I will head for the harbor which Spencer Trefoyle offers and reread Machiavelli at my leisure. . . .

Zoe found herself looking toward the window as if the famous hurricane were blowing right outside, remembering Spencer Trefoyle's dark face in the photograph on Annabelle's table. She took a deep breath and turned to a small sheaf of entries for the early months of 1939, which were written on a brittle onionskin paper that crackled as she read:

(Friday, April 28, 1939) . . . We have had a very sweet little party here today for Baby Arthur's first birthday. I am pleased to say that in spite of certain upheavals in his parents' household, our little one has had a quiet, even uneventful year. Proud as could be, he toddled down the Mall today in his nice new shoes, and fell with a gurgle into my outstretched hands, thus taking his first steps here in front of our home— which is now his as well. . . . Although Laura and Eugene have made all the self-serving noises one would expect of such a pair, when Celia came to me last week, very distressed to say that they were not managing at all well over there in Brookline, I said, of course, that we would have them in. This is good news to Annabelle, particularly in Trefoyle's recurring absence, and she is eager to have her pet just down the hall. I feel as if we have history repeating itself here on Commonwealth Avenue with yet another generation of Hillyards taking refuge in my house. It is precisely as my father intended, though perhaps through forces he did not anticipate . . . but it is not the first time that we have had an imperfect confederation under this old (new!) roof. . . . They should be well ensconced by next weekend at the latest.

Zoe paged swiftly through the summer and fall of 1939, thinking of the little boy, "in his nice new shoes," who had become her brother. He had stepped in for Spencer Trefoyle so much earlier than she had ever imagined. A tingle of pity for Annabelle came and went, just a shiver of sadness, as she read on through Christmas of 1939 and the new year:

(February 14, 1940) . . . Ah! My poor Anne. As my papa would say, her troubles are all over. I held a weeping Celia Wheelwright to my heart this afternoon as they laid her mother's casket in the Lowell vault. Anne Higgins Lowell: my last friend. I feel that I am outliving everyone I know. So many are gone—Zachary, Mathilde, Sarah, Alex, John . . . and Eugene. Everyone is gone and I sit here, aged but upright, taking what I confess to be an immoderate and unbecoming pride in being the last to go. And yet I am alone, alone with memories too rich to bear, and with regret too close for comfort, though I fight it off. . . . I have loved more fully and more deeply than anybody ever knew, nor was I *myself* aware until (belatedly) I ranged my ghosts around me and declared my devotion to each one. If I did Anne Lowell a disservice while she lived by lack of love expressed (though felt! Oh, deeply felt!), because I did not have the wisdom, courage, spirit (which? all?) to tell her what was in my heart, my tears for that omission cannot, as the poet tells us, wash it out. But love her I did, more than she knew, and so I must tell her now, in this strange way. . . .

As Zoe set the page aside, an old-fashioned sepia portrait fell out of the bundle. It was a photograph of a young woman in a wedding dress, the train of the gown swirled about her feet, a slight, anxious smile upon her lips. She held a small cascading bouquet of white flowers. An inscription in a copperplate hand read: "To my beloved Augusta—my true, eternal 'Maid of Honor.' Your faithful Anne. May 11, 1881."

Zoe was unaware that her mouth was open in a wide, astonished smile. Anne Lowell was the great-grandmother she and Arthur shared with Claudia. Zoe looked carefully into the young bride's sweet, pensive face, searching for any elusive resemblance to the woman Claudia Wheelwright had become. Though everyone always said Claudia favored the Wheelwrights with their blue eyes and robust constitutions, there was a gentleness, an innocence, in Anne Lowell's gaze that Zoe recognized at once.

She tucked the picture back as she'd found it and paged through the rest of 1940, the warm spring, and the early days of the war in Europe, of which Augusta wrote with an almost personal dread. "As I reflect on past wars," she wrote on June 17, "the one into which I was born and the horror that they said would end all war, I have an intuition that this one will far surpass that other nightmare—the times are more egregious now and life is more cheaply held."

Zoe frowned and read on, noting the family's damp and quiet Christmas, the unsettled atmosphere in the house, Annabelle and Laura circling each other like "competitive lionesses," while little Arthur—according to his Grandmère, blissfully oblivious to the conflict simmering around him—spent his days happily nestled away in the back parlor, playing with some little trains, endlessly listening to his music box. As she gently touched Arthur's name in Grandmère's handwriting on the page, Zoe could not shake off the feeling that she was like a member of an audience at a Greek play, centuries ago on a hillside in Thessaly, waiting, knowing the ending, but unable to drag her eyes and thoughts away as the inevitabilities unfolded.

Her eyes came to rest on an entry from the spring of 1941, written in obvious heat, the writing still black and clear.

(April 10, Thursday) . . . The situation is now complicated in a way I probably should have anticipated. That damned Spencer Trefoyle is lurking about the house more and more, dividing his attentions, in a very strange fashion, between Laura and Annabelle. Annabelle has never looked with any affection upon Laura (this in spite of the fact that she brought sweet little Arthur into the world), and her dislike is now exacerbated by Spencer's behavior and his gifts to Laura, which cannot really be viewed as "fatherly" in spite of the fact that she insists they are but friendly tokens meant only as homage to her "delicate condition." It is so hard to know what to make of it, but I've decided that as it is all so disruptive, he must not be permitted to present himself here again.

Whatever debt I may have had to Spencer Trefoyle on the account of my house is, as far as I am concerned, now fully paid! I said as much to Annabelle this evening after dinner. I told her that I would no longer allow him under my roof whatever role he may have played in its replacement. I fear, in retrospect, that I rather badly outsmarted myself by doing so, but there it is. Although I realize that with this high-handed "lady of the manor" approach I may have done irreparable harm to whatever remains of my relationship with my younger daughter, I am more concerned with trying to create at least a *semblance* of peaceful family life for little Arthur's sake. His elders will have to play out their wretched little melodramas elsewhere—we have had far more "theater" here today than suits my taste. . . .

Grandmère then wrote nothing at all for nearly two weeks. As Zoe fingered the pages and read the April 10 entry again, it occurred to her that Jim had rather pointedly avoided mentioning Eugene and Laura Hillyard today at lunch, though there had been opportunities aplenty. Perhaps he knew this miserable little story but was loath to hurt Zoe's feelings by the telling of it. The tawdriness was distasteful to her, sickening.

As she was about to put the page aside, however, she recalled that until Saturday afternoon in the hospital, Annabelle had never (at least not that Zoe could remember) actually spoken ill of her mother. Even the act of closing up Augusta's room, treating it as a kind of shrine, had always seemed to Zoe and Arthur to be a kind of devotion—a memorial—although they were only children in those days and could not, of course, have perceived a nuance. Zoe frowned at the page from April 10, wondering if she had misjudged Annabelle, if she herself was seriously at fault for having spent decades thinking of her only as—what did Arthur call her?—a "self-absorbed, frivolous old bitch." Of course, all that was true enough, but was there more? Zoe realized she would never, never know.

She turned several pages in her haste to get away from Laura, Eugene, and Spencer Trefoyle, but an entry from the end of October proved that she could not so easily elude them. The disruptions their behavior caused affected everyone, and Augusta was clearly at her wit's end with them.

. . . It seems to me that on no account should a young man with a small child and a very pregnant wife even be *thinking* about dashing off to an undeclared war, and yet young Eugene talks about this all the time. He is a selfish, foolish boy who hardly has the stuff of heroism in him (if that is indeed his fantasy). Just last night as Annabelle and I were listening to the radio reports of the terrible torpedo attacks off the coast of Iceland, he came rushing into the back parlor wailing about how he wanted to be "involved," as he called it, to join up! He snarls that he was "cheated" out of the Spanish Civil War (which so inconveniently coincided with his marriage) and does not intend to be cheated out of this one. He is just appalling.

Laura, of course, makes no attempt to hold her tongue, to let his adolescent fantasy play itself out—as it would doubtless do if Eugene were simply left to bluster on. But Laura is not known for her forbearance, her wisdom, or her tact, and their incessant bickering is wearing very thin indeed. Laura makes all the use she can of her pregnancy to try to haul her silly husband into line, but he is every bit as selfish and pigheaded as she. I lay awake the other night listening to their latest squabble, hard put not to run down the hall in my nightgown and throw them both into the street. They are an exhausting pair and no mistake!

Zoe leaned back against the side of Grandmère's bed and read about her parents once again, searching in vain for a sense of pity or tenderness toward those petulant, unloving children. They seemed to her to be hardly more than cardboard characters in a story spun by Grandmère. An egg and a sperm, Zoe thought, wincing; that's all they were to me.

But as she read through the last days of 1941, Zoe's sense of being just a spectator fell away:

(Monday, December 8, 1941, midnight) . . . The cold winter sun set today on the entry of the United States into the war—and on the newest Hillyard. If there is a prayer left in this old heart, it is that there be no omen here.

At two o'clock this afternoon, in the midst of flying snowflakes and the reverberations of Mr. Roosevelt's Declaration of War, Laura Wheelwright Hillyard was brought to bed of a girl—the first baby born in this house in over fifty years.

So suddenly did her labor come upon her (virtually at the *crest* of yet another violent argument with Eugene!), that there was no time, particularly in such dreadful weather, to travel to the Lying-In as planned. Doctor, nurse, family all watched, horrified, as the battle raged between the parents even as the baby, plump and healthy (with black eyes like my own Anthony), was brought into the world. She was at once washed and wrapped and handed to Grandmère to hold, and I carried her away at once, down to this very room, out of earshot of the cries and recriminations of her distracted parents.

I think Laura scarcely felt the pain; it was merely an inconvenience. She even refused to hold the child—indeed, it seemed she barely noticed as it was taken from her body, for she was too locked in conflict with Eugene to give so much as a glance to her new daughter. What should have been great joy in the child's arrival was eclipsed completely by the bitter argument between them (which has raged on all autumn long!)—over selfishness, over deceit, over Eugene's ridiculous insistence upon going off to war. Although the doctor tried to calm her, Laura would not be silenced. Her attention was all upon her husband (in attendance at the birth, shocking one and all!), who vows that he *will* leave, will go to the war which was also born today.

Celia, who arrived before noon, eager for her third grandchild, carrying lovely blush-pink roses out of season, and a silver cup given to Laura at her own birth by the Lowells, left the house in tears mere hours later. Fortunately, Annabelle and little Arthur went with her, off to the Wheelwrights, and Annabelle has telephoned to say that they will stay the night.

. . . I am a sensible woman, always have been. I walk under ladders; I have bought opals for myself. . . . I kept a black cat once for years. But there is one superstition I will not turn my back on: I cannot let the sun go down on an unnamed infant. Of course, since we are but two weeks from the solstice it was dark by four o'clock, yet the symbol seemed strong to me. I set the baby in Zachary's cradle (retrieved from the cellar last week and cleaned for this occasion), and while Veronica watched and rocked her, I went as briskly as I could to Laura and Eugene to ask them for a name.

Though she was desperately tired, Laura's ferocity toward her husband seemed unabated. She waved me away with an indifferent hand when I explained my purpose.

"The child must have a name," I said.

From her pillow, Laura shrugged and looked at the ceiling.

"Grandmère," said Eugene, "do whatever you want," and so saying turned back to his wife.

Pertinaciously I stood there, asked again. "You must have talked about this," I said, "made a plan. What is her name?"

Laura, white-faced with pain and anger, turned her Wheelwright eyes to me and sighed—in exhaustion or disgust I can't be sure. "It doesn't matter . . . it can wait."

"It can't," I said.

"Pick it out yourself, then, Grandmère," Eugene cut in. "Whatever you choose will be fine."

And they never knew that I had left the room. . . . I came back here and took the baby into my lap, watching as she sucked with her little lips upon a warm bottle of thin milk. After a few minutes she loosed her tiny gums and, as I fancied it, looked with her bright new eyes into mine. Even now, with midnight passing, and the baby fast asleep beside me, it gladdens me to think that her first view of the world was of her Grandmère's face. There may not be a proper mother for this precious child, but there will be love enough from her Grandmère. I felt this afternoon—and feel more strongly now—that she is as my own and not two generations gone between us. . . .

I sat in the warm firelight, holding her as she burbled softly and soon slept, and rocked her in my arms and sought a name. What name, I wondered, for a child come to her life on the first day of a war that promises to burn and thunder for hard years to come? And ZOE came into my mind—the Greek for LIFE . . . and AMERICA—our country that we cherish and now fear for.

I hope I live long enough to see this baby girl grow up to learn with what great love her Grandmère has welcomed her into this beautiful and sorry world.

ZOE AMERICA HILLYARD: A fine name. It should last her.

Zoe began to cry, and cried with her mouth wide open the way animals and little children do, fists curled hard against her stomach—rocking back and forth with a primitive, rhythmic shudder, losing her breath and sobbing in little shrieking sounds as the oxygen flooded in.

". . . Oh, God . . . Grandmère . . . I'm sorry I'm sorry sorry sorry . . ."

She stood up on stiff, unwilling hips, the tears pouring down her face and falling to the wrinkled page to magnify the words. Still shuddering and swallowing, ragged sobs escaping from her throat, she made her way to the bathroom down the hall, where she blew her nose and held palms full of cold water to her eyes. She slipped down to her knees on the chipped marble floor, her wet hands in her tousled hair, and cried some more.

At last she got up, washed her face again and dried it, and went downstairs. Arthur's cheap scotch was where she'd seen him hide it, and she poured an inch or two into a glass and drank it slowly with two aspirins. She began to see flashing white lights in her peripheral vision and sat down on the floor and put her head between her knees, trying to absorb the sense of conversion to an unidentified cause. And cried again.

Edwina came in, making small whiny sounds, and pushed against her, licking her hand until, ignored, she wandered over to her basket in the corner to fall asleep again. Zoe leaned all her weight against the refrigerator and sipped the scotch, feeling dizzy and nauseated, emptied of everything but what she'd learned.

There was so much history she had never known—all the myths and legends from decades already decades out of mind—family lore filled with tales of seashells and scandals, hurricanes and wedding parties, bisque angels and silver services, feuds and childhood friends. Others knew these stories, had been part of them—had been characters on that bright stage.

But here, precious and infinitely secret, one final story, beside which all legends paled, a story known to no one but the only living female descendant: that Augusta Hillyard had kept a diary and in that diary, on Zoe's first night on earth, was recorded not only the child's name, but more than that: her claim on a place in the wide circle of the ghosts who came before.

Zoe held the glass against her forehead, then slid boneless and exhausted to the floor, closing her eyes against the lights, against her own still-flowing tears. . . .

. . . And on the dining-room table, after three whole days of feeding on mere slivers of light, the water in the vase unchanged for all that time, the lilacs—well and truly forced—were open.

Part Three

MASTERPIECE

You are reaching a time when you will find out what my own father pointed out to me at a very trying time in my own career: that family is more important than the individual, that a family must be solid before the world no matter what the faults may be of a single member, that a family has a heritage to hand down which must be protected.

—JOHN P. MARQUAND, *The Late George Apley*

THIRTY

*Z*oe awoke late Friday morning with a blazing headache, confused at first to find herself lying in her nightgown on the damask cover of Augusta's bed. Full, bright daylight streamed through the curtains. She felt disoriented, exhausted, and lay still for a minute staring at the ceiling medallions, slowly remembering that she had come back, close to dawn, to gather all the scattered pages of the diary and put the oval green box back in the armoire. She was not sure why she felt so relieved that she'd done it before she fell asleep.

Back in her own room, Zoe changed into slacks and a gray sweater, then went slowly, still in a daze, down to the kitchen. She put the kettle on, took two aspirins, and sat finally at the table, both hands around the cup, watching the foam swirl on the surface of her instant coffee. For the first time in over a year she really wished she had a cigarette.

She was waiting blankly for the first jolt of caffeine to have a chance to settle, her mind clearing slowly, when the phone rang loud and long. It was almost a minute before Arthur's sobs receded and he could talk.

"When?" Zoe whispered. "When, dear?"

Arthur managed to sniff and blow his nose. "About . . . half an hour ago. . . . I was there . . . I was right there, by her bed, thank God, and . . ."

"I'll be right over. Arthur? . . . Arthur, dear, go to the main lobby and wait for me, okay?"

His weeping started again, and she heard him hiccoughing and blowing his nose again.

"Okay. . . . When can you come, Zo?"

"Right *now*. Just wait for me."

As soon as she hung up the phone, Zoe poured her coffee down the sink, ran to grab her bag and jacket from her room, and hurried back to the kitchen to call Claudia and a taxi.

When she came through the wide main doors of the hospital about twenty minutes later, she immediately saw Arthur sitting hunched on a small sofa near the gift shop with a big white plastic bag in his lap that had "Personal Possessions" stamped on it in blue letters. He looked up at her with a confused, dull expression, and sank against her willingly when she sat and put her arms around him. They were still sitting there, Arthur weeping again, silently, when Claudia, Eddie, and Uncle Jim arrived.

Jim sat down and put a hand on Arthur's knee. "Let's get on home, son. We'll take you home."

Claudia dug into her purse for Kleenex and gave a bunch to Arthur, bending over to kiss him on the forehead as she did so.

"Come on, sweetie, let's go," she said, squatting in front of his knees to smile gently up at him. Eddie, hands deep in his windbreaker pockets, stood back and watched them all, his lips pressed tight together.

By the time they got back to Commonwealth Avenue it was well after one o'clock. Arthur, still grasping the handles of the plastic bag, went to the kitchen cupboard for his scotch and emptied the bottle into a Road Runner glass. He opened the door to the back alley and sat on the top step, staring at nothing, until Claudia gently ruffled his hair and led him into the dining room to join the others, who sat clustered at one end of the long table, eating Zoe's now-ripened Bosc pears and passing plates of crackers and cheese and a bowl of oranges back and forth.

As they stirred sugar into their coffee, Zoe watched them, trying to absorb the fact that it had only been a week since the last gathering at this table—all of them, except for Jim, making small talk under the dirty chandelier, with Zoe herself but minutes off the plane from California. Now they ate the fruits and cheeses she had bought, and drank the coffee she had made, and tried to figure out how to put a funeral together by Monday, the day Arthur—for reasons no one else could fathom—was insisting on.

"You know, guys," said Claudia, looking up from the cracker she was meticulously covering with Brie, "the Marathon's on Monday."

"Oh, goodness, that's right," said Eddie, pouring more cream into his tea. "They leave Hopkinton what? Noon?"

"Noon sharp," said Claudia, licking her knife, her vivid blue eyes looking like her father's or her grandfather Wheelwright's, or Laura's—Zoe couldn't be sure. Arthur sat staring morosely at his glass of scotch, seeming still to be the "sweet little man" who had taken his first steps nearly forty-four years ago into Grandmère's waiting arms.

"So we'll have to be back here before two at the absolute latest," Claudia was saying. "That's when the winners start coming into Copley Square—two, maybe ten after." She looked at Arthur, hoping for a suggestion, a compromise, but he nipped silently at his scotch, ignoring everyone.

Uncle Jim got up and gently pried the plastic bag out of Arthur's fingers and put a cup of hot coffee in front of him. He moved the glass full of scotch into the center of the table near the thick purple lilacs.

"We've got to make some decisions here, son," he said softly, hitching up his trousers to sit. Zoe had a flash of "young Jimmie Forbes," leaning toward imperial old Augusta Hillyard, perfect in pearls and a large hat, enthroned in the one decent chair in his shabby office, almost fifty years ago.

"You sure you want the funeral on Monday? That's a little tight for planning. . . . You're going to want everything to be nice for her, Arthur, isn't that right? 'Course it is. . . . Arthur?"

Arthur turned slowly toward Jim, inhaled, and nodded. "Monday's best," he said. "No reason to delay it, or anything."

"Okay," said Claudia. "Fine. Monday it is. Now, what about a wake?"

"A what?" Arthur, galvanized somehow by the word, looked in horror at Claudia, his eyes large behind his smudged spectacles.

Claudia sighed. "A *viewing,* dear, in the funeral home."

Arthur shook his head back and forth in rapid short movements. "Absolutely not . . . no!"

"All right, that's all right . . . no viewing. But don't you think we should have some sort of refreshments here . . . a reception after the cemetery? It's going to be in the *Globe,* after all. People will want to come over."

"Well, we're going to have to get the house ready in that case," said Eddie, glancing around the grimy dining room.

"Look," said Zoe, rousing herself. The headache, which had receded from necessity, crept back again, settling down behind her eyes. "First things first. If we want to have the service on Monday, we've got to get squared away with the funeral home as soon as possible. Arthur . . ." She leaned toward him across the table. "Honey?"

"I'll call over to Leape & Neames," Jim said, his hand still tight on Arthur's shoulder. "Let them know we're on our way. We'll get it all figured out here this afternoon."

"Want us to go ahead and take care of it, Arturo?" said Eddie, looking up from his tea, his forehead creased with uncertainty.

"How about that, son?" said Jim. "You could probably afford to get some rest. You can do that while Zoe and I—"

"No! No, I'm going. Let's go." Arthur struggled to his feet and shambled off to take the plastic bag upstairs.

"You think they'll really come?" Claudia said morosely after Arthur left the room.

"Don't you worry about that," Jim said. "You'll have a raft of old ladies here falling all over themselves trying to get to the sherry. They'll be here, all right. Hell, you won't be able to breathe for the Shalimar."

When Arthur came downstairs a few minutes later, clutching a bright blue dress of Annabelle's clumsily wrapped in tissue, everyone agreed it would be best if Claudia and Eddie stayed behind to get a start on the cleaning, while Zoe and Uncle Jim took Arthur over to Leape & Neames to make what Jim called "the arrangements."

At the funeral home, the tall, soft undertaker, his prominent red-brown eyes shiny with expert sympathy, led them to the casket showroom in the basement. Zoe leaned against a cement pillar while Arthur followed Mr. Leape from walnut to oak to bronze, cautiously touching the satin linings with his long fingers. Zoe's headache looped faintly through her eyes as she watched them, thinking most particularly of money, guessing she should have taken Jim's gentle but clear advice and thought of it before.

Upstairs in the "family room," after a few awkward courtesies, they took their seats around the long polished table and got down to cases. As the conversation progressed, Arthur receded, staring into space, finally going to the windows that looked out over the garages, where men in shirtsleeves and Celtics T-shirts were polishing the hearses and limousines, sweeping flower remnants and bits of ribbon briskly onto the driveway. Zoe thought suddenly that this was exactly what Arthur had done when they'd gone to see the social worker—gazed into the middle distance with his back to the action, to the reality of it all.

". . . and from the church. . ." Mr. Leape asked, eyebrows inquiring as the voice did not.

"We want to have the service here," Zoe said, imagining the Marathon winners zooming into Copley Square, mere yards from the church, and the crowds of screaming people who would not be interested in making way for Annabelle's cortège.

Mr. Leape consulted his records. Hillyards, Lattimores, and Wheelwrights had been buried from Trinity Church for years, and of course Leape & Neames had always handled "the arrangements," which had been virtually the same for generations.

"Surely the pastor . . ." Leape began, disturbed at this irregularity.

"Oh, he'll be here," said Jim. "Matter of fact, I'd like to use your phone, sir, if you'd be so kindly; haven't had a chance to call Bob as yet." Leape led Jim into a small office and closed the door behind him.

"Now, Miss Hillyard," he began again, giving Zoe a deferential smile. He clearly regarded her as the head of the family, despite the fact that she had arrived at his white-columned establishment accompanied by two men. In his experience, women mourned and men arranged, but this did not seem to be the case with the current Hillyards.

"Mr. Leape, may we wrap this up, please," she said, pulling her checkbook from her bag and looking toward Arthur, who had not moved from the window—and who produced no checkbook of his own. She went over the expenses on her fingers, glancing at the printed list of charges Mr. Leape was reading upside-down, pointing out the line items one by one with his gold pen as he explained them once again. Zoe thought it was like storyboarding the end of Annabelle, nothing forgotten but the six black horses with ostrich plumes (which Annabelle would probably have wanted).

"Are you sure about the limousines? Only two?" Mr. Leape found her choice of such spartan arrangements disconcerting; surely the clan would gather? After all, no Hillyard had died since that old bastard Anthony had departed this life nearly thirty years ago. Leape had heard stories from his father and old Mr. Neames about *that*.

"Two is plenty. And no flower car."

Leape was privately horrified at this crass disregard for tradition, but he carefully rubbed out the dollar figure after "flower car" and made a little "-0-" on the line.

When Jim came back from the phone, Zoe was writing a check. Arthur still stood against the window, his nose nearly pressed to the glass. He had not turned around at all, not even when the final figure was mentioned. Jim stood behind Zoe's chair as she handed the check to Mr. Leape.

"It's all set," he said, reaching into his pocket for Eddie's car keys. "Spoke to the pastor himself. He says ten o'clock is fine, but he'd take it as a favor if everyone was real punctual about it—seems he's got a wedding in the afternoon."

"Splendid. Oh, Miss Hillyard . . ." The paperwork was evidently incomplete, as was the check. Zoe signed her name to the balance, looked once again into Mr. Leape's gingerbread man's eyes, and, corralling Arthur, they left.

When they got back to the house, Claudia was on the phone in the kitchen, but Eddie, in his undershirt, was busy in the parlor. He had rolled up the huge, dusty Sarouk, pushed all the furniture into the middle of the room, and was sweeping the baseboards with an old broom. The late-afternoon light was slanting through the rippled glass of the bowed-out parlor windows, illuminating the mess.

Though she had eaten nothing for a whole day, Zoe's headache was gone, and as she went to join Claudia in the kitchen she felt a kind of second wind as if the hours at the funeral home had refreshed her. An important tribal task had been dispatched, even though she knew perfectly well that the check she'd handed to Mr. Leape with such aplomb would bounce sky-high unless Roger covered it at her bank in California.

Eddie came in to wash his hands and volunteered to go up to Boylston Street to get some take-out from the Peking Grotto, even over Claudia's protest that Chinese food was too festive.

"You're nuts," he said, kissing her on his way out the door.

"Well, it's true," Claudia said to Zoe, waving at Eddie as he disappeared down the alley. "I guess I just associate Chinese food with good times. Remember, Zo? It was always offered to us as a reward when we were kids." Claudia frowned in annoyance at herself. "I guess I'm being silly, huh?"

Zoe, leaning against the stove with a glass of wine, felt an intense rush of affection and went over to put her arms around her cousin.

"Thanks for everything, Claud," she mumbled into the frosted hair. "Everything—and all that's coming, too, I guess."

Claudia smiled up at Zoe and kissed her on the cheek.

"What do you say we just slurp up that Chinese food and get on home, okay? Let you guys get some sleep. I'll be back in the morning and you and I can have at it again." Claudia hoisted herself onto the sink rim and sipped the wine Zoe poured for her. Her loafers dangled from her toes.

"Listen," she said, looking at Zoe, who was sitting in the alley doorway, "do you have something to wear?"

"Wear? Oh! To the funeral. My goodness, I never thought of that; I certainly can't wear anything I brought with me. Think we can pick up something tomorrow?" Uncertain, Zoe looked up at Claudia, who brightened at the thought of shopping.

"No problem. We'll do it in the morning. Lord & Taylor's just around the corner. Okay with you?"

"Sure."

Claudia slid off the sink and stepped over Zoe's legs to sit just below her on the chipped alley steps.

"Doesn't seem right to be eating Chinese food and going shopping," she said, "but dammit, Zo, I'm not going to miss the old bag, and that's the truth."

Claudia looked unhappy and embarrassed; she took off one loafer and scratched furiously at her instep. "Sorry . . . that just popped out."

"Don't worry about it," Zoe said. She put her hand on Claudia's shoulder. "Look," she said, "I just want to concentrate on helping Arthur survive the weekend and the funeral. And then . . . jeez, I don't know, what should I do, Claud? Maybe take him back with me for a while? Couple weeks? But oh God, I've got so much work to do on the picture . . ."

Or nothing, she thought, clenching her teeth. But she knew this was not the time to think about what had thus far been so studiously avoided, pushed so far away. There seemed to be no room in all this busy mourning for Frye, for that charlatan Gianfranco Sessa, no time for what she had, until so recently, supposed to be her only life.

By the time Zoe said good night to the Trouts and Uncle Jim, Arthur was already in bed. Exhausted as she was, she went through the downstairs rooms, checking the locks on all the doors, turning off the lights. The parlor was ghostly in the reflected light from the avenue; the furniture, clustered in the middle of the floor, looked like a child's fort. She went to the window and parted the curtains with her fingertips, startled to see that the same white Cadillac she'd seen last Sunday night was parked at the curb; the same man was standing with his elbows on the car's roof, smoking, and staring at the house.

Zoe quickly drew back her hand, but the curtains, rigid with dirt, remained just slightly parted, and she could watch without touching them. After a while, the man pitched his cigarette into the street, got into the car, and drove away. Zoe stood there, even after the Cadillac was completely out of sight, and thought of Arthur sleeping upstairs, dead to the world—consumed, perhaps, by more than grief?

Too weary for either curiosity or apprehension, she turned off the hall sconces and pulled herself up the staircase in the dark. She went into her room and sat on the edge of the bed, feeling light-headed and a little sick at her stomach, wondering if she could get away with waiting until the morning to call Roger. She was a little worried about covering the check to Leape & Neames, though she knew it couldn't bounce until Monday, maybe Tuesday.

But after a minute or two of fretting, Zoe admitted that the check had nothing to do with it. She longed to talk to Roger, to tell him about Grandmère and the diary, and all she'd learned about the past. But as soon as the idea came she knew it was out of the question. These were secrets meant to be kept. If she was to keep faith with Grandmère (than which nothing in the world seemed more important), she would have to deny herself forever the joy of telling anyone: not Roger, not Arthur or Claudia or Jim. No one. Ever. That is the promise you made when you turned the first page of Grandmère's diary, she said to herself. When you kept reading, when you knew you weren't going to stop, you made that bargain. . . .

Roger immediately offered to come to the funeral. "It's no problem, darling, I can get to Boston in plenty of time."

"I know, but there's really no need. I'll be back probably Monday night, Rog. I thought I'd get a flight right after the reception."

"Zo, you sound like hell—you must be exhausted. You sure about this?"

"I'm sure, yes. I'm really tired, but I think all I need is one good night's sleep. I'll be okay."

Roger was chewing on the apple he'd been eating when she called. She could hear him through the wire, her eyes smarting.

"How much was the check again?" he said.

"Eighteen fifty." Zoe put her cold hand on her forehead.

"That's not too bad, actually, for a Brahmin funeral," Roger said, chuckling a little through his teeth. He thought of the plain pine boxes in which his family were buried.

"That's just the down payment," Zoe said. "There's another five grand to go, *not* counting the casket. Jesus, Rog, you should see it— it's covered with carved rosettes and there's a pink satin lining. I can't imagine what came over Arthur. Anyway, do you think you can help me out?"

"Of course, honey, of course. I'll be at the bank first thing in the morning. Don't worry about it." Roger scraped at his apple with his top teeth. Zoe could see him doing it, thought of the nibbly way he liked to eat things like apples and carrots, and felt a sudden rush of hot familiarity. Listening to him eat his apple seemed intimate, precious.

"Zoe, look, I know this is a bad time, I know everyone's depending on you there and you have to handle everything, you have a lot on your mind, but .. "

Dear Roger, protecting me from what? Zoe wondered, though she knew the answer.

"Something happening with Sessa, is it?" she said with a small, ironic smile.

" 'fraid so."

"But he's not in L.A. Is he? I can't believe Frye would—"

"Sidney called about an hour ago to tell me Frye's coming back from Mexico sometime this weekend and Sessa will definitely be with him."

Zoe realized then that she hadn't in the least absorbed what Roger had told her Wednesday night; her sneering disregard for Gianfranco

Sessa's abilities had no force at all against the reality of his coming back from Mexico to take her place.

Zoe sighed and thought a minute. "Didn't the sketches come?"

"Not yet. You sent them when?"

"Um, Thursday? Yesterday? Yes, yesterday morning. Noonish, I guess it was. They'll probably get there tomorrow, Rog. The man said they do deliver Saturdays."

A moment went by in silence; another moment. Zoe shook her head slowly.

"What can I say, Rog? What can I *do* about it?" She let herself slide down onto the hall carpet runner with her back against the posts of the banister. "I seem to have sort of shifted gears, somehow," she said. "In the last two weeks, I . . . things seem very different to me."

Roger knew that. Last night he'd lain rigidly awake, looking blindly into the darkness of his bedroom, and found himself reviewing, comparing, all the conversations they'd had since that Sunday afternoon in Zoe's kitchen almost two weeks ago, when she had exploded into such angry fear at the thought of going to that place that she did not now want to leave.

"I can understand that," he said finally, his voice thick to his own ears. "I can, honey, but . . . Zo? You there?"

"I'm here . . . I'm here. I'm just awfully tired. I guess I'm feeling like I need a hug," she said, surprised to find herself very close to tears. "From you."

"Zoe, I could . . ."

"Oh, Roger . . . I miss you, I really do, but I . . . I think I have to take care of all this myself."

"Oh, Zoe, Zoe!" He sounded so angry that Zoe, who had some experience of Roger's slow but genuine capacity for anger, was instantly contrite.

"I'm sorry, Rog, I know I'm being weird, but please try to understand . . . even if I don't. I just know I have to stay with this. I have to stay *here*. Look, the drawings, the notes, all those photos will come tomorrow, and . . . Christ, I can't beg Julian anymore, I just can't. The stuff I sent him is really good, and it'll just have to be enough. It'll have to go however it goes with Sessa, Rog. I can't help it. I have to be here."

When Roger didn't answer, Zoe sniffed and stood up slowly. "I guess

I'd better get to bed," she said. "Claudia's coming over in the morning; we've got a zillion errands to do."

"Zoe, I won't come unless you want me to, but if you change your mind . . ."

"I know. Thank you, sweetheart. I . . . will."

Zoe hung up the phone and brought both icy hands to her cheeks. She thought of calling Roger back—apologizing, begging him to come be with her—but she didn't. She felt suddenly, physically sick and put her head down in her lap, trying to breathe slowly and think nothing.

After a few minutes she felt a little better and tiptoed up the stairs to Arthur's room. He lay in his old-fashioned underwear on the top of the bedclothes, his mouth slightly open, his silvery hair spread out on the pillowslip. Edwina snored in the crook of his arm. Zoe covered them with an old afghan she saw folded up on a chair and tucked the edges carefully under the mattress. As she bent over, Arthur's breath, smelling of scotch and fried rice, gusted gently into her face. She felt the same vague envy she had the other night—for the plenitude of his grief—and she thought again, as she stood in the doorway watching him sleep, Who do I love? Who's on my list? And understood, for the first time, that she knew the answer.

It was very late when Zoe slipped into Grandmère's room and pulled the door tightly shut behind her. There was something comforting about finding the green boxes just as she had left them in the bottom of the armoire, something that threw a veil of entitlement and ownership over them that was as compelling as it was irrational.

She took out the square box and carefully set aside the topmost layers, bit by bit excavating toward the bottom, not sure what to read next. She knew she had seen only snippets compared with the reams of paper Grandmère had covered with that close, clear writing, day after day for what appeared to be more than sixty years. Some days there was just a single line or two, but on other days, when Grandmère's thoughts and feelings seemed most urgent, she would write several pages, often on both sides, on and on. And there seemed to be gaps, too, of weeks at times, months perhaps. Zoe couldn't be sure; she had read so little.

After the briefest consideration she chose a bundle of pages and sat on the edge of the brocaded cover, then swung her legs up onto the bed and leaned against the carved headboard with the pages in her lap.

Carefully untying a narrow green ribbon, looping it around her neck, Zoe read with an aching heart about the earliest days when the house was brand-new and glowing with gaslight and fresh fringed velvet (surely in those days the showplace Jim Forbes had imagined it to be), the time when Augusta took such pleasure in her husband's rise to fortune, in the family which was gathering, growing around her.

Zoe's eyes flew down the pages as she read of long, sunny afternoons in the cottage in Nahant in the years when even the clematis and wisteria were new, just starting their twining creep up the latticed sides of the pergola that Potter constructed on the lawn overlooking the sea. A happy young Augusta, her hair glittering in the sun, sat writing on the veranda while her children laughed and tumbled on the grass and into the flower beds.

Zoe turned the yellowing pages and read of picnics on the beach, lit by fireworks, echoing with singing voices; the sweet corn was mere hours off the stalk, still smelling of the warm farm air. The guests arrived in landaus and phaetons, in dogcarts and on horseback, their arms filled with flowers.

Later, in winter, as she listened to Mozart and Fauré, Augusta's happy eyes glowed above her sable muff. She was swept away by the deep thrum of the orchestra, the soaring violins. "Oh, what blessings!" she wrote on a December night in 1898, returning from a concert. "How thrilling to hope that life can truly be a thing of joy, of beauty, of satisfaction, and that these glories can be not only *real,* but mine."

Then, on paper fastened together with a tiny sprig of dried clematis, skewered with a common pin, was an entry written on the morning of May 30, 1902. As Zoe read the description of Augusta's fortieth birthday party, the smile never left her lips; she hardly breathed, aware of nothing but the words. There had been a splendid high white cake, festooned with real roses, cases of iced champagne, giggling happy daughters and a disheveled little boy bearing a crusty pink seashell, and—just as Augusta prepared to make her entrance, to greet her happy guests—there was Eugene Hillyard, his dark eyes gleaming, silently pulling Augusta's earrings off with his teeth.

> . . . As I stood speechless and smiling, he handed me a small blue velvet box, which I recognized at once as from Tiffany's in New York, where Eugene had gone last month, as he said, "on business."

Well! The earrings within were sparkling with a life of their own: diamond earbobs set in platinum. The stones are the size of almonds, fastened with clasps of smaller pavé diamonds encasing a black pearl. I held them in my hands, feeling the weight of them, and stared wordless and openmouthed at Eugene, who looked down at me with his wry sardonic smile as he fastened them to my ears. He kissed me on the cheek and took my arm to escort me to my party. Not one word passed between us. . . .

As I lie in bed this morning, writing these words, I have (with a great frivolity none would believe of me) fastened on my diamond earrings once again, and they send the sun's fire to the farthest corners of the room. . . .

Zoe leaned back against the headboard of the bed with the loose pages spread across her lap, the small dried flowers weightless and whole in her palm, and gazed into the splitting darkness beyond the window.

 $\mathcal{T}$ he splendid chandelier that had hung for nearly a century over the dining-room table was half polished. When Zoe and Claudia returned to the house well after three o'clock, having spent most of the day going to liquor stores and supermarkets, bakeries and Lord & Taylor, Claudia had looked around with a vigorous expression, crisply contemplating all the cleaning that they could not possibly do before the reception on Monday afternoon.

"Look," she'd said, pacing the length of the dining room with her arms folded, "we can probably only give it all a lick and a promise, as Mother would say, so let's make a good choice. How about the chandelier?"

"Get serious," Zoe had said, making a funny, horrified face, looking up. The dangling prisms were so filthy they barely reflected the light from the weak bulbs in the fixture. "Grandmère's crystal chandelier?"

"It's the most bang for the buck, Zo," said Claudia, already moving the vase of lilacs onto the sideboard and kicking off her shoes. "Barefoot's best," she'd said. "More traction. You can always polish the table."

"But my God, Claudia, look at it."

"No, we can do it. Plus, it's so big everyone will notice it and forget the rest of the mess. Come on. You go first, you're taller. You get the top tiers and then I'll do the lower ones. You got any lemon juice? Go see."

Not waiting for an answer, Claudia folded up the stiff vinyl cloth, stuffing it into one of the trash bags they had bought, and moved the heavy mahogany chairs out of the way. Zoe stared at her for a minute, biting her lip, and went to look for lemon juice.

They had worked over an hour on the highest crystals, Zoe easily reaching the topmost pieces and carefully handing them down to Claudia, who washed them in a solution of ammonia and lemon juice with hot water. Now, half cleaned, even without the discarded lightbulbs, the chandelier looked almost otherworldly, as if the glittering top crystals were raining light on those beneath.

Zoe stared at it for a minute, slowly shaking her head, and then climbed off the table, stepping onto the seat of a chair that they had covered with a towel and down to the floor. When she came into the kitchen, Claudia was leaning into the refrigerator with her hands on her knees, looking for something to drink.

"I'll get it," Zoe said. "You sit down—your turn on the table is coming, don't forget." She took Claudia by her shoulders and sat her in one of the wooden chairs and then got glasses, ice, and two of the cans of ready-made tea they'd picked up at the market.

"Great," Claudia said, as Zoe handed her a tinkling glass. "Umm, hits the spot."

Zoe laughed and put her bare feet up against the sink rim.

"Mother loved iced tea," Claudia said, taking a big gulp. "Used to put a little cognac in it, said Grandma Celia taught her that." She reached into a Dunkin' Donuts box that had been on the countertop since morning and took out a plump doughnut. When she bit into it, bright red jelly oozed onto her palm, and she bent her chin to lick it off.

"I thought you were on a diet this week," Zoe said, sipping her tea, smiling past the ice cube that was clicking against her teeth.

"I need to fortify myself," Claudia said, popping the rest of the doughnut into her mouth. She took out a long twisted cruller and broke off a piece, offering it to Edwina, who had been watching, cranky but alert, from her basket by the pantry door.

"You know, Zo," Claudia went on, riffling through the *Globe* she had brought along with the doughnuts early in the morning, "Annabelle couldn't really abide either one of us, and here we are doing all the work for her, uh, departure. Hard to believe, hmm?"

"Ironic," Zoe said dryly. "That's the word."

Claudia had newsprint and confectioner's sugar all over her fingers. "Yeah. Ironic. Listen, take out the dress," she said, letting Edwina eat the rest of the doughnut from her hand. "I want to see it in this light."

"I put it upstairs already," Zoe said, not moving her feet off the sink.

"Go get it. I want to see."

"Okay, okay." Zoe sighed melodramatically and ran upstairs to get the dress, returning minutes later with the big Lord & Taylor garment bag in one hand and the dress on a wooden hanger in the other. Claudia wiped her hands before she reached for it and pulled it, rustling, into her lap. It was a dark burgundy silk with flowing long sleeves and a wide belt. It had seemed to Zoe that Beatrice Holland would wear such a dress—this deep color, this swishing skirt.

"You know," said Claudia, squinting critically and holding the dress up by the shoulder pads, "you could easily wear this to a nice dinner party, Zo—you'd just need something here at the neck."

"I think it'll be fine for Monday," Zoe said. She hooked the hanger over a nail that stuck out of the wood of the door and stood back to look at the dress from a distance. "I'm glad you talked me into it," she said, grinning at Claudia, who had immensely enjoyed her job as "coach," as she called it, racing back and forth from the racks to the dressing room to bring Zoe new dresses to try on, squatting on the floor to pull at hems, reaching up to straighten plackets and collar facings, bustling around Zoe and the distracted saleslady with great importance.

Claudia reached into the box for a loose piece of cruller and glanced up at the clock.

"I can't believe Arthur's still not back," she mumbled through the doughnut in her mouth. "And it's obvious he didn't come home while we were out, because all the same doughnuts are still in the box, including the chocolate glazed that I happen to know is his absolute favorite."

Zoe shrugged. "He was such a mess yesterday, I think I'm just glad he's out, not holed up in his room."

She thought Arthur either had miraculously recovered from yesterday's dementia and was off doing something sensible, even useful, or had flipped out completely. But the worry she felt was blurred somehow by the fact that she had not yet quite returned from last night's journey down the tunnel of Augusta's youth; the glow of summers in

Nahant seemed to blend in her mind with solemn images of Arthur walking all alone by the river, or sitting in the cellar of Leape & Neames, his head on Annabelle's coffin.

"Maybe he's gone over to Cambridge to play the piano or something," Claudia suggested, getting up to open the alley door for some air, then taking the dress into the dining room where she hung it in the crook of one of the ornate sconces by the fireplace. Zoe thought about the massive Chickering on the third floor, Chopin's *ballades* crashing through the darkened house. But she said nothing, going to the sink to rinse out the large plastic dishpan and mix up more of the ammonia solution.

She went back into the dining room to find Claudia standing in the center of the table in her bare feet, her hands on her hips, looking up at the chandelier. Zoe had already cleaned the branching rack of ornately carved bronze arms, and the fanciful leaves and buds of the design shone with a dull gleam.

"My turn," Claudia said, smiling down at Zoe, who had carefully set down the pan of water and was unfolding a stack of fresh linen cloths from the upstairs closet.

Claudia gingerly unhooked two crystals the size of pears and passed them down to Zoe, who had everything arranged on thick towels to protect the table. They worked silently in a smooth bending-dipping-wiping-reaching rhythm; every time Claudia replaced one of the gleaming prisms, they looked at each other and smiled, enjoying the slow, perfect process of bringing Grandmère's chandelier to life.

Zoe dunked one long pointed piece and was absorbed in drying it off when Claudia, doing hip stretches on the table above her, suddenly asked, "Did you actually know that man in the restaurant, Zo?"

"What man, dear?" Zoe was bending down to pick up a linen towel that had fallen to the carpet.

"The guy with the dark auburn beard. Came in when we were just finishing lunch."

"Who now?" Zoe handed the long thin crystal up to her.

"The man with the *beard,* Zo. Tall, tweed jacket—in the restaurant."

They'd had a bite of lunch at a place on Boylston Street, renowned, so Claudia promised, for their cheeseburgers. They took a seat by the window and wound up talking until almost two o'clock. They discussed the menu for Annabelle's reception and segued to other stories of old parties, old friends, old times they hadn't shared. From there, the conversation moved easily from Claudia's ideas for accessorizing Zoe's new dress to Lowie and his endless string of hobbies, thence to reminiscences of rainy summer days when they were kids. They cast *The Gilded Affair* with long-dead actors, and Claudia giggled over a few of Zoe's old Italy stories, Zoe carefully emphasizing the fun, the excitement, the glamour, offering small glimpses of De Sica and Fellini. Watching Claudia's delighted face, Zoe knew it was best to edit out those anecdotes less glittering, more venal; she was eager to entertain her with these stories, rather than to disguise her own long struggle.

Zoe felt a little blue all of a sudden, realizing that they could never really catch up. They could go only so far with their common childhood memories—there was so much more that had not been shared for twenty years. But a moment later, watching Claudia stir three sugars into her coffee, Zoe remembered, as if it were something she'd forgotten, that they could go forward, were indeed doing so—making new memories, new stories for some luncheon conversation twenty years from now.

Just as she thought that, a tall man had come into the restaurant alone. He passed them and walked with long strides over to a table in the corner. Zoe swiveled slowly in her chair and followed him with her eyes, saying nothing to Claudia.

"*Did* you know him?" Claudia asked again, leaning down with another oval crystal, not letting go until Zoe had it firmly in her fingers.

Zoe looked up, feeling startled, and then quickly bent to dip the crystal in the dishpan, swishing it around and around.

"Oh, no . . . no. He just for a minute looked like a friend of mine. It was silly to think it could be he."

"Somebody back in L.A.?" Claudia thought she saw a light go on in Zoe's eyes as she looked up at the dripping crystal, her crescent smile just about to widen. "Somebody special, Zo?"

"Well, yes, I guess you could definitely say special. Very special." Zoe kept her attention on the wet prism, well aware that Claudia's delighted blue eyes were twinkling down at her.

"Who is it? Someone in movies?"

Zoe laughed at that, thinking of Roger's generalized stupefaction at the "crazies" Zoe worked with. "Oh, God, no—Roger's an art dealer; he has a gallery in Century City. He's definitely not in 'the business.' "

Zoe laughed again and handed the sparkling prism back to Claudia. "He's a real person."

Claudia strained upward to hook the crystal in its place. "So what's the story?" she said, grunting. "How long you guys been together?"

"Oh, almost a year, it'll be a year next month, and he's very . . . Claud, get that pear-shaped one next," Zoe interrupted herself, pointing.

"Oh, okay." Claudia had to stand on tiptoe to reach the piece, sticking out her tongue in concentration.

Zoe silently dunked the crystal and stood with her hip against the long mahogany table, drying it with a fresh towel, rubbing it over and over, saying nothing.

Claudia, watching her do it, squatted down until their eyes were nearly level. Zoe glanced at her with an arch, teasing look, savoring the hesitation. Claudia's eyes narrowed with affection and anticipation.

"He's a wonderful man, Claud," Zoe said softly, thinking of Roger's voice on the phone last night, of how hard she'd pushed him. "Just lovely. Our relationship's been a little strange, a little bit at arm's length for one reason or another, mostly because of *me,* but now . . . here," she said, reaching up with the pear-shaped prism glittering in her fingers.

"Now . . . what?"

"Now, well, I don't know. I feel so many things changing somehow. It's as if while I've been here in Boston, I've sort of . . ."

"Seems like you've been here forever, doesn't it?" Claudia said, unhooking a small, octagonal piece. "Can you do two at a time?"

"The little ones, sure, give them to me."

"Have you two talked since you've been here?" Claudia asked, handing Zoe two of the eight-sided crystals and wiping her dusty hands on the towel hanging from her pocket.

"Oh, yes," Zoe replied, nodding over the dishpan. "Several times. Last night, in fact." She brushed her hair away from her face with her forearm. Looking up at Claudia's intense expression, Zoe felt a now-familiar shiver of amazement at her cousin's sense of other people's feelings.

"Is it serious?"

"Serious?"

"With this 'friend' of yours. With *Roger.* Is it serious?" Zoe looked as if she did not know what the word meant. Claudia bent to take the two clean crystals from her, her lower lip pushed out with amusement, and challenge. As she reached up to replace them and unhook two others, it occurred to her that Zoe, only forty years old, after all, could still have children; lots of women were doing that now, waiting. She was healthy, strong. Claudia felt herself getting all excited at the prospect, although, wisely, she said nothing, waiting Zoe out. But Zoe simply reached up to take two more grimy pieces from her, silent as before.

Half an hour later they were finished. Zoe wished Grandmère could see her chandelier now, it sparkled so. Rainbows shot into the corners of the room, seeming to ricochet off the walls and back again to be gathered into the crystal heart of the chandelier.

She sat down on the window seat, to look at it from a longer angle. She had a sudden flash of the superbly corseted ladies from *The Gilded Affair* seated in their bustles and jewels around the table, all the champagne glasses and scalloped silver glittering down its length. She saw Laurence and Beatrice gazing with hopeless adoration into each other's eyes, the huge basket of orchids on the sideboard. . . .

Claudia finished changing the bulbs and climbed down from the table. "Is that gorgeous or *what?*" she cried out, laughing up at the blazing chandelier.

"Sensational," Zoe whispered, leaning back against the window. "It's sensational."

"Grandmère would be so thrilled," Claudia said, carrying the dishpan into the kitchen to pour the dirty water down the sink. "Eddie says I'm a complete dope about it, but I always think how I hope Grandmère's not up in heaven someplace looking down at what's happened to her house."

Zoe stood in the kitchen doorway watching Claudia putting on her shoes and socks. "I suppose you want another snack now."

Claudia arched her eyebrows. "You bet your ass I do. I deserve at least two snacks, maybe four."

"Okay. Let's see." Zoe bent to look into the refrigerator at all the food they'd gotten at the Star Market. They had loaded up two shopping carts with cold cuts, ready-made salads, pastries and cookies, and a fully cooked, chilled turkey.

"Gee whiz, take it easy, Claud," Zoe had said when she saw Claudia hoisting the huge bird into her basket.

"Never mind—it won't go to waste, believe me."

Now the turkey took up the whole bottom bin of the refrigerator. Zoe pushed it back as far as it would go and reached for a little plastic container of German potato salad.

"How about this?" she said, handing Claudia a fork.

"Perfect. Yum." Claudia dug into the salad, shaking her shoulders with pleasure. "I guess I'll have to start my diet officially after the 'wake,' " she said, whispering the word and looking furtively around the kitchen as if Arthur could be hiding under the sink. Edwina nosed about her ankles, hoping for a taste, and Claudia dropped a forkful of potato salad between her sharp little teeth.

"Maybe it would be nice if he came, you think?" she said with a disingenuous smile at Zoe, who was sipping iced tea from a can.

"Who?"

"Who? Roger."

Zoe looked up, her black eyes shining like onyx. She put her feet up on the rim of the sink as before, her long legs crossed at the ankles. She listened to Claudia eating her potato salad, seeing, just at the corner of her eye, that she was watching Zoe's profile with a twinkly but pensive look.

"Zo," Claudia said with a small frown, throwing the plastic dish into the trash and getting herself a can of Diet Coke from the fridge, "Zo, let me sort of stick my neck out here for a minute."

Zoe snorted with a sudden burst of laughter. "Be my guest, dearie."

"Well, tell me what you meant when you said your relationship with Roger was a little, uh, 'strange,' I think you said. What did you mean?"

Claudia knew that this was prying of Olympic proportions, failure to "mind her own business" at a level that would give Eddie apoplexy if he ever found out. But she felt sure that Zoe would be eager to talk about Roger if given half a chance, sensed that she had never before done so, not with anyone. Confidences came hard to the Hillyards, as Jim had pointed out the other day. Zoe and Arthur, superficially so different, were identical, Claudia believed, in some deep hidden core. They kept their secrets, and they suffered for that pride, that stubbornness, in ways too powerful to tell.

When Zoe said nothing, Claudia got up and leaned back against the sink, resting her hand, cool from the soda can, on Zoe's ankle.

"Do you love him, Zoe? Is this a man you really love?"

Zoe took a deep breath and looked up; there was not the slightest hint of girlish, pajama-party, giggling curiosity in Claudia's blue eyes, only a willingness to hear the truth—and keep it to herself.

"Claudia, it's terrifying . . . terrifying."

"Ah. A definite sign."

"I know."

"But why is it, Zo? Terrifying. Doesn't he love you, too?"

"Oh. Oh, no. In fact, that's probably it. He does love me, more than . . . more than I ever imagined anyone ever . . ." Zoe blinked and looked away, thinking of Grandmère and Arthur, her mind blank for a moment. Then she said:

"I haven't been that good to him—certainly not as good as he deserves. He's been so patient, Claud, so loving, so faithful, and he's taken so much crap from me you can't imagine. All these months with the movie, I've just been *obsessed* with it, and Roger's had to stand by, take a backseat; I always seem to be making him wait for something else to finish in my life."

Zoe broke off, an expression of terrible pain clear on her face. She swung her legs off the sink and put her elbows on the table, swiveling away from Claudia.

"I suppose some shrink would say I'm trying to force him to leave me, seeing how far I can push him before he tells me he can't stand it anymore."

"Are you?" Claudia said, squatting down beside her, her hand on the back of Zoe's chair. "Is that what you want?"

"No." Zoe turned and looked right into Claudia's eyes. Their noses were inches apart. "No. The truth is I don't know what I'd do if I lost him—I really don't—but I can't seem to . . . Heaven knows I've been around enough to know there's no one like him, no one I would ever feel this way about. . . . 'Love.' God, what a word."

Zoe paused and sighed, her black eyes narrowed in surprise at what she'd just revealed, as much to herself as to Claudia.

"I think he should know all that, Zo," Claudia said. "If he doesn't already. And even if he does, he'd probably like to hear it straight from the horse's mouth, so to speak."

"I know," Zoe said.

Claudia pushed herself up and began gathering her parcels, which were all in a heap by the alley door. She threw the Coke can into the trash and looked at her watch. "I have to go get the kids," she announced in a disappointed tone. She went into the dining room and looked around with tense annoyance. "Now the furniture looks like shit. Maybe I could . . ."

"Just go ahead and pick them up," Zoe said, helping Claudia with her bags and totes and shoving her toward the front hall. "Don't worry about it. I was going to polish everything in here anyway. You think we can deal with that miserable parlor tomorrow?"

"Oh, of course. Eddie will help us. We'll be over bright and early." Claudia yanked her purse over her shoulder and suddenly stopped.

"Listen," she said, "I have a great idea. Let me take Edwina. She's going to be cranky and obnoxious and . . . where is she? Edweeena, get in here, baby . . ."

Zoe frowned. "I thought Lowie was allergic to her or something."

"Oh, no, no. I'm going to drop her at the vet's. It's one of my all-time best ideas, Zo. Get her out from underfoot."

Claudia leaned forward into Zoe's waiting embrace, just as Edwina came waddling in from the kitchen as fast as she could go, her sequined leash already in her teeth.

After Claudia left, Zoe worked on in the dining room, rubbing vigorously at the table, sideboard, and chairs with a dish towel damp with lemon oil. She polished the marble mantel and attacked all the surfaces with an old feather duster. She washed the majolica tureen in the deep sink in the butler's pantry and set it on a doily in the middle of the table. When she was all done, she sank into the armchair at the kitchen end of the table and looked down its length to the broad bay window.

The late-afternoon light beamed across the polished furniture, filtering through the long discolored curtains that were dragging on the floor. The tureen shone under the dazzle of the chandelier, the embossed pattern of fruits and fishes once again colorful and bold. Idly, Zoe wondered if there was time to go out for flowers—they would be so beautiful in the tureen. Small pots of impatiens would be lovely for a centerpiece. Perhaps grape ivy? Or clematis, Grandmère's favorite, climbing in such profusion over the trellises at Nahant.

She looked up from the imagined flowers to the tall, smiling man she suddenly found seated at the other end of the table, his dark red beard shining in the sunlight, his glass raised only to her. Zoe leaned slightly forward, smiling straight at him, and anyone watching would have sworn there was a full glass of champagne in her hand.

THIRTY-TWO

*A*t dusk, Zoe went up to Grand-mère's room and sat cross-legged in the center of the bed with sections of the diary from the second, oval box spread out around her. She had just gotten a group of the entries that seemed to be from the late 1920s arranged on the brocaded coverlet, trying reverently to keep it all in order, when she heard the slam of the front door and soon after the sounds of Arthur doing something in the kitchen.

"Oh, good," she mumbled to herself. "Good." She swung her legs off the bed, pulled the door of the room tight into its warped frame, and ran downstairs to find him.

Arthur was standing by the sink with five or six of Annabelle's ornate silver picture frames, disassembled, stacked on the countertop beside him. The pictures of Spencer Trefoyle were scattered on the floor, on the gas burners, even in the sink. Arthur had the jar of silver cream in his hand and was smearing the pink goop in sloppy haste on all the blackened frames.

Zoe put her hand in the middle of his back and leaned around his shoulder to look. She stood up on her tiptoes and kissed his cheek. "I'm so glad to see you. What in the world are you doing?" She laughed a little and rubbed the space between his shoulder blades. "What is all this, kiddo?"

Arthur was applying the cleanser with a fragment of sponge, rubbing with random energy at the curlicues and scrolls, which remained black in their centers.

"I have a chance to sell them—I have to hurry." He had a cigarette burning in a saucer on the sink drain and took a drag, leaving the dirty pink goo from his fingers all over the filter.

"Well, then you should do a slightly better job, Arthur," she said dryly, smiling sideways at him. "But what do you mean, you're selling them? What's all this about?"

"Flowers." The gooey cigarette dangled from his lips. He hadn't shaved for two days, and a silvery stubble roughened his cheeks.

"What?"

"Annabelle needs flowers for her coffin, Zoe," he said with some exasperation, as if anyone with half a mind would realize there was a problem here. "I'm a little short of cash right now, so I'm selling them."

Arthur threw the limp cigarette into the sink and lit another, getting silver cream all over his lighter.

"You're going to *pawn* them?" Zoe stepped over toward the stove so she could look more directly at him. "Now? Arthur, we can easily buy flowers for her tomorrow. Claudia and Eddie can drive us out to the—"

"No, no. There's a place in the Combat Zone where I can sell them tonight. Oh, Zoe, she loved roses—especially pink . . . pink roses to match the casket." He pushed his glasses up on his nose with a smeared knuckle and kept rubbing at the frame in his hand with frantic industry.

Zoe wondered if this ranting was just the irrational anger of grief, or something more. Something serious.

"Arthur . . ." she began. She had been about to ask him where he'd been all day, but she began to see that that was probably a subject best left unexplored. He had an intense, desperate look on his face that was starting to alarm her.

"I have to do this right, Zo, don't you see? It has to be the best for her."

He pushed up his glasses again and rinsed the heavy silver frame under running water. "I bet I can get twenty, maybe thirty bucks apiece for these, easy," he said, drying the frame on a tea towel. It looked awful—uneven and smeared, almost greasy; old scratches that had been hidden under the tarnish now showed clearly.

Zoe, really worried now, moved to take the frame away from him. She managed to pull him into a chair, and he looked up at her for the first time, suddenly smiling brightly.

"We should call those people at the funeral home, Zo, maybe get a special hearse or something, maybe two flower cars instead of one."

"Arthur, you weren't listening yesterday," Zoe said. She pulled up a chair and sat facing him; their kneecaps touched. "We're not having a flower car, honey, don't you remember?"

He looked at her blankly, breathing through his mouth, each breath shallow and rough as if he had been running.

Just moments ago, coming down the stairs, Zoe had vaguely planned to say something about expenses for the funeral, thinking that she might set the stage a bit, maybe take him out for supper, find a way to start. But now she saw that it was too late for such indulgences.

"The funeral's already over ten thousand dollars, Arthur," she said softly, not sure she could go through with it, but knowing she had to take a shot. "And you heard Mr. Leape tell me he's going to want the rest of the money on Monday, remember? . . . Arthur?"

He hasn't heard a word, she thought, covering his limp hands with her own. His eyes were round behind his glasses.

"Arthur," she said quietly, dropping her hands and leaning slightly away from him. "Do you have any money at all for the funeral? Anything?"

The dim look seemed to go out of his eyes. "Oh, well—I can get it—that's not the point . . ."

"But, it *is* the point, isn't it? And let's say we can cope with the funeral, that's just one thing. . . . " Zoe felt the words coming out of her throat as if entirely of their own accord, just as they had the other night. She swallowed and tried again. "Look, for example, the hospital bill will probably come next week, and it's bound to be twenty thousand dollars at least. I want to help you all I can, whatever is needed, but . . . well, you need to tell me the . . . the *scope* here, Arthur."

Zoe paused, thinking of Jim's advice—get the facts, he'd said. Well, she'd certainly left all the fact-gathering for the last minute, hadn't she? She sniffed and tried to get her breath, worried that her voice might have sounded too impatient, strident.

"We have to talk about these things. We really do," she said more quietly.

Arthur was looking down at his hands, opening and closing each one in turn. "I'll get it," he said. "It's no problem. Besides, there are still things in the house to sell."

Zoe's eyes widened. "You've sold stuff from the house?"

Arthur, shrugging with what he thought was a gesture of bland, guiltless indifference, tried to make light of it. Zoe realized all at once that he'd never meant to say it.

"A few things, over the years . . . just some knickknacks, the stained-glass lamp in the library, a couple of the smaller orientals, some jewelry. No big deal." He said all this with a stiff jerk of his shoulders, as if flinching before being struck.

Zoe suddenly thought of the jewelry drawer in Grandmère's bureau, the tumbled boxes, little loose squares of cotton . . . and the diary. But before she could open her mouth, Arthur raced on, trying to close the door he'd so foolishly opened.

"See, it was all for Annabelle, Zo, all of it—she needed so much; all the things . . ."

"*What* jewelry?"

"Oh, well, just a couple of pieces of Grandmère's jewelry—little things." Arthur pressed his back to the slats of his chair; his eyes were still focused on his sticky hands.

" 'Little things'?" Zoe was whispering.

"Sure. Well, for instance . . ."

After more mumbling and muttering, he told her that a few years ago Annabelle had given him the key and sent him to Grandmère's room to look for a pair of diamond earrings old Eugene had bought her as a gift, ages before.

"But they weren't there, Zo. I looked all through the bureau drawers. Annabelle was absolutely furious. She thought Anthony'd gotten them somehow—way back when."

Arthur coughed and began to polish his glasses on the tail of his plaid shirt. "There were just a couple of pins, brooches, something with garnets and little pearls. It wasn't all that much," he finished, as if that made it all all right.

Zoe stared at him, simply grateful that he didn't seem to know about the diary, feeling sure he would have mentioned it if he did. She tried to work through the possibility that he did know and wasn't saying, and then she realized with a shudder that she was completely losing her sense of the priorities.

"Arthur," she said, "if you don't have the money for Annabelle's funeral, you really should tell me so we can make some sort of plan. And you must have other bills," she went on, a terrible thought just coming into focus. "I know it's hard to talk about dear, but this is *me*. You can tell *me,* can't you?"

Arthur put his glasses back on without looking at her. He stood up and went over to the cupboard under the sink. "I can't get into all this now, Zoe."

She saw that she had let him crouch behind his grief too long. The sweet, organized conversation she had hoped for was completely by the boards.

"We *have* to talk about it now," Zoe said, a kind of sad anger rising in her. "We have to. Dammit, Arthur, we haven't talked about anything at all. There's the funeral, the hospital bills . . . okay, that has to be thirty thousand, at least, right there. What else? . . . Arthur, put that down and talk to me!"

He had pulled a large grocery bag from under the sink. Zoe jumped up and snatched it out of his hands. Arthur, astonished, looked at her with his mouth open, and then his arms fell slowly to his sides. All at once, the foggy expression left his eyes and in its place came a look of infinite, unbridgeable regret. He seemed to shrink, to capitulate to something.

"What else?" Zoe said, dropping the bag and sitting again at the table. "What else?"

Arthur lit another cigarette and, sighing, smoked for a while as if daring her to interrupt. "Well, there's my MasterCard."

"Yes."

"And VISA, and Filene's, also some doctor bills, the guys before Mainwaring . . . oh, and heating oil. They were going to cut us off, but the law says they have to make deliveries until April if there's an elderly person in the house." He took a long drag on the cigarette and smiled at her in a wily way as if he'd gotten away with something for which he deserved praise. Zoe said nothing.

"And . . . and some loans from my, uh, friends. . . ."

Zoe took a deep breath and looked at Arthur's cigarette, wishing she had one. "Claudia and Eddie?"

He looked up at her quickly, his eyes wide open. "*No!* Never . . . never . . . not Claudia!"

"Okay, so how much?" Zoe whispered. "The loans."

"Another six, maybe eight. Thousand. I don't exactly remember."

Zoe felt as if she were rappelling off a cliff, the pit at the bottom filled with smoke. She had never actually imagined there would be so much. Arthur just sat puffing diligently on his cigarette, twitching slightly.

Zoe stood up and looked in the refrigerator for some wine. She offered none to Arthur and took her glass back to the table.

"Okay," she said at last. "Looks like—what? Forty, fifty thousand?"

"More. Fifty-five. For everything."

Zoe blew out her breath in short puffs, eyeing the pack of cigarettes on the table between them.

"What about Annabelle's will, then?" Arthur was silent.

Zoe thought again of her conversation with Uncle Jim—about a small mortgage on the house. How "persnickety" she wondered, could they be? How minuscule a mortgage would it take?

"Well, look, the house is yours now," she said, "at least as soon as the will is probated, which we could probably get speeded up. A tiny mortgage?" she said softly, through her teeth. "I know it seems awful to do it, especially after what Jim said the other night, but maybe just a fraction of what you could borrow on the whole thing, enough to get going on some of the bigger bills—give you a clean slate? The house must be worth a fortune, Arthur, even though it's in such abysmal shape. A small mortgage would get you on your feet."

Zoe bit on her back teeth and waited for a response. None came. Arthur didn't even look up. He put his cigarette out with great attention, pushing out every little spark.

"You know," Zoe went on, trying to speak as calmly as she could, "I stand to make some pretty decent money on the movie. I'd be happy to work out a way to help pay it back. You want to try that? I could cosign, or whatever."

"No. No." Arthur was shaking his head again in that infuriating robotic way he had.

"Well, I know it's hard to deal with; a mortgage on Grandmère's house *is* sort of extreme, I guess, but under the circumstances, we could—"

"No!"

Anger ignited in Zoe like a struck match. "Arthur, Christ! What are the alternatives?"

"*No!*"

"It's not the end of the world!"

"*NO!*"

"*Why not?*"

"Oh, Zoe! It's already mortgaged!" Arthur finally looked up at her, his mouth wide and contorted. "All of it! *All* of it!"

The abrupt silence lay between them like fresh, wet cement. Zoe stared at him, her mouth inches from the rim of the wineglass.

"I don't believe you," she said a minute later in a soft, uninflected voice, knowing as she spoke that she did, absolutely, believe him.

"I'm sorry, Zo. It's true. It happened about five years ago," he said in a harsh breathy voice not at all like his own. "We just couldn't go on the way we were. We had to have money. We had to. Annabelle was . . . she said she . . ."

"I don't understand," Zoe interrupted, watching his eyes and mouth. "Annabelle mortgaged the house?"

Arthur shuddered. "No . . . no. She never knew. She gave me her power of attorney actually about ten years ago. She said she didn't want to bother with the trust anymore, it was too much trouble for her, so she appointed me 'successor trustee,' it's called, and she herself resigned. . . . And then about five years ago I saw a chance . . . I thought I could make it better for her, you know? . . . Zoe, I was so sure! I mean, I was teaching almost every day, playing piano pretty often at night. It seemed so easy . . . and of course I was actually the trustee then, so . . ."

Arthur got up and backed away from her, flinging his arms about with pent-up energy, as if he believed that the faster he talked and waved his hands around, and the farther he backed away, the more Zoe might believe him.

When she got up and started toward him, he was pressed flat against the sink edge.

"Of what, Arthur?" she said in a hoarse voice. "Trustee of what?"

"I was sure I could handle it, Zo, honestly I was—that I could pay it back. I kept some of the money especially *for* that."

"What 'trust'?"

Arthur took another deep breath; his cheeks filled with it. "See, shortly before she died, Grandmère made a trust—mainly just the house and contents—and Annabelle was the trustee." He spread his fingers out on the sink as if he'd thoroughly explained everything. Zoe looked into his eyes, forcing him to continue.

"Well, and there was this guy," Arthur went on, his voice clotted with saliva. "Conrad. The guy who slid the letter under the door the other night."

The man with the white Cadillac, Zoe thought. Yes.

"I met him in Cambridge," Arthur went on in the same thick voice. "A few years ago. He handles properties, mortgages, loans, and so forth—I guess he's into all kinds of things like that—I don't actually understand it too well. And so one thing led to another and he offered to cosign for me. . . ."

"Arthur," Zoe said, feeling almost frightened, reaching toward his arm, "why don't—"

But he couldn't stand it, couldn't stop.

"Conrad said the bank wouldn't lend me the money otherwise, that I wasn't a good credit risk except for the house. So we did the mortgage at Grandmère's original bank, where the trust was, and then we took the money—"

"Arthur, I *still* don't understand. Why was there a trust?" She had come closer to him, looking up, her eyes blacker than he had ever seen them. "Why didn't Grandmère just bequeath the house to Annabelle? Why didn't she simply—"

At that moment Arthur gave it up, crying into the air between them:

"Zoe! It's yours! The house is *yours!* Grandmère left it to *you*—in trust for *you!*"

Zoe turned her back on her brother's sudden explosive weeping. She bent double from the waist and put both her fists on top of her head. Blinding white lights flashed at the sides of her vision, though her eyes were closed.

"See," Arthur said, appalled at himself, racing on in the same high-pitched, singsong fashion, "see, the house was for Annabelle to use for her lifetime—it's called a life estate or something—but you were a little child, of course, when Grandmère died, so in her will she appointed Annabelle to be the trustee. There wasn't anyone else, after all—certainly not Anthony, not Dad—Mother was dead . . ."

Zoe sank into a chair and put her head on the table. She sat absolutely rigid and still, unaware of her own thoughts, blank as could be.

After a while, she had no idea how long, she became aware of her own body, the slight ache of her hunched posture, and then, a few minutes after that, she started to think again, to remember what he'd said. She found herself wondering if she was going to be able to live through such unending revelation.

"How much?" she said at last, her chin still on her folded arms on the tabletop, her eyes level with the glass of wine.

"What?"

"The mortgage. How much?"

Arthur didn't answer at first. He opened the alley door a few inches and stood leaning against the jamb, inhaling the chilly outside air.

"About ninety thousand, ninety-five . . . but we put that in another bank. Conrad said it was smarter."

Zoe looked up. "Why smarter?" she said slowly.

"Well, because Conrad said he knew people there, and besides then I could write checks to myself." Zoe's eyes narrowed at this, but she said nothing.

"I know it's illegal," Arthur said. "Worse than illegal. I know that as the trustee . . . Well, Conrad said the other day I could actually go to jail; he never told me that in the beginning."

Zoe drank all of her wine at once and said tonelessly, "What did you do with the money?" She held the empty glass motionless in her lap.

"We lived on it," Arthur said, eager to explain. "I bought things for Annabelle. First I had to give Conrad five thousand for his fee, and then I kept out twenty-five in a separate account to repay the first few years of the mortgage . . . and I did, Zo, I did, and . . . and everything went along really well for a while. See, I was sure I'd be able to pay the other sixty-five or so off without any problem, get the house back. . . . I made some investments, too, but they didn't actually, uh, pan out. See, I really thought I could . . ."

"But you couldn't."

Arthur shook his head and sat heavily, slowly, in his chair and looked over at her. There was none of the fireworks he had so dreaded. The conflagration of anger, loathing, disgust that his fantasies had told him would follow this confession—that had blazed up every time he had rehearsed this very moment in his mind—was instead a cold and glacial wall, Zoe's calmness worse than all anticipated fire.

"How bad is it?" she asked, in a still, calm voice. "How close are we to actually losing Grandmère's house?"

"Pretty close."

"How close?"

Arthur swallowed. "Well, I've missed the last three payments, and in another week or so it'll be four . . . and when Conrad reads the obituary he'll know that my power of attorney is over and the house is yours."

"How much will it take?"

"Zoe, it's not really the money—I don't think he'd even actually take the money now. He wants the house. He wants to *live* here." Arthur held his hands out, palms cupped, as if beseeching an invisible Conrad to take handfuls of coins. "I was three or four payments behind about two years ago, and he let me pay him that time, because I guess each time *I* pay, the amount he'd have to come up with himself, for the bank—I mean, if I were to blow it completely—would go down . . . but now . . ."

Zoe had already realized that, seen the strategy.

"He was expecting you to default all along, wasn't he?" she said in a calm, factual voice. "To miss payments? From the first?" She felt a sudden complete understanding of Conrad, of an astute malice that would be hard to equal, even in Hollywood.

"See," Arthur was saying, talking as fast as he could, "the missed payments to the bank go back to January—that's when the heating-oil trouble started. I used the money for that, and now the twenty-five thousand I set aside for the house is all gone. Conrad has made all those payments to the bank himself—that's about nineteen hundred dollars just there, which isn't all that much—but I don't think he'll take it. I . . . don't know. . . ."

Arthur took a deep breath and put his face in his long, fine hands.

Zoe pulled her chair up again, close to him, brushed her hair out of her face with one hand, and took a breath.

"Just tell me one thing, Arthur, one thing: why didn't you call me long ago—years ago, before this happened? When you started to realize it wasn't going to work out, why didn't you let me know?"

Arthur's silence told her that he'd thought of it.

"Was what happened ten years ago so terrible we couldn't rise above it? Oh, Arthur—how did this happen to us? How did we get to where we are from where we started?"

Even as she spoke the words, Zoe remembered the mesmerizing power of the inertia that had silenced *her* for so many years—kept her away from him, from making the first move. She felt thoroughly, irrationally guilty for never having intuited, in all those years, that something terrible was happening to Arthur.

"Why didn't you tell me—call me—let me know? I would have come."

"I *couldn't,* Zoe," he said, shaking his head. His blue eyes dragged their focus up to her face. "I couldn't take the chance that you would hate me, turn your back on me for good. I told myself it was for Annabelle's sake—and it was, it *was!*—but I knew it was no more than stealing. I knew it all along, but I really believed I could pull it off, and I thought, 'If Zoe finds this out, if she ever realizes what I'm doing . . .' I didn't want you to hate me, Zoe, like I hated myself . . . just in case in the future, we could . . . get together again. . . ."

Arthur broke off, nearly out of breath. He was sick of himself and his chronic, panicky unhappiness. Sick.

Zoe chewed on her upper lip for a minute. "So all along you were thinking you'd find a way to pay it all back and I'd never have to know."

"Yes."

"But then Annabelle had her stroke and Claudia called me to come and you panicked because you didn't have any more time—any more options."

"That's right."

Zoe sat for a moment with her eyes closed, her dry lips pressed together. Then, rising, she leaned forward to grasp Arthur's shoulders. She wrapped her arms around him and held him tightly to her, this lonely, brave man whom she'd missed so badly for so long.

"But you kept it going," she whispered to him, her arms firmly around him, her chin in his hair. "In spite of everything, the house is still standing, after all."

Arthur just leaned against her and said nothing. She could feel his muscles shuddering through the wool of her sweater.

"We'll find a way to keep it," Zoe said. "We have to . . . and we will."

She moved away and closed the back alley door, which had been slightly ajar all this time, letting in wet breezes. The sky, so blue and soft all day, had leaded over, and droplets of unpredicted rain pinged onto the steps.

"Look, we'll just pay the bank," she said. "We'll get the money somewhere and rewrite the mortgage in my name—get that Conrad person out of the loop."

"I don't think we can, Zo."

"Why not? Sure we can. We'll just—"

"He has the deed, Zoe."

Zoe stopped right where she stood, her hand on the chain lock. "What in the world do you mean? The *what?*"

"Back then, in the beginning, we made a kind of side deal—like collateral, I guess you could say. Conrad insisted. So I, um, gave him the title deed to the house, which he could just record—register— if I missed three payments, and then the house would be his, and—"

"Wait a minute. Wait a minute. You gave him the *deed* to Grand-mère's house?" Zoe looked at him as if he had not actually said any of this in English.

"That's where I was today," Arthur said, his face back in his hands. "I went to try to find him so I could maybe talk him out of . . . I mean, since he's paid the bank, he's basically—"

"The holder of the mortgage now, not the bank."

"In a way, yes."

Zoe paced the short length of the kitchen, pushing back her hair with both hands, in some part of her mind trying to remember if there had ever been a time she hadn't cared about all this.

"Then we have to get the deed away from him . . . somehow. We'll scare him, threaten him. I'm sure he's guilty of all kinds of other things. Maybe we can get all the money, he'd take it *all,* I'm sure . . . or the bank would . . . cash . . ."

Arthur said nothing. The notion of default, which he believed he'd nearly learned to live with, had never quite encompassed such suffocating shame.

He got up from his chair and gathered the scattered photographs of Spencer Trefoyle, pausing only for a moment to look at them. The faces, their eyes as depthless and black as the tarnished silver frames in which they had spent half a century, looked back without passion. Suddenly, Arthur tore them into little pieces and dropped them in the sink. He took his jacket from its hook and opened the back door Zoe had just closed.

"Ah, Jesus, Arthur, where are you going?" Zoe said. "Let's try to think this through."

She took him by his sleeve, but he gently pulled his arm away and went out onto the steps. He turned to her with a flat, deadly look she had never seen before in his pianist's eyes.

"I'll call you later, Zo."

"Arthur!" Zoe looked up at him standing over her, tall, shadowed, his hair shining in the backlight from the alley.

"Arthur!"

But he walked quickly down the steps and through the alley. Zoe ran a short distance after him, calling his name, but in a moment he had turned the corner onto Exeter Street and disappeared.

Swearing under her breath, she came back and closed and locked the door against the rain. She gathered up the clanking silver frames, still tarnished and damp, and jammed them into the paper bag. She put the jar of silver cream away and wiped up the sink and counter with a paper towel. There was an inch of wine left in the jug in the refrigerator, and she drank it and threw the bottle into the trash along with the frames and the pieces of Spencer Trefoyle.

THIRTY-THREE

*T*he rain strengthened into vertical, cold sheets. Magnolia branches sagged under the weight of the water, and chilled petals, already melting into pale brown around their edges, fell to the soaked ground. Gusts of northwest wind tilted the rain and blew it against the bow windows of Augusta's room.

The diary was spread out on the bed as before, the top pages of the bundles luffing ever so slightly as random breezes sneaked past the warped, imperfect sashes of the windows, shaking in the wind. Zoe sat in the middle of the bed and read odd entries from 1927 and 1928 out of sequence, feeling daunted by the hundreds of pages, skimming without purpose or understanding, thoroughly distracted by Arthur's confession.

It crossed her mind that the diary, this very paper, was now hers. "House and contents," if Arthur was to be believed, and oh, she had indeed believed him. *("Zoe, it's yours! The house is yours!")* A renewed sense of entitlement flared up in her, but was as quickly smothered. This was the second assault on Grandmère's house in less than a week. The threat posed by the social worker, of course, had been nullified by Annabelle's death—but this? What in the world, Zoe thought, can I possibly do about *this?* It may be too late already.

Let it go? Is that an option? But Grandmère's father bought it for her one hundred and one years ago! How can I let that man have it? No!

How can I *do* that? But what are the alternatives? *It's so much money!* "Oh, Grandmère," Zoe whispered aloud, "when you left me your house, did you know this would happen? That it would be like this?"

Zoe pushed herself against the headboard, where carved swans floated in a lake of flowers. Idly, she reached for the bisque angel with the stiff tulle wings and the chipped hands. She wet her finger and scrubbed at the grimy cheeks, then licked the cheeks with her tongue and rubbed with her sleeve at the blush appearing. She propped the figure against her legs and looked with what seemed like old acquaintance into the angel's wise and tiny eyes.

Zoe knew by now about this angel, twice found by surprise. The guardian of her childhood trinkets was in fact the old Lattimore Christmas angel, misplaced for years, only to be discovered again in 1904, at Christmastime, seen then as the greatest of prizes, a token of past joys. Augusta had written that she washed it with her own hands and set it on this rosewood table by the bed. Somehow the angel found its way to little Zoe's bureau years ago, then to the breakfront in the library, and just two nights ago Zoe herself had brought it back here to Grandmère's room, where the journey had begun . . . now to be thrown out with the trash, perhaps? Sold for a dollar in a yard sale? Or to guard the Hillyards for another hundred years?

Zoe put her face in her hands over her bent knees, cradling the angel in between.

"I don't know what to do," she said aloud from behind her hands.

The wind pressed against the sashes and battered the cleft tree on the Mall. Zoe got up and went to the window, parting the curtain to look out into the rain-swept street, but after just a minute or two, she went back to the oval box and picked up a bundle labeled "1932 to 1934" which Augusta had tied tightly with a piece of red-and-silver Christmas ribbon. Zoe blew her nose and sat on the bed again, tucking the angel carefully against her hip as she began to read.

In the autumn of 1932 the Hillyard fortunes deteriorated, as did Augusta's patience with Anthony and young Eugene, who was now, against all reason, off to Harvard.

Zoe held the packet of pale blue paper cradled against her legs. It seemed to her that Augusta's handwriting had changed from the early years at Nahant she'd read about the night before; the letters were more pointed, the words placed closer together.

"He has turned out to be little more than a foolish child," Augusta wrote of the second Eugene in mid-September. "Our sweet, long-suffering Frances would have become a splendid mother for this tiresome boy—would have taught him discipline, forbearance, all that he will never learn from his father. I know I tend to view my grandson with a somewhat disapproving eye, but it is clear to me that Eugene has no business at Harvard: neither his intellect nor the times are auspicious."

Zoe, though somewhat amused at Augusta's bitter humor, found her father's early life distasteful and irrelevant. She sensed that whatever messages she might be looking for were not to be found with him. But then, on the top page of a small sheaf of ruled white paper, along the margin of which Augusta had drawn a pretty sketch of falling maple leaves, she wrote that she had heard again from her old friend Mathilde Gaylord:

(October 30, after luncheon) Mathilde's letter is a delight—every line filled with humor and spirit. She writes that she has some new friends— art students at the University—young and filled with life, projects, dreams. No adversity seems able to dampen their spirits. Mathilde's health is better, her cheeks still "rosy" from her summer in Beauvais. "My dear Maman," she writes, "would be scandalized at what the sun has done to my complexion!" My goodness, but I miss her.

Closer, Zoe thought, not quite sure how this applied to her . . . but closer to some sort of comfort, yes.

Then, turning several pages at once, she smiled as for some reason she always did when she saw Hortense's name. At Christmas 1932, at the end of what Augusta confessed had been "a bitter year," the Dukes traveled up from Savannah for the holiday. They had originally planned to stay for several weeks, but a sudden crisis in Eliot's business affairs made it imperative that they return south in early January of 1933. Before their departure, Augusta, fearing the times and longer separations, planned a special dinner party. She wrote on January 8:

As of old, the Lattimore Coalport is out and Potter is hard at work, polishing the silver . . . doing double duty what with Veronica in bed for the fortnight since Christmas, having caught a chill after church. We've had the doctor for her, but he just gives her some pills and syrups and waddles out into the snow, shaking his head. . . . And so tonight we had our farewell dinner for Hortense and Eliot, a festive occasion—unsullied, I am happy to report, by untoward behavior from Anthony, who arrived downstairs looking very handsome indeed and quite ready to be cordial and attentive to his departing sister.

Anne was with us, accompanied by granddaughter Laura, who is still at home and champing at the bit that Celia has, I think wisely, put between her pearly teeth. The Wheelwrights, unfortunately, were unable to join us, as Celia and dear James were in Rhode Island as houseguests of the Forbeses—the parents of young Henry's bride-to-be. I would venture to guess that the growing involvement of Henry Wheelwright and Miss Paulette Forbes does not sit well with Laura—she dislikes having attention diverted from herself. In spite of Laura's attractive appearance, a young gentleman who might hope to find in her a suitable companion is rather abruptly put off by her sharp tongue. Somehow, however, our young Eugene finds this appealing—further proof (in Grandmère's judgment!) of his foolishness. He *is* a trial. . . . They were nevertheless seated together at dinner (*my* choice, vicious old prune that I am)—and although I don't think we could quite describe it as "sheep's eyes," there seemed to be some thin rapport between them. I'm sure we shall have more anon. Annabelle partnered her brother, not quite as sour as of late, in spite of Mr. Trefoyle's not having been invited, but of course Annabelle knows better than to think I would consider it.

So, all in all, we were a very cheerful group; the conversation rollicked along until nearly eleven o'clock, thanks in large measure to dear Eliot, who *is* a talker! My papa would have loved him! Hortense, the lamb, sits quietly admiring him. They will no doubt dance into eternity in such a *pas de deux!* The food was delicious: how Potter and Win put together a crown roast in such circumstances, I have no idea. The vegetables were crisp and perfect, the beef succulent, the *crème de marron* divine, divine, divine! I confess that as I grow older the delights of the table make more sense to me than they did when I was younger and savored different pleasures. Those now being unavailable to me, I am just as happy to content myself with glazed pears and *crème de marron!* Shall I conclude from this that a taste for frivolity is not confined to youth?

How different, Zoe thought, holding the pages against her chest, from that other dinner party, the one she had created in that room, just the other day. Yet they were alike as well, both opulent, elegant, filled with handsome guests, with Grandmère's Coalport and her crystal, her lovely silver with the shells carved in each piece . . . and both splendid settings created to support loss, farewell, and separation.

In the spring of 1933, in May, Potter died at the age of seventy-six, quietly in his sleep. Zoe, lost in the pages, felt irrationally sad to learn that he was dead. Augusta, who had known him from just after her marriage when he came to serve Eugene, had not been sure of his age. It turned out he had dyed his hair. He was buried, at Augusta's expense, in the Hillyard section, two graves west of Eugene.

The loss of Potter, sincerely mourned, drove Augusta closer to Veronica, who, after all, had shared her life in so many ways over the years. Veronica had been but twenty years of age and "green off the boat" when she arrived at Commonwealth Avenue in the winter of 1891 to care for Annabelle and Zachary, then just four months old. The tie was, in Augusta's view, "ultimately binding."

Truly affected by that phrase, Zoe looked back at the early spring of 1933, to the months before Potter's death, and noted something that had slipped her attention before, a brief entry dated "February 19," written on a small piece of tablet paper, inserted into the bundle as if Augusta could not bear to leave unrecorded something that, in her view, was of real significance:

> . . . and so they are all as loyal and dear as they can be, this in spite of the fact that I was obliged to gather everyone just last Tuesday, after weeks and weeks of poring over my account books, to announce that there will be no wages for a while—a roof and food only, and perhaps a ha'penny or two for pocket money. This is terrible news, of course, and afterward I was so beset that I actually confided it to Anthony. But he inadvertently made me realize that I had taken a correct if unhappy course. He suggested that they all be *dismissed!* As if one puts one's family in the street!

Augusta was unable to restore the women's wages, even after Potter died, but Veronica and Winifred didn't seem to mind at all; they would not think of going, of leaving the mistress. Augusta wept openly when the two of them came to her to say that as far as they were concerned, this was their home, too, and they would never leave it of their own accord. Zoe saw the affection and loyalty commanded without gesture or word and thought again of Jim Forbes's remark about Augusta's fineness of character, which he had thought was unappreciated.

As the hot summer of 1933 crawled by, the family's situation became far more straitened. Anthony had taken to disappearing more and more, sometimes staying away for several nights in a row. The contributions he had promised Augusta for the table grew less frequent, and the small legacy from Alex was slowly but surely squandered away (as Augusta viewed it) on food and small necessities. Annabelle had returned to her old habit of staying home, "locked in her room, even on the loveliest days, only to bolt off from time to time in bursts of enthusiasm that can have only one source. I am able to time Trefoyle's comings and goings by the clock of my daughter's temper," wrote Augusta in late July.

In September, the Hillyards set about their annual housecleaning. The chores that other people usually did in spring Augusta always planned for fall: the rugs were beaten senseless out on a line stretched across the alley, the walls were scrubbed, the curtains washed and pressed. But all those heavy tasks being now too difficult for an arthritic Veronica and an aging Winnie, they settled, in September of 1933, for what Augusta peevishly felt was "the merest tidying up!" And the plumbing, she wrote in a firm, angry hand, was faulty and the roof a disgrace. Rainwater was caught in buckets on the fourth floor, and Winnie was obliged to move down to sleep in Hortense's old room. Anthony could not be persuaded to help out.

Augusta spent some money, frantically hoarded for the plumbing, on taxes, arguing with Anthony right in the downstairs hall, over money, over obligation, over pride:

He has come again to ask for my diamond earrings, "for an investment," he says, for an opportunity too good to miss. I am disgusted with him and his pettiness, his shortsightedness. He seizes moments only—never concepts, never ideas. He seems not to understand that tomorrow *does come*. He is like his father in that, and I am sorry to say it of him. But at least Eugene could be generous when he had it!

Augusta, infuriated by Anthony's greed, his temerity, refused him her diamonds (as she had the year before), but she wavered only a moment before giving him one thousand dollars—the rest of the plumber's money and next year's taxes. She took to her bed after that, but arose after just one day, feeling more resolute than before.

Toward the end of the month, as the labor of "tidying up" neared completion, Augusta thought she noticed a few items missing from the house, but the losses were so minor she could not be sure. She wrote on a Sunday night in late September, "that Meissen vase has also vanished, along with the gateleg table from Nahant that we have always kept in the back parlor, covered with a scarf, and possibly the silver fruit compote that belonged to Aunt Sallie Cabot at one time."

But the plumbing problem seemed to improve all by itself, and Augusta, at first suspicious, then very close to "a kind of shame that I cannot acknowledge—even here," decided not to press the matter with Veronica.

Zoe read all this with her breath held in her throat, her shoulders hunched over the pages in the poor light. She felt brilliantly alert, and hungry, too—she had not eaten since lunch with Claudia, had drunk only the one small glass of wine in the kitchen with Arthur. Still, she refused to move, though her hips felt stiff and achy. She stretched her leg muscles until she was a little bit more comfortable and then forgot her physical self again and read on without stopping, though the next few pages were badly wrinkled, some words smudged and hard to decipher.

On Monday, October 16, 1933, Augusta went to New York on the day train by herself. She stayed away for two days, returning on the Wednesday:

> I cannot imagine how I ever fancied I would not be exhausted. I have returned feeling like a fish which has swum upstream on a journey lasting years, and yet it has been only three days since I set off from Back Bay Station with what I felt at the time to be a sprightly step, my decision firmly made, my excuses well in place. And yet, when I returned this afternoon, I was obliged to throw myself on the bed, fully clothed— hat, gloves, coat, and all—to fall into a sustaining stupor. When Win returned from market and found me there, she fussed and clucked in that sweet way she has, helped me on with my wrapper, and brought me some beef tea, and I spent what remained of the evening here on the chaise, at last feeling equal to putting down some of these thoughts.

As I must—for there is a momentousness even in so loathsome and final an act.

The truth of it is that after the past many months, nay years, of making do, of scrimping, of squeezing the odd drop of juice out of the bitter, withered onion that our fortunes have become, watching Winifred and Veronica selling trinkets for urgent repairs to the house, and the greatest trinket of them all twinkling in the darkness of my bureau drawer . . . I went.

I have scant experience with traveling alone, and yet everyone believed my story that I was going to see Mathilde, supposedly on a brief visit to New York. I think they believed me; it really doesn't matter. They would have no way of knowing that dear Mathilde is far away in France. They thought I was to be with her and all her fancy friends, and dear Winnie, with needless care, wrapped up my gray chiffon dinner gown and tucked it into my valise, where it remained—unneeded and unworn.

The Belmont being far beyond my means, I stayed in a little place in the Murray Hill district, which was possibly not a good choice for a lady of my years, and yet I'm sure I looked quite suitably drab. No one would ever have suspected that in my little satchel there were diamonds.

On Tuesday morning, after a night's rest that can only be described as fitful, I forced myself to Tiffany's and stood outside on Fifth Avenue for more than an hour, pacing slowly back and forth on the pavement as the crowds surged past, until my behavior caught the eye of a policeman, who approached—to my horror!—asked me my business, and sent me on my way. Trembling, I went into an "automat" on 57th Street, got a cup of tea for a nickel, and sat, my diamonds still in my purse, fearing of course to take them out for one nostalgic look, but squeezing them from outside; the finger marks are still pressed into the leather of the bag.

But an hour later, feeling somewhat strengthened by the tea (or the *necessity!*), I went back . . . how could I not go back! The banisters are broken! The wallpaper droops in shreds! My tax money is gone! My house is coming to pieces! How could I not go back? I walked inside the great brass doors of Tiffany's and stepped with what I hoped was just a speck of grandeur to the counter and took out the earrings, still in the blue box in which Eugene presented them to me more than thirty years ago. The almond-sized diamonds blazed up at us from the black velvet tray on which the man placed them. How they sparkled! How they gleamed! How they blinded the clerk! He looked up at me with a mixture of pity and awe that I do not believe I care to see again. He called the manager over, and I was made to stand there, trying so hard not to appear supplicatory in my posture, as they whispered and turned away and put their mouths to each other's ears and turned back to me—and made their offer. . . . I had planned to bargain. I had planned to transform myself into the Augusta Hillyard who used to ride past that store in a lacquered barouche with four matched sorrel horses! But I quietly accepted their cheque, and all I can say for myself is that throughout this most bitter of transactions I did not drop my gaze. The cheque was made out for who knows what fraction of the value of the earrings. What is "Value"? My home is falling apart, and that compels me.

And now I'm back, safe in my own room, which feels just a trifle tomblike on this warm October evening. The window is slightly open, breezes ruffling these pages, a portion of wine in a glass beside me at which I sip as if to make it last when I would gulp and gulp again if I but had the stomach for it. I had the oddest (and most foolish) thought of going to Eugene's grave tomorrow to apologize and then reminded myself that those famous earrings—my "Birthday Earrings"—were bought with my own money all those years ago . . . and yet that's not important now.

For tenscore millennia and more, my earrings grew in the earth, the silty carbon hardening, congealing into diamonds, and then Eugene bought them for me and thirty-one years flashed by and I sold them back to Tiffany's and we shall pay the taxes with the proceeds. There is really nothing else to say about it.

Zoe sat back against the headboard of the bed with her hands unconsciously cupped as if to cradle the diamond earrings that just tonight Arthur had said Annabelle once sent him up here to Grandmère's room to find. It was clear to Zoe that Grandmère never told anyone that she had sold them. The stairs were fixed, the taxes paid, the banisters repaired . . . and no one asked where the money came from: Augusta was expected to provide. That she did not wear her famous earrings in the twelve years between the trip to New York and her death apparently occurred to no one; obviously not even Annabelle had realized they were gone. Augusta had evidently thought long and hard about selling them, and yet there was a suddenness to the resolve to do it that impressed Zoe—a decision made virtually in an instant, the necessity unquestioned.

The Tiffany entry ended in tiny letters squeezed at the bottom of the paper, the writing cramped and spiky. The very next page was dated more than a year later; if there had been anything of note, of celebration or catastrophe, between the selling of the diamonds and Christmas Eve of 1934, it was impossible to know.

"I have not very much to say about the last year," Augusta wrote late on the night of December 24, 1934. "I have felt no need." Zoe looked up from the page and imagined she could see Augusta's upright figure by the window, where, she wrote, she'd stood for over an hour, thinking and staring out at the snow.

If there is anything I've learned in this year it is that others suffer more than we do, that the time for counting blessings does *not* pass, that the sundial that records our gratitude must have no shadows. . . . I think all the trials and tribulations of these dreadful times—those we shared and those we were spared (or rose above)—have helped me navigate a year of quiet joys and quiet suffering. Perhaps after years of excess I have learned to steer the middle course.

I can't imagine why I have resisted coming here—to this "confessional"—but I think after I sold my earrings I went a little mad. Not from regret for the glitter of the possession, or for the luster of the symbol. Not for fond memory of my wicked (yes, wicked) and beloved (yes, beloved) husband, not from loss of youth, for I lost that long ago, and not even from joy and relief because my house was safe. . . . No, I think I went a little mad because I have realized at last that my life has not turned out as I once thought it would, and I know now, at my great age, that the only act that defines us is how we accept such knowledge and the truth it tells.

I am philosophical this evening; the dotty old dear is philosophical. I would laugh at myself, were I not so eager to make clear—if only to myself—that these thoughts might mean that I have at last found a passage through these shoals, and settled down within these walls, yes, within these pages. And if I last for many years more and this is all there is of Augusta Hillyard—never seen, never known of by anyone—so be it.

Tears flooded Zoe's eyes at this, and she was glad to find an old tissue in her pocket so she did not have to move. It had never before, with all she had read—even the death of Zachary, the loss of Anne and others—been as clear to her that Augusta had suffered this much pain. And no one knew it, not even Jim Forbes, who remembered only the strong, imperial Augusta. In spite of all his reverent love, he never saw this side, so unapproachable had the matriarch become.

. . . and so, in spite of everything, we are planning as fine a Christmas as the purse can stretch to. Veronica and Win have engaged themselves upon the poulterer; I pity the poor man—confronted by my darling harridans, determined to have the finest bird in all of Boston and not willing to take no for an answer. There has been the smell of baking in the house, and the fruits are sliced for the trifle. Dear Potter, looking down, as one imagines, from the skies, must be smiling to himself, because there is indeed champagne chilling in the snow. I think I will have only the tiniest portion of brandy this evening, smoke one last cigarette, and rest my bones for the exertions of the morrow. All are coming—it should be quite festive. Dinner is planned for four o'-clock, then coffee and Veronica's famous Christmas trifle afterward in the parlor. Many Wheelwrights, many Hillyards, an opportunity perhaps for poor Eugene to press his suit on snippy young Miss Laura? I am not entirely pleased with the developments I see there, but perhaps it is high time, after so many years, that the Wheelwrights and the Hillyards intermarried. . . . . It happens in novels; it can happen here.

Zoe smiled at that and blew her nose again; she knew the ending, after all—knew all she needed to about her parents' screamed recriminations and their early deaths and realized that it didn't matter, couldn't matter, never had. As far as Zoe was concerned, the generations between herself and her Grandmère were only dust.

Christmas Day, 1934, dawned icy cold and clear, the morning sunshine brilliant. Augusta woke and ran barefoot to the window—enthralled to hear sleighbells on Commonwealth Avenue. Zoe smiled again as she read Grandmère's descriptions of the shimmering tree, the pots of poinsettias clustered in the center of the table—of the smells of cinnamon and oranges, wafting from the kitchen. But the day ended on a far less felicitous note:

(Christmas Night) . . . in short, I threw him out. Bag and baggage, never to return—and if he thinks the crazy old fool (as he called me) is going to relent, he is much mistaken. I see now that we've had this coming, Anthony and I, for half a century. Our "disaffinity" (no word is adequate!)—which I will mourn until the last day of my life—has hovered in the air between us from his childhood, waiting only for the critical moment in which to play it out. This came tonight.

An interruption. As I was putting down the lines above, more than an hour ago, Annabelle stormed unannounced into my room demanding that I take Anthony back. I have just finished explaining to her that she understands nothing, that all of this is none of her affair, and have packed her off to bed precisely as I used to do when she was a tiny girl. It is really too remarkable that Annabelle should think it her place to defend her brother, particularly in view of her own behavior, yet there is a romantic pathos to poor Annabelle's extravagant errors that her brother cannot hide behind:

He asked me for my *house!* Demanded that I give it to him! On Christmas night—after our happy guests had all departed home—my eldest child sought me out and asked me for my house! I was horrified, yes, speechless. Anthony wanted me to give him the house—to *SELL!*

How did I so completely fail to show my children that the sanctity of home is all we have—the preservation of that home our greatest burden and our chiefest joy—the symbol of our family? When did I lose the chance to teach them there's a fortress here, these walls unscalable by all adversity, so long as they are valued and preserved? How did I fall short when the lesson which I learned in my bones has not (it is now clear) so much as grazed a single hair of their unthinking heads? And I do not blame Eugene: the lesson of the home, the sanctuary, the family, is Mother's job to teach. If Anthony believes the essence of his family is disposable, replaceable, unimportant—that's not Eugene's fault. It is mine.

My God! I know it's but a house, a structure—a pitiful thing of stone and wood, plaster and scrap. I know that! I am not so utterly the daft old fool my son would make me out. He tells of yet another "deal" gone bad, an opportunity slid by unseized, and he could "bail it out," he says, if only he could have the house to sell. "Don't worry, Ma," he said to me, a charming smile upon his curving lips, "I'll get you a nice flat in the South End. Just help me this one time and then we'll all be rich again." Then, his parting shot, before I threw him out, his satchel already in his hand—forgetting the citrines, the tax money, the pearl cabochon, not understanding, blind to all distinctions, oblivious to symbols, baubles and fortress all one to him—he peevishly reminded me that I had refused him my diamond earrings, too. But I, in turn, reminded him that I refused them *twice.*

The doubts may seize me later, but tonight I am too furious to think I might have wronged him. If the dawning of another day—be it a fortnight or a decade hence—should prove me wrong, unfair, unfeeling, or lacking in perspective, charity, or proper mother's love, I do not care tonight. Anthony has given up his place, and I will not offer it back to him. If he comes begging? Well, he won't—he sets no value on his home; he finds no sanctuary here. If Anthony would abdicate, would sacrifice his place—in the family, in our home, and in my heart—let him live with his choice.

The pages fell to Zoe's lap and fluttered one by one to the bedcover and the floor. After a while, she went to the window again, pressed her forehead against the damaged pane, and watched the rain sluice down the darkness of the avenue.

THIRTY-FOUR

*E*arly Sunday morning, Zoe stood in the doorway of Arthur's room. His bed had not been slept in; the old afghan was smoothed over the narrow mattress in a semblance of tidiness. Near the bed was a large plastic dishpan filled with Arthur's unopened mail. Zoe pushed it flush against the wall with her toe and went downstairs to make some coffee.

Though she was bone-tired and a little nauseated this morning, Zoe felt alert to her worries, and not really comforted at all by the fact that Arthur had called last night, as promised; it was nearly midnight when the phone zinged through the upstairs hall. His voice had been dry, hushed, as if produced without saliva. He did not say where he was or when he would return, whether he had murdered Conrad and escaped to South America, or gone to sit by Annabelle's casket in the dark cellar of Leape & Neames—only that he was "okay" and would see her "later."

Arthur's call had served to pull Zoe away from Grandmère's sad reflections on the death of Mathilde Gaylord, her words so clearly those of someone who had done her weeping before setting pen to paper. "How I will miss her!" Augusta wrote in May of 1936, just after one of the young art students Mathilde had befriended sent a letter to Boston with the news. "Her charming humor, our wonderful long talks—my goodness!—I have so many precious memories of her . . . and yet that unquenchable thirst to *have more*—is life itself. Dear Mathilde, from her tomb, would agree, I think."

Zoe put the page down and gazed around the room, at the beauty with which Augusta Hillyard had surrounded herself, the calm elegance of this sanctuary where, Zoe now realized, she had spent the most important hours of her life. Zoe's eyes narrowed in confusion; in spite of the brave words about those happy memories, she felt terribly sad and lonely for Grandmère's own sake.

The diary entry that told of Mathilde's passing was separate from the rest of the packet marked "1935 to 1937." It was written on a single sheet, the paper clipped to a thin rice-paper envelope with an intricate ribbon closure of a type Zoe knew had not been manufactured for years. Inside was a matte-finish studio proof of a dark-haired young woman, somewhat exotically posed against a flower-bedecked terrace balustrade, her chin resting on one hand. Like the wedding portrait of Anne Lowell, the picture had been placed in the diary at the time of the dear friend's death and not tucked in with a happier occasion. And, like Anne's, it was inscribed:

Ah, ma chère Augusta: amie—confidente—exemplaire!
Mathilde, 1907

Zoe could not remember ever having seen a photo of Grandmère; there were a few hints of her own view of her appearance in portions of the diary Zoe had already read, but as far as she knew, no photographs remained. Zoe had a blurred memory of an afternoon many, many years before, she and Arthur crouching, terrified, behind Annabelle's open bedroom door, on the day that news was received of Spencer Trefoyle's death in New Mexico. They had watched as Annabelle, shrieking and sobbing, methodically ripped up almost all the family pictures, the old leatherbound albums strewn about her on the carpet. Though it seemed logical that a few might have survived, that Annabelle had not destroyed every single one, Zoe knew that for now she would have to content herself with her imaginings and the memory of scented warmth that still remained.

By the time the Trouts and Uncle Jim arrived, the late-morning sky was full of light, and Zoe, Arthur's toolbox on the floor beside her, had already begun to dismantle Annabelle's huge bed. Eddie instantly ran to help her, and together with Claudia they carried the wooden pieces to the cellar and then lugged the mattress and box spring out to the bin in the alley.

The arrangement in the long parlor now seemed more spacious, returning step by step, Zoe imagined, to what once had been. She and Claudia selected odd items from the other rooms—a small tub chair from the back parlor, and a floor lamp that had stood for years in Eugene Hillyard's library, a tall, cloisonné monstrosity with four black-enameled elephants couchant at the base, complete with gilt howdahs. They found a few pieces of bric-a-brac and a lovely pair of porcelain candlesticks in the music room and set them on the parlor mantel next to Annabelle's precious Staffordshire dogs. Eddie unrolled and vacuumed the immense Sarouk, and they all stood back to admire the effect, pronouncing it more than adequate for the purpose.

"Well, that's done," said Claudia with a brisk look around the room. "It could still stand a good swabbing down, though," she muttered, sniffing the air.

"And a paint job." Eddie looked critically at the ceiling. Even from floor level the grime crusted in the dentils of the Italianate cornices could easily be seen.

Jim Forbes, who had been rather quiet all morning, sat on the small divan they had pulled from a dark corner to a spot across from the fireplace. Zoe brushed and dusted the divan and was pleased to see that the thick upholstery had survived decades of disinterest. It had once been a deep Prussian blue, sprigged with fanciful flower designs in gold thread, but was now so worn that the color and pattern could be seen only under the seat cushions. Jim sat down with a sigh and ran his hand slowly over the arm of the piece in a caressing gesture.

"Augusta Hillyard always liked her guests to sit here," he said. "She'd take a straight-backed chair every time herself, and the tea would be just here." He put his hands in the air before him, pouring in pantomime from an imaginary pot. "Then she'd settle back with her cup and let *you* talk." He chuckled a bit at that and sat back himself.

"Room's pretty bare now, but she used to keep lots of stuff in here— always seemed awful crowded to me. Had a bust of somebody or other up there," he said, pointing to the ornate mantelpiece. "Dante? Shakespeare? I can't seem to remember. . . ."

"How's about a snack, everybody?" Claudia said, sensing her uncle's somber mood. Zoe was no picnic this morning either, silent but without yesterday's warm serenity—closed off somehow. She assumed that Zoe was worried that Arthur had not come home last night, though it had not been discussed beyond the observation that he was not there.

"I don't much feel like a snack, honey," Jim said, kissing her cheek. "I'd like to see us finish up around here, though, not drag everything out past poor Zoe's tolerance." He looked at Zoe, who was leaning against the fireplace surround, head to one side, arms and ankles crossed.

Zoe shrugged. "Maybe a cold drink's not such a bad idea," she said, rousing herself and leading the way down to the kitchen.

"Well, *I* think we need flowers," Claudia said, as she watched Zoe reach into the refrigerator for the big bottle of Gatorade they'd gotten at the market. "Eddie," she called over her shoulder, "why don't we get up to Mahoney's hon . . ."

Eddie had been looking forward to his lunch; he knew there were deli sandwiches and chips in one of Claudia's plastic bags. But when he came into the kitchen he saw an unmistakable look in his wife's eyes.

"We're almost done here, Zo," Claudia said, glancing at Eddie again. "I think it might be good to get some greens in here, lots of cut flowers; it's prime time for tulips in pots. Eddie, don't you think so, honey? And some nice blue hydrangeas?"

"Claudia, honestly, you don't have to . . ." Zoe began. She had not said one word since they came into the kitchen. Neither had Jim. He stood in the alley doorway with his hands in his pockets, gazing out at the trash bins.

"No, no, we really need some *fleurs*. And I think definitely a centerpiece of some sort for the dining room, too," Claudia said, slinging her big tote bag over her arm. "I like the tureen in the middle of the table, by the way, Zo, looks just great. . . . Eddie, bring the sandwich *with* you, sweetie."

Uncle Jim closed the alley door behind them and sat down at the kitchen table with his glass of Gatorade. Zoe went into the butler's pantry and came back with the bottle of gin she knew Arthur kept there and held it up with its label showing, raising her eyebrows at Jim, who pointed to his glass and nodded. She fixed the same for herself and sat across from him in the chair from which Arthur, just last night, had spilled out his secrets.

"Feel like drying eight million plates and glasses?" she said. "I'll wash." She gestured with her glass toward the dusty stacks of china and glassware by the sink. "Took them out this morning. Look like enough?" She smiled a small forlorn crescent, unlit by amusement.

Jim put his glass down and looked at her with his bright eyes. "Fine with me," he said after a moment. "I think I'd rather gab awhile though, digest my drink."

"Uncle Jim . . ."

"Plain to me you got something on your mind, honey—plain to that sweet Claudia, too, the way she shanghaied Eddie out of here. Care to tell me what it is?"

Zoe shrugged and looked at the table. "I'm just tired. Didn't get much sleep."

Jim sat back in his chair and crossed his legs, nodding thoughtfully. "You know, Zoe, I been chewin' on something since the other day at lunch, little remembrances nagging at me, couldn't quite put my finger on it until now."

As he spoke, Jim gazed out the window of the back door, though he could see Zoe's face from the corner of his eye.

"What would that be?" she said in a small, dry voice.

"Well, all weekend long I been thinking you remind me of something, someone, wondering who it might be, and here finally it's come to me. Yep. I can see it now just as plain." When he looked at her, his eyes were calm and narrow.

"I always had the impression I look like Anthony," Zoe said. "When I saw Annabelle in the hospital last week, we . . . we talked a little, not much, of course, she really wasn't making all that much . . . but she said I look just like him."

"Yes, you do have his eyes, that's for sure. I realized that last Sunday over at Claudia's, saw it right away. And that's a compliment—Anthony Hillyard was a fine-looking man, Zoe, no doubt about it. But that's just superficial, if you follow me, just physical. No, what I'm talking about, what I been trying to put my finger on, is different . . . different."

Jim looked sharply at her over the glass of greenish gin as if waiting to be contradicted. Zoe said nothing, but the muscles seemed to move slightly in her face.

"Seems to me you generally tend to be a very contained kind of woman; you don't fidget around, poking at your hair and all the way a lot of gals do. Your great-grandma was like that, Zoe dear. She could sit for an hour without moving her hands out of her lap—talk the whole time, mind—loved to talk when she wasn't forcing someone else to do it, but she tended to do it without moving. Most people wave their hands around, pick at themselves. She didn't. And neither do you. . . . At least that's my impression."

Zoe took a deep breath and crossed her legs, saying nothing.

"You know, honey, could be that when Annabelle saw you in the hospital, mostly out of her head as I guess she was there toward the end, you were reminding her of Augusta more than anything—that stillness, that control. That strength. Annabelle never could deal with you or her mother either . . . just got you two mixed up in her poor mind."

Zoe wet her lips and looked at the floor. After a moment, she pushed herself up from the table and went over to the sink to start in on the glasses.

She had found forty-six gold-rimmed sherry glasses in the uppermost cupboard of Potter's pantry, above the Coalport, neatly stowed but opaque with decades of dust. She began washing them, one by one, saying nothing. Jim came up beside her, took the first glass out of the drainer, and dried it slowly with a linen towel.

"Only Augusta Hillyard would have so many matching sherry glasses," he said, making little chuckling sounds. "Paulette told me once about how much she loved to entertain—in the old days, long before Paulette came into the family—heard it all from her mother-in-law, Celia, I expect. Actually, from all I've ever heard, this 'do' for Annabelle's bound to be the biggest party this old house has seen in many a year . . . many a year. Ironic."

Jim wiped the clean glasses in a lazy way, each swipe of the towel alternating with a swig of the Gatorade and gin.

"What do you think Grandmère would say if she knew that this was a farewell party for her house?" Zoe said softly without looking up from the sink. "What do you think she'd say to that?"

Jim took a deep, careful breath and dried one more glass. "Meaning what?"

"Meaning it could very well be just that."

Jim reached around Zoe and turned off the water. He moved his hand to her shoulder and pulled her away from the sink, handing back her drink with his other hand.

"Come on over here and spit it out, honey. Spit it out."

And Zoe, after only the briefest hesitation, told him all about her talk with Arthur—everything he'd said about the mortgage, the unrecorded deed, Conrad, Augusta's trust. She did not editorialize, she did not weep. She told him everything.

"Well," Jim said at last, setting his glass gently on the table with a precise gesture, "I can't say I'm surprised. Not at all. She just doted on you, Zoe, never made a move without you in those last years. 'My sweet Zoe' this, 'my little Zoe' that. I remember, let's see now, it must have been in '43, I was here in Boston on a short furlough before they shipped me out to godforsaken Guam."

He leaned forward, thinking. "That's right, May of 1943. . . . Zoe, there was nothing on that island but Quonset huts and about a million cases of cheap Canadian whisky. . . . Anyway, even with all the rationing, they had a nice lunch party for me over in Celia's back garden. You were toddling all over the place, but you never did get too far away from your Grandmère, patting her skirt, reaching for her hand, and she'd whisper to you, take you into her lap if you fussed." Jim chuckled and looked up at the ceiling with shiny eyes. "She sure did love you, yes indeed."

Zoe just clamped her teeth together and watched him. After a moment she said, "Arthur believes Conrad's going to show up here, sooner or later—wanting the house, or a lot of money, or both."

Jim looked back at her and nodded. Though she'd doubted it at first, it soon became clear that he'd heard every word she said.

"I'm sure he will," Jim said. "No doubt about it—gloat, brag, whatever turns him on. Threaten." He leaned forward again, frowning slightly.

"Arthur pretty sure he hasn't recorded the deed yet?"

"I think so," Zoe said. "Arthur feels he wouldn't do it, you know, quietly. He'd want to make Arthur squirm some more—the bastard. He has missed all those payments, though."

Jim sniffed in agreement and poured some straight gin into his glass, thinking about what she'd said.

Zoe sprang up from her chair and paced up and down the small open space in front of the sink.

"I wish to hell Arthur would get his ass back here, for cryin' out loud!" she cried in a voice filled with angry frustration. "Jim, he's been gone since last night! I just . . ."

Zoe broke off and fell into her chair. Her black eyes were sparkling in her flushed face.

Jim just sipped quietly at his drink and watched her with a thoughtful expression, realizing with some surprise that she did look exactly as Anthony Hillyard had in one of the rages that had punctuated his later life, though he thought better of pointing that out to her.

"He's probably been out all this time looking for that damn Conrad!" she said in a thick, tense voice.

"Nothing much you can do about it now, sugar," Jim said. "Though I admit he could very well be off making one last brave stand. That sort of quixotic behavior kind of runs in the family, too, now that I think about it. But like it or not, you'll have to wait it out."

"But he should have told me he was in trouble," Zoe insisted, her eyes still luminous with all that she was feeling. "Jesus, I'd like to wring his neck! Why didn't he *tell* me? I would have helped him, Uncle Jim, I would have."

Suddenly, tears flooded her eyes and she got up to get a Kleenex from the box on the counter, keeping her back to him as she blew her nose and hooked her hair behind her ears.

"You know," she said, "until last week, Arthur and I hadn't seen each other in over ten years." She turned and, sniffing, looked at him carefully. "Hadn't even talked on the phone."

"I know that, honey."

"Or written, even."

"I know." Jim got up to add some Gatorade to his drink, nodding all the while. Before he sat down, he put his hand on her shoulder, just for a second, looking at her until he saw by her tiny smile that she had most of it out of her system.

"Okay," he said. "Listen up, now, Zoe dear—let's look at all this carefully."

And Jim talked and Zoe listened, her elbows on the table, eyes intent and calmer now. He explained to her in detail about mortgage deeds, title deeds, laws of property.

"There's a prejudice in the courts, and in the boardrooms of most banks, too, in favor of the original owner—lousy public relations to let it get out that owning your own home is not a pretty safe proposition."

Zoe was nodding. "Right. I can see that. You're not saying there's a slim skinny ray of hope?" she said, raising her eyebrows, smiling just a little.

"Well, there's always rays—slim and slimmer. But it's a pity about that side agreement, though. How many payments was it?"

"Arthur says three—if he missed three payments Conrad could record the deed and get the house. But next week it'll be four."

"And this Conrad made those payments to the bank?"

Zoe nodded. "Arthur says he did. He's the cosigner, after all."

"Uh huh . . . uh huh." Jim looked at his watch for a second. "And he has the deed?"

Zoe nodded again.

"The actual title deed?"

"That's right."

Jim pursed out his lips and sucked in his smooth cheeks for a second. "Okay," he said. "Any lawyers involved in that little private deal?"

Zoe shook her head, trying to follow his thinking. "I don't think so."

"Figures. Well, that just could be for the best. Still, remains to be seen what that sumbitch has up his sleeve. How much you say Arthur still owes—house and everything?"

Zoe told him.

"Whoo-eeee! That is a bunch of money, all right."

"I don't have it, you know," Zoe said, getting up to stand in the open alley doorway. "At least nowhere near *all* of it. And I have to tell you, Uncle Jim, I don't have the faintest idea where I could get it—not the faintest."

"I don't think that that's today's worry, honey."

She turned and looked at him with a tortured, uncertain expression, unable to take it one step at a time as he was obviously planning to do.

"I thought I'd promise him just about anything," Zoe said, her voice rising as she spoke. "Tell him whatever he seems to want to hear— worry about the consequences later—tell him I *have* the money and then try to get it any way I can—shit, I don't know how, but any way at all." Zoe's hands rose into the air as if the answer was there to be clutched.

"Well, that's a start, you know?" Jim laughed in his snorty old man's way. "I always did admire that Mr. Nick Machiavelli. He was a lawyer, Zoe—I don't think a lot of folks realize that. Always admired his mind. Guess that's why I decided to get into this line of work, way back when. Heh! . . . Zoe, my friend, deception's not such a bad place to start, under the circumstances. Been my experience that not too many folks are interested in turning down money, and this Conrad fella's obviously no exception to that. Sounds like a greedy so-and-so to me, else he wouldn't be where he is today."

"Which is where?" Zoe asked with an amused expression.

"In big trouble with the Hillyard family is where. Now, Zoe dear, I believe I'm starting to get an idea, something I'd like to gnaw on for a while, and I'm going to have to ask you to trust me on this. . . ."

Jim put his penny loafers on the other chair and pulled his lisle socks up over his skinny ankles. "I were you, I'd expect him tomorrow at that wake thing you're having. It's in the paper, isn't it?" he asked, tapping the Sunday *Globe* that lay on the table where Claudia had left it, open to the obituaries.

"Yes. So?"

"So, he'll be wanting an audience—if what Arthur says is true. Right? Crueler that way. Nickels to doughnuts it'll be tomorrow. And you'll be ready. Just give me a little time here."

In spite of herself, Zoe expelled a snuffling laugh and went to the sink to start in on the dusty glasses again. With an energetic movement she yanked the sleeves of her sweater up over her elbows.

"I'm loaded for bear right now!" she said, pushing her hair out of her face and turning on a blast of water.

"I can tell," Jim said, reaching for the dish towel. "But I promise, you'll get your chance."

By the time the Trouts returned from the nursery, Jim and Zoe had washed all the sherry glasses and the stack of gold-bordered Haviland luncheon plates and piled them on the dining-room table. Hearing Claudia and Eddie at the front door about four o'clock, Zoe ran to let them in, laden with pots of azaleas and hydrangeas, their arms full of bouquets of spring garden flowers—red tulips and delicate Japanese iris, pink freesia and Peruvian lilies.

Jim helped Eddie carry a five-foot palm tree into the parlor while Claudia bustled into the kitchen with all the cut flowers, quite aware that Zoe, though she smiled and exclaimed over the beautiful blossoms, was still in a quiet mood, simmering, but perhaps a little less tense and edgy than before.

Claudia dumped all the flowers in the sink and then, to Zoe's surprise, kissed her on the cheek and handed her a single pink carnation.

"How you doin', kiddo?" she said with a wink. "Feeling better?"

Zoe shrugged, smiling in spite of herself. "Oh, okay. I wish my idiot big brother would get himself back here, though."

"I know," Claudia said, unwrapping a fat bundle of pale yellow jonquils, "but I'm sure he's all right, Zo. He'll be back when he's ready. Not to worry."

Claudia climbed on a chair to reach the cupboard over the sink and lifted down half a dozen filthy vases. Zoe took them from her and stood them in the deep sink in the butler's pantry.

"That nice Wedgwood thing should be perfect for the freesias, Zo. Want me to help?"

"It's okay."

"Sure?"

"I'll let them soak. I can fix the flowers later," Zoe said, swishing water in the vases. When she turned back, Claudia was watching her with a thoughtful, almost analytic expression.

"All right." Claudia paused, as if reconsidering something she'd meant to say, thought better of, and then couldn't bear to leave unspoken.

"What?" Zoe said, with a little smile.

"Did you call him?"

Zoe was drying her hands on a paper towel; she shook her head and looked at the floor and then up into Claudia's astute blue eyes.

"No. I was going to . . . I was. Last night. But . . . I didn't get to do it."

"Then call him now, dear," she said. "Tell him . . . whatever needs telling. Lots of otherwise very clever people don't seem to know things unless somebody just *tells* them. Know what I mean? I'll bet you anything he'd come in a minute if you asked him," Claudia said, not waiting for a response. She gave Zoe one of her one-armed hugs and stood back to look up into her face.

"See you first thing in the morning, okay?"

And without another word, Claudia took Eddie and Uncle Jim and went on home, knowing, with the certainty of a woman who had almost no privacy herself, when someone needed to be left alone.

$\mathcal{B}$y late afternoon, the masses of flowers were arranged in Augusta Hillyard's antique vases and placed on tables and mantels in all the downstairs rooms. Zoe brought one of the huge pots of blue hydrangea upstairs and set it on the writing desk beside the chaise in Augusta's bedroom.

She knew this was a perfect moment to call Roger. It was just three o'clock in Los Angeles, and Roger (in some very irritating and utterly lovable ways, a creature of habit) would probably be home doing his little household chores, getting ready for the week ahead, undoubtedly thinking of her, hoping she would call and ask him to come, tell him she wanted him with her. Edgy, nervous, Zoe wandered listlessly around the room, finally going back to pick up the entries for early May of 1942 that had scattered on the carpet. She straightened the pages as best she could, leaned back against the pillows of the chaise, and began to read, hoping for messages.

On May 3, Augusta wrote that Celia Wheelwright had begged to be allowed to be the hostess for Augusta's eightieth birthday celebration. But the festive preparations, begun by an eager Celia nearly one month early, were dampened by the selfish behavior of Annabelle and Laura, who were locked into a silent hatred for each other that affected everyone in the house.

I have no particular objection to a nice party, even though as "guest of honor" I will be required to bask in a spotlight which I can never tell poor Celia is so unwelcome. . . .

But it is so dear of her to think of me that I am trying to be as gracious as I can, offering comments on the menu, and expressing all sorts of "preferences," though I am well aware that Celia and Paulette are doing all this work themselves without any assistance or encouragement whatsoever from those two ungrateful witches, and were I not so fearful of somehow spoiling the party, I would take them to task for it and no mistake. I sometimes wonder if I would prefer bickering and shouting to the dry, bitter silence that vibrates so between them. I see the hand of the wretched Trefoyle in all of this; I spotted him out by the street lamp on the Mall the other evening, and soon after Laura made some flimsy excuse to leave the house. . . . Oh, I suppose it could all be innocent enough, and it does not do to brood lest an unwelcome truth lurk in the speculation!

In spite of her misgivings, though, Augusta enjoyed her party. Apparently she had insisted that it be in the afternoon so that "my baby" would not be left out, and the festivities had an almost childlike tone. Zoe, reading the pages with a small smile, grimaced when she learned that she smeared French vanilla ice cream all over her "nice new party frock." Augusta fretted that her darling had missed her nap, though "the dear little thing didn't seem to mind at all, as if aware that the party was something special for her old Grandmère." Zoe chuckled when she read that Celia Wheelwright had had to open all the presents and hold them up for Augusta to see because Baby Zoe fussed whenever someone tried to take her from her Grandmère's lap.

. . . and Hortense sent a lovely knitted bed jacket all the way from Savannah; it really is quite splendid—all hand-done, with pink ribbons woven in and out. It seems my Hortense is an artist, after all! I also had a sweet garnet-and-pearl brooch from Veronica and Win and a wonderful stack of books from Paulette, which, I am delighted to say, included *The Grapes of Wrath,* which I have thus far only read *about,* and the latest from poor, dead Scott Fitzgerald, *The Last Tycoon.* I shall enjoy reading about the evils of Hollywood. I suppose if I were a trifle younger I could consider traveling off to California to see the New Babylon for myself! . . . oh, and of course I also had a new bottle of Nuit de Noël and a nice card from Celia. There is probably scant need to mention that I received no note from young Eugene on this occasion, though there was a fine sentimental remembrance from dear Jimmie Forbes, who was unable to join us; a lovely bouquet accompanied his card.

Annabelle (who had some fancy bonbons for me) left for one of her famous, not-so-secret trysts before Celia served the ice cream, and directly afterward Laura established herself, sulking away, in an old rattan chair at the bottom of Celia's garden, claiming not to feel quite well. Anthony did not appear, although he sent over a small nosegay by the florist's boy, which is rather more than I expected.

Zoe put the pages down and stared out the window, thinking of Anthony Hillyard—and rubbed her hand over her face, feeling her bones, her skin, wondering. But in a moment she shook her head as if to clear it of such unwelcome, unsettling comparisons and read on, still wondering.

In April of 1943, Spencer Trefoyle left Boston on one of his extended trips to New Mexico, and Augusta noted some settling of the tension in the house. Trefoyle was not expected to return until midsummer, and as "young Eugene" had been for nearly a year, in spite of all the threats and importunings from the women in his family, far away in the Pacific, the house was "quite feminine in aspect. After all," Augusta wrote one night in early June, "were not Medusa and the Furies female?"

Four generations cheek by jowl in an uneasy alliance born of the merest necessity! I daresay were there funds and opportunity to go our separate ways, both Laura and Annabelle would be out the door. I, of course (aha!), would remain here with dear little Zoe, who toddles after me everywhere I go. I took her down to Jordan Marsh on Thursday and found the most charming apple-green corduroy overalls with little straps and pockets. My girls, of course, wore only starched pinafores and petticoats, even for playtime, but these funny little overalls are ever so much more sensible.

Zoe paused again in her reading, restless, impatient, not finding in Augusta's words the perspective she was looking for. She put the diary down and paced the room again, nervously touching the picture frames and porcelain boxes, flaring out a filigreed ivory fan that caught her eye, tucked behind a figurine on the mantel shelf. She went repeatedly to the window, parting the curtains with twitching fingers as if Arthur might appear on the sidewalk below at the very moment that she looked.

Then she threw herself on the chaise again and riffled through the summer of 1943, noting the many references to herself and her childish accomplishments, Grandmère's pride and pleasure irking her somehow, as if misplaced. She could not believe that Jim Forbes had for even a split second compared her with Grandmère.

In August of 1943, Augusta experienced a series of short, yet debilitating "indispositions," as she called them: "They are probably nothing more than small losses of energy," she wrote on a sultry afternoon as she sat at her writing table, gazing out onto the Mall:

> . . . Still and all, it's clear enough that I am in the last decade of this great voyage, and bluster though I may, I shall not be able to outrun the "thousand several shocks the flesh is heir to" after all. But I'm damned if I'll take my old woman's mewling complaints to that fool doctor, which would certainly be convenient enough, since he's here nearly every day consulting with Laura. Nevertheless, the "sensations" I have had this winter (that dreadful feeling of looking at the world through the back end of a telescope—the lights!) all make me realize that the old girl must obviously be about her business.
>
> It is really too bad that young Jimmie Forbes is so far away; I would much prefer to deal with him at this time, but have all the same written to let him know that I am obliged to make other arrangements. I haven't given any attention to this tedious and distressing matter of a will since shortly after I lost Eugene, and procrastination clearly will no longer do. . . .

There were no further entries for the summer of 1943, and though Zoe looked with great concentration through several bundles of paper, she found nothing at all to indicate that Grandmère had indeed gone to a new lawyer and prepared a final will. But as she read of Augusta's enjoyment of the warm, dry October weather, her peaceful afternoons with Paulette and Celia and the children in the back garden of the

Wheelwright house on Bay State Road, it seemed to Zoe that the fresh serenity infusing Grandmère's mood was acquired through actual effort, by dint of a clear-minded and deliberate choice:

I strolled today around the Public Garden, wandering down every little bordered walk, kicking the fallen leaves out of my path as I went. The Garden is so somber at this time of year, yet beautiful in its own way. However does Nature manage to astonish us with its beauty even in this season of withering? The gathering in of the year has always been a favorite time for me. I think the dry metallic edges of the leaves, the fire faded, sometimes seem more lovely to me than the silky bits of green from which they started. What, I wonder, might the leaf have learned with the passing of the long, hot summer? "We know neither the day nor the hour," as some Irishman once wrote, yet I have begun to suspect I shall not be kept waiting overlong.

Zoe sat with her legs uncomfortably folded under her, realizing that even the contemplation of serenity eluded her; and though she read the words again, Augusta's voice, relaxed nearly to somnolence, could not communicate itself to her, and she gave it up at last. She had hoped to skim some solace, some instruction, from these pages, from this woman who could talk with her hands in her lap, whose genes were swimming in her blood, but for now, at least, she could not.

"I'm freaking out here," she mumbled as she put the diary away. Though the sky was overcast and the evening air looked cold, she felt a need to do her waiting out of doors. She closed the armoire doors and then plumped the pillows of the chaise with slapping hands. She got her jacket and went to sit on the Mall, to wait for Arthur in the chilly, lengthening twilight, realizing that it was the merest assumption that he was actually coming back. She would eagerly have gone looking for him had she the slightest notion where to start.

The eve of the Boston Marathon seemed to inspire amateur runners of every generation. They made their way down the Mall in their special shoes, elbows up, eyes glistening with effort. Zoe sat on Eugene's stone bench, her jacket buttoned up against the brisk air, and watched them struggle past, chests heaving. Lights glowed in the ornate street lamps and began to twinkle from windows and doorway fanlights all up and down the avenue as the evening lost its shine. The runners thinned out, either from exhaustion or the coming of the dinner hour, and searchlights crisscrossed the western sky toward Kenmore Square—in celebration of the Marathon, Zoe guessed, or perhaps just for the Red Sox.

It was nearly full dark when Arthur Hillyard, at the wheel of an old Dodge pickup truck, complete with heavy-duty tires and silver flames painted on the sides, screeched up Commonwealth Avenue and lurched to a stop directly across from Zoe's bench. His arm rested jauntily on the edge of the open window as he shouted across to her: "Meet me in the alley!" Zoe jumped up, running across the grass toward him, screaming his name, but he gunned the engine and the truck rattled off around the corner in a cloud of unmufflered black smoke.

Zoe sprinted across the street, oblivious to the traffic, up the steps, and through the dark house to the kitchen, yanking open the alley door just as Arthur pulled in among the trash bins. He climbed up into the bed of the truck and grasped an enormous flat parcel, wrapped in quilted movers' pads and tied with yards and yards of gray rope.

"Come give me a hand, Zo!" he yelled as he tilted the huge rectangular package carefully onto its side and leapt to the ground to grasp it from the other end.

"Arthur! Oh, you're back—I was so worried! Where the hell have you been?" Zoe cried, infected with his shrill excitement, almost laughing with relief as she kicked a chair against the kitchen door to keep it open and ran to help him.

"Arthur! Arthur! What *is* this?"

"Get that end, Zo!" Arthur shouted, grinning even as he ground his teeth with concentration. "Watch it! Watch it! Don't let it bump the side!"

Together they tilted the object down and out of the truck bed, grasping the heavy ropes for leverage, and sidled cautiously through the back door, Arthur yelling, "Careful! Careful, Zo!" every two seconds. He was laughing all the while with a powerful euphoria Zoe could not remember in him . . . not even at the piano.

"It weighs a ton!" Zoe shouted back at him, as though they were calling to each other across a chasm, water roaring, tumbling far below. "What is it? Dammit, Arthur, tell me what it is!"

They edged through the dining room, Arthur leading, turning on lights with his shoulder or his nose as they made their way to the parlor, finally leaning the object against the bare south wall, both of them bending over from the waist to catch their breath.

"Okay, Zoe," Arthur panted, "go away for a minute—go sit in the kitchen or something—don't come back until I call you." Arthur reached into his pocket for a utility knife, flicked the blade out, and began to saw away at the rope.

"Arthur, where in the world have—"

"Zoe! *Go away* a minute. I'll *call* you." He turned to her with a broad, cheeky grin. *"Go!"* This was Arthur Hillyard?

"Okay, okay . . . I'm going."

"Don't even peek until I tell you!"

"I'm going."

Zoe backed out of the parlor and ran to the kitchen to close and lock the alley door, then crept to the hallway and leaned against the wainscoting, still breathing hard, not entirely sure, the first ecstatic reaction now receding, whether she should laugh or cry.

After about fifteen minutes, Arthur came to find her and stretched out his bruised and dirty hand.

"Madame," he said, bowing slightly from the waist. His blue eyes twinkled as he looked down at her, satisfaction beaming from his calm and handsome smile. "Step right this way, if you please."

Zoe sucked in her cheeks and tilted her nose into the air in an ironic imitation of his courtly pose, and allowed him to take her hand and escort her with elegant slow steps into the parlor.

John Singer Sargent's portrait of Augusta Hillyard was propped against the far wall. Arthur had turned on all the lamps, and the painting glowed against the stained wallpaper, which faded into insignificance behind it. The gilded frame was more than six feet high and nearly five feet wide. The woman in the portrait, life-sized, stood tall and relaxed, just a touch of contented self-awareness in the fine features of her face, cognac hair piled high with combs over an ivory forehead. With one hand she held the skirt of her shell-pink, beaded gown; it fell in perfect silken folds against the background, which melted into shadows behind her; a tapestry bergère, a chinoiserie screen were barely discerned against the strength of the woman's presence.

"Oh, my God . . . Grandmère!" Zoe expelled the words as a greeting—a salutation. She sank down on the rug in front of the painting and put her hands over her mouth. "Arthur . . . is it?" she said in a hoarse whisper from behind her hands. "Is it Grandmère?"

"Oh, yes. Augusta Florence Lattimore Hillyard. Absolutely."

Arthur went over and squatted down by the lower right-hand corner of the painting. "Look here, Zo." He pointed to the artist's signature, clear as could be: *John S. Sargent. 1905.*

Zoe sat cross-legged on the Sarouk about ten feet away from the painting, leaning forward as if ready to enter the world she saw there, but not quite ready to go too close, not ready to touch it. Rocking slowly, back and forth, she was almost afraid to blink lest she open her eyes to find the portrait gone.

"Oh, God," she said again. "Oh my God, John Singer Sargent. Arthur . . . you have to tell me everything now. Everything."

"Let me get a drink."

Arthur got to his feet and stood with his hands on his hips for a moment, watching with her. Then he went to check the locks on all the doors and soon came back with one of the clean sherry glasses from the dining-room table filled with scotch; he sat down on the blue divan, hunched forward. Zoe hadn't moved an inch in the few minutes he'd been gone.

"You remember," Arthur began in a soft, slow voice, "you remember I told you that Annabelle sent me up to Grandmère's room about five years ago—to look for a pair of diamond earrings?"

"Yes."

"Well, the portrait was there then, on the long wall near the fireplace, and . . . and I was just stunned, Zo, stunned, because I realized what it was. Instantly. I knew it had to be Grandmère, of course . . . but, well, seeing the signature just took my breath away, because even though I don't know that much about art, I thought . . . a *Sargent,* for God's sake. . . ."

Arthur paused for breath and took a sip of his scotch, wiping his mouth with two fingers. Zoe glanced at him and then fastened her eyes to Grandmère's face again.

"But I left it there," he said. "I left it just where it was and locked the door behind me. I didn't say a word about it to Annabelle, and I never gave her back the key either, by the way, which for some reason she didn't mention. . . ." Arthur took another deep breath and paused for a moment, clearly thinking about something else.

"Anyway," he went on, "I more or less forced myself to forget about it, and then about two, two and a half years ago—that was the first time I was late with a couple of the mortgage payments—well, I went up to Grandmère's room again and looked at it and thought about how much money it might bring and all. I was starting to think maybe the time had finally come."

Zoe looked at him again, inhaled, but decided to say nothing.

"I know how this sounds, Zo," Arthur said quickly, his eyes flickering as if he'd read her thought. "I knew the painting belonged to you, but I also realized right away that whatever else I was screwing up, making such a mess of, I just couldn't consider . . . I was terrified, see, that if it all really went to hell with Conrad he could get the portrait right along with the house! Please believe me, Zo, I knew selling it was out of the question . . . out of the question, no matter how . . . how desperate and . . ."

Arthur paused and looked up into Grandmère's eyes. It was as if the breathing woman were actually in the room with them. Several minutes went by while he took a gulp of his drink and got up to walk back and forth in front of the painting, caressing the carved frame with his fingertips.

"So then I got the idea that I should try to hide it, just in case, and so what I did was I wrapped it up and took it down to one of those do-it-yourself storage places. It was basically a private warehouse, down in South Boston actually, near where the Trefoyles used to live, believe it or not—and I left it there. As I say, that was about two and a half years ago."

Arthur paused again and took another swig of his drink, swallowing carefully as if he were afraid of choking on the scotch. He lit a cigarette and sat down on the border of the Sarouk, placing one of Annabelle's enameled bonbon dishes for an ashtray on the bare floor beside him. He looked up at the portrait for a long moment and shuddered, remembering. Zoe still said nothing, but she could feel her thoughts begin to come together, could sense her understanding of so many things growing—as Grandmère had written of her diamond earrings— as if for millennia in the earth.

"I never once went back to the storage place to look at it," Arthur was saying. "All that time, I never did. I guess I just didn't want to think about it. Anyhow, so a couple of years went by, and I sort of, you know, got through it, until it all started going down the tubes here right after Christmas. But I still didn't go back. I was too scared to . . ."

Arthur stopped in midsentence and pressed his lips tight together for a second. "Anyway, this past Monday night I met with Conrad and he . . . he basically said he'd had it with me. He was disgusted and sick of dealing with me, and, like I told you last night, he said he was going to go ahead and record the deed and take away the house. And so . . . I realized I had to do something pretty fast."

"Arthur," Zoe began, pulling herself into a kneeling position and leaning toward him. "Arthur, this is—"

"Please let me tell you, Zo," he said, not looking at her. "Let me finish."

Zoe got slowly to her feet and went to lean against the fireplace, her arms folded tight against her body. "Okay."

"So then on Thursday, when you went to lunch with Claudia and Jim and I said I had to stay in the hospital with Annabelle, remember? . . . Well, actually that was the day I went down to the storage place. I took a taxi and got over there and I had my locker key and everything and I went right to it and . . . and, oh Jesus, I absolutely panicked, Zo—it wasn't *there*. I got hysterical. Absolutely hysterical."

Arthur wiped his free hand over his face; a sudden flush of the same, remembered hysteria overcame him, and for a second he couldn't even breathe. Finally, he turned and looked at Zoe, who was standing with her shoulders flat against the mantelpiece, her black eyes deep in shadow.

"I mean, I'd paid religiously," Arthur said, his voice thick. "The storage rent was up to date. I knew it was! I used to pay it about six months at a shot to sort of . . . sort of protect it from myself and . . . Christ, Zo, that was the only financial thing I was ever really good about, especially in the last year or so, I . . . I had the canceled checks and everything."

He looked away from her for a second, shaking his head rapidly back and forth, his mouth open. "Zoe, I absolutely freaked out. I thought I'd just die. Thursday. In fact, I'd only just gotten back to the hospital when you called to see if I was coming home. I don't even know what I did afterward. I can only remember that I left the hospital again, just to get away. I don't know . . . I was just walking, trying to think."

Arthur set his drink on the floor and polished his glasses on the tail of his shirt, trying to compose himself. Though the portrait was there right in front of him, Arthur looked aghast and terrified, as if the memory of his panic on Thursday were more compelling to him than the reality of the painting itself. Zoe watched him rub at his spectacles and waited.

"Well, it turns out the storage company expanded a few months ago and moved some of the stuff, but I didn't get to find any of this out until this morning, because . . . because of Annabelle. They actually showed me a copy of the letter they sent, back in January, but I tend not to open my mail, since it's generally so miserable, so of course I didn't know about it. Anyway, this morning I finally tracked down the manager; he'd been off all weekend, and the kid working at the warehouse yesterday was new and didn't know anything. . . ."

"Take it easy," Zoe said softly from the fireplace. "It's okay, Arthur. Just take it easy."

Arthur took another swallow of scotch and sat up on the divan again, crouched over, the glass gripped in both hands.

"Anyhow, I reached the manager at his girlfriend's place and found out where they moved it to. It was nearby, actually, just a few blocks away from the older warehouse, and I called one of the teachers at my school to see if I could borrow his truck—isn't that some truck, by the way?—and so I had to go all the way back to Cambridge for that."

"You did all this on the 'T'?" Zoe said, unable to imagine it.

"Or taxis." Arthur laughed, a humorless bark of a sound. "I'm definitely out of money now, believe me, completely out."

Arthur raised his glass to Grandmère and drank the rest of his scotch. "I'm surprised I didn't have at least a heart attack. Christ. But you can see why I didn't tell you last night when we talked about the house and all. . . . I still didn't know for sure that the portrait wasn't lost, and I thought even if I located it, it might be damaged, ruined. As a matter of fact, the guys at the warehouse had all they could do this afternoon to make me open it, unwrap it, so they were off the hook for damage, whatever. I was so scared . . . I just didn't want to know."

Arthur put his head down on his bent knees for a minute. "I have to tell you, I don't think I could have lived through it, Zo, honest to God. . . . I know I really lost it for a while, last couple of days. But I just panicked . . . I freaked."

"I remember," Zoe said dryly, standing up straighter and wrapping her arms around herself. "Arthur . . . Arthur, you are amazing," she said in a hushed voice. "Absolutely amazing." She repeated the words to herself in the same disbelieving voice, heartsick that he had borne this all these years alone. How had he been able to keep it to himself?

Arthur went and knelt by the painting. He took off his glasses, peered at the signature again, and touched it carefully with his finger as if imagining it would smear.

"Think it's really real, Zo?"

Zoe knew she would find out tonight, would go to Grandmère and find out all about it. In a small part of her mind she remembered cryptic, unexplained references in the diary to "my painting." She thought she dimly recalled a passage or two about Potter rehanging something in the bedroom, or the parlor—changes seeming to be associated with Augusta's shifting moods and fortunes—but Zoe had paid little attention, seeing those short passages only as tiny ripples in the great ocean of the diary.

She felt a little lurch of panic, thinking perhaps she should have stopped to wonder, to ask herself what painting Grandmère could have meant—but she couldn't even remember if anything had brushed her mind at the time, confused her. Yet, if she'd skidded right by Augusta's story of her portrait and her relationship with John Sargent, what else might she have missed? Her breakneck, disordered reading, her efforts to absorb so much in so short a time, might have robbed her of much more. She leaned against the marble entablatures of the fireplace, over-whelmed for a moment with an urge to run back upstairs that very second.

Zoe wiped her eyes quickly with the tips of her fingers and for the first time moved close to the painting, to where the lights of the room fell on the painted beading of the beautiful pink dress. Of course, the real one, the original, was hanging upstairs in the armoire. Zoe's arms tingled with the memory of holding it.

She stopped a foot away and stared, entranced, at Grandmère's face and the fabulous diamond "Birthday Earrings" that had been sacrificed to save this house—this home for which sacrifices were again de-manded. Zoe's mind sprang forward, and she knew at once she'd do it if she had to—make the choice Grandmère would surely make: if the portrait was an authentic Sargent, if they could prove it was, they might have to sell it to save the house again. It came down as before to a choice between symbols.

"You think it's real, Zo?" Arthur asked again.

"Yes, I do," she replied, her face tilted up to stare into Augusta's painted eyes. "Yes. Absolutely."

"What do you think it's worth?"

Worth? Worth?

"What is Value?" Grandmère had written with such anguish the night after she sold her diamond earrings. And now, as in 1933, the only measurement that mattered was the amount it would take to save the house.

"What do you think, Zo?"

"I don't know." Zoe blew out her breath and turned to Arthur, her eyes widening. "I have no idea."

"Think it's enough to save the house?"

There was a loss of strength that was not quite weakness creeping back into Arthur's voice, as if the act of retrieving the painting from its hiding place, of driving a truck with flames painted on the sides, had emptied him of all the force he'd ever had. He looked exhausted, the natural letdown overwhelming him now. He took no pride in what might be viewed as a heroic effort—catastrophe had come too close.

"Arthur, we can't think about that tonight, but sure, I guess so. I can't imagine that it wouldn't be enough."

"But what if Conrad won't take the money? Oh, Zoe! What if he doesn't?"

Zoe moved to within inches of the portrait—close enough to feel Augusta's breath, to smell the aged pigments, the sour dust of the warehouse, a fragrance. The woman in the picture was taller than Zoe had imagined, not really smiling, but thrilled somehow—the deep bosom seeming to rise and fall as the artist created breath. She reached up to touch the earrings with her little finger.

Painted jewels take their color from the surroundings, soaking up the prism of the setting: Sargent had used gray and blue, pink and gold. As Zoe came closer still, his tiny perfect strokes of titanium white turned into diamonds at her touch. Augusta's eyes, too, nearly level with Zoe's as she stood on tiptoe to look directly into them, were, seen so close, painted with the full palette of the portrait itself. Yet as Zoe moved the slightest distance back, the individual brushstrokes disappeared and the subsuming occult light of whatever Augusta had been thinking suddenly engaged.

"He'll take whatever we decide to give him. Anything . . . or nothing," Zoe said, and turned, calmly smiling, to her brother.

$\mathcal{S}$unday night, Zoe stayed by herself in the parlor, staring up with wordless joy into Grandmère's eyes. Her first impulse was to run to the phone to call Roger, but almost instantly came a terrible fear that he might think she only wanted his advice about the portrait. Stunned by that thought, Zoe left the house and walked for almost an hour, clutching her jacket against the chilly dark, awash in panic and regret, remembering how awful she'd been to him on the phone Friday night, and the anger Roger had tried and failed to hide.

When she got back, still confused and sick at heart, she stood for a minute in the parlor archway, looking at the portrait, before she went slowly upstairs to the phone.

She stood with her fingertips on the receiver, not sure she could bring herself to do it. But he has to be here, she thought. I have to find a way to make him understand all this.

She knelt on the floor in front of the bridal chest, breathing as evenly as she could, and slowly dialed the number. Roger picked it up on the first ring.

"Rog?"

"Hi!"

"It's me."

"I knew that."

"Will you come here?"

"Tonight?"

"Um . . . yes."

"Of course."

"You will? Oh, Roger, you will?"

"Certainly. Just let me call the airline and I'll call you right back."

"But . . . you don't even . . . Roger, I need you here with me because . . . because I . . ."

"Zoe, I'll be on the first plane. Let me just find out what time it gets in."

"But don't you want to hear . . . ?"

"I hear it, Zo—I heard it the minute I picked up the phone, darling."

When Roger called back, not fifteen minutes later, Zoe had marginally composed herself and felt able to tell him about everything that had happened since they'd spoken Friday night: the trust, the house, the mortgage, the deed, and the portrait. As Zoe talked, Roger believed he heard the echoes of convictions only recently embraced, but knew he would have to wait a little longer for her to tell him what they were. An hour later he was on his way, grinning as he sprinted up the concourse to his gate, flying across America in the dark because she'd said she needed him.

And Monday morning, standing in the shabby, magnificent foyer he had so well imagined, Zoe gripping his hand, Roger remembered the lyrical sound of her voice on the phone, the way she looked at him when he got out of the taxi, running down the broken stone steps to throw herself into his arms. And as he had during all those silent hours on the plane, Roger wondered what had happened to her here in Boston, in these eleven endless days. Something, he sensed with vivid hope, had made it possible for her to love him back at last—or, at last, to know she did.

When the family arrived at Commonwealth Avenue, they were pulled forcibly through the front hall by an exuberant and natty Arthur. His dark blue suit was perfectly pressed, though it smelled faintly of naphtha, and a Harvard tie was knotted high and tight against his jowls. Zoe stood smiling at the bottom of the great staircase, looking elegant in her burgundy silk dress. Roger, his eyes bright and exhausted, was right beside her.

"Folks, this is my friend Roger Horvath," she said, quickly explaining that he'd come all the way from California and was only moments out of his taxi from the airport. Roger shook hands warmly all around and smiled indulgently at Zoe, who was telling everybody that he'd come for the funeral somewhat unexpectedly, since she'd called him just the day before.

"That's 'night' before," Roger said dryly to Uncle Jim, with a calm, tired smile, winking at Zoe. "Caught the red-eye."

Everyone went into the dining room for juice and coffee, but after just a few minutes Arthur looked at his watch and pulled Zoe into the hall.

"Now?" he whispered urgently.

"Yes . . . yes."

They made everyone wait in the foyer while they ran up the staircase to the second floor. They had wrestled the painting up to Zoe's room late Sunday night after an impassioned review of their options. Arthur was afraid Conrad might show up at any moment.

"He'll come and steal it. I know he will!" he said to Zoe, offering to spend the night on the blue divan in the parlor.

"Arthur, that's ridiculous. Let's just carry it upstairs; we can put it in my room, and I'll sleep with the door locked and the bureau in front of it if that'll make you happy." She had looked at Arthur with a wry, affectionate expression, shaking her head. "Conrad's not going to break the door down tonight, particularly. He doesn't even know Grandmère's portrait exists, for God's sake."

At dawn, they had moved the portrait from Zoe's bedroom to the wide space at the top of the stairs, propping it carefully against the deep curve of the wainscoted wall, then going down a few steps to turn and gauge the effect. Now at last the audience was here.

"Okay, everybody," Arthur called out. "Come on up!"

They all gasped when they saw it. Claudia and Eddie seemed momentarily confused, but Roger whistled softly with pure admiration as he looked up at Augusta Hillyard, poised, as if alive, at the top of the stairs.

Jim Forbes leaned against the banister, breathing heavily with more than the exertion of climbing the stairs. "I'll be damned," he whispered. "I will be damned."

Zoe went down and hooked her arm through his, leading him up the last few steps to the landing. The old man went over and touched Augusta's painted cheek with reverent fingers, nodding all the while.

"Isn't that a wonder," he said, almost to himself. He pulled his hand away with a self-conscious gesture as if it were a rude familiarity to touch the canvas.

"It's a fine likeness, but even the great Mr. Sargent couldn't do her justice. Used to hang in the parlor," he said, turning to Zoe, "years ago, and then, before the war, or maybe just after—can't quite recall—it was gone and, well, I never thought about it again. I must have been too young and frisky back in those early days to really appreciate . . . Oh, my Lord, will you look at that face," he said as he turned back to the portrait, his hand reaching out, but not quite touching.

" 'Nineteen ought five,' " he read in a hushed voice. "And do you know, that's exactly how I remember her, even though I didn't know her until thirty years later. The essence . . . never changed."

He sat down suddenly in the armchair beside the painting and took out a big handkerchief, blowing his nose loudly as everyone stood mute around him, so affected by his reaction that no one moved until one of the limo drivers rang the doorbell.

When they left the house for the service at Leape & Neames, Jim shepherded the Trouts into the first limo, and then led Zoe, Roger, and Arthur to the other car, climbing in after them. They were riding down Beacon Street in an easy silence, the Trouts' car already far ahead, when Jim leaned forward and said to the driver, " 'Scuse me, friend," and pressed the button to roll up the divider window.

He smiled at their expressions. "Seems a bit mysterious, I guess," he said, "but I got something to say to you kids, and I didn't have a proper chance back at the house. And I know Dr. Roger Horvath here is family, so . . ." He grinned at Zoe and then turned to Arthur, letting him know right off the bat that Zoe had told him all about the house and mortgage. "She was right to tell me, Arthur. Don't be upset with her now."

Arthur had pressed himself deep into the corner of the seat, a mixture of pain and relief clear on his face. "I never for a minute imagined it would all go to hell the way it did, Jim," he said. "Believe me, I—"

"Now you listen here to me, Arthur. You did what you had to do. You had a helluva problem, and you shouldered that burden all alone for a long, long time. And from what Zoe tells me, you handled everything with that wonderful portrait just right. Took a lot of courage to make those choices, son. Don't you go blaming yourself."

"But what difference does it make?" Arthur cried out, throwing up his hands. "Conrad's going to take that deed I gave him, and——"

Zoe leaned forward and smacked him lightly on the knee. "Arthur, will you please shut up! Let Uncle Jim say what he's got to say! You always keep getting *ahead* of yourself."

Jim smiled and put his hand on the back of the seat to keep his balance as the limo swerved onto the bridge over the Charles River.

"Now Arthur, far's you know, did that Conrad record the deed yet?"

Arthur shook his head. "No. But last Monday night he as good as told me he would—he threatened to."

"Okay. But not for sure?"

"No, I don't think so. He'd want to tell me to my face, rub it in." Arthur's eyes were bright behind his glasses.

Jim and Zoe exchanged the briefest of glances, and Jim sat back, smiling and brushing invisible specks off his trousers.

"Well, I made a phone call last night that I want to tell you about." He sniffed and thought a moment. None of them moved. "I called over to my old friend Mr. Franklin Chadwick. I've known Bud Chadwick must be almost fifty years now—pal of mine from law-school days. He works at your bank, Arthur; actually, I understand he's the board chairman over there. . . ."

Jim let this bomb sink in and recrossed his legs. Zoe clasped her hands in her lap and looked at Arthur, who sat up straighter and stared back at her.

"Well, anyhow, we had a nice chat. I told him a bit about this little problem we got here, and he seemed to think it was pretty interesting. Had a few suggestions, too. . . ." Jim smiled at Zoe in a private, comradely way and leaned back against the velour seat. "I did one or two favors for ole Bud in years gone by, and he was just as happy as could be to do me a little something in return." Jim chuckled to himself for a moment and went on.

"Now what we're going to do, see, is transfer some money from my account, which happens to be at Bud's bank, by a very strange coincidence, into that Conrad feller's, which Bud says is no big deal—they'll find it on their computer. . . . Zoe, honey, now hold on just a tad . . . hold on. It'll be just enough to reimburse Conrad for those three-four payments he made, and then, why, we'll scoot some more money over to Arthur's mortgage account and try to get a little ahead on that. It's all on the computer, see, easy as pie. Bud says it'll be posted against your payments bright and early this morning." Jim looked at his watch. "Should be happening right about now."

"Uncle Jim, my God!" Zoe said, leaning toward him; she was the first to realize exactly what he'd done. "This is what you were talking about yesterday, isn't it? 'Trust me,' you said."

Jim laughed out loud at the expression on Zoe's face. "Well, yes, I started to get this little brainstorm yesterday when we were talking there in the kitchen. Between you and me, Zoe, I admit it has a little fighting-fire-with-fire flavor to it, but I'd say that's the sort of tactic that's called for right about now."

Jim leaned toward her, suddenly serious, and took her hand in both of his before he spoke.

"Zoe, honey, I never had a chance to pay Augusta Hillyard back— not to my own satisfaction—for her many kindnesses to me, for the privilege of knowing a person like her. I just thank the Lord I've got this opportunity to do it now. Yes, indeed. I'm just thrilled to be able to do it." He patted her hand as if doing so would close the mouth which was still open in astonishment.

"I'll pay you back. I swear!" Zoe finally said in a hoarse voice, turning to Roger and Arthur as if for confirmation. She knew from Claudia that Uncle Jim was far from wealthy.

Jim smiled and nodded slowly. "I know you will, but there's no hurry. Bud said there's plenty of time for details—paperwork and whatnot. I wish I could make it a gift, but . . . it's not a lot of money, Zoe; altogether it's just eight or nine payments, but it ought to cancel out what Conrad paid *and* tide you over until the fall, anyhow, help you catch your breath. You and Arthur have some terrific expenses here, isn't that a fact? I'm just as pleased as I can be to help out a little. Don't you worry about it now."

Arthur couldn't stand it. "But what about that stupid side agreement?" he burst out. "What if he *did* record the deed? What if he's already done that?!"

Jim shrugged. "Well, I ain't saying there won't be any litigation, particularly if he tries to exercise ownership rights. It's not impossible, Arthur. Timing's a factor in these things. As a matter of fact, I asked

Bud if he thought maybe he could backdate the transfers a day or so, more or less for old times' sake. Who knows? But still and all, the payments are made, and that'll surely help in case you get into court with that feller. And it sure doesn't hurt that today's a state holiday—Registrar of Deeds is closed up tight as a drum!"

The limousine approached the Fresh Pond Parkway and moved into the long slow curve from Memorial Drive. Zoe peered out the tinted windows at the budding trees that lined the river. Roger, who had been silent as befit his role as newcomer, cleared his throat and put his arm around Zoe's seat back.

"I only had a few minutes to take a look at that painting, but it seems absolutely genuine to me, and well, perhaps . . ." He looked around at them all, smiling faintly. "Zoe, you said something on the phone last night about a trust?"

"Hillyard Family Trust," Arthur said, as if pleased to be able to offer a comment, but it suddenly occurred to him that he was still the trustee, and the realization shut him up at once.

Roger nodded. "Right. Now, Mr. Forbes—"

"Jim's the name, son."

"Jim." Roger flashed a smile, his teeth showing through his beard. "As you know, it's not unusual for trusts to claim the value of works of art. . . ."

Jim looked at Roger with respect, his eyes narrowing to wink at Zoe. "Smart fella you got here," he said, enjoying the blush that flooded her pale face and then receded.

As he spoke, the car crunched onto the gravel driveway of the fake Georgian manse that housed Leape & Neames. Claudia and Eddie and the boys were waiting in the porte cochere, and Yancey ran over to make faces at Arthur through the car window.

"I can see this conversation is tabled for a bit," said Jim, laughing and waggling his fingers at Yancey. "Let me get back to Bud later on and ask him where his folks stand on secured loans and such. Properly handled . . . Yancey, you're getting your fingerprints all over the man's glass now!" He slid out of the limousine and, taking Yancey's hand, escorted the family into Annabelle's funeral.

Arthur finally dissolved into tears at the cemetery, as Zoe had expected. She kept her arm tight around his waist as the minister spoke his final prayer and the casket was put into the ground. The Hillyards lay dead all around them, their marble stones bathed in the flood of sunlight, lined up in rows before a huge monument, topped with a rampant stone angel. The single word

HILLYARD

was carved into the slab.

At the eastward rim of the plot, at the feet of the angel, was Grandmère's grave, between Eugene and Zachary, her brother Hugh Alexander Lattimore in front of her, and Annabelle now next to him. When the graveside service was over, Zoe took a spray of lilacs from one of the many bouquets that had been brought along in the hearse and went across the grass to Grandmère's stone.

AUGUSTA FLORENCE LATTIMORE HILLYARD
MAY 29, 1862–DECEMBER 25, 1945

was carved in unbending Roman letters in the marble. No epitaph, no Latin, not even an etched flower had been added.

"I wonder if she chose this," Zoe said, turning to Roger, who had come up behind her. He kissed her forehead and read the words on Augusta's stone to himself, his lips moving slightly.

"You think it's real, don't you?" Zoe stooped to arrange the flowers just so against the marble, and then stood up to brush a speck of lilac from her dress.

No transition of hers was too fast for him; Roger smiled when he answered. "It's not my period, honey, and I haven't done any of the auction research, but the signature, the brushwork . . . yes, I do think so. Still, as I told you, I'd like my old buddy Harlan Janeway to take a look. He'll know for sure—he did his dissertation on Sargent. You know, the fact that the painting is so beautiful is almost as important as the fact that it's a Sargent. And she's lovely, Zoe," he said, pressing her shoulder tightly against him. "Absolutely lovely."

"What do you think it might bring?" she asked. "Enough?"

Roger had been thinking about that all morning. Zoe's synopsis of the situation on the phone last night and the conversation in the limousine had been very clear.

"We'll find out when I get hold of Harlan. Come on now, dear, everyone's getting ready to go."

He took her elbow and turned back to the road, where the limousines were parked. They had gone several yards down the path when Zoe turned and looked back at Grandmère's grave.

"I hope she really wanted it to be like that," she said. "Just plain. I hope it was her choice." But then she let him lead her past her father's stone, at which she barely looked, and around the tumble of Annabelle's flowers to the road.

"Someday you might like to add something for her," he said. "There's room. A saying . . . or a flower . . . ?"

"Maybe," Zoe said, glancing back one last time at the marble slab that seemed to gather in all light. "Maybe clematis . . . maybe not. . . ."

The speeding limos got back to the house only minutes before the first group of guests. Nine or ten of Annabelle's cronies tottered through the foyer together, obviously ready for a party, eager to speed Annabelle on her trip to the "next world."

"She was a chaahming woman—chaahming," said one old gentleman to Arthur, who bent over to listen with his perfect courtesy, even as he threw comic anguished glances to Zoe and Claudia, who were circulating with trays of sherry. Uncle Jim moved smoothly through the crush, bowing to everyone in his courtly, old-fashioned way, his Phi Beta Kappa key dangling from a chain across his tummy.

Lowie and Yancey, watching the festivities from the alcove near the butler's pantry, had been extremely sedate all day long, well confined both by the gravity of the situation and by their dress-up outfits. They grinned with relief when Zoe came up and led them to the back parlor, where she settled them in with full plates of turkey sandwiches and cake, promising to turn on the TV as soon as most of the guests had gone.

A moment later, she found Jim and Roger chatting in the parlor archway. "How you holding up, honey?" Jim said, kissing her cheek. "This girl of yours did a helluva job, sir," he said, turning to Roger. "Helluva job, and no fancy caterer either—she and my Claudie did it all themselves. Yessir, Bedouin hospitality. . . ."

Smiling broadly, Zoe left Roger to the early stages of an onslaught of Jim's recollection of past parties and went to look for Arthur.

She found him out in the alley at the brick border of what had once been Veronica's kitchen garden, a small plot barely four feet square, where, Augusta proudly wrote, she'd "cultivated some fine vegetables and a few lovely petunias and marigolds." Arthur was leaning against the wall of the house, smoking a cigarette, looking up at the blue sky.

"Well, it looks like Annabelle had more friends than I thought," Zoe said, coming up beside him. "Or are they just here for the free food?"

"Zoooeee!" Arthur gave her a wounded look.

"Joke! Little joke!" Zoe laughed and kissed his cheek. "Pretty hard to take it all in, isn't it?" she said more softly, handing him a glass of punch.

"I can't believe he'd do that for us," Arthur said. "I just can't believe it. I've been thinking about it since he told us in the car. I'm absolutely knocked out." He paused, ground out his cigarette in the dirt, and lit another. "But how the hell are we going to pay him back? Sell the painting? What if Conrad . . . oh, God, you think he's going to come? I thought he'd show up at least by now, Zo."

"He'll *be* here, Arthur—I'm positive he will. Let's try to take it a step at a time, dear."

"I can't believe Jim did that for us," Arthur said again. "It's amazing to me, amazing."

"Well," Zoe said, spreading a paper towel on the stoop and gathering her skirt to sit down, "you remember what he said—how did he put it?—that he thanked God for a chance to do something at last for Augusta Hillyard. And I really do think it's as simple as that, Arthur. He feels indebted to her, and now he's found a way, as he sees it, to pay her back."

Arthur leaned against the back wall of the house and squashed his fresh cigarette against the pavement. "But what if that banker friend of Jim's doesn't want to—"

"Arthur, you are impossible," said Claudia, who had been standing behind them in the kitchen doorway. "Right, Zo?"

"That's for sure. Shape up, Arthur," she said, getting up and briskly dusting off her skirt with both hands. "Try to pretend, just this once, that everything is not actually going straight to hell."

Arthur's blue eyes squinted down at her as if she had completely missed the point. "Conrad's vicious, Zo. Vicious. You can't believe the slimy—"

"Shoot. He's just a guy, Arthur. Just another son of a bitch, exactly like—"

"Give it a rest, you two," Claudia said. "You have a million guests here, for Lord's sake." She waved them both back into the house. "They're all in the parlor just dying to tell you about how much they miss Annabelle. Arthur, get in there and be nice."

THIRTY-SEVEN

*J*im Forbes had been absolutely right about the smell of Shalimar. It lay with near-visibility in the air of the parlor, mingling with apparently equal portions of Chanel No. 5 and the scent of the roses Claudia had brought over in the morning. Eddie opened all the front windows and the kitchen door, but the afternoon air was still and warm, and dilution of the rich atmosphere seemed impossible. The "turnout," as Claudia called it, was better than expected, and when she and Zoe went back into the crowded parlor she stood on tiptoe in the archway, chin up, as if counting the house.

A trio of old ladies came fluttering up to Arthur and began telling him stories of Annabelle's salty sense of humor, her love of a good time.

"She was a pistol, dear, and that's a fact. Mrs. Willis, isn't that a fact? . . ."

"I just love these Haviland plates you've set out; my mother used to say that you can always tell Haviland because . . ."

"Another sherry, Miz Louise? I'd be happy . . ."

"What a lovely service, wasn't it, dear? Lovely. When my Cornelius passed away we had . . ."

"Yes, she just loved a joke, Annabelle did . . . used to tell the one about the debutante and the mountain lion . . ."

Roger smiled at Zoe from across the room. He was being so patient and lovely, chatting away, attentive to the old dears, jet-lagged though he was. He nodded warmly at everyone and sipped the coffee Claudia had perked just for him, gamely returning the tipsy smiles of the flirtatious old ladies who gathered around him in their lavender curls and picture hats.

A few names rang small bells for Zoe, echoes from the diary. Nannie Pickman was there, escorted by her teenage nephew, who looked desperately out of place, aching to be anywhere but here, Zoe thought, but solicitous of Nannie just the same. The feather in her immense hat smacked against the boy's face as she gripped Zoe's wrist and pointed out the remains of the old families as they inched their way across the Sarouk, nephew in tow.

"Now that old coot over there," she croaked in Zoe's ear, "his mother was a Binney; your people knew the Binneys back before the war." (Which war, Zoe wondered, catching the agonized eye of the nephew.) "You can check on that. . . ." Nannie Pickman, a debutante in 1915 or so, Zoe remembered vaguely, was now an aged maiden lady with quail feathers on her hat.

By late afternoon, the two cases of sherry were nearly gone, and even though people were starting to leave, Eddie decided to dash up to the liquor store on Boylston Street to get a few more bottles. Jim, quite content to "make do" with a gin and tonic, flashed Zoe a wolfish look as he disappeared into the back parlor with Roger and the children to watch replays of the Marathon finish. He put his feet up on a threadbare tapestry hassock while the boys flopped down on the rug with a big bowl of grapes and a plate of Mint Milanos between them. Zoe poked her head in.

"You guys hiding out?" She winked at Lowie, who colored up and looked quickly back to the TV.

"I'm taking myself a break," Jim said. "Old folks make me tired. Besides, all the women are after me—I need to build up my strength before I can go back in there." Zoe gave Roger a look of pretend exasperation, waved at them all, and went to look for Claudia.

She found her in the dining room, trapped against the window seat, cornered by a skeletal woman in a dusty black crepe cocktail dress, over which was draped an immense fringed shawl which may once have covered a piano. The woman's jet-black hair, showing an inch or so of white roots, was back-combed and lacquered into a coiffure that threatened to snap off, Zoe thought, at any moment.

"Zoe!" cried Claudia. "Come and meet, uh . . . Ms. Perry."

The woman whirled to greet Zoe, the fringe swinging across her chest; her large square teeth showed in a smile.

"Aha! Arthur's *sister!* Isn't it? I'm Edwina's *cousin,*" she said with great meaning.

Zoe's mind shorted out for a second, then she remembered. "Oh, yes . . . yes. Hello." Edwina Perry, Arthur's escaped wife.

"You weren't at the wedding," the woman said accusingly, as if it had been a week instead of nearly a decade before.

"Uh, Ms. Perry, that was many years . . ." Zoe began.

"It was a *grand* occasion! Simply grand—and the Hillyards were *not* well represented!"

"Well, you know, there aren't really all that many of us left," Zoe said, suppressing a sudden urge to giggle, not sure where the conversation was going. She knew that Arthur's wedding to Edwina (hardly "grand") had taken place in a judge's office in Cambridge; the witnesses had been two graduate students who happened to be chatting in the parking lot.

"Well, it was a splendid affair, and you missed it!"

The square teeth were again revealed by a grin that Zoe realized was reflexive only, habitual—not indicative of humor.

"And he just broke her heart! Isn't it? *Broke* her heart!"

"Really?" said Zoe softly, looking straight into Ms. Perry's pale eyes. She felt a rush of amusement that was completely discourteous, but she couldn't help it, couldn't quite control the sudden bubbling up of the strange manic energy she'd been feeling all afternoon. "I heard it was the other way around."

"Not a *word* of it is true," Ms. Perry hissed mysteriously. She grabbed a full glass of sherry from the tray on the table and loped off toward the parlor, her piano shawl trailing on the floor behind her.

Zoe leaned on Claudia's shoulder and exploded in a sudden fit of laughter.

"How could she *do* that!" Claudia coughed and started to giggle; she pulled a tissue out of her suit pocket and gave it to Zoe, wiping her own eyes with another.

Arthur came up to them, looking like a large, nervous bird. "He here yet?"

"Oh, sweetie, no, he is not here." Zoe blew her nose into the Kleenex and tried to control her gulping laughter. She wondered if she might be just a bit hysterical, if there was a spasm of violent sobbing trying to escape from all this laughter. She'd heard that people sometimes became hysterical with relief at funerals—because they themselves were still alive. "That unquenchable thirst to *have more*," Grandmère had written, "is life itself."

But her own feelings seemed different to Zoe. Not even her wild, thrilled reaction on the day the movie contract came compared with this. Looking at Claudia and Arthur, at the glittering chandelier, the laden table, thinking of Grandmère and Roger and Jim, she felt a sudden flush of incomprehensible joy and knew that problems and all (and they were monumental), she felt more brilliantly happy—more alive—than she had in all her life.

"Did you see your former relative, Arthur?" Claudia said, wiping the tears from her cheeks. "She just went back in there."

"Oh, Ilona—'Il-*loon*-a'? I saw her come in." Arthur pulled up a dining-room chair and sat next to them. "She always shows up at times like this. It's her hobby. She reads the obituaries and goes to the, uh, receptions. Edwina couldn't stand her—always said she was bananas. Zoe, it's after four o'clock. Where is he?"

"Arthur, did he *say* he would come?"

"No, but . . ."

"Sweetie, if he comes, he comes." Zoe got to her feet, leaning her weight on Arthur's shoulder. "He could show up any second." Arthur watched her go out of the dining room and with a sigh took out another cigarette.

Zoe stood in the wide archway of the parlor, her arms folded over her chest, her shoe tapping against the marble floor of the hall. In her mind she transformed the thinning crowd of guests into a film crew with cameras and cables and techs everywhere. The embossed ceiling was more than high enough for all the cranes, lights, boom mikes. She saw a smiling, handsome Laurence Thane, at ease in an Empire chair, across from Beatrice Holland, who stood poised by the Hillyard fireplace, her hand reaching toward the tiger lilies on the mantel, while a girl from the makeup crew powdered the shine off her face and the cinematographer called to Zoe to come look in the camera and see if she liked the lens he—

"Are you a Hillyard?" A little round woman in a felt hat was standing at Zoe's elbow, peering up into her face. Zoe smiled down at her, wrenching herself away from the daydream.

"I'm Zoe Hillyard. Thank you for coming, Mrs. . . . ."

"Hanrahan. Katherine Hanrahan. I'm sorry for your trouble, miss. This is my daughter Alma." Zoe shook Alma's dry hand.

"I just wanted to pay my respects. Your grandmother, old Mrs. Hillyard, was very kind to our family—"

"Augusta Hillyard was my great-grandmother."

"Is that a fact? Well, I just wanted to say that my Aunt Vee kept house for her for many, many years . . . used to say that old Mrs. Hillyard was just good as gold to—"

"Housekeeper?" Zoe leaned over the tiny woman, her eyes sparkling. "That wouldn't be Veronica?"

"Yes, miss. My Aunt Veronica was the housekeeper here until, well, let's see now . . . Alma, when was that?"

Alma was a tired-looking woman in her late forties. Her brown eyes were calm and intelligent behind her glasses. "Miss Hillyard, what Mother's trying to say is that your great-grandmother was so generous to our aunt, long ago, that when a friend called last night to say she'd seen an obituary in the Sunday *Globe,* well, when we heard the address, we knew it had to be the same Hillyards, and Mother insisted we drive up."

"Good as gold," little Mrs. Hanrahan piped up. She had an empty sherry glass clutched in her fist. Zoe put a hand on her shoulder and looked intently back to Alma.

"You see," Alma was saying, "Aunt Veronica used to have Mother up here from Providence to visit from time to time when Mother was just a little girl, and she always remembers how sweet Mrs. Hillyard was to her. And then when Aunt Vee passed away—"

"When was that?" Zoe asked softly.

"The summer of 1948. She was in a nursing home, down in Westerly. Mrs. Hillyard paid for that, you see. Left instructions in her will,

I suppose, that Aunt Vee was to be looked after, and, well, she never married, never had a home of her own . . ."

"This was her home," Zoe said in a thickened voice, quickly swallowing her saliva. "My great-grandmother cared a great deal for her."

"Yes," Alma said, smiling just politely.

"It's going to get dark, Alma," Mrs. Hanrahan said, looking doubtfully toward the bright fanlight above the front door.

"We have to be going now," Alma said, putting her arm around her mother's shoulder.

"Thank you—thank you for coming," Zoe called as they moved slowly toward the door, and then she suddenly remembered something and ran down the long hallway after them.

"Mrs. Hanrahan! Can you wait just a second, please? Just a second? I'll be right back."

Zoe hiked up her skirt with both hands and ran up the stairs, two at a time, to Grandmère's room. She took one of the pretty little porcelain boxes from the mantel, rubbed it quickly on the back of her skirt, and sprinted back downstairs.

With a smile she leaned over Mrs. Hanrahan and pressed the box into her hands. "This is just a little something, but it belonged to my great-grandmother, and I know she would like you to have it."

Alma looked at Zoe with a complicated expression of gratitude and resentment that Zoe almost didn't catch. "Isn't that nice, Mother," was all she said.

Zoe opened the front door and led them out onto the top step. Feeling vaguely unsatisfied, she watched them out of sight around the corner of Fairfield Street and then leaned against the pilasters of the doorway, looking distractedly across the Mall.

Just then, a white Cadillac drove up on the far side of Commonwealth Avenue and stopped, double-parked, in front of the old Mason house. The driver cut the engine and looked first at his watch and then across the Mall toward where Zoe stood, until he was sure she had become aware that he was looking at her. He lit a cigarette and smoked it down with long voluptuous puffs, enjoying it, in no hurry to move. Boston-style, oncoming cars ignored the double-parked Cadillac, merely swerving left around it.

Several elderly people came out of the house together, chortling about something, squeezed past Zoe, and tottered off down the sidewalk. Zoe stood absolutely still and watched Conrad as he blew the cigarette smoke out the open window of the car.

Good, she muttered to herself. Finally. He knows I see him, too. She went back in the house and walked quickly upstairs to her room. Augusta's portrait was leaning against the bedroom wall where Arthur and Eddie had replaced it before everyone left for the funeral. As Zoe stared into Augusta's eyes, they seemed to look back at her, a smile of recognition just starting to form in their painted depths.

"He's here, Grandmère. He came. . . . He wants our house."

Zoe stood with her face inches from Grandmère's, one finger barely touching the brushstrokes that made the perfect cheek. She thought she could smell a lingering whiff of Nuit de Noël and the musty odor of the eighty-year-old gown, could almost hear the dried-out rustle of the skirt.

"Tell me what to do, Grandmère. Just tell me and I'll do it."

Zoe moved back just a few inches, as she had downstairs last night, and saw the brushstrokes of titanium white harden into diamonds. And suddenly, as if in answer, there was no gentleness in that patrician gaze; the dreamy softness was gone, replaced (in Zoe's thudding mind) by a look of utter self-possession.

"What, Grandmère? Tell me. What should I do—what should I say to him?"

All at once it was clear to her that Augusta Hillyard would be unintimidated by these events—she would barely have perceived them as "events" at all. Her heart would not be quivering in her throat, her palms would not be damp. Never. A threat against the house, posed by the likes of Conrad, would not have seemed real to her; she would feel only a momentary satisfaction as she dismissed the intruder with an elegant shrug, an imperious word. How could Zoe have forgotten, even for a moment, that this was a woman who had, almost without hesitation, sold off heirloom diamonds and banished her only living son to save this house? That Conrad, that anyone, might actually succeed and take away her home would not have crossed Augusta Hillyard's mind.

Zoe heard the doorbell and then a muffled commotion from downstairs and knew he had arrived at last. She touched the earrings with her index finger, caressed the painted cheek, and then went out to the landing at the top of the stairs.

The family were lined up facing Conrad, who was standing in the hall looking poised and fit in a rather handsome sport coat which shone faintly in the back light of the open door. When he saw Zoe at the top of the stairs, he looked up into her eyes and smiled, showing his excellent teeth. Zoe was surprised to see that he was actually sexy in a skewed way, as if he relished acts that people seldom spoke of. She walked briskly down, not touching the banister, and Roger and Eddie moved apart to let her walk between them. She stopped about three feet from Conrad and looked slightly down into his yellow eyes.

"Get out of my house," she said.

"But I've come to pay my respects to the dead," Conrad said, waving his arm in a broad gesture to include the family, who stood close together behind Zoe. At the very rim of her peripheral vision, Zoe saw Arthur separate himself from the family group.

"Get out," he whispered to Conrad.

"Artie! My dear! I didn't see you hiding back there! I read of your loss in the *Globe*. My condolences. You should have told me sooner, Art. I would have sent a spray."

"Conrad, just go away." Arthur moved toward him and stopped side by side with Zoe, who had not taken her eyes from Conrad's animated face.

Conrad appeared shocked. "But Art, my boy, this is *my* house. You weren't thinking of asking to *rent*, were you? Dear me, I hope not." He looked around the marble foyer with a critical, ironic glance. "It would be awfully inconvenient."

Zoe came closer to Conrad, and for a moment she thought she might actually touch him. There was something wiry, muscular, in Conrad that seemed to quiver as she approached.

"You're trespassing," she said in a low, calm voice, "and if you don't leave at once, I will call the police. This is *not* your house."

At her words, Conrad's smirk ignited into hissing anger.

"Sister dear, you have been misinformed. Your beloved brother has fucked you over; did he mention that? I have a little piece of paper here that will explain everything."

Conrad reached into his jacket pocket and took out an envelope. "It's called a 'title deed.' Ring a bell, Art? Which, by the way," he said, turning to Zoe with a flash of teeth, "your adorable brother *gave* to me. I was very generous with him, you know, said he could miss not two but three payments, and heavens to Betsy, this week it's going to be *four!*"

"Did you record it?" Arthur burst out, unable to help himself. "Did you?"

Conrad immediately recognized Arthur's fear and confusion. A film seemed to come down over his amber eyes. He fanned himself languidly with the envelope and ran his fingers over the wainscoting. "What nice molding," he said, ignoring Arthur. "Looks original. Needs paint, though. I thought you folks had taken better care of the place."

Zoe moved even closer to him and pointed at the envelope. "I don't know what you've got in there—a deed, or your laundry list—but it's of no interest to us. . . . Now get *out* of my house." She could feel his breath, could nearly see her own breath ruffle the threads of his jacket, she was that close.

Suddenly Conrad screamed at her, waving the envelope around with sweeping movements of his arm. "You bitch! 'Get out of my house,' " he mimicked, his voice quickly rising to a shriek, all the affectation gone. "Who the fuck do you think you're *talking* to? You goddam aristo-crats—"

All of a sudden Conrad stopped and passed a hand over his face; it seemed that for just the briefest moment his body swayed toward the foyer wall.

"Forgive me," he said in a strained, sarcastic voice. "I'm a passion-ate man, though I thought I had learned not to let my passions get the better of me." He smiled lasciviously at Zoe, looking up into her eyes.

Zoe knew many professional actors; she thought he was not all that bad for an amateur. But his arrogance betrayed him, ruined his per-formance. With his outburst, she saw that Conrad was little more than a small-time bully—a man who could not survive without a victim. He had obviously anticipated immediate submission, such as he had learned to expect from Arthur and, doubtless, many others; he was not prepared for Zoe's ability to resist him. Her commitment, her ne-cessity, was far greater than his, but he had revealed himself—and she had not.

"Actually," Conrad said, looking thoughtfully at the ceiling, "I came here to make you an offer." He shot Zoe a flirtatious glance, which she ignored.

"I don't want to hear it," she said, looking down into his eyes, aware of his tiny pupils, the sheen of perspiration on his skin. "You are so pathetic, Conrad. You are so ridiculously small-time."

"You listen to me, cookie—"

"You miserable thief. It doesn't matter at all what you've got to say or what you've got in that silly envelope—"

"I'm willing to make a deal!" Conrad started to say, backing up ever so slightly, brushing the envelope against his leg with vicious, slapping gestures. "I've decided to let you give me money for the house!"

"Go to hell," Zoe said calmly, "and take your 'title deed' or whatever it is with you. I don't need 'deals' or anything else from someone like you."

As she moved slightly closer to him, it seemed to Zoe that she advanced in just millimeters of distance, as if she were actually pressing the air of the hallway against Conrad, pushing him out. The family, gathered behind her in a tight group, had barely moved. Only Jim, his arms folded casually across his vest, was aware that it was not yet over.

"This house is mine!" Conrad screamed, starting to move slowly backward. *"Mine!"*

"That's enough! You listen to me and you listen carefully. This has been my family's home for one hundred years. It is not yours," Zoe said, her voice almost a whisper, each word perfectly enunciated. "And for your information, there is no mortgage. It has been paid off—one hundred percent. So just get out or the police will be here before you can say 'fraudulent lending practices.' "

Conrad laughed then, an ironic hawking sound. "You're blowin' smoke, lady. There's no way you could have paid it off. I don't believe you."

Zoe shrugged, suddenly knowing that he did indeed believe her, but feeling an almost euphoric indifference to him, his envelope, his very presence in her house. "You know, I really am surprised that you're so remarkably stupid," she said in a conversational tone. "You don't have the brains to pull off even this little scam, do you? I'm disappointed, Conrad, I really am. I thought you'd be more of a challenge."

Conrad lost control of himself then. His eyes glittered and the muscles jumped in his face; his words sprayed saliva.

"You friggin' bitch!" he screeched, his lips pulling away from his teeth as the words pounded out. Claudia winced, but Zoe barely paid attention.

"You goddam Hillyards are dead—obsolete—*finished!*"

"You weren't listening to me," Zoe said, leaning toward him as they moved together toward the open door in that strange, sliding dance. "Just get out of here before I decide that it would be a good idea to have you prosecuted for fraud and extortion."

"You can't touch me!" Conrad yelled, even as he sidled backward toward the open door. "Bitch! I already recorded it! *Ha!*" He was holding on to the door molding with one hand, still clutching the crushed envelope in his fist. As he shouted at her he raised it high into the air, waving it back and forth. "I did it today!"

Zoe laughed at his theatrics—a low, unmusical sound. "No, you didn't. The registry was closed for the holiday. But if you try, I promise you the state attorney general is going to get very interested, very fast, in every deal you've got going."

Zoe's hand was already on the door; she turned slightly away, as if boredom and contempt had suddenly gotten the better of her.

"You can't do a friggin' thing to me!" Conrad wailed. "I'll *show* you . . ."

He was actually standing on the top step, outside the doorsill. As he wrenched open the envelope, tearing it along with whatever was inside, he took his watering eyes from Zoe's face, and her hand flattened against the edge of the heavy door and slammed it shut.

There was absolute silence in the vaulted hallway. Zoe moved to the rippled glass panels next to the door and peeked out. Conrad had gone down the steps and was standing on the sidewalk, the torn paper still in his hand. Zoe leaned all her weight against the door panel and threw the dead bolt home.

THIRTY-EIGHT

*I*n a soft, vermilion twilight, Zoe and Roger walked hand in hand toward the Public Garden through the shadows of the trees that lined the Mall. Zoe felt a little let-down, light-headed, and was glad of this chance to be alone with Roger in the cool, fresh air.

"I didn't realize I missed Boston," Roger said in a dreamy voice.

"How long since you were here?" Zoe asked.

"Twenty years? Eighteen? I'm not sure—it's all a blur," Roger said, smiling at something.

As they crossed Dartmouth Street, Zoe slid her hand through his arm, leaning against him. They talked quietly about Roger's years in Boston, doing fellowships at the Museum of Fine Arts and the Gardner, sharing a miserable apartment in the South End with his friend Harlan Janeway.

"So you know him from back then?" Zoe said.

"Um-hmm. In those days Harlan was spending almost all his time at the Gardner—hours and hours every day soaking up the old lady's Sargents and Whistlers."

Zoe thought of Grandmère's erstwhile friend Isabella Stewart Gardner and her "fake palazzo on the Fenway," her fancy New Year's Eve party, and her circus of a funeral, recalling Augusta's tart comments with a smile she kept to herself.

"And you think he's really the best one to show it to?"

"Oh, absolutely. Jesus, is he ever going to drop his teeth when he sees Grandmère's portrait."

Roger had wandered the house in the afternoon, unnoticed by the guests, unimpeded by the family. He prowled through all the rooms, frowning over the stained wallpaper in the library, the broken dentils of the parlor cornices, the faded old Piranesi renderings in the dining room. At one point, he got the key from Zoe and went up and sat on her bed, staring at the portrait, mesmerized, for almost half an hour.

"Of course, the whole surface has darkened," he said after a minute. "And I saw some flaking, too. I don't know enough about Sargent's pigments to talk about repairing it, but considering it wasn't well cared for, it's in pretty good shape. Could be a great one, Zo, a great one."

"I hope so."

Roger smiled in the descending darkness and pulled her closer against his side, bending to kiss her forehead, then, very gently, her mouth.

"Harlan will know," he said. "But in any case, I think you and Arthur should be really careful about how you handle it. There's lots of ways to skin this cat. Selling the painting is not your only option."

Zoe shivered a little when he said that and leaned closer to him, but made no reply.

"You feeling okay?" he whispered into her hair. "Are you chilly?"

"No . . . I'm just tired. I guess I'm feeling sort of anticlimactic, you know, because of Conrad."

"You were magnificent with that bum. Just magnificent."

"Isn't he the worst?" Zoe said, making a face. "I told you I saw him a couple of times out the window, didn't I? But meeting him today, I can really see for the first time how desperate Arthur must have been. . . . Jeez, what a creep. He was probably a movie producer in a previous life," she said.

As they crossed Clarendon Street the sky faded to tangerine, to peach, to palest cream. The wind shifted silently to the east.

"Did Jim tell you if he's calling his pal Bud tonight or tomorrow?" Roger asked.

"I'm not sure . . . maybe tomorrow? God, I can't even stand to think about it." Zoe pulled away and wrapped her arms around herself. "I can't lose it, Rog. I can't. . . . Oh, what if . . ." She put her face in her hands, imagining Bud Chadwick telling Jim it was all a mistake, that he'd have to take back his money and give Conrad the house after all.

"Zo! Zoe!" Roger pulled her into his arms, rubbing her tense shoulders. "Darling, come on now, come on. It'll be fine . . . it will. Don't 'get ahead of yourself,'" he said, smiling.

Zoe wiped her hands over her face. "That's exactly what I said to Arthur in the car this morning, isn't it?" she said, laughing in spite of herself. He reached for her hand, kissed it, and tucked it through his arm again.

They walked on slowly, crossing Berkeley and passing the statue of Alexander Hamilton just across from the Ritz Carlton Hotel. It had grown rather cool; the Mall was dark and deserted, and they were quite alone. Roger sat down on a fancy iron bench, gathering Zoe to him; they sat quietly, facing the French Consulate. Roger felt Zoe relax, just a bit, inside his arm. After a moment of reflection in which he decided several things, he softly cleared his throat.

"Did I mention that Sidney had a little dinner party Saturday night?" he said. "At the beach house."

"Oh?" Zoe tried to sound indifferent, twining her fingers through his, thinking she'd probably better hold on to something.

"Yes. Only about nine, ten people. Frye . . . that famous old English actress who's playing Lavinia Griffith . . . also the new cinematographer, a guy who used to work for Kubrick . . ."

"And Mr. Gianfranco Sessa?" Zoe asked through her teeth, not moving her head from his shoulder.

"Uh-huh."

"So he's actually in L.A., then." It was not a question, and Roger held his breath and gave her a minute to absorb it.

"Was he obnoxious as always? Did he do his 'I used to be a noted *enfant terrible*' number?"

"Zo . . ."

"Did he?"

"Well, he was just his usual pompous self. Criticized everything, said the paella was 'too dry,' insulted various people. He's a real jerk. I don't see how Frye can stand to work with him. As a matter of fact, the boss man himself," Roger went on, "seemed rather on the subdued side that night, which I thought was interesting."

Zoe twisted and looked up at him; her black eyes focused intently on his face. "What do you mean, 'subdued'?"

"Oh, 'apprehensive' might be a better word."

"Julian Frye? Roger, not a chance."

"No, that's the word—or 'uncertain.' He seemed very nervous, as if Sessa were some sort of Frankenstein he never realized he'd created. All evening it was as if Sessa was playing to *Frye's* audience. Very weird. But then when Frye showed everybody your new sketches of Mrs. Griffith's sitting room, the ones you did in Grandmère's back parlor, he really got a rise out of Sessa."

"He brought my stuff to Sidney's? Why would he do that? What's the name of *this* little game?"

Zoe jumped up and paced up and down the walkway in front of their bench. The lights from the Ritz Carlton ballroom shone out into the night behind her.

"Those sketches are signed! They are protected, and Julian Frye damn well knows it!"

Roger nodded slowly. "Of course he does. Zo . . . Zo, come sit down. Don't you see? He was trying to provoke Sessa."

"What?"

"Look. Come sit, darling. . . . What I got out of it—and yes, it was play-acting, vintage Frye—is that the 'game' is now between him and Sessa. Sessa, believe it or not, seems to be insisting on studio sets, and Frye's not so sure anymore, and they went on and on about that, with Frye using your sketches as . . . well, I can see now that the atmosphere in a studio would be wrong, Zo, just as you were explaining to me all winter. I mean, especially now that I've been here, in the house."

"*A* house."

"Whatever. The point is that everything you sent really impressed him. I think you should get Frye to come here, see it with his own eyes."

"Oh, Roger, good Lord."

"You know you've thought of it, Zoe—shooting the picture in your Grandmère's—your—house. You told me so yourself, on the phone."

"Oh, Rog, it's not what it was!" Zoe broke off and held out her arms as if to gather all of the rich old magnificence of Commonwealth Avenue into them. "Uncle Jim said there was a time . . . it was such a *showplace,* he said. But that's gone, Rog. It's gone."

"Zoe, think a minute," Roger said in a calm tone. "There has to be more than enough in the production budget to repair the house . . . re-decorate it? In fact, it might well be cheaper to do that than to build sets from scratch, no?"

Smiling at her expression, Roger stood up, took her arm, and led her across Arlington Street, now nearly deserted of traffic, into the Public Garden. They wandered down a gravel path that curved around wide beds of spring flowers. Zoe leaned against an enormous linden tree and jammed her hands into her pockets. Roger came close to her in the darkness and kissed her softly on the cheek, waiting for a response, and then tilted her chin up and kissed her mouth, closing his eyes when he felt her lips open and move, felt her tongue on his teeth.

Zoe felt warm, molten; she seemed to sag under her own weight, and Roger's arms tightened around her. She kissed his neck and the edge of his beard and his parted lips and let herself sway back against the linden tree, her hands still on his shoulders.

"It's time for you to come back, darling," he whispered.

"I know . . . I know." Zoe touched his face again and then turned away. She bent over an oval bed of azalea bushes and plucked off a small bloom, gently stroking the limp flower with one finger.

"You know," Roger said after a moment in which Zoe never so much as lifted her eyes from the flower, "Frye also brought along your drawings for the dinner-party scene. He had them blown up in his lab, and, well, they just knocked everybody out. They're sensational, Zo—looked just as if Grandmère herself were going to walk in and sit right down at the table."

Zoe looked up at him. "It's the most important scene in the movie," she whispered. "It's where everything comes together."

As she said that, Zoe felt herself brightening a little, as if she'd been winched up out of her strange, dreamy mood by the memory of how she'd felt in the dining room last Wednesday morning, setting that scene, furiously polishing Grandmère's silver. She took a deep breath and threw the azalea stem aside.

"Oh, and get this," Roger said. "I can't believe I almost forgot to tell you. At Sidney's the other night there was also a huge argument about that last scene, about using it—"

"Argument?" Zoe said, squinting up at him. "I thought that issue was all settled. I told Frye at least a month ago I thought he should use it. The contrast is so exciting, so romantic—seven years later, when some of the stolen art mysteriously shows up again and the audience starts to realize that Laurence Thane is the one who made it happen, and . . . !"

Zoe thought of the poignant symmetry she and Frye had already discussed, Laurence and Beatrice at opposite ends of the crowded, palatial room—he now hidden behind a dark beard, his hair going silver. "And it's Christmas, too, Roger. It balances the *first* scene! He *has* to use it!"

Roger was nodding all the while. "Yes, and that's what several people said. Even Frye's publicist got all excited when it came up. He was leaping around the room, saying that it's 'dramatically essential'—that it's what the picture is all about. He got very upset, Zo. It was a riot." Roger laughed a little, remembering. "Anyway, Frye seemed to be listening very closely, and right then and there he asked Sessa to do a few sketches, maybe a model of the grand drawing room decorated for Christmas."

"And is he?"

"Nope. Refused to do it."

"He turned Frye down? In front of everybody?"

"Right there on Sidney's lanai."

"He's scared of the period," Zoe said softly, thinking hard. "And turn-of-the-century is even harder to do. You know, that faker, I bet he hasn't even read the script."

"Well, he flat out said he wouldn't. And Frye was obviously furious. Zoe, Sessa's really taking advantage of the situation, and I think Frye's beginning to see it. This is the perfect time for you to . . . well, resume your rightful place."

Zoe looked down at her clasped hands. "He thinks Sessa is distinguished," she said softly.

"Well, I suppose he is, in his own way. But *The Gilded Affair* is not about *banditos*. Frye needs you, honey, not a hot dog like Frank Sessa."

"He'll never admit that."

"Probably not, but so what? Everything's backfiring. He screwed up and he knows it. It's time to give him a call, sweetheart. It is."

When Zoe looked up at him, Roger saw that her eyes were shining with more than the lamplight. A thin fog had descended on the Garden, and the dampness settled into the air around them.

"You really think I should call him?"

"I do. Tonight. And I think you should tell him about the house, too, ask him how he might feel about using it. Offer it, show him the advantages of shooting the picture in Boston. Invite him to come see for himself."

"That son of a bitch? Give in to him?"

Roger sighed. "Zoe, Julian Frye needs to be in control more than you need to go back to square one."

When he said that, Zoe made a groaning noise in her throat and pulled away from him. She walked slowly down to the ornamental lake, starting to cry, her hands deep in her pockets. She saw the tall iron lamps on the curve of the water only as blurred yellow circles in the black cave of the Garden.

A moment later she felt Roger's arms around her shoulders, his warm fingers on her cheeks.

"Zoe . . . Zoe, darling, what is it? . . . What is it, dear?"

Zoe turned slowly and put her face in his shoulder, weeping in an involuntary, motionless way, as if the source of the tears were somehow outside herself, and bottomless. In some part of her mind, even as she leaned all her weight against him, Zoe knew that she'd had this coming for days, weeks maybe, possibly longer. Roger just held on to her, until—as silently as they had started, and flowed—the tears stopped.

Zoe felt herself no longer crying, sensed the dull, not unpleasant throbbing in her head, and slid her arms around Roger's waist.

"Zoe. What happened to you while you were here? Do you want to tell me? *Can* you tell me? Do you know?"

She turned in his arms, gazing out toward the dark, stone-pillared parabola of the bridge that crossed the serpentine, ghostly in the light. Underneath, in the shallow water, the famous swan boats swayed, knocking with dull, soft thuds against their moorings.

Without a word, Zoe reached for Roger's hand, and they walked in perfect step up the incline of the bridge. They stood by the iron railing, looking across the still surface of the water. The sky over Back Bay was heavy with gathering clouds; all color had fled with the darkness, and fog blurred the outlines of the Ritz Carlton and the John Hancock Tower. Zoe wished that Grandmère, who loved the Public Garden so, could see it now in this magical absence of light.

"Wouldn't it be wonderful," she said suddenly, "to have Grandmère's portrait in the picture? In that last scene—maybe at the other end of the drawing room from the Christmas tree. . . . It would be so beautiful," she whispered. "So perfect."

She'd thought of using the painting almost at the moment she'd seen it for the first time, last night. But the idea of Grandmère's portrait hanging in Beatrice Holland's home—a home created inside Zoe's own mind, Grandmère's life reflected in the movie—had been almost too much for her.

"Laurence and Beatrice made the wrong choice," Zoe said, a phrase from the diary starting to dance around the edges of her thoughts. "In that final scene there's such a . . . such a terrible lack of . . ."

Of what? she wondered, and then there it was, the heartfelt, luminous passage Grandmère had written at the time of Anne Lowell's death, coming back to her:

". . . a terrible lack of wisdom, spirit . . . *courage!* Oh, what a mistake they made! He could have gone up to her—or she could have just walked the thirty feet to . . . There was a chance! She was the only one who recognized him!"

When Zoe turned and looked eagerly up at him, a glint of something like desperation in her eyes, Roger looked down at her, frowning slightly, filled with a sense of waiting for some awful revelation.

"Tell me what happened here, Zo, what really happened. Please tell me."

Zoe blinked, trying to put into words the exhilaration and dread she had been feeling for days.

"I've waited years to feel this way, Rog, and these last eleven days have been so . . . Oh, I can't let it get away from me again! Don't you see? And even if there's a chance for me with Frye, with the movie—I can't go back!"

"What do you mean?" Roger said, straining to see the expression in her shadowed eyes. "Why not?"

"How can I go?" Zoe cried. "I can't leave with everything up in the air the way it is, the mortgage, the portrait—Grandmère's house! I can't leave until I've finished."

"Zoe, Zoe! I'll *be* here. I'll stay here and take care of all that for you. I planned to, just so you could go back. Didn't you realize that? I expected to do that all along!"

Zoe looked up in amazement. "You would do that for me?"

Roger was completely disconcerted to see that she viewed as some great sacrifice what he considered simple and obvious.

"Zoe! Goddamn it! How can you ask me that? How can you doubt it? How can you not *assume* it? Oh, Christ, Zoe—what the hell do you think's been going on between us? How can you not know there isn't one thing in the whole world I wouldn't do for you? Wouldn't you do anything—the *equivalent*—for me? Zoe, *would* you?" His shout was almost swallowed by the heavy, wet air of the Garden, but his shocked anger was plain in his face.

"Would you?"

"Of course I would!" she cried, horrified that he would ask. "Good God, Roger! Of course I would!"

"Why?" Roger's voice was less of a shout, but deep, thick with what he was feeling. He put his hands on her face and made her look into his eyes. "Why?" he whispered. "Why?"

Zoe gasped, understanding completely what he meant. Tears flooded her eyes.

"Oh, Roger, I don't want it to happen to us. I don't want to be looking at you across some room, years from now, scared to death to make the first move . . . wishing everything were different . . . regretting . . . that I never told you how much . . . how much I love you. And for *so* long."

Roger took his hands away from her face and stood back as she said it again, more softly, and more clearly. "I love you."

But even as she said the words Roger had begun to fear she'd never bring herself to say, Zoe was looking up at him in a way that seemed to implore even in the very act of declaration. And then he knew that they had reached that long line drawn in the sand of Zoe's past that he'd told himself she had to cross before he had his chance with her. But he had not understood, not until now, that he had to *hold on to her* while she stepped the last millimeter over and beyond it.

"Tell me again," he whispered, grasping her hands and staring with joy into her smiling face. "Tell me you love me, Zoe."

"I love you," she said, pulling him closer. "I love you. Yes I do."

Zoe sat on Eugene Hillyard's stone bench by herself and watched Roger go up the steps and close the heavy door behind him. Lights were on all over the house, even up on the fourth floor in Arthur's room; only

Grandmère's window was dark. She could see Yancey and Lowie passing in and out of view through the bay window of the dining room, setting the table for dinner.

The wind shifted to the northeast and brought, on the floating fog, a chill that made Zoe pull her jacket closer around her shoulders. A good solid Boston night, she thought, a night to pace your widow's walk and wait for tall, four-masted ships to return to harbor. Schooners, clipper ships, brigantines—all coming back.

The leaves trembled against each other, and small needles of rain began, isolated at first, slowly gathering into veils that slipped down the tunnel of the trees along the Mall and washed the lamp-lit path. Then the notes of a *ballade,* thin and misty, transformed into rain and light, came from somewhere not too far away.

At the door of Zoe's house, a man and a woman, arm in arm, their heads as close together as her large, extravagant hat would permit, their intimate laughter faint, upwind, walked up the broad steps and went inside.

Zoe followed them.

Epilogue

The plane reached its cruising altitude over the Susquehanna River Valley. Zoe sank back in her seat and sipped from a plastic cup of wine the stewardess had brought right after takeoff, a rusty, dark zinfandel that really wasn't all that bad. It occurred to Zoe that she probably shouldn't be drinking wine, that she should fill her blood with caffeine, the better to fence with Julian Frye when she got to Los Angeles, though Roger had dryly pointed out that conciliation, felt or not, would be a wiser course.

"It looks like he's handing it back to you, sweetheart," he said when she came down to the dining room to report on her call to Frye. Everyone was sitting around the table drinking leftover sherry, while the boys, giggling about something, dried dishes in the kitchen.

"Not exactly," Zoe replied. "This is no silver platter, Rog. It's not for sure. He made that perfectly clear—he said 'maybe.' You know he's not going to miss another chance to make me crazy."

What Frye had actually said, when Zoe reached him at the studio in Los Angeles after Claudia's fine family dinner, was more along the lines of "Get your ass out here by tomorrow afternoon and we'll see."

"My flight's supposed to get in about two your time," she told him, having called the airline beforehand.

"I'll try to send someone over to LAX to pick you up," he'd replied in his hoarse, silky voice. "Oh, by the way," he added with exaggerated unconcern, "those, uh, photographs you sent?"

"Yes?"

"Let me get this straight. That house is really yours?"

"Yes. It belongs to me," Zoe said with a *frisson* of joy, glad Frye couldn't see her face.

"And we could use it—shoot all the interiors there?"

"Yes."

"This doesn't necessarily mean we're going with practical sets, you know," Frye had grumbled. "I haven't made my final decision yet."

"Well, we can talk about it tomorrow," Zoe answered, wondering if he realized she knew all about Gianfranco Sessa, Sidney's party, models of formal drawing rooms. Were shoes sliding onto other feet so soon?

"Also, I'm considering a different costume designer," he said. "Marco pisses me off."

Zoe frowned into the phone, holding it with both hands. "Well, I know he can be a very abrasive guy, Julian, but he's really terrific—don't you think? I'd recommend keeping him." But she smiled as she hung up, hearing in his words a way to make a bargain.

An hour later, Zoe was standing on the steps with a very teary Claudia, who held her tight while they watched Roger and Arthur, down on the sidewalk in the misty drizzle, help Eddie get the palm tree into the station wagon.

Zoe had insisted that Claudia take most of the plants and all the flowers back home to Newton. "Our two favorite bachelors are *not* going to take care of them, after all," Zoe said, laughing and hugging her back.

Eddie came up beside them in the doorway and took Zoe's hand in both of his, reaching deep into his mind for the perfect farewell phrase; failing to find it, he pulled her into his arms, pounding her back in lieu of words, while Claudia watched, chuckling at both of them, wiping her eyes.

Minutes later, just as the ritual flurry of gathering and packing and retrieving was declared complete and Eddie announced that it was time to go, Zoe led Lowie and Yancey into the back parlor and plunked them down side by side on the old love seat. She took Zachary's conch shell from the mantel where she had placed it earlier and got down on one knee in front of Lowie.

"I want you to understand that this is a very special shell, honey," she said in a low voice. "Did Mom ever talk about Grandmère to you guys?"

"All the time," said Lowie. "But she's *yours,* right?"

"Sweetheart, she's all of ours. She was my great-grandma, mine and Arthur's, that's true; but Uncle Jim knew her real well, and she loved your mom when she was just a little girl."

"You sure?" said Yancey, his blue eyes wide and suspicious at the same time. It had never occurred to him that the mythic "Grandmère" had ever actually loved anybody.

"Absolutely. Now, this shell was hers—her son gave it to her for a birthday present, long long ago. Lowie, I want you to take very good care of it and remember how special it is, okay?"

"Yeah," said Lowie in a reverent voice as he took it from her hands; he was accepting the magnitude of the occasion on faith.

"And Yance, kiddo," Zoe went on, straightening her knees and ruffling his hair, "I am going to bring you something terrific from California next time I come—promise."

"Well, I guess there's nothing in Auntie Annabelle's house for me, huh? For a . . . what do you call it, Lowie?"

"A memento," Lowie said, blushing as he glanced at Zoe's face.

"Yeah. It's okay." Yancey was philosophical, but waiting was hard. "When you comin' back, Cousin Zoe?"

"Pretty soon, sweetheart. Pretty soon."

Jim waited until the others were out at the curb before he led Zoe into the deserted parlor. Arthur and Roger had replaced the portrait right after dinner, and it was hanging from the hooks still solidly planted high in the south wall. Jim walked the length of the room to the painting and looked up at it, the tips of his fingers caressing the hem of Augusta's beaded gown.

"Last couple of days I've come to realize how much I miss her, Zoe. I surely do miss her."

"So do I," she said, coming up behind him, putting her hand on his shoulder, rubbing the fabric of his suit coat back and forth.

"I don't want you to worry about anything now," Jim said. "May have to send you stuff to sign and whatnot, time to time."

"Fine," said Zoe.

"I think we've got things pretty well organized here for now," he said more briskly, turning away from the painting. "How long's your Roger planning to stay?"

"As long as it takes. He's already got a call in to his friend Harlan; apparently he's been out of town, but he's supposedly due back tomorrow or the next day. . . . Oh God, Uncle Jim, what if Harlan . . ."

"One step at a time, honey," he said, turning to wrap his arms around her, pulling her chin tight against his old cheek. "You've done a helluva job—handled things just the way Augusta would have wanted you to—clear-minded, resolute. But there could be some hard choices coming up, Zoe, hard. Takes a lot of perspective."

"I know."

Zoe kissed his taut cheek and stood back, looking up at the portrait. If something had to be stood back from, looked at from a distance in the weeks, years ahead, it would definitely not be Augusta Hillyard's house. The choice between symbols seemed no choice at all.

"Oh, but Jim, I don't want to lose it!" she cried, as she had to Roger just hours before. She gestured widely with both arms, reaching toward the portrait.

"Zoe dear, one step at a time now, don't go getting yourself in a state. We'll get this figured out. Franklin's calling me back tomorrow about the painting and the transfers and all the rest of it. I liked what I heard when I talked to him here this evening, but remember, it's early days yet. You just concentrate on knocking 'em dead back in Hollywood."

"Roger said he'd call me the minute Harlan sees it."

He gave her one of his sly looks, his old man's snort of laughter. "That Roger's a smart man, and a nice one, too. Thinks the world of you."

Zoe pulled her gaze away from Augusta's face and smiled, the creases around her eyes crinkling up. "Isn't he wonderful? I'm so . . ."

When she trailed off, Jim chuckled. "I sure hate to sound like some philosophical old geezer, Zoe dear, but there's only one thing worse than having no blessings and that's having them and not knowing it, or not believing."

Zoe went back to the front window and, parting the lace curtain, looked thoughtfully into the street, watching Eddie and the boys making a final arrangement of Claudia's parcels and plants in the back of the station wagon.

Jim came up beside her, buttoning his jacket.

"How am I going to thank you for this?" Zoe said, looking with intense concentration into his face. "How can I ever do it?"

"I don't need thanks from you, my dear. That little bit of cash is not what's important here, and you know it."

Zoe clenched her teeth together and looked with narrowed, shining eyes into his, unable to think of another thing to say.

Jim smiled and kissed her hand. "Zoe Hillyard," he said, "I am proud to know you."

Later, when the house was locked up tight and Arthur and Roger were both asleep, Zoe settled herself on the blue divan in the parlor, facing the portrait, and spent several hours working out some ideas for the final Christmas reception scene. She sketched the ornate fireplace surround (adding a bronze bust of Dante with a holly wreath around its neck), and the broad sweep of the bay windows with their rippled panes, clustering dozens of potted poinsettias on the broad window seat. She placed a Christmas tree in the center of the long wall opposite the fireplace, dazzling with burning candles and velvet bows. She changed the old Hillyard Sarouk to a forty-foot Savonnerie carpet, indicating the colors—peach, gold, pink and green, wine and cream. And finally— dominating the room—a full-length portrait of a tall, beautiful woman in a pink silk dress with beaded shoulders, her face glowing with the sparkle of her diamond earrings.

It had been almost two in the morning when Zoe finished the sketches. She went silently upstairs to the third floor, to what had once been Hortense Hillyard's bedroom. It was still pretty in its fussy Edwardian way, the darkness hiding the stained and shredding ribbon-stripe wallpaper. Roger was sound asleep, his face deep in the pillow. Zoe knelt by the bed and laid her cheek on his, kissing his hair, his eyebrow, the side of his mouth, feeling his shoulders move under the thick comforter. He smelled of sleep and soap and the last chocolate truffle he'd eaten before she tucked him in, hours before. She rubbed her nose against his neck and kissed his shoulder, smiling as he smiled, still fast asleep.

She softly closed the door and walked slowly down all the curvings of the staircase and along the carpeted hallway to Augusta's room. It was warm and dark, dawn still several hours away. The bedside lamps cast dim and filtered light. Zoe took the two green boxes from the bottom of the armoire and carefully straightened out each one, tightening and smoothing the ribbons, arranging the packets just so, placing them in date order as much as possible, keeping out a small bundle, tied with a gray ribbon, marked "Autumn 1944 to Winter 1945."

After she put the lids back on the boxes, she sat on the floor and leaned her head against the brocade cover of the bed, looking up into the depths of the carved ceiling medallions, seeing the same pattern of flowers and angels and twining vines that Grandmère had gazed at in the night a century ago. Zoe could not help but think, and with a deep shiver of regret, of all she had not read, all she might not have a chance to learn for months to come. But she knew that for now, lying here holding the last pages of the diary in her lap, she could content herself with the hope that in finding an authentic, excavated plain on which to set *The Gilded Affair,* she had also dug deep enough to find a place to put herself.

She ran her fingers one last time over the embossed letters on the box lids and hefted them back into the armoire, squatting to push them back as far as they would go. Hiding the diary elsewhere—in the cellar, the attic, the library breakfront—was pointless, unnecessary. Arthur seemed to have sensed that in her time in Boston his sister had acquired a secret of such depth that even he, architect and bearer of so many secrets, was not to know it.

Even that morning at the airport, as he and Roger walked her to the gate, Zoe had a moment of suspecting Arthur might ask her if she had anything else to tell him, anything to add to the plans and instructions, schemes and speculations they had already discussed with such exhausting thoroughness. But all he did was hug her to him and kiss her cheeks and her clasped hands. No, Arthur had wisely held his tongue, but Zoe sensed in him, even at that last moment as he waved goodbye, an awareness that there was ground here which was not his to tread. He would not be going into Grandmère's room.

The stewardess took Zoe's lunch tray away and stage-whispered that the movie was starting, would she please lower her shade. Zoe took one last look at the hills of southern Indiana far below, the April land seeming almost emerald-green to her through a haze of midday sun. She snapped the shade down and unfastened her seat belt so she could reach the satchel under her feet. The pages of the diary for late 1944 and 1945, still neatly tied with the pale gray ribbon, were in a large envelope right on top. Little beams of north light glinted around the sides of the window shade, their angles changing as the plane curved into a southwest heading, illuminating the paper she pulled into her lap.

From the first pages it seemed clear that Augusta, at a time of life when people often narrow down their spheres and look increasingly inward, was trying to turn her own thoughts away from family travails and toward the wider world. Yet it was with misgiving that she wrote of the entrance of the Allied forces into Germany, of Roosevelt's fourth election, and of the Dumbarton Oaks Conference, which strove to symbolize what hope it could.

"The war is with us every day," Augusta wrote on a cold November night in 1944.

The news on the radio is filled with it, just as Europe is filled with the booming of cannons. The shaking of one old woman's fist to Heaven will not keep these boys from dying, any more than it did those other poor children a quarter century ago. This anguish is too global.

The first war blew the world apart, ending forever the way of thinking and the style of life that I knew as a girl: the nineteenth century, one might say, ended in Belleau Wood. . . . But *this* war! This war has simply stopped the world, I think, by the sheer force of its commanding every creature on the planet to be a part of it. The millions dead include animals, trees, birds, flowers; fish die when submarines fire their torpedoes! The world is dead in its tracks from this war. I fear we have come a long way from believing that war is sin—if indeed we ever did. But we must have hope—hope that the ideas of Dumbarton Oaks will survive us all. May it become a shrine to which our children travel only on their knees.

Shortly after Christmas, Augusta hired two boys from the neighborhood to carry her portrait back upstairs. "I do not think I will be moving it again," she wrote on a sunny afternoon late in January of 1945.

. . . But I am pleased to have it with me every day now that since my accident I do not venture down the stairs so much. It's silly of me to consider it, I suppose, but silly of Veronica, too, to think she can prevent me. She's grown remarkably stout this past year and stood winded in the doorway when she brought my tray today, though she tried to hide it when I protested I was well enough to take my meals downstairs.

"Tommyrot! The doctor says you're not to attempt the stairs!" says she. "Not even holding the banister?" says I (butter wouldn't melt in my mouth). "Doctor says you must stay upstairs, and I won't hear any more of this foolishness." And, so saying, she lumbered from the room and left me here with my omelet, my muffins—and my portrait.

Zoe put the pages down on the tray table. She knew it was probably fortunate she hadn't read this section before Arthur brought the painting home. It was hanging, that very minute, in the parlor on Commonwealth Avenue, high on its original hooks, and though Jim Forbes thought it might need to hang for a while in Bud Chadwick's office in the bank, or maybe in the vault, held for a kind of ransom, it was too soon to say if it would serve the Hillyards as collateral or loss.

Unwilling to linger on the thought, Zoe took another sip of the zinfandel and read on, noting with a strange, dull sadness that Augusta wrote less and less all through the spring of 1945. She turned the pages over, shook the envelope, thinking there must be more, but the well of words, thoughts, feelings, hopes, and daydreams seemed to have been emptied. When Grandmère did make an entry, the writing was cramped, even crooked, and she admitted that she wrote the sloping words in defiance of a chronic dizziness which had plagued her since her fall in January.

"I find I sleep a good deal, which vexes me no end," she wrote in early April.

. . . But when I wake I see the portrait there before me, and though it will be forty years in June, sometimes in my old lady's sleepy fancies I become—for just a moment—the woman I was then. The very gown is in the armoire as I write, though out of fashion, heaven knows, the silk rotted through in places, and the beading littering the floor. I wonder if I made a mistake when I sold the earrings instead of the picture? . . . An idle wonderment, I suppose at this remove, but the choice seems correct, as I have not missed the earrings, have I? I could not wear them now, however festive they might look with my old flannel bedgown and my robe, but John's painting can be looked at, can stir memories I welcome. It will survive, I fancy, to be sacrificed another day. The loss of diamonds is not enough for us; the future Hillyards may outdo us all in prodigality. Now I want to take my fill of my picture before my eyes close on it forever. . . . It occurs to me that Anthony will doubtless snatch it up before I'm cold in my coffin, but it won't much matter then.

That's right! Zoe thought suddenly, staring wide-eyed at the page. Anthony didn't take it! Why not? How was he prevented? He surely, just as Grandmère guessed, would have gone straight from her graveside to the house to get it, but . . .

Ah, Annabelle? Annabelle—who locked up Grandmère's room and kept the key? Had there been some drop, some thread, some unsuspected spark of sentiment in her? Zoe shuddered, imagining the possibilities, realizing that she would never know.

She tilted the shade away from the window and pressed her face into the shining little gap next to the glass. The Mississippi River lay below, platinum and twisted, slicing through the middle of the country, the earth curving far to the north beyond the river end.

Augusta spent the summer of 1945 alternately joyful at the waning days of the war and reading somber poetry—from Donne to Tennyson to Frost—transcribing whole passages into the pages of the diary. On a hot afternoon she copied out the last lines of "The Kraken," finding metaphors there that she did not explain:

> There hath he lain for ages, and will lie
> Battening upon huge sea-worms in his sleep,
> Until the latter fire shall heat the deep;
> Then once by man and angels to be seen,
> In roaring he shall rise and on the surface die.

Zoe paused, wondering. Perhaps the bombing of Hiroshima and Nagasaki in early August had made her fear for little Zoe and the world she would inherit? Then, at the bottom of the page, written in pencil, was blurred evidence that Grandmère had tried to find her own words for such obliteration:

I have thus lived from "The Gilded Age" to what the journalists are now calling "The Atomic Age," as if we should be satisfied and pleased to have a name for all this madness. The haze from the explosions has moved eastward on the wind, like Krakatoa years and years ago. I remember well how frightened we were then—the ash from the volcano darkened the very sun for weeks. It seems now, however, that we have not only defied the gods but overtaken them as well. What thieves we are.

The Japanese surrender one month later did not cheer her. Throughout September she wrote fiercely and much more frequently, though with a fragmenting of thought and expression which was (to Zoe's eye and ear) so different from the language of years gone by—an almost despairing recitative of what had been missed, lost, plundered; catalogues of all who died, of all that went before.

"Only Zoe remains," Augusta wrote in October. "But I will have no chance with her; she is as lost to me as those long dead, because she will outlive me for so long. Oh! How will she do without her Grandmère to love her?"

The remainder of that entry was almost completely illegible, the lines of writing crooked and smeared.

"Oh, please, Grandmère," Zoe whispered. "Don't give up!" She knew, of course, that Grandmère had died at dawn on Christmas, a final stroke taking her life in a heartbeat, but even so she gripped the arms of her seat and stared at the writing, begging Augusta not to die.

Then, on the night of what would have been her sixty-fourth wedding anniversary, October 22, 1945, after weeks of sometimes incoherent, always anguished rambling, Augusta seemed to come to herself once more. She made a plan:

I have lain abed all day today, reflecting somewhat sourly on my quite odious behavior of the past few weeks. I can't think why I do this—to myself, to precious Zoe, to dear, patient Veronica, little Arthur. Even Annabelle deserves better from me than the ravings of the demented old woman I've become. Do I have, perhaps, some strange and awful knowledge? Premonitions far inside my mind? Or is only a reluctance, a loathing, to face the necessity (coming soon!) to leave it all, knowing there can never be enough time left for adequate regret or joy? I know I must try to think it through and maybe see it whole . . . and so I have decided to do something I assumed I never would have the courage (or the foolishness) to do—I am going to read it all. Every word, from the day Eugene and I were married to last night. I must try to do it, though

I have barely the strength to pull out these damned boxes and begin at the beginning . . . but I must. I shall make a parting ceremony of it— as why not? I shall be missing my own funeral service, after all.

Tomorrow morning, after breakfast, I will start, and I hope the dizziness, the pain, the lights—always those lights!—will subdue themselves long enough to let me finish.

The words trailed from the page, and Zoe drank the dregs of her wine, tasting nothing of it. She now knew why she had found the diary in such perfect order. She took a deep breath and turned to the very last entry.

(Dawn, Monday, December 24, 1945) . . . Well, then. I have lived it, read it through, and neatly tied it up—I am done with it. It was very difficult to resist the urge to edit and to annotate—to become my own amanuensis—to change my own Fortune! But by the time I got to the morning of Anthony's birth, I knew I had to read without my pencil in my hand, and, to my amazement, the need to change it, once resisted, fled, and I read on. Births and deaths, gains and losses, anger and joy— the stuff of life all glittered by—all in these pages. And not so bad for all of that: a balance reached. It's true that my journeys in the wider world were fewer than I'd hoped, but many were the nights I lay awake in the darkness of this very room and saw before my inward eye the scarlet, sunset-frosted deserts of the West and forests made of trees as old as diamonds; I saw cities cluttered with towers and steel, and I saw wheat, green and blowing in a wind that came from distances farther than any eye could see. I saw fish leaping in cold lakes and strange gold flowers blooming in snowy crevasses where the only footprints were my own. I know these are sights I will never see, but may still dream of through that endless, arriving sleep.

. . . and now the white-and-silver Boston dawn is slipping through the window, and I smile as I write these last few words, taking some comfort in the thought that I shall end my days, in unison with Mr. Thoreau, having "traveled much in Concord."

Darling Zoe, if I could, I would leave these words for you to read someday. Someday in the far future when you are a grown woman and cannot remember your Grandmère, you should have these poor words to learn how well she loved you. If I dared, Zoe, I would keep this for you in my cupboard, in this room, in this your house, but I don't dare. No. I shall bring you to my lap this afternoon and tell it all to your young, uncomprehending ears—and on this Christmas morning coming I will burn it.

Zoe held the empty cup against her mouth and let the window shade come up so she could see the Rocky Mountains just ahead. Grain and gold, iron and water slid under the plane as they flew through the glowing western sky that Augusta Hillyard had gone to her grave dreaming she could see.